POTARIUM

THE JESTER'S JOURNEY

POTARIUM

KYLE SORRELL

4 Horsemen
Publications, Inc.

Potarium
Copyright © 2023 Kyle Sorrell. All rights reserved.
4 Horsemen Publications, Inc.

4 Horsemen
Publications, Inc.

1497 Main St. Suite 169
Dunedin, FL 34698
4horsemenpublications.com
info@4horsemenpublications.com
Cover by J. Kotick
Typeset by Niki Tantillo
Edited by Devora Gray

Library of Congress Control Number: 2023933508
Paperback ISBN-13: 978-1-64450-901-2
Hardcover ISBN-13: 978-1-64450-902-9
Audiobook ISBN-13: 978-1-64450-903-6
Ebook ISBN-13: 978-1-64450-904-3

DEDICATION

Dedicated to my loving parents, Gary and Patricia,
my little brothers Samuel and Jacob, and everyone
else who put up with my weirdness!

Fiddle

Cynkz

TABLE OF CONTENTS

TABLE OF CONTENTS

CHAPTER 1

Every star
Near and far
Waits for us
To just
Reach out
And accept them…

A LONE SPIRIT DRIFTED ALONG ON A sunless sea. His mind sat firmly in the strange haze between the waking world and that of dreams. The dark ocean blended with the black night sky, with little else for his mind to focus on beyond the thin line of reflected light marking the horizon. The ocean reflected the sky, and in turn copied its speckled brilliance. From afar, it would be impossible to tell one apart from the other, providing a pleasantly unobstructed view of the universe, if not for the lone soul drifting along the border.

Even in the dark ocean's embrace, Cynkz could recall the poem. His mind was as lost and wayward as his body, pushed back and forth against the flat sea waves, yet his thoughts often returned to the cryptic verse. Even in his perpetual soporific state, the poem stayed with him. The soothing waters and twinkling night sky impressed an intense torpor upon him, giving him no choice but to let the world take him where it may. For once, he was completely vulnerable to the unknowable hand of fate.

The thin gleaming light on the horizon reminded him of the thread—its divine otherworldly brilliance sticking out in his mind like a needle gently pressing into his thoughts. Memories surrounding the angelic twine allowed for images to overlap in his mind—the lavender, night-ridden deserts and forests of Dulrot, the po and their glowing auras dotting the dark landscape like stars in the night sky, the many animals and birds and their calls and chirps singing from the dark, the stony sentinels who watched over the land, and the rare visits of gleaming, brilliant entities from beyond—the apostles.

Memories of his old home faded as new lands came into view—the dark and murky bog, the shifting gray mountains, the yellow haze of the swamp, the glistening black desert, the caustic pink fog, the maze-like forest, the turquoise grotto and the layered colony housing the Sisters of Elm in the ground below.

He could remember the scruffy silhouette of his friend, the imp, leading him to the company of several old, hunched women. Their grayed skin and sharply wrinkled faces did little to hide their warm expressions and strangely affable nature. The bright face of a young woman stood tall among them. Every face had a name, yet for the moment they escaped him. His tongue drew a blank as potent as his mind as he tried time and time again to say them. The sting of frustration sharpened his thoughts, and he remembered something that stood out—the missing Sister of Elm.

A name! Or a title at least. That was enough to get him thinking of more specific details—the fifth chair, the four sisters, Orla taking the position of the lost Sister of Elm.

Orla...

Orilay...

The mysterious woman from Cynkz's earliest visions came back into view. He could remember the weight of his strong connection to the woman, who only spoke a single verse to him as far as his memory served. He thought of the missing woman, and the missing sister. It helped to force connections between his memories, as loose as they were. Yet the more he tried to think of the enigmatic fifth sister, all that filled his mind was darkness. With little else to go on, his mind resorted to a darkened silhouette piercing the light of his other visions.

He couldn't help but think of her departure, why she left, and the effect it must have had. The impact of her one simple decision seemed to cast a great shadow over her sisters, and in a way, the rest of Munderworld who bore the consequences of the sister's trauma. The more he pondered the fifth sister's motives, the more her darkened silhouette pierced the light, its shadow expanding wide over the rest of his mind. It wasn't long before his visions returned to darkness, and he retreated to his floating slumber.

Time seemed meaningless, and as for how long Cynkz drifted in the sea, even he couldn't tell anymore.

Yet something caught his eye. It was large, unnaturally straight-edged—and broke the line of light on the horizon. It was enough of a contrast that he was able to turn his head against the flat, gentle water carrying him to get a better view of what was approaching. As it cut through the water and its size grew, he realized what the strange object was—a boat! He swore he could hear voices moving back and forth across the vessel, though he wondered if it was just the shifting of waves around him playing tricks on his mind.

Exerting such effort caused him to grow tired, and he let his head rest back in the cool, black waters carrying him. The water felt chill and smooth, like an ethereal silk blanket carrying him along the sky. It was easy to sleep when fate took the burden of existence off of your shoulders.

CHAPTER 2

THE SOFT TOUCH OF WATER GAVE WAY to coarse rope, and then the firm press of many hands gripping him, pulling his body up by every available limb. Cynkz's heart sank for a moment as he was reminded of the formless hands that pulled at him within the dark eye at the bottom of Munderworld. Fortunately, the pleasant warmth and soft grip of the new po helping him complimented the soothing ocean, keeping his mind calm.

With the hollow thud of his body being laid on flat wood, he inhaled, and could feel life being forced back into him for the first time in what felt like ages. As his gasps calmed, the voices of working po began to take over, and he finally opened his eyes. He was greeted with the view of sailors shuffling back and forth over the slick deck of the sea vessel. A few of them were close by, with a couple reaching out to help him sit up and get his bearings. Before the jester could speak, his body began to convulse as he coughed up foreign water from his lungs. He felt the soft patting of a warm hand on his back as a new voice spoke to him.

"You're alive!" the new voice said. "Not that the great ocean would actually drown anybody."

The husky sailor, wide-shouldered and unusually calm for one out in the middle of an infinite ocean, looked at the jester, who could hardly maintain eye-contact as he continued to wheeze in a desperate attempt to clear his throat.

"It's fine, take your time," the sailor said. "Just breathe and relax. You're safe now. You finally made it!"

The jester gave a final rattling cough that settled him and replied, "Th-thank you."

"No need to thank us. It's always a pleasure to fish out new souls just before they reach Potarium."

The sailor gave the jester another look. "You know, you're awfully heavy for such a lean guy. I was about ready to pull out a crank. You'd make for a good anchor!"

The jester took in his first unhindered breath and looked around. He returned his gaze to the sailor, presumably the captain, considering his calm demeanor and being the only po not shuffling frantically across the boat's hard wooden deck.

"You said ... something about Potarium?" the jester muttered.

"That's right. The land of po, where all souls are destined to return."

"Ah, I see. I finally made it…"

As the jester leaned back in relief, he noticed that he had solid support on both sides of his body. At first he did not think much of it, until he realized something was wrong—his arm! He had lost his left arm to the corrosive mists of the pink mountains deep in Munderworld, but it was back! And as healthy as ever, as far as he could deduce. He was not sure if his head felt light as a result of the ocean, or the surreal realization that he had somehow been healed. Even his sleeve was still torn where his pale arm jutted forth from its opening, only partially draped by his dark half-cloak. He couldn't help but stare at it for a few moments.

"Are you alright, stranger?" the sailor asked, leaning in ever so slightly, his gray eyes shifting back and forth to look the jester over. "Most of the po we save are either scared witless and crying or ecstatic. You seem to be quite serious, however, as if you have other things on your mind."

"No, no, I am fine. You will have to excuse me." The jester took another deep breath, and confidently pushed himself up, trying to get a feel for his new arm as it shook slightly under the pressure. "Where are my manners? My name is Cynkz."

"Cynkz?" The sailor's brow twisted as his head turned. He reached up with a hefty hand to scratch at his broad chin, an oddly delicate act for such a husky figure. "That's a weird name if I've ever heard one. You'll definitely stand out among the other po in the city! How is it spelled?"

"C-Y-N-K-Z. But the 'z' is silent. It is pronounced like sink, as if sinking into, well…"

"Sinking into the ocean?! Ha!" The sailor caught himself in the middle of a hearty laugh, only partially stopping to continue, "I'm sorry, it's just too perfect.

Well, it's a pleasure to meet you, Mr. Cynkz. I am Bellor, the captain of this humble vessel."

Cynkz looked up and out to the ocean, squinting to see anything in the dark of early morning. He took the opportunity to take a few steps away toward the taffrail and angle himself away from view. With a swift gesture and a slight puff of colorless smoke, he conjured a proper sleeve for his bare arm, once covered by his dark cloak.

I still have my abilities, he thought. *That's good to know.*

"You know," the captain said, "most po have little more than whatever rags they were wearing in Munderworld with them. Yet here you are with an entire getup: a dark cloak, a fancy red and purple pattern on your shirt and pants. And even a hat to boot? How did that manage to stay with you all this time? Did it somehow get stuck to that long braid of hair you're carrying?"

"Heh, it's hard to say, I—" Cynkz interrupted himself, eyes wide as he remembered the thread. He frantically reached for his breast pocket, his palms sliding clumsily over the smooth wet material of his shirt and cloak before catching the opening's edge with a sharp fingernail to pull it open. A brief flash of otherworldly light peered out from the dark cavity before he closed the pocket flap just as quickly.

Cynkz couldn't help but exhale in relief. He also noticed the crude twisted ring Foa had given him in Munderworld. Its metal was so dull, worn, and sandy in texture that it hardly reflected anything. Seeing his belongings in order put his mind at ease.

"You're a strange one, ain't ya?" the captain said. "But it's alright. Potarium welcomes all kinds. I figure I'd be a bit scattered too if I had just been fished out of the ocean."

Cynkz readjusted his shirt and cloak as he turned to address the captain. "What can you tell me about Potarium, if I may ask?"

The simple act of moving on solid land, getting the opportunity to ask questions and investigate, filled Cynkz with confidence. It felt more than good to get his bearings and to begin making progress on his journey again, even if he was now doing it alone.

"It's the city of po. In fact, it's said that all po souls are destined to eventually make their way to its shores. Strangely enough, we haven't been getting as many po coming in as we used to. You're the first we've seen in maybe, ah… Hey, Jaid!" The captain turned his head to one of his crewmates. He lifted his heavy hand to his mouth to amplify his already boisterous voice in the direction of a young lad pulling in ropes from over the boat's edge.

"Hey! Jaid!"

"Y-yes, cap'n?"

"When was the last time we saw a po wash up in the dark ocean? Five years? Maybe six?"

"As far as I know, it's been 'round twenty full years, at the least, sir."

"By all that the Creator—"The captain ran his wide palm along the side of his head. "Twenty years already? Time sure does fly here."

Cynkz's eyes began to dart around as he worked through the implications. *Twenty years? Surely it couldn't have been that long. It hardly felt like a night's dream since I last spoke with Fiddle and The Munder King down in the abyss. But what if it's right? That such a simple decision to move forward could lead to entire decades just gone…*

"You alright, stranger?" The captain's voice broke Cynkz out of his pondering, and the two greeted eyes once more. "You seem awfully distressed for someone who was just saved." Bellor hoisted himself up, readjusting his belt as he took in a weary breath. "Welp, whatever you went through in that hellish pit, it's over. It's all good tidings from here, friend. We'll be arriving at the docks soon enough."

"Earlier you were talking about Potarium?" Cynkz said, trying to refocus the conversation.

"Oh, yeah! Potarium is a beautiful city. A giant mountain of fancy buildings and towers. Golden grass and colorful birds humming all around it. Once it starts to get a little lighter you'll see it reflecting across the horizon like a lamp against a mirror."

"Is it that bright? Like a glowing city?"

"Well, you've gotta take into account that all po souls glow. You get a million of 'em all cooped up in one place with a bunch of bright, shiny buildings, and it's gonna be a real sight at first."

"It sounds painfully blinding."

"Aye, but your eyes'll adjust to it real quick. We fishermen and sailors have to deal with it the most. Going out into the dark waters just to come back, and needin' to look at the city time and time again. But you get used to it."

"You still have to fish? Even in heaven?"

"Well," the captain ran his square knuckles against his chin again, a tick that Cynkz couldn't help but take note of. "We don't *have* to do anything. But they say that even in Heaven, it's good to know the joy of earning your keep. It's worth it, too! The fish and food here is unlike anything you've likely had back on Peara."

"Peara…" Cynkz looked down as he struggled to recall as many details about the planet as he could.

"Yeah, Peara. You know, the world? Though I've heard it no longer exists. What madness could have brought that about, huh? You weren't there, were you? When Peara was supposedly bathed in 'destructive light,' or whatever the priests say happened?"

"No, I… I don't think I was there." Cynkz couldn't help but notice how unsure he felt all of a sudden. He could feel his head weighing heavy as he looked down at his feet, and his shoulders bearing down on him as they slumped. What little confidence he had was gone as he tried to think of ways to fit in, to make it sound as if he was not some strange alien who had never heard of his own world.

"Well damn. It'd be nice if at least *someone* could give us a firsthand account of what happened. It sounds way too interesting to be left up to interpretation."

"Who knows," Cynkz said, forcing a soft smile. "Perhaps I will be the one to find out what happened? You just have to learn how to get to the right people and ask them the right questions."

"Maybe, maybe, but that's way too much sleuthing for me." The captain rested his hands on the ship's railing, almost looking dismissive of the idea. He kept his eyes on the horizon for a while. Cynkz wondered what it was in particular he was looking for.

"Ah! There!" The captain excitedly pointed a stocky finger at something in the distance.

Cynkz's eyes followed the line the captain's arm formed. At first, he couldn't see anything distinct in the darkness, no matter how hard he squinted. Yet when he least expected it, Cynkz's sharp eyes became wide as he noticed an intense glimmer of light cutting through the exact middle of the scene before him, right where the dark ocean met the sky.

The fierce light rose out from the horizon. Its center revealed what appeared to be a golden mountain, one that was oddly detailed and intricately patterned. Upon further viewing, its truth became evident—it was a layered piling of exquisite architecture. Rows of shining gold lined the edges of countless, creamy white walls and formed deliberate barriers of the many buildings that composed the city's silhouette. The metropolis engulfed the horizon, its borders seemingly unending as it unveiled itself. The smaller, milky white structures at the base of the city eventually gave way to rows of gleaming towers behind them, and even greater unknown structures behind those. The many rounded edges and jutting spires lining the upper columns bordered on pomposity, as if the architects knew no limits, be it money, space, or time. Taking in a whole view of the city from afar gave the impression of an abstract painting, and its theme, if there was one, was that of indulgence.

At the center of the rising mass of structures a colossal tower stood out above all others. It was a pure, solid cylinder of gold that reached up into the heavens. From the top of the tower several smaller pillars reached out in all directions, like the fingers of a mighty hand. Potarium itself appeared to hold up the sky.

The final detail that stood out was the sky itself. Rather than a flat plane of color and clouds, it resembled a clear, ethereal marble. The atmosphere looked as if it were bending upward, as if it were attempting to swallow the cosmos. The rounded, orbed effect distorted and reflected the countless lights emanating from the souls below as they moved back and forth. Their movement streamed across the surface of the marbled sky in arcs reminiscent of shooting stars. Parts of the city could be seen reflecting off of the far side of the orb, though the image was distorted in such a way that it was nearly impossible to determine anything specific.

Much like the rest of the city, it was easy to relax the mind and soak everything in as a single large piece, letting the various elements and lights and colors blend together into something abstract and holy. Despite its supernal impression, its overwhelming presence inspired the undeniable temptation to reach out and embrace it.

Cynkz stared at the city in silence for a long time, hardly noticing the early dark morning turning into day. Every other sound was drowned out by his fixation on the land set before him—the soft brush of foamy waves, the thumps of shuffling po on the ship's deck, even the sharp whistle of faint winds that carried the vessel forward. As they drew closer, Potarium's splendor amplified his fixation. It was physically challenging to try and take in every detail set before him.

As soon as he mentally surrendered himself to bask in the city's glory, the ship banged against a concrete pier jutting out from a stone dock and into the ocean. The resulting shock jolted his body back and forth, and his senses returned to him.

Cynkz could hear the frantic scurrying of the po manning the ship as they hurried to obey the orders of their captain. Just as he turned to watch the scene unfold, his eyes met Bellor's, who seemed to be waiting for the right moment to address their passenger.

"Alright, we're finally here, stranger. Once we set the gangway onto the dock you're free to go."

"Thank you," Cynkz said. "Where should a newcomer such as myself head first?"

"Well, by all rights you're free to do as you please." Bellor's voice strained as he struggled to reel in a heavy rope connected to the towering sails above. "I'd suggest you wait a moment and meet one of the holy men who will show you around. There's always one or two waiting near the docks to help new po get their bearings."

Just as Bellor yanked on another thick rope, the heavy clunk of wood on concrete caught Cynkz's ear. A new opening in the vessel's railing led to a makeshift bridge leading down to a stone pathway above the water.

Cynkz made his way to the path and had to stop himself short of stepping onto its planks. Considering that he still had his powers—such as shapeshifting and presumably flight, and their related attributes, such as his immense weight—he remembered that he had to take great care not to break anything he stepped on. Not wanting to draw any more attention to himself, he concentrated his gait upward, hovering ever so slightly above the surface before stepping forward. It took only a dozen soft steps before he reached the cement dock at the bottom and could relax.

He had hoped his act would go unnoticed, yet as soon as he rested at the bottom of the walkway, it seemed he had the attention of one po in particular all along. Cynkz met the man's eyes and took note—average height, evenly tanned skin, a clean-shaven head and luxuriously smooth and simple robes colored like a deep grape wine with gold accents.

At first the po seemed unknown to Cynkz, yet the way he watched him and smiled said that he was familiar with him. Cynkz stared and squinted for just long enough, and suddenly his memory was jolted at the realization of who his watcher was.

"Kadd!"

CHAPTER 3

CYNKZ COULD HARDLY BELIEVE HIS luck. It was indeed the same po he had talked with back in the depths of Munderworld, trapped between the shifting gray mountains of Horgafell, though now Kadd was much more presentable. Despite his change of clothing, and his clean-cut hair, he radiated the same calm, dignified air that stood out to Cynkz in the abyssal realm.

"Cynkz!" Kadd called out, releasing a thin, tapered hand from one of the baggy sleeves of his robe to wave. "It's been far too long. You and your imp friend have some nerve!"

Cynkz caught himself staring a moment too long and pushed himself toward his friend. Once within arm's reach and before he could say anything, Kadd stepped forward and wrapped his arms around him for a warm hug. Cynkz couldn't help but smile and return the gesture, though realizing he was still wet forced him to speak up and start the conversation proper.

"Ah, my apologies, Kadd. I still reek of the ocean—"

"Nonsense!" Kadd pulled back, the tanned skin of his cheeks pressing in tight balls toward his eyes, his hands pressed firmly on Cynkz's shoulders. "You and your friend have some gall."

"How so?" Cynkz asked.

"You and Fiddle come along, and within mere moments capture the attention of a forlorn group of po whom I had been looking after for only Paithos knows how long, and then you lead us on a harrowing adventure to an entirely new realm, giving us the opportunity for ascension. Then what? You just leave? I could have sworn you possessed better manners than that!"

Paithos?

"Well, I cannot speak for Fiddle," Cynkz replied, his head bowed, "but I at least try to ensure each of my own interactions begin and end proper—"

"Cynkz, I'm only joking." Kadd's words sputtered through a half-chuckle.

"My apologies…"

"Weren't you a jester?"

"Yes, but… I hardly remember anything of my time alive."

"Ah, that's right." Kadd stepped back, folding his arms into the billowing sleeves of his shining robe. "I remember you mentioned you lost your memory of your life back on Peara."

"What I am interested in is how you ended up here? Fiddle and I barely made it out of that swamp unscathed. I tried to follow and help the other po but—"

"Cynkz, it's alright." Kadd patted the jester on his pointed shoulder once more. "I know you did what you could. We all knew the risks of what we were attempting to do. The fact that I, and several others, were able to make use of the opportunity to eventually ascend means you did more than enough."

Cynkz couldn't help but press his own cheeks up into tight knots as he smiled back at Kadd. It was difficult to tell if he was merely dripping wet, or if actual tears were beginning to form in his eyes.

"Thank you, Kadd. That means a lot."

"In truth, it was not long after we got separated that I was able to lead Harla and a few others toward a maiden of Elm."

"Harla? I remember her. She was the ... 'interesting' older woman with the sharp tongue?"

"That's the one." Kadd's expression loosened as he shrugged and shook his head. Cynkz could only guess at the sort of burden Harla had been back in Munderworld.

"Is she here too?" Cynkz asked. "How did you manage to make your way through that swamp? And how did you end up here before me? Fiddle and I blazed through the remaining realms in what felt like record time."

"Really? It's been some years since we last saw a po wash up on our shores, at least fifteen, maybe twenty years since I last saw you two."

"Twenty years..." Cynkz rubbed his chin and jaw as his eyes darted around, as if trying to follow his frantic thoughts. "So, what the sailors spoke of was true... But how? It could not have been *that* long. It hardly felt like a night's dream since I last spoke with Fiddle and The Munder King at the bottom of the abyss."

"Wait..." The priestly po's eyes shot wide, his arms loosened from his sleeves as he looked the jester straight in the eye. "You actually *spoke* with this 'Munder King'? You found him? He's real?!"

"Yes, very real, and just as terrifying as you would imagine a lord of darkness to be."

"By Paithos..." Kadd stumbled back so clumsily that it looked as if he might fall over. Cynkz widened his stance, bracing himself to lunge forward and help if need be. Before he could do anything, Kadd caught himself and raised one hand as he rested his head in the other.

"I—I'm fine, Cynkz, thank you."

Paithos... That name again... Cynkz thought. Kadd had said the name enough times that it stood out as significant.

"Is it really that shocking?" Cynkz continued. "I mean, considering all of the oddities in Munderworld, meeting the king does not seem so far-fetched an idea that it should be surprising."

"It's not that... The Creator—or Paithos, as we call Him in Potarium—none of his teachings mention a Munder King. In fact, much of Munderworld does not exist in the old texts or scriptures."

"Well, that is odd—"

"It's more than odd." Kadd returned his arms to his sleeves, his expression now stern to match his stately demeanor. "It is near blasphemous that such a thing even exists. Nothing is supposed to exist beyond Paithos' guidance."

"Kadd, I did meet The Munder King, as did Fiddle."

"Oh Paithos, Fiddle met this 'Munder King' too? Hopefully, he didn't anger him? Though considering you are here, it must have gone … decently?"

"Yes, in fact. Actually, believe it or not, Fiddle is one of The Munder King's offspring—"

"What?! How…" Kadd took in a deep breath, perhaps realizing that he was betraying the otherwise dignified impression he was trying to uphold.

"Fiddle was just as shocked as you to learn of it."

"From where did you two learn of this?"

"The Sisters of Elm. We got to meet them and had an interesting exchange."

"You … also got to meet the Sisters of Elm? Personally? And they told you all of this?"

"Yes. They helped us move forward and tasked me with finding their long-lost sister—"

"There's *more* of them?!"

"Yes. Just one. Her name is Yla."

"I have never heard that name before. If there is a 'Yla' here I've certainly never met her. But… by Paithos…"

"I am sorry, I did not mean to—"

"No, no, it's fine, Cynkz. But you have literally just arrived! You're still dripping wet from your time in the dark ocean, and of course, the first thing you do is come along and relay world-shattering information to me. This is all too much!"

"My apologies. I only wish to be candid."

"That you are, Cynkz. In fact, it is why I like you! Simple, straightforward and honest, like any respectable po. But come along." Kadd turned and gestured toward the city behind him. "I have been working these docks as often as I possibly could in the hopes of getting to greet you if you ever arrived. Now that you're here, I'd like to fulfill my duty as a humble deacon and help introduce you to our lovely city."

Cynkz's eyes followed the line formed by Kadd's pose, his vision trailing along the po's robed shoulders, his thin extended arm and finally resting on the mass of gold and white buildings that layered upon one another just ahead. He looked back at Kadd and smiled.

"Of course," Cynkz said. "Lead the way."

The subtle combination of sweet and salt in the air faded as the two walked further into the city and away from the shore. It was fortunate to have a proper guide, as only one word could adequately describe the new world Cynkz now walked through: overwhelming. He saw detail upon detail, layers of cream-colored stone and golden edges, exquisite arches supporting the many, unnaturally colored trees and plants—they were everywhere Cynkz looked. His eyes felt overworked, though in the exciting way a child may feel upon visiting somewhere new.

Despite the abundance of elements at play, everything was meticulously designed. The curvature and coloring, and even the way the divine light shone upon the many glistening edges did well to lead the eye naturally in the right direction. It was easy to deduce where one would need to go in order to walk from one area to the next. The wide streets and clean brickwork were also inviting, allowing the overflow of po bodies to shuffle back and forth effortlessly in every which way.

Cynkz took every opportunity to look around, always keeping Kadd's humble silhouette in view from the corner of his eye. The bright whites and golds constituting the majority of the architecture made the numerous flags and ribbons hanging off every available nook stand out. Most of these banners were dark and silky, brilliantly mirroring the realm's radiance with complimentary reflections. Deep crimsons gave off pink shines, weighty ultramarines were lined with sky-blue lighting, and even thick and woolen eggplant colors expressed lavender shades when dancing against the light. In many of these pieces of cloth intricate threads of gold were woven into unknown symbols consisting of carefully considered curves and swirls that formed their embroidery. As if that weren't enough, within many of the designs were clear cut outs, and as the wind blew through them, the air hummed sweetly. There were so many of these flags and ribbons, and yet their many songs against the wind never clashed. They inexplicably harmonized in a way that one could not believe, even when experiencing it directly.

The angelic whistling of the flags and ribbons seamlessly led the ear to the excited chirps of numerous small birds buzzing and dancing their way across the open air. Unlike the hanging cloth, their colors were not afraid of delving into the lighter hues, some so bright they were indistinguishable from the glistening reflections of gold.

Cynkz had remained mostly quiet on their tour, so that it seemed as good a place as any to start his light-hearted inquisition.

"So, what is with all the birds?"

"Hmm?" Kadd turned his head slightly to the side, keeping his sight in front of him but an ear toward his guest.

"The birds," Cynkz repeated. "There are a lot of them. Their song is lovely, but creatures are often not the most sanitary things to have going about."

"Ah, the hummingbirds. Potarium's representative animal."

"Representative?"

"Yes." Kadd finally stopped and turned, revealing a warm, simple smile as he spoke. "A national animal, like a symbol chosen to represent a people, something to embody them in a romanticized, artsy way."

"They are beautiful, but why hummingbirds?"

"Well, they're colorful, energetic, clean, full of active energy and life, and the constant beating of their sharp little wings creates a pleasing hum. But, between you and me," Kadd leaned in, going so far as to place a hand up to his mouth, akin to a child about to share some wily, arcane knowledge with a friend, "my favorite thing about them? It's their snoring."

"Their ... what?" Cynkz was taken aback, literally, in that he had to stop himself from leaning too far back as he raised a curious brow.

"They snore. At night, they always go to sleep at the same time, and you can hear them snore well into the night. It's absolutely adorable."

"Seems as though it would be hard to get any sleep."

"That's the best part." the humble holy man spread his arms wide, his billowing violet sleeves waving around like wings. "Their snoring synchronizes! They always come together into a single, calming tune. It's like getting your own personal angelic choir to lull you to sleep. I swear it sounds a little different every night, but it's pleasant all the same."

"That sounds lovely." Cynkz had to restrain himself from smiling too wide as he witnessed his friend's enthusiasm for the little creatures. He even wondered if he could turn into a hummingbird later and join in the nightly chorus for fun, perhaps to add a little bit of himself to the holy air.

"I'll admit, it's a bit of a childish thing to gush over." Kadd returned his hands to his sleeves and looked upward. "The fact that they are so reminiscent of the most glorious, though subtle, part of our city cannot be understated."

"And what is that?"

"I mentioned it earlier, but their little wings create a constant buzz, a soothing hum that fills the ear like warm honey. That hum is much like a proper *huum*."

"A what?"

"A huum. You're hearing it now."

Cynkz looked around, unsure of what precisely the man was talking about.

"I can only hear the buzz of the songbirds and the hustle of po in the street. I do not—"

"Listen more closely, Cynkz."

For the first time since their walk, Cynkz stopped and rested his mind. The cacophony of buzzing wings and shuffling feet, of whistling wind blowing through open flaps sewn into cloth—everything merged into a single harmonic sound. It was difficult to describe in terms of sound, but it could be felt easily. It was akin to a thick, balmy water swelling up within the soul that gently pushed its way up from the core and to the face. It was like sharing the warmth of another's heart with his own.

Cynkz didn't feel sad or mournful, yet the heat of oncoming tears lined the bottom of his eyes. The only thing that stopped him from staining the otherwise pristine brick roads with his newfound emotions was the regular soft pats of hands given by passing po upon his shoulders as they greeted him:

Welcome to Potarium.
Praise be to you, newcomer.
May Paithos guide you.
Potarium welcomes you.

The difference between the cold ocean water and the warm, loving air proved too much, forcing Cynkz to finally raise his hand to wipe away a single tear. The bulbous drop flattened and blended in with the rest of his slightly damp skin.

"What... what was that?" Cynkz asked.

"That was huumming, Cynkz," Kadd replied.

"I—I still do not understand, not fully."

"Song is the light which can touch things beyond the dark. We huum for Him. The effect is more powerful in groups, as you have no doubt just witnessed."

"So, it is like singing?"

"Not necessarily. It's like humming from the soul. It's a means of pushing forth your inner warmth out into the world around you. All po can do it! Give it a try?"

"I, uh, have no idea what I should do."

"Start simple, try humming."

Cynkz paused for a moment but took solace in his friend's confident expression. He took in a soft breath, cleared his throat, and gave his best attempt.

"Hoom… Hoooommmm… Hyooooommmmmm."

Kadd's smile immediately flattened, then the sharp edges of his mouth curled up like a dried leaf as his lips split to let out a hearty laugh. Cynkz couldn't help but smile back.

"Well," Kadd said, "it's a start. Nobody gets it fully on their first attempt."

"It all seems lovely, regardless."

"That's the important thing, I suppose. It means you have a heart, and you are, in fact, a real po."

"Was there any doubt of my po-ness?"

"Considering what you can do…"

"Fair point. But you know…"

"Hmm?"

"I remember the sentinels possessing some intensely deep roaring abilities. Is that at all similar to—"

"Ah, those stony beasts from the abyss? No, it is not the same, I hope. Huums are specifically meant for po to express and enjoy. They are a way of celebrating Paithos' brilliance and love. To huum for anything less is a grave sin, and certainly is not a privilege permitted to creatures of the dark."

"That makes sense."

"Let's keep going. This city is so large it'll probably take us a solid year of daily walks just to see it all."

With so many sights and sounds competing for his attention, one thing captured Cynkz's eye: the massive golden tower and the strange orbed sky it held.

The tower appeared like a shining marble filled with pure, clear water and perfectly reflected the world below. It radiated an aura similar to the apostles that would occasionally appear in Dulrot, a sight that demanded one to stare, yet no matter how much one looked, they could never quite make full sense of it. It was a beauty that escaped all logic, which only made the enchanting effect more potent. This formed a relentless feedback loop of furious thoughts leading into awe-inspired acceptance. Once the mind settled, more thoughts forced their way into view as it attempted to deduce what was being seen. On and on the process went through Cynkz's mind before he could hold his curiosity back no longer.

"What is that, exactly? Up in the sky?"

"I figured curiosity would get the better of you at some point. In truth, we know very little about the phenomenon."

"What of the tower, then?"

"That's an easy one to answer. It is called the Hand of Po, though most merely call it the golden tower, to appear a little less pretentious."

"It almost looks like a giant hand holding up the sky."

"Yes. It is believed to have been one of the first things the po built as tribute to Paithos. Before all of these buildings and roads and whatnot, there was just the mountain."

"Where do the resources come from? This city seems to radiate abundance."

"Believe it or not, countless resources grow within the mountain and below it. No matter how much we mine into the ground, there is more space and more materials to be found."

"Was gold the first thing the early po found?"

"No, but it appeared to be the most significant, or perhaps symbolic."

"How so?"

"Look to the ground, around the trees."

Kadd stopped and pointed loosely in the direction of a nearby oak. At the base of its silvered trunk stood countless small threads of gold. Save for its color and sheen, it seemed to behave as normal grass, except for one distinction. No matter how much the strands swayed, they never crossed paths or met one another. They stood in perfectly straight order, moving in harmony as they danced against the soft breeze.

"The grass itself used to cover this entire mountain," Kadd said. "It is a staple material of Potarium, lovingly called 'tinsel weed,' though it has many names. I believe the 'scientific' name for it is tinsel fescue, but many resort to much more pleasing terms, such as angel hair or Omun thread."

Cynkz couldn't help but chuckle beneath his breath, knowing what he did and carrying a truly divine thread in his pocket.

"Yes, the term 'weed' may seem a bit derogatory," Kadd continued, "but it is in good spirit. The unique golden grass is stubborn and strong and will grow anywhere it gets the chance. Some believe the soil it grows from could possess a number of practical uses of its own. It's both incredibly durable and flexible. No doubt you've noticed the golden lining on much of our cloth?"

Cynkz looked over Kadd's robes at the golden seams that poked out against a sea of dark silk. Another look around him and he noticed similar, though more restrained, threading in much of the other clothing the passing po wore. What would be simple shirts and trousers and skirts seemed elevated by the soft shining edges of gold outlining their silhouettes.

"Indeed, I have noticed. It looks very nice, almost ostentatious."

"Well," Kadd released his crossed arms to shrug his shoulders and smile. "When you have an eternity to look forward to, you may as well make the most of it. We could find you a seamstress to help you blend in. Your cloak and dark attire make you stand out quite a bit."

"I am used to standing out, whether I want to or not."

"I can imagine."

"How big is this city? How can it continue to accompany so many souls?"

"Good question!" Kadd's excitement overtook him and his voice was loud enough to rise above the buzz of birds and the brush of the crowd, catching at least a few strange looks.

"Look up to the sky again. You can see the other side of the city reflected on it, though it may be a bit distorted."

Cynkz could see countless glowing dots sliding back and forth along the clear silver surface of the curved sky. It no doubt mirrored the many po as they moved back and forth through the city underneath.

The golden tower covered most of the bottom of the sky, and the light reflected so intensely that the top of the structure seemed to blend into the orb itself. He could see some part of the bottom edge of the orb as it curved away from the tower on the opposite side. The faintest line stretched across the circular edge in a bleach-white strip that cupped the sky.

"You see it?" Kadd asked. "On the other side of this mountain, you can see an infinite desert, or at least we believe it to be infinite. Many have tried to travel into it and reach its edge, but no matter how far we go, we could never find its end. We gave up trying to travel across the thing, and nowadays we are just grateful for the free real estate!"

"A desert does not sound too inviting."

"No, no, but here's the amazing thing about the land," Kadd lowered his hand, gesturing toward the golden grass before them. "The fertile soil itself slowly expands. In fact, if you stand on the edge of Potarium's border and stare long enough, you can see the ground changing color and texture as it reaches outward."

"Ah, sort of like the burning horizons in much of Munderworld."

"In a sense, yes. Though the effect is much, much slower here. It's wondrous at first, but soon loses its novelty. I liken it to a more exciting form of watching paint dry, to be perfectly honest with you. Though I am grateful all the same."

"The abundance present in nearly every facet of this city makes a lot more sense now. How interesting."

"Interesting, indeed! It's surreal, isn't it? We have ever-expanding lands to cultivate, an endless sea to fish from, limitless minerals from the ground, and all the space and time eternity can offer."

"And no sentinels or muns to get in the way of pursuing more peaceful, productive endeavors."

"Exactly!"

Again, Kadd was loud enough even Cynkz was beginning to feel uncomfortable. Once again Kadd drew a handful of strange looks. Fortunately, it gave many po an opportunity to give their greetings as they passed by.

Greetings, Father Kadd.

Good day to you, Father.

Morning, Father Kadd.

"Father?" Cynkz asked, his curious brow raised enough to poke uncomfortably into his forehead.

"Yes, well," Kadd said, finally quieting down. "I've spent enough time here to get on good terms with most po. I figured rubbing elbows with the religious authorities was a good way of getting along."

"It seems like a perfect fit for you, I would say."

"Why thank you!"

Again, Cynkz's guide was loud enough to garner more attention from passersby. Even the occasional passing hummingbird stopped to give the man a quick glance.

He must be doing this on purpose, Cynkz humorously thought.

Kadd seemed to calm down, and he looked back up at the sky, staring on for a moment too long for Cynkz to consider comfortable.

"Many believe that an even greater land lies beyond the sky," Kadd said, his voice returning to the more solemn tone Cynkz remembered from their first meeting in Horgafell. "We have a name for it, a sort of unofficial title for what many believe to be the land of the Creator, Paithos, and his loyal Omun. It's called Omundisia."

"Omundisia…"

Cynkz joined his friend to stare in awe at the divine orb. The streaks of light reflecting the po strangely reminded him of stars shooting across the night sky. Of course he was reminded of his time stargazing in Dulrot, as such things always did. He felt overwhelmed, almost suffocated, by the barrage of new details this strange world was giving him. He longed for the comfort of the still, night sky and its motionless stars, their positions ingrained in his mind like an old map.

Yet something new stirred within him—thoughts of what he would do, and where he would go after accomplishing his task to find Yla, the missing Sister of Elm. Returning to Munderworld was not all that appealing, but strangely, neither was staying in Potarium. His mind still felt incomplete, and he knew spending another eternity watching the sky, even if it was in a newer, brighter place, would not satiate his unending curiosity. Whatever answers he sought, he knew he would most likely have to go further than he ever thought possible.

If what Kadd said was true, then everything he could ever want to know must lie in the land of Omun. He had found his way to the enigmatic Munder King; what was there to stop him from at least attempting to reach the Creator?

"We should get moving."

"Hmm?" Cynkz responded sharply, as if a trance had been broken.

"The days go by quickly in Potarium, and I'd like to grab a bite to eat before retreating to my home for the night. If that's alright with you, that is?"

"Of course. It is not as if I have anywhere else to lay for the night."

"What kind of food do you like? I imagine your palate is sick of whatever cuisine Munderworld offered?"

"Well, I was never that picky. Normally, I would just catch some small fodder and Fiddle would cook it with his flaming breath."

"Ugh!" Kadd's face twisted with displeasure, the first time Cynkz had seen him with a cold expression since his arrival. "You two are such animals! Come on, let's get you some real food. Maybe steak? Seasoned vegetables? I'd offer seafood, but considering how long you must have spent drifting in the ocean, I could understand your distaste for such things."

CHAPTER 4

T HE WORLD WAS DARK, WARM, AND comfortable. The rejuvenating veil put Cynkz's mind at ease, despite residing in what could be described as an unending abyss. A dark eternity stretched out in every direction, yet held his heart in tranquility.

A single light in the far-off abyss caught his attention. The tempered cadence of its twinkling was soothing for the soul. With little else to use as a reference—not even his own body—the sight of the single light growing larger made him think he was somehow approaching it. Or perhaps it was approaching him?

It felt like too much effort to break the peace by questioning it. Except the one thing that stayed with him longer than the poem—his curiosity—forced him to examine the vision further.

He looked hard into the abyss, and into the light and its piercing quality. What was once airy and tranquil soon weighed heavy with dread. The calming, suppressive touch of the darkness now felt encumbering as if something, or someone, was holding his mind in place. The cradle of the dark revealed itself to be the cold grip of countless invisible hands hiding just beyond his sight. The dancing light resembled the tip of a dagger as it stretched into a long, sharp pupil.

The sharp, vertical slit continued to burn its way toward him. The once-flat plane was engulfed in the frayed, dancing edges of a menacing eye that peered directly into him, and spoke in a voice that was felt, rather than heard.

The thread…
Power…
Freedom…
You are but a wayward child… You grasp at the dark,
blind to the freedom, the power, sitting right before you…
Give it to me, then…
The thread!
Give it to me!!!

Howls of the damned flew past Cynkz's ear. The woeful groans blended with the crackling, frayed edges of the light burning against his vision. When movement failed him, he tried to speak. Nothing but coarse sand spewed forth.

Cynkz smothered himself with cries of agony as the blinding light and cold grasp of the damned consumed him.

A quick, shallow breath returned Cynkz to the waking world. The contrast of chilled sweat mixing with the warmth of his bed helped bring him back to his senses. He could do little in that moment except stare at the dark, blank ceiling.

It was just a dream…

Cynkz could hardly remember most of his dreams, and nightmares were rare. Even though he knew better, the few times he experienced anything in his slumber often stayed with him far longer than they should. It took a lot to affect him enough to return from a dream or a nightmare. Despite everything he had experienced thus far, such a short meeting with the dark eye—Eshra'Tel—seemed to offer the appropriate amount of trauma to have a long-lasting impact. He wondered if Fiddle ever experienced something similar.

As his breathing slowed, he reminded himself that he was safe and merely lying in a simple bed in Kadd's humble home on a cool evening night.

He looked to his side and could see the edges of a bowl, half-filled with crackers that sat next to a half-filled glass of flat ale. He remembered Kadd mentioning the risks of eating just before going to sleep.

Even heaven itself can do little to protect you from your own mind. Snack away at your own risk, Cynkz.

As Cynkz recalled his friend's warning, he couldn't help but chuckle. He thought it was a fitting reward for expressing such restraint during the day's walk. He remembered the look on Kadd's face as he practically shoved all sorts of food into his face: finely roasted vegetable skewers, exquisite crabs and lobsters that reflected odd colors in the light, and steaks seasoned with golden … something. Kadd never told him exactly what it was, thinking it would be more fun for him to just 'try it' and see what he thought.

Being inside such a small space was odd. He had spent so much time soaking up the infinite air of Dulrot, with nothing to restrict his freedom or his shapeshifting. Anxiety's sting slowly overtook him as he sat himself up to stare into the dark room.

A subtle, sharp chirping coming from outside a nearby window set his mind at ease, reminding him that freedom was but a few feet away. With an invigorating breath, he picked himself up and made his way to the clear pane, making sure to grab his trusted cloak and pointed hat along the way.

A creak of the frame and he heard a passing breeze carrying a trill symphony throughout the night. From every corner of the city, tiny trailing echoes fluttered in perfect harmony. When the sleeping hummingbirds would breathe in, a soft whistle flattened the air. Then came a pause. Then a handful of rolling chirps tickled the ear. They started off high in pitch, then trailed off into the night like wind. This rhythm repeated, over and over, complimenting the otherwise silent night the way a rocking chair creaking back and forth on a wooden deck would.

A quick glance around the neighborhood revealed the coast was clear. Quickly, the jester stepped up and flew outside, sticking close to the side of the building to finally rest on top of the slanted, shingled roof. The roof's angle ran almost parallel to the rest of the city, with its many short buildings, tall and winding trees, and various odd structures, including intricate street clocks, shining flagpoles and golden railings sitting perfectly on the mountain's side.

As he looked into the far distance, he could hardly see the line where the city ended and the flat, dark ocean began. Everything had a pleasing way of melding together; one element had a way of naturally leading to another, setting the mind at ease with little more than a slow look around. When he sat down and leaned back, the quick shift in perspective as he lost sight of the ground instilled the sense of his center of gravity being thrown to the wind. It was a freeing sensation, complimented perfectly by his first deep breath of fresh air.

The night sky in Potarium was odd to Cynkz. He could see most of the same stars and constellations he knew back in Dulrot, yet the general brightness was distracting. Back in Dulrot, the darkness had a way of dulling the other senses, making the stars stand out all the more potently. In Potarium, despite it being the dead of night, most of the world was clearly visible. This, along with the city's excessive detail and flair, made stargazing difficult for Cynkz for the first time. Regardless, he resumed his rest and focused himself completely on the stars, looking for the usual constellations: the many stories the night sky told.

In the center of the sky, from his perspective, was a small bundle of four stars that formed a distorted, rhomboidal shape. It was said to represent the shield of an ancient hero, simply named Olcgahen. Many said he was strong enough to thwart half an army on his own and needed no weapon. He only began to carry a shield to help protect his friends on the battlefield.

Farther down was a loose collection of no less than eleven stars that, when connected, formed a crude spiraling shape. This was meant to represent Fairia, the first po, or the po mother, as some called her. Cynkz had heard many speculations, from scholars and the like whom he and Fiddle had met in Dulrot, concerning what exactly she was meant to be holding. Some said it was her first child; others believed she was merely holding her hands up to her heart. Some of the oldest art depicting the constellation merely showed a po woman huddling around something, concealed by a long elegant robe that cloaked her entire body.

Cynkz's favorite theory, however, was that she was holding a precious egg and was using her warmth to incubate an unborn phoenix. Just to the right of her constellation was another collection of stars, around fourteen in total, though sometimes as few as twelve could be seen depending on the lighting or time of night. These stars were meant to represent one of the oldest creatures in po mythology, a great fiery bird named Hagharaia the Sky Flame. It was depicted as stretching out its wings to Fairia, giving her warmth and strength as she birthed the first po.

It was rare for the stories concerning constellations to overlap, but Fairia was notable as the first to do so. Cynkz often wondered what exactly she looked like. Such thoughts led him to think of the mysterious woman who told him the poem. This, of course, always led to Cynkz reciting the poem in his mind:

Every star
Near and far
Waits for us

To just
Reach out
And accept them...

Perhaps he could find her, somewhere in the massive city. And if not, maybe he could go to the Creator, Paithos himself, and ask him what it was supposed to mean, or why he had held on to the memory for so long.

His mind went quiet, and then he lifted his head from the slanted shingles of the roof and looked at the top of the mountain city. First, he saw the giant golden beam reaching up to hold the glistening orb that defined the sky. In the dark of night, it was much easier to see the many reflections of the world below, though from so far away very little could be discerned. Everything reflected on its surface melded together into countless swirls of colors and shapes, looking similar to a giant divine marble melting into the rest of the sky.

As it always did, curiosity pierced his mind, letting loose countless simple questions regarding the phenomenon:

Omundisia...

What is it exactly?

What is stopping me from just going up to it and...?

That was the moment Cynkz knew he had to do something. If watching the stars wasn't enough to quell his mind for the night, he may as well go forth and do a little exploring. He was still on a mission after all, and it did no good to sit idly by and watch time pass. Who knows, perhaps he'd find an important clue regarding the missing sister? Endless possibilities ran through his mind, giving him a burst of energy that could be contained no longer.

Cynkz began to ponder his method of attack: *I suppose I could fly up there to the top of the tower if I really wanted to, but ... I would rather not draw unnecessary attention if I can help it. I doubt the good people of Potarium would appreciate a cloaked figure slithering across the night sky.*

Another pensive look around, and the jester made his way up the slanted roof. Once he dropped behind the lip of the gray-shingled rooftop, a quick puff of colorless smoke was all that remained. In his place, a small cream-colored mouse could be seen venturing off to the first open alleyway behind the humble home.

In the guise of his diminutive new form and under the shade of the bright elaborate architecture, Potarium revealed a new side of itself to Cynkz.

One thing that stood out to him during the day was how wide the buildings in the city were. Most structures didn't surpass three, maybe four stories as far as he could tell. The relative height of any building seemed to rely mostly on its placement on the mountain. Near the pier were many larger buildings that seemed squat and short when compared to a single restaurant or simple shop placed upon a fabulous perch. From below, so low that Cynkz's long whiskers dragged along the smooth sandy brick in the many roads, everything appeared massive. The extravagant architecture and the many looping arches and flared edges only seemed to exaggerate the effect. Cynkz did his best to stick close to the walls and railings as he sped along. The open inviting layouts now seemed intimidating.

Another aspect of the city that stood out to him were the many stalls placed meticulously alongside the proper buildings. None of them were being manned during the day, at least as far as he could tell. Most had little occupying their shelves, and their specific purpose escaped Cynkz, though there were a number of stalls that did have something nearby: puppets. What would normally be little more than knee-high bundles of loose, wooden joints and simple caricatured faces appeared as resting colossi to the mouse.

Cynkz had to take great care not to trip on any of the many strings attached to them. Their size and variety were as bewildering as many of Potarium's other details. They were so different from one another that Cynkz began to wonder if each one was made for a specific person in the city. They did have one unifying trait, however. A single, wooden chute shot out from their heads. Most had at least a single feather sticking out like fanciful plumage, and most, if not all of their strings came from the chute. It seemed as if someone happened upon a genius innovation for puppet construction, and the practice spread like an epidemic over the entire city.

Perhaps Cynkz could get one made for him. If puppetry was so beloved in Potarium, he would do well to get along with the other po and learn the trade, or so he thought.

The strange mouse seemed to enjoy getting a chance to truly stretch its legs. He almost seemed to make a game of it, going out of his way to jump between arches and somersault over railings. Whenever a path or alley offered no obstacles for him, he took it upon himself to hit his stride and carry his momentum onto a nearby wall, running along the vertical edge for as long as he could manage before gravity finally had its say.

He could never get truly lost, no matter how much he tried, as the golden tower always loomed overhead, pointing him in the right direction. Flat roads led to layered steps, leading to inclined walkways. Railed paths lined the ground with winding pedways clearly designed for leisurely strolls by those who had nothing but time on their hands.

The closer he got to the tower, the more inefficient and ornate everything became. The relatively utilitarian square blocks of the buildings near the ocean gave way to elaborate cream-colored residences and golden arches with countless flags and ribbons. Further up, the residences gave way to huge terraces, grassy parks, and gated mansions. They were the first buildings he saw that exceeded the usual three or four stories of the buildings below.

The scent of fresh water flowing through fountains and man-made ponds caught his nose. As things were even more open and spread out, he finally had a clear view of the golden tower in its entirety. The base of the structure appeared like an elaborate castle, though the tower as a whole seemed remarkably simple in its design. It was golden, but it was little more than a massive rod of sparkling material, with nothing more than a number of windows dotting its sides as one looked up.

Cynkz wanted to find a high place somewhere to rest for a moment and survey the land. A dangling branch from a nearby tree on the edge of a small estate seemed the perfect place.

The countless taps of his tiny claws against the pavement immediately turned to coarse scratches as he pulled himself up the tower of bark. From high on a branch, he could hear the wind again, and felt the slow breeze forcing the woody limb to wave ever so slightly to the world. As he caught his breath, he relaxed to the tune of the hummingbirds lulling the world to sleep with a quavering lullaby.

Yet something felt wrong. He couldn't quite put his paw on what felt off, but the small hairs stiffening on his back and the tensing of his whiskers seemed genuine. He thought about how Potarium did, in fact, have animals, and if it had animals, it must have predators. For a moment, Cynkz wondered what kinds of predators the city housed, and then he heard something behind him—

A prolonged scratch against the tree's bark, followed by a mellow, trailing hiss.

Cynkz froze in place, unsure of how to react, when he heard a new voice calling from the distance.

"Frallion!" a young po woman cried out. "Frallion! Here baby, here kitty! Come here already!"

Kitty? Of course...

Slowly, the mouse turned and locked eyes with its stalker. The feline's immaculately fluffed fur and rounded patterns did little to hide the intent in its expression. It was a beast, staring with a deathly glint that sharpened its wide, round eyes. At that moment, the world was still and silent. Cynkz couldn't even hear the hummingbirds. If he could sweat in mouse form, he may have been worried about making a mess of the pavement below.

What should I do? Cynkz thought to himself. *Normally, I'd just transform and get away, but how would I explain this to the woman? The last thing I want is to be the source of strange rumors, as some odd, shapeshifting miscreant making trouble in the—*

Before he could finish his pondering, the beast leapt, forcing the dangling branch up and down as it pushed off. Cynkz could do little more than release his grip and fall to the ground. For a moment everything was a blur, but a quick thud and a pain in his tiny shoulder brought his senses back.

Driven by nothing but pure instinct, Cynkz quickly picked himself up and ran straight ahead, faster than his little legs had ever managed before. He could hear the shriek of the woman behind him, and worse, the pounding of padded paws gaining on him. He thought he was fast, but the predator on his trail seemed nigh impossible to match. It didn't help that he had no idea where he was going, only barreling forward in fright. The lip of a heavy wooden door misaligned with the ground caught his eye. Salvation was in sight!

A quick dash and his head flew under the door. A weighty thump followed him, and he could see the shadow of the lumbering beast poking through the slit of light coming from outside.

Before he could take his first breath of relief, a long, furred arm shot under the door and scratched around, grasping in the dark for its prey. Without thought, pure instinct driving him once again, the rodent bit the beast's knuckle, forcing a blood-curdling shriek as the furry fiend withdrew its weapon.

Finally, things were calm enough for Cynkz to recollect himself. As his adrenaline settled, he could hear soft footsteps hurrying to the scene.

"Frallion! Thank goodness. I didn't think I'd be able to—Your paw! How did—? Ugh. Let's just go home."

The shadows peeking from beneath the door lifted and faded away, and the world was quiet. He couldn't hear the hummingbirds from inside.

Cynkz attempted to look around but couldn't see much in the dark. What caught him, however, was an odd combination of scents. Clean, manufactured oak and steel and stacks of wooden barrels were tucked away in what little room his temporary safe haven offered. What was even more peculiar were their contents. The smell was coarse, textured, though it possessed the faintest hint of something sweet, like a fresh plant that had recently been pulled from the soil. It was tinsel weed soil!

He remembered Kadd's words regarding po researching possible uses for the material. If what he said was true, then it made sense for them to store it somewhere neatly. As much as he wanted to investigate, he reminded himself that he was on a mission, and could sense the coast was clear.

The tiny rodent cautiously poked its pink snout from below the door to give a final glance around for potential danger. The tower was so close that it took up much of his vision. Around its base was a multitude of pristine shining plants whose green and blue edges reflected the golden light of the tower. They were the perfect place to transform into something capable of flying up to the tower's crown.

A quick dash led to the ruffling of grass and leaves as he entered the brush. A quick puff of colorless smoke brushed the surrounding fauna like a gentle breeze, and a simple white dove began to make its way through the air.

⁘

The small white bird perched itself at the top of the massive tower. With a few hops, it was far enough from the ledge to conceal itself from prying eyes. A burst of smoke revealed the cloaked jester, as he finally rested, relieved to have reached his destination.

Cynkz took care not to get too close to the edge, so as to not accidentally reveal himself to any who may notice him. The structure was so large that the horizon was barely visible from his position. There was nothing else up here. Perhaps its immaculate condition was owed to being constantly windswept. He was still able to move and get a good look around—for the first time getting a full view of the entire city.

To one side, he witnessed the usual flood of rolling hills and cream-colored buildings that dotted the mountainside. He even wondered if he should call it a mountain; it was such a large mass it could merely be called an oddly raised continent. His sharp vision allowed him to pick out many of the city's usual charming details, but he struggled to focus on anything farther out to the horizon. Like the edge of a painting, the flat, dark sea bordered the top of his view of the city. It seemed to stretch out infinitely and was eerily calm, presenting itself as little more than a massive, world-framing line of black that shone subtly against the night sky.

In the opposite direction, Cynkz looked out to see more buildings and terraces and streets that wound together into a mass of architecture. Cynkz struggled to make sense of the structures at the far end of the city, yet Potarium's border blended into what appeared to be a desert. Waves of bleached, pristine sands created a wavering line on the horizon against the dark sky. It too seemed to go on without end. Taking in such a vast, clearly split landscape gave the impression that he was standing on the invisible line between light and dark.

All that was left to consider was the orb itself: a clear glassy curving of the sky whose surface bowled into the golden hand beneath it. Strangely, Cynkz could hardly make out his own reflection in the structure. The orb seemed to distort anything that reflected off its surface. The images it expressed were stretched every which way, and he could see hints of the starry night sky twinkling through it. The positions of the stars were equally distorted but clearly visible. He swore that he could see a shooting star or two fly across its curved form.

Cynkz felt awestruck, if only for a moment. He couldn't help but laugh at his trepidation. He went through quite a bit of trouble to get here, yet he struggled to take the final steps. The orb hovered so close he could nearly reach up and touch it from standing on the tower's roof. Despite its clear, potent form, it didn't look like something that could be touched. It was as if one were looking at a mirror in a dream.

Still, Cynkz's curiosity could not be sated with a mere glance, and he finally lifted himself off the ground and drifted to the orb. He reached out, and his pointing finger was the first to establish contact. A brief all-consuming chill ran through him before immediately dissipating. It was as if he were touching nothing at all. Confident, he gave a smirk and thrust himself into the dreamlike surface, his entire body disappearing into the ether.

Upon which, he was shot out instantly, his form flying out as quickly as he entered. The impossible shift in his perspective caused him to pause, his mind empty and unable to make sense of what just occurred. He turned around, gave the orb another glare, and threw himself into it once more, this time more vigorously, or perhaps anxiously.

Yet again, he found himself spat out. His expression began to twist, reflecting his frustration. He turned around, took a deep breath, braced himself as best he could, and threw himself in once more with every ounce of strength he could muster.

The world had become a blur, but a quick thud and a sharp pain in his shoulder brought him back to his senses. His ejection from the orb was such that he created several tiny cracks in the building's otherwise immaculate, golden material when he landed. Once the sting in his shoulder settled, the only thing he could recall was the sense of a bitter chill running through his body for a brief moment upon entering. The sensation seemed to dissipate as quickly as it came.

Cynkz picked himself up and brushed himself off. He gave a final look to the ominous orb as he decided on his next course of action.

I think that is enough for tonight. Perhaps I should fly home for now…

After staring at the orb for a moment too long, he gave a deep breath, a weighty sigh, and a hearty stretch before retreating to the edge of the golden tower. With a puff of smoke, the cloaked jester descended into the form of a simple white dove and flew off into the night.

CHAPTER 5

THE AIR FILLED WITH ROLLING twangs, plucked harpsichords, and boisterous horns. Sharp calls and trill chants filled what would have been silent air between each sound. The deep, rhythmic thumps of flat hands and smooth wooden mallets being slammed on top of wide drums could be felt tickling the inside of the listening ear. This was enough to finally wake Cynkz up from his deep slumber.

It took a moment for his eyes to adjust to the light. Fortunately, he only needed a moment before the over-whelming radiance calmed, and he could comfortably look out onto the city.

Kadd's home was a humble little building, or at least, it was humble when compared to the rest of the architecture that sprawled across the landscape. Cynkz noticed the shingles of the roof he sat on were actually a dark, dull red. If he positioned himself just right, he imagined the harlequin pattern of his attire could partially blend in with them.

The night's choir could be seen littering the air with colorful streaks of feathers and shining needle-sharp beaks. It was fun to try and keep track of the hummingbirds as they zoomed back and forth. It was surprisingly difficult to separate them from the vivid combinations of dress and plumage worn by the po gathering in the street.

In contrast to the almost humble attire of the day before, many of them wore extravagant outfits and carried unknown objects and accessories. Dark wooden staves dragged countless trails of cloth as they waved flags through the air. Loose pants and long coattails dragged their way across the immaculate streets. Shining bodies peeked out from beneath an infinite variety of masks, each one seemingly unique and tailored specifically for the wearer.

The masks were interesting, as they reminded Cynkz of his visions dancing with partygoers and courtiers in banquet halls of old. The odd shapes stood out to him. They were huge impractical curls of material with eye openings carved into all sorts of expressions that did little to hide the smiles and laughs hiding just beneath them.

The creaking of heavy wood directly below caught Cynkz's ear, and a familiarly robed man stepped onto the short stone pathway that separated his home from the street. The man looked back and forth before turning his head to look up to his home's ceiling. Once his eyes met Cynkz's, the two shared a smile and a wave.

Without a second thought, Cynkz pushed himself forward and hopped down, making sure to slow his descent as he drifted toward the ground. It wasn't until his foot touched the brick pathway in front of the home that Cynkz realized his mistake.

"Whoops," Cynkz mumbled to himself.

"What's wrong?" Kadd said. "Seems like you've taken to the great huum quite well."

"The what?" Cynkz raised his brow as he turned toward his friend.

"There," Kadd continued, pointing toward something far off in the distance, embedded deep within a wave of clean white structures. "Farther down the mountain of buildings—you see the great flag?"

"Indeed, I do. It is quite large."

"Yes!" Kadd turned back around to face Cynkz, placing his hand back within the end of his baggy sleeve. "Those flags are embedded at key locations across Potarium, sitting at the center of a Temple of Paithos. As the wind passes by, the huums inscribed within them emit a most powerful aura that protects all living po."

"A greater huum?"

"Yes. Specifically, the Huum of Peace."

"What is so special about it?"

"It can sense oncoming danger and will swoop in to spare a po from any imminent injury. Say if you were to, I don't know, jump off of a building? Your descent would soften long before you reached the ground."

"That sounds amazing. I doubt even The Munder King would be capable of such a thing. Though I did not feel anything affecting me as I came down."

"Really?" Kadd revealed his hand to scratch at his chin. "It's rather potent. Many describe it as feeling as if one's body were swiftly enveloped in warm air, thick enough to almost smother them as it takes effect. It can even detect one's intent! One would not be able to willingly harm another under its effects."

"That does not seem too different from the many huums I've experienced already. I did not feel anything significantly different."

"I see... And you said you still possessed your powers?"

"Yes."

"Extraordinary. Almost as extraordinary as your preference for sleeping outside like an animal."

"My apologies, Kadd, I did not mean to—"

Kadd interrupted Cynkz with a smile and a quick pat on his shoulder. A small huff of air took the place of what Cynkz presumed would be another chuckle.

"Cynkz, I'm joking again," Kadd said. "You're free to do as you please here in Potarium, even sleep outside like a beast."

"I've grown so used to being outside, completely unobstructed." Cynkz tipped his head toward the ground. The tip of his hat poked forward into his sight, leaving little else aside from Kadd's sandals to look at. "Being inside any enclosed space makes me quite anxious, unfortunately."

"Why's that?"

"Well, shapeshifting is quite demanding, both in terms of the energy it requires and space needed to move about."

"That makes sense I suppose but," Kadd pulled his hand back to his chin to scratch the smooth, tanned surface that stretched to follow the contours of his wry smile, "you could always just shift to something smaller, right?"

"Of course, but shapeshifting is not so simple."

"But you make it look so effortless!"

"I assure you it is anything but. Whenever I shift into a new form, I adopt the perspective of whatever it is I turn into."

"Perspective?"

"Yes. Say, for instance, I turn into a mouse. I would then see everything the way a mouse would. A space that would seem unimpressive to us would appear gargantuan."

"Sounds frightening."

"Sometimes, yes. Because of that shift in perspective, I could easily overestimate the free space available for future transformations. I could be a mouse in someone's home, and in the spur of the moment, believe I have enough room to shift into an elephant."

"What happens if you turn into something too large for the current space?"

"One of two things will occur. The space itself will give way to my new form, or I'll collapse under my own weight."

"Holy... That sounds, um, unpleasant, to say the least. Has this happened before?"

"Only once. Fiddle and I were hiding in a large tree. As I was in a hurry to get us out of there, when the coast was clear I transformed preemptively and the tree burst. Fiddle was none too happy about the incident. He was picking splinters out of his fur for days. It was so long ago that I hardly remember the circumstances—perhaps we were hiding from a sentinel we played a prank upon?"

"You two really are troublemakers! Who would have the gall to prank sentinels?"

"Heh, yeah, but what else is there to do in Dulrot?"

"Fair point, my friend."

A moment of quiet settled between the two, giving Cynkz an opportunity to look past Kadd's shoulder and toward the festivities growing in the street.

"What is with all the activity so early in the day?" Cynkz asked, finally letting loose a burning question he had held onto like a hot coal.

"Ah, there's a parade today," Kadd replied. "I forgot to mention it yesterday during our walk."

"Does Potarium host such festivities often?"

"Yes! So much so that it's difficult to keep up with them all."

"I suppose the open layout of everything makes more sense now."

"Great observation, Cynkz. But alas, I have a request for you, before we partake in the festivities."

"Of course, Kadd. Anything you need."

"I'd like for you to join me in early morning service before the parade kicks off in full."

"Service? As in church? Of course. What better way to begin learning more of what holds your heavenly city together?"

"Splendid!" Kadd loosed both hands from his billowing silk sleeves. A quick step to the side and a hand on Cynkz's shoulder opened the way forward. "Let's hurry, then. We're late enough as it is."

Just as the day before, Cynkz found himself overwhelmed by the deluge of colors and architecture. He began to notice a consistent trend with Potarium's design. Nothing could ever be simple. Every single thing needed an extra flourish, whether it was the odd twisting at the end of an arch, or the ribbed stone surface of a pillar exposing intricate designs and symbols, or even what should be a plain ribbon shining at its edges with golden threads woven into flowery patterns. The flat shirts and trousers of the previous day were covered in tapering coattails and puffed sleeves.

Up close, Cynkz noticed the many masks and costumes the po were wearing also reflected much of the light around them. The constant flutters of the hummingbirds zooming back and forth only added to the multitude of hues bouncing between the shining surfaces. It was one thing to witness a rainbow from afar, but as he followed his guide through the streets, he felt as if he had fallen directly into one. He was grateful Kadd was wearing something dark and dull in comparison; it made him easier to follow through the crowds.

Finally, Kadd approached the magnificent red oak doors of a tall pointed building. Its basic design accentuated its one flourishing element—excessive height. Cynkz couldn't help but stop to look upward, as if trying to meet the towering points in some way.

"Right this way, Cynkz," Kadd said.

Cynkz snapped his attention back to see Kadd resting a delicate hand on one of the heavy wooden doors. He stepped forward as quickly as he could.

"One final thing," Kadd pointed at Cynkz's crown. "It's common courtesy to not wear a hat inside, stylish as it may be."

"Of course." Cynkz hurriedly removed his pointed hat, taking care to not ruffle any of its tips. He noticed Kadd looking him over and smiling, and Cynkz wondered what he was up to.

"Have you ever considered getting a haircut?" Kadd asked.

"A haircut? I do not think so. Why? Is something wrong?"

"Not necessarily. It's just that your braid of hair is massive. From a distance, it looks like the dark tentacle of a beast! It can't be convenient lugging all of that around."

"I've grown used to it," Cynkz released a hand to rub the side of his head, combing his ink-black hair with pale, pointed fingers. "Plus, Munderworld does not give much room for such luxuries, as I'm sure you know."

"Very true."

"If it is that bothersome, I could perhaps transform—"

Kadd's expression froze, and he promptly leaned toward Cynkz, catching him off guard.

"I would advise against transforming out in the open," Kadd whispered. "We do not know how people will react to such a display, or what your powers mean in Potarium."

"Ah, of course."

Kadd leaned back into the door and pushed it open. The creaking of the dense wooden door immediately gave way to the sound of distant preaching. An effect of the tall open space inside, every sound within seemed to echo, giving the impression that everything was farther away than it really was. Kadd noticed a few heads turn toward them, and he quickly bowed and gave a silent greeting before hurrying to an open row of seats in the back. Cynkz followed close behind, trying to ignore the eyes staring at him as he walked by and sat down next to Kadd. Once they were seated, everyone's attention returned to the man giving a passionate sermon.

The priest stood behind an exquisite deep red podium beneath countless colorful lights shining through the stained-glass windows that made up the sides of the chapel, their extravagance only matched by his attire. Long coattails led up to long, billowing sleeves and tapered to thin shoulders that held up the older gentleman's head. It was adorned by the tallest hat Cynkz had ever seen. From a distance, it appeared like a gleaming pike was cutting through the waves of colored light that coated the walls and floor as his head moved back and forth to match his impassioned display. Whatever material his hat was made of seemed to split and cross near the top, leading to two tiny golden spikes that gave his tapering silhouette a final unnecessary bit of flair.

Cynkz was beginning to see what Kadd meant by him standing out. None of the jester's attire came close to the ostentation on display in much of the city. He tried to imagine what he must look like from afar and could only imagine a dark tendril weaving its way through heavenly mists of light.

Cynkz finally quieted his mind and focused his attention on the priest's teachings.

"Hear now, beloved children of Paithos the Creator! See how even in this humble building the light shifts and paints the world with beauty. It is through His blessing that we po have been capable of focusing His splendor. By harvesting His materials, and by the vigor of His blessing, we can meld the very elements into something orderly and divine. All light in Potarium— we must remember—comes from Him, and it is this light that allows us to see the world in front of us. He literally grants us vision to witness beauty. Is there any greater gift?"

Rows of murmurs rolled through the audience:

No, father.

No, my Lord.

Of course not.

"Of course not," Kadd whispered.

Cynkz looked at his friend and smiled before looking back to the priest.

"We must always remain grateful of His glory, and we must never take it for granted. Remember, we always huum for Him."

The crowd muttered once again:

We huum for Him.

We huum for Him.

The priest continued, "Let us finish today's sermon with a simple huum."

The priest flipped open the top of the podium and revealed a brilliant crystal. It was a perfectly cut pyramid, and one could see a number of glittering particles suspended inside. The second he revealed the crystal, the rainbow of colors lighting the chapel seemed to focus on the object. What was once a sea of varied colors melded together into a soft, milky golden hue.

Cynkz quickly leaned to his side and whispered to Kadd, "W-what is that?"

"That is a medium," Kadd whispered back.

"A what?"

"A medium. I suppose you can add that to the list of things I forgot to mention on your first day."

"What does it do?"

"In truth, they can do lots of things. Remember how I told you about the scripture sewn into the flags making huums? Well, you can carve huums and scripture into almost anything for a variety of effects. You can even communicate with others over a long distance."

"Like telepathy?"

"Heh, not quite."

"What else can they do?"

"Well…" Kadd leaned back and crossed his arms. "Some believe it possible to do nearly anything, if we could only figure it out. Some even think teleportation might be possible."

"Teleportation?"

"Yes. If we could channel the appropriate huums into the appropriate mediums, we may be able to transport materials over long distances instantly."

"Wow… I would not believe it normally, but considering everything else I have seen and heard thus far…"

"Indeed! Perhaps we just need to—"

"*Ahem.*"

A new voice interrupted, and they met eyes with a stern looking po seated in front of them. All three stared at one another for a moment before the two realized their transgression and ceased their discussion.

Kadd seemed to know exactly what to do. He leaned forward, clasped his hands together, and began to hum. Cynkz noted the welling feeling of an invisible, warm energy surrounding them as the crowd's huum grew in intensity. He seemed to be growing accustomed to the effect, but noticed he was the only one not contributing.

"Kadd! Psst, Kadd!" Cynkz said, desperately leaning toward his friend with one hand covering the side of his mouth and the other lightly tugging at Kadd's sleeve the way an anxious child might.

"Yes, Cynkz?"

"What do I do?"

"Just huum. Remember how we practiced?"

"Yes, but I still don't think I can—"

The sharp clap of a single pair of hands silenced the room. Cynkz's sharp eyes grew wide as they darted to the front and met the eyes of the priest.

"I see we have a newcomer," the priest said. "How wondrous! Come forth, child. I would love to give you a blessing."

"Kaaaddd!" Cynkz's whisper could hardly be considered as such as he frantically accosted his friend. "What do I do?"

"Just relax and follow the good man's lead." Kadd softly patted Cynkz's sharp shoulder, reassuring him, even if only a bit. "Oh, you can leave your hat with me."

"Thank you."

Cynkz relinquished his trusty hat to his friend, drew in a deep breath, and stood up. He walked down the long aisle splitting the room in two. The intense light beaming from the front forced the benches to cast short, hard shadows on the ground. He tried not to look directly into the light as he walked forward and kept his eyes downward. He could see the soft, rounder shadows of the po as they shifted in their seats, presumably to watch the strange newcomer. Indeed, he appeared as a dark tendril cutting through a wave of light. The huums continued, and he felt as if he was walking through a warm cloud. The sharp lines of the red carpet lining the aisle guided him through the shining haze.

Cynkz finally reached the steps leading onto the stage and found himself stopping just before climbing to the top. He looked up and was greeted by the open arms of the priest. He seemed much shorter up close, but he still needed to look up to the holy man. It took everything he had to not turn his eyes and gawk at the towering tips of his chapeau.

"Welcome, my child." The priest's voice felt both heavy and tender, much like the air around them as the crowd's huumming continued. "I do believe you are a new soul. It has been some time since we last had the pleasure of greeting a newcomer. Indeed, it is a pleasure to welcome you to Potarium."

"T-thank you," Cynkz muttered, his stuttering weakening what little confidence he had beforehand. He felt so much more sure of himself walking blindly along the shadows in the ground. He missed the dark nights of Dulrot more than ever as he forced himself to greet the light head on.

"Come! Stand before me so I may share His blessing with you."

Cynkz climbed the final step and stood squarely in front of the priest. Having to look down at the short man put him at ease.

At least, until the priest started speaking, stringing together nonsensical words in a rhythmic fashion, almost singing along with the chorus of huums emanating from the crowd. The priest closed his eyes, placed a light hand on Cynkz's sharp shoulder, and began waving the other one forcefully around his head.

Cynkz almost laughed as he watched the towering cloth on the priest's head wave back and forth. He wondered how such a thing managed to stay on his head, though he also wondered about his own hat, and how it managed to stay glued to him no matter what turbulence he underwent. Pondering these mysteries was enough to stay any potential chuckling.

He noticed that the priest's hand was getting dangerously close to his own head. He thought about Kadd's words, about the great Huum of Peace protecting everyone in Potarium.

Surely, he would not hit me? Cynkz thought. *Though he is getting awfully animated. I do not wish to be rude, but I cannot keep track of his movements without turning my head to watch. Though that would look quite silly if I—*

Smack!

The priest's palm pressed squarely into Cynkz's forehead. The impact cut through the air with a harsh pop as flesh collided with flesh, and the collective huumming of the crowd immediately stopped.

Cynkz's mind was blank, save for a single word: *Oww...*

It was then that Cynkz noticed the priest's heavy gray eyes were now wide as he looked at him. His shock was enough to make Cynkz uncomfortable, and his eyes began to move around in the hopes of settling on something less striking. He could sense a similar expression on the faces of dozens of po in the crowd from the corner of his eye and froze.

The priest quickly pulled his hand back, stumbling over his words as he said, "M-my child! You truly are blessed! To take the full force of His love so elegantly, especially for a new soul unaccustomed to the church? Wondrous, indeed. You may return to your seat."

Walking away from the light was an easier affair than pushing toward it. Cynkz couldn't help but notice his pointed, towering shadow piercing the radiance reflected off of the floor. More and more he could feel how out of place he was in this heaven. He wasn't uplifted, he wasn't chosen or asked, at least not initially. He may as well be an invader, a new darkness trespassing in an otherwise peaceful realm. He reminded himself that at least the Sisters trusted him with an important task, though it did little to quell his growing anxiety.

As he approached his seat, the jester noticed Kadd looking at him with a new expression. The puzzling twist of his brow and a squint in his eye led Cynkz to believe he was trying to figure something out. In truth, Cynkz was just glad to be out of the limelight, able to fully retreat to the back of the chapel, out of view of the audience.

⁓

The end of service came quickly, and the shuffling of bodies toward the exit matched the growing tempo of the festivities in the street. Kadd adorned his usual warm expression and moved toward the door. Cynkz hurried close behind, a small sliver of confidence coming back to him as he donned his trusty hat once more. He remembered that the pointed tips used to have bells on them but was grateful that they were merely silent, frayed edges of cloth.

A familiar, heavy voice called out to them before they could leave.

"Excuse me! Newcomer? Father Kadd? A moment, if you please."

It was the priest, currently shuffling toward the two as quickly as his short legs could manage.

Kadd stepped forward to greet the man. "Ah, you'll have to excuse my poor manners, Vicar Reindall. I've been so focused on showing Cynkz around Potarium that I nearly led us out without sharing our usual morning greeting."

"It's fine, old friend," Vicar Reindall said. He turned his attention toward the tall jester, his pupils flitting around in an attempt to try and make sense of the strange new soul standing before him. "So, your name is Cynkz? That's a most interesting name."

"So I've been told," Cynkz said through a soft smile, hoping to put the awkward situation on the platform behind them.

"Well, I wanted to apologize greatly for the, uh, incident on stage. Surely Father Kadd has told you of the great huum protecting Potarium? I figured I could go about my usual proceedings without risking an assault."

"Think nothing of it, great reverend," Cynkz said with a slight bow. "I have made it through far worse."

"I can imagine… And 'great reverend?' Not even Father Kadd addresses me in such a way!"

"I could begin right now if you want me to, great reverend?" Kadd said, the edge of his mouth curling into a tight smirk.

"No, no, it's alright." Vicar Reindall continued, "Considering what I put our newest guest through, I dare not call myself great at anything. But Father Kadd, I must ask, how has the court been? They've been awfully reclusive lately."

"Your guess is as good as mine." Kadd shrugged. "They haven't summoned me for anything in quite some time."

"The court?" Cynkz asked.

"Ah, yet another thing I failed to mention," Kadd said. "I suppose you can add it to the list."

"Yes, the Royal Court," the vicar adjusted his shoulders and quickly cleared his throat. "It is where the nobility of great historical distinction resides and rules over Potarium. Kings and queens of old sit high in the magnificent golden tower holding up the sky and manage the laws and such of our great city. Surely, you've noticed the great structure?"

"They're an interesting bunch," Kadd said. "Honestly, you can spend enough time with them and realize they're just as silly and quirky as everyone else is in town."

"Only you could get away with such a whimsical assessment, Father Kadd."

"I'm no more special than anyone else, pastor."

"Yet you have, in a short time, garnered the good-will of so many of Potarium's children. Why did you continue to stay below and work as a mere deacon of the docks?"

"I always wanted to be the one to welcome the po who helped me back from the abyss." Kadd reached over and placed a soft hand on Cynkz's shoulder, squeezing it tightly and smiling.

"Oh my! So it was you!" Vicar Reindall, hardly capable of containing his excitement, reached out and grabbed Cynkz's hand, shaking it vigorously. "We are so honored you could finally make it! Father Kadd has told us crazy stories about that wretched abyss, and how you valiantly led him and others through the darkness! You have done Potarium a great service already, young Cynkz."

"It was nothing, really," Cynkz said.

"Ah! And humble too?" The priest pulled back and cupped his hands over one another, holding them close to his chest as he smiled. "I think you will fit right in, Cynkz."

Cynkz smiled, but ultimately couldn't shake the feeling he had earlier as he walked through the chapel.

As different as he was, it was comforting the po welcomed him so earnestly.

"We should get going," Kadd turned himself toward the open chapel door. "I don't want Potarium's newest guest to miss his first parade."

"Of course. We'll speak more later, old friend."

The two shared a final bow, and Cynkz followed suit when the vicar looked to him and did the same. Once they began walking toward the bustling city streets, Cynkz took advantage of the moment alone to ask a burning question.

"I still cannot get over the new title," Cynkz said.

"Yes, well, po love to organize things with names and titles," Kadd said.

"The vicar mentioned you were close to the royalty here in Potarium?"

"Sort of, but I've no further ambitions beyond helping Potarium however I can, even if it is just greeting new souls and spreading the good word of Paithos."

"Such humility seems to be a great way to become loved." Cynkz stepped forward to address Kadd more straightforwardly. "Do you think the Royal Court could assist me in finding Yla?"

"Perhaps, but…"

Kadd stopped walking, as did Cynkz. As Kadd looked to the ground, Cynkz wondered if he was asking for too much from his friend. He noticed that his dark grape-colored robe stood out against the bright creamy whites and vivid greens that decorated the walkway in front of the chapel.

"Is something wrong?" Cynkz asked.

"I'm not sure if it's a good idea to bring up Munderworld with the nobility. Many are working through their traumas borne of their time in that place."

"My apologies. Perhaps it is too much to ask."

"In truth, I have no means of demanding an audience with them. The court comes and goes as it pleases, as you can probably imagine. Though many may speak highly of me, I do not have that kind of pull."

"I see, I meant no—"

"But imagine how funny it would be! Imagine the looks on their faces as a tall, dark stranger addressing the highest nobility in Potarium—legends in Peara's history—brings a small piece of Munderworld to their very doorstep! It's exciting!"

Cynkz was caught off guard by Kadd's enthusiasm. He could see the same excited, even childish, whims of fancy that he enjoyed in Fiddle. As much as he too enjoyed it, he remembered that it was also his own whims for adventure that put him and others through great peril as he ventured through Munderworld. He knew he had to take things more seriously and to think through any potential ramifications. Still, it did warm his heart to be in the presence of a happy friend, regardless.

"Even more exciting?" Kadd leaned in to whisper to Cynkz, something the jester found quite humorous considering they were all alone on the stone pathway in front of the chapel. "The court has been dealing with a growing issue. There are rumors of strange sightings in the night, even hooded figures skulking through alleys doing only Paithos knows what."

"How interesting…" Cynkz's thoughts returned to his excursion the night before. It seemed to be the right call to keep his shapeshifting hidden, despite the danger it put him through.

"Indeed! And who else could be of assistance than a great, shapeshifting jester?" Kadd leaned back and shot his arms out, as if presenting Cynkz to a crowd on a stage.

"Oh boy…" Cynkz scratched at the side of his head, wondering what he was about to get himself into.

"If we could garner an audience with the highest lords and ladies in the land, surely you could do what you do best, shake things up, help out po in need, and of course, make your way forward?"

"Make my way forward…" Cynkz looked up at the marbled, orbital sky.

"What's on your mind, Cynkz?"

"I was just thinking… You said that it is believed Omundisia lies beyond the sky, correct?"

"Yes, or so we believe. No mere po can venture into the sky or the land of Omun, of course."

"I am no mere po, however."

"Cynkz, you're not thinking of—"

"I still need answers about Munderworld, the Munder King, Peara, and about who and what I am. What better place to find them than at the source of everything?"

"I… I don't know if such a thing is possible! Though if anyone would know, the Royal Court might. I'm sure they of all po would possess deeper arcane knowledge of the land beyond."

"I guess we'll just have to find out," Cynkz said with a shrug and curled his lips into a faint smile to match.

"Ha! This is why I always wanted to meet you again, Cynkz! You always make things interesting."

"In truth, I do not try to 'make things interesting.'"

"Exactly! It's so effortless for you. All the better, huh?"

"I suppose so."

"Come on, we can start dreaming up plans and ideas for your adventure later. The parade is well underway, and I know a good spot where we can watch and get a good view of the action."

CHAPTER 6

W HENEVER CYNKZ HAD TO MAKE HIS way through the crowds, an anxious feeling returned. With so many bodies and po and noise swirling around him, he wanted nothing more than to fly away. Of course, he knew better than to make such a scene in the middle of a crowd and merely kept his focus on the violet-robed back of his friend and guide.

Except his friend was now gone!

He was completely lost in the crowd. The noise and music only seemed to get louder as Cynkz desperately tried to push his way past the flow of bodies swarming him. Worse still, the steady beat of heavy drums began to overpower everything else, and the crowd began to dance. Women in extravagant one-pieces and shining masks carrying large, brightly colored and feathered sashes twirled around him. Many would throw their sashes across the necks of po caught in the crowd.

Oh no… Cynkz thought, fearing the worst.

There was a thin separation between two bodies only a few feet away that led to the corner of a nearby shop. Salvation was in sight! Cynkz slithered his way through what felt like countless bodies, each shifting and swaying and gyrating, proving to be near-insurmountable obstacles for him. It felt as if he were worming his way through a battlefield, and the countless colored hoops and trails of shining confetti presented themselves as dangerously as fiery bombardments and flame-tipped arrows.

Just as he stretched his first foot to safety something loose and soft flew over his head and wrapped itself around his chest. He could hardly make sense of what it was before being pulled back into the mass of dancing po. Pulled through a sea of coattails and ornate masks, he came face-to-face with his captor, a young extravagantly dressed woman bearing her own glittering asymmetrical mask that did little to hide her beaming expression, or the many freckles dotting her face. Upon closer inspection, Cynkz noticed a blend of features he had never known: countless freckles dotting an otherwise pale face, rows of curled, intense auburn hair that shone similarly to the many dark flags dancing above poking from beneath her feathered headdress, and two piercing paradoxically ice-cold amber eyes. He was instantly reminded of Orilay—the woman in his visions who told him the poem he now held on to—and the pause in his thinking delayed his reaction long enough to induce a prolonged stare.

By the time he realized what was happening, it was too late. He was caught in the woman's web.

For a moment, he was lost in both mind and spirit. He felt completely vulnerable to the whims of this stranger as they pranced and twirled in step with the crowd. As he looked down and into her, and her back into him, his senses flittered peacefully into the void of an otherwise still mind. A quick glance around revealed his trusted hat had been knocked off at some point during his capture. Strangely, he didn't feel all too bothered by it, and figured that, at least for the moment, he could relinquish it to the whims of fate.

It was difficult to keep up with her. She was a bouncy youth, brimming with the sort of tireless energy one would expect. Cynkz did what he could but knew full well that he was out of his depth, only making him stand out even more. She didn't seem to mind however, so much so that she continued to pull him toward her. The grip on her sash, still wrapped around him, was rising. The accessory was resting firmly on his neck! Still, she pulled him in, closer and closer. Many of the other dancers were doing the same in the crowd.

Cynkz grew bashful and tried to break their gaze. He noticed how difficult things became when he couldn't transform to get away or deflect opposition. *Is this some sort of courtship ritual?* It was the first clear thought that had come into his mind since their dance began, and it left just as quickly as it came.

Her pull grew firmer, and Cynkz drew closer. The cool breeze of the wind seemed to merge with her soft, warm breath between them. It weighed heavy like an anchor, pulling down on an invisible rope that tied the two souls together. Everything seemed to paradoxically move too quickly and too slowly at the same time; she was pulling him in at a rate that he felt gave him little time to think things through, yet everything seemed intense, every passing second growing thicker and thicker, feeling heavier than the last. The only consistent element he could keep track of was his heartbeat rattling his chest.

As their faces were only inches apart, Cynkz took in a much needed, though quiet breath, and finally relaxed. He leaned in, as did she, and finally—

Smack!

A quick, sharp pain shook him out of his trance. Their heads recoiled, leaving Cynkz with only a single thought: *Oww...*

He instinctively reached up to rub his forehead, only to notice that she had done the same. Cynkz couldn't help but nervously chuckle, but stopped when he noticed the look of shock on his pursuer's face. He wasn't sure what to make of it. She seemed more surprised than anything, with just a hint of perplexity to round her expression out.

Cynkz was confused, then remembered: *The protective huum! That's right. This is just like what happened with the priest...*

A firm, friendly grip on his shoulder interrupted them. Cynkz turned around to see the calming, smiling visage of his friend, once thought lost, just in time to save the day.

"Cynkz! There you are," Kadd said, loud as ever. "I found your hat!"

"T-thank you," Cynkz said as he nervously took his hat and returned it to its proper place.

"I'm so sorry, ma'am. Cynkz here is new. If you'll excuse us."

With a slight bow and a smile, Kadd led them through the crowd and to an open corner, the same one Cynkz tried—and failed—to reach prior.

"I'm sorry, Kadd, I got distracted and—"

"There's nothing to apologize for, my friend! It's easy to get lost in the madness, but—" Kadd took in a breath and held his chin between his forefinger and thumb, smiling wryly, "what happened there? The poor young woman looked shell-shocked."

"I, uh, I'm not entirely sure." Cynkz couldn't help but bring his hand up to his neck, rubbing the skin where the woman's fluffy sash had caught him. "She pulled me in to dance, and I guess we got too close and, well, we bumped our foreheads together."

"It was similar to the priest, wasn't it?"

"Yes. How could you tell?"

"You have a nice pink mark on your head from the collision."

"Oh…"

"It seems as if you truly are out of place here, Cynkz."

Cynkz's sharp eyes grew wide, matching the perplexed state of the woman from a moment ago. "W-what makes you say that?"

"Actually…" Kadd paused, cross-examining the jester the way a researcher might their test subject, "Nevermind, it's probably nothing."

"If you say so…"

"Let's get going. We're almost at the good spot I mentioned earlier, nestled safely away from any potential po wranglers."

"Ah, that sounds lovely. Lead the way."

Even Potarium's back alleys, covered in their own shade, gleamed brightly in the morning light. Despite their winding path, it was easy for Cynkz to stick close to his guide as they made their way ahead. To his right, there were buildings layered as high as the eye could see, dotting the great mountainside, and to his left, the backs of the many small shops and stands lined the edge of the street. Perhaps it was due to their stability, but he found it a more comfortable environment to navigate. It was cramped, but it was also much easier on Cynkz's mind, not having to constantly worry about gently brushing past po bodies as he moved.

Kadd gestured toward a small set of gray steps that followed the back of a simple, two-story struc-ture. The claps and flops of Kadd's sandals echoed up the steps, and Cynkz followed the sound as he kept his eyes downward, taking great care to manage his weight so as to not cause any damage. The dull shade of the back alley immediately disappeared as he reached the building's roof, and the infinite colors and flairs of the parade took up much of his vision.

Despite being relatively high off the ground, many of the march's attractions found their way to reach up and past them. Feathers, ribbons, sashes, twirling string and even a few masks and shirts were being thrown to join the cacophony of cheer filling the air. Just above the fray many hummingbirds sang, their chirps barely audible among the chaos below. They followed close enough to act as a vibrant crown to top off the moving show.

Kadd shuffled to the building's ledge and took a seat, dangling his legs over the side. Cynkz noticed he didn't care to adjust his robe to keep it from getting dirty or ruffled. He appeared to put comfort above all else, and Cynkz saw no reason not to follow suit. Once he sat down next to Kadd, he began to point out the more notable aspects of the parade.

Many of the po dancing in the flamboyant march wore equally colored and accented masks, each bearing a unique visage. Some were simple caricatures of easily digestible expressions. Happy, sad, crying, one even tried to mimic the puffed cheeks of someone on the verge of puking. Others were more interesting, often being split with one side trying to express one feeling, and the other side pulling in the opposite direction. Not a single mask was placid. Despite the variety, none of them did a particularly good job of hiding the many smiles and laughs peeking out from every edge below their coverings.

Some of the po were smiling so hard Cynkz could see their puffed cheeks stretching the string keeping their masks attached to their faces. Yet what stood out most was the excessive plumage sticking out of nearly everything that seemed capable of handling it. Great bundles of billowing feathers and fur weaved through the air. Fortunately, their colors were brighter and more varied, even more pure in that they needed no further accentuation, unlike the flags and ribbons with their gold threading. Rainbows of fluffed gradients made it easy to keep track of most of the individuals that filled the parade as it marched forward.

Sharp clicks and clacks caught Cynkz's ear, and he turned his gaze to see strange creatures being led alongside the procession. They looked like elongated equines–light in coloring and much taller and thinner than one would consider healthy for a standard horse. They too wore a number of elaborate dressings. Smooth, silky fleeces sat loosely on their backs, dripping down to nearly touch the ground. The muted colors provided equal contrast to each beast's otherwise bright peach and beige coats. Their manes were long, straight and finely edged, showing the extensive care put into their health and appearance.

The elegant beasts moved lightly, as if riding on the air itself. In spite of their thin frames, they worked collectively to pull a number of large, wine and oak-colored carriages bearing the usual assortment of golden flourishes.

As they drew close, Kadd leaned forward, noticing his friend's new fixation.

"Those are Hirlwen steeds. They're beautiful, aren't they?" Kadd said.

"Yes, I think I've actually seen those before," Cynkz said.

"Truly? Perhaps from your time back on Peara?"

"Yes. I remember seeing them littering the fields outside our homestead."

"Really? Were you from Hirlwe?"

"I believe so."

"I never figured you for a simple farm boy. There isn't much out in the country aside from grassy plains and hilly glades."

"You've been there? To Hirlwe?"

"Yes, but it was only for a short time." Kadd leaned back and looked at the sky.

Cynkz couldn't help but lean back as well, giving him his full attention.

Kadd continued, "It was back when I was a bandit."

"What?"

"Yes, I was a roaming bandit in my early years. My group never amounted to much, though we traveled quite a bit. Mostly just hiding out on ships we shouldn't have been on to invade places we shouldn't have gone to."

"I never would have taken you for a bandit, of all things."

"Well, I didn't take up the profession until after I left home, after my father and mother died."

"I... I'm sorry, Kadd."

"No, it's fine! It feels good to open up about these things."

"Did you ever ... do anything unsavory?"

"You mean like murder? Paithos, no! We weren't capable of such a thing. We mostly resorted to stealing, sometimes for ourselves, sometimes for the benefit of others willing to pay a good coin."

"I see... Well, you have become a much better person as far as I can tell, Kadd."

"Indeed. In a way, it gave me the confidence needed to lead other po, a skill that followed me into Munderworld. It wasn't much, but helping the few other lost souls that I could find in Horgafell and leading them to whatever cave or nook or cranny we could find to rest—It felt good. It taught me a lot about dealing with people. Every po has their own story, you know? Everyone just wants to be heard and comforted."

"I can see why the people of Potarium like you so much."

"Yes. I think in a way it is an unending attempt to try and make amends with my own father. He was a preacher, you know."

"Really? How did you end up as a bandit?"

"I was already young and reckless. I was more interested in chasing my vices and seeking fun than hanging around a boring congregation. We had good money, which I of course took for granted until my parents were murdered while traveling. I was off on the far side of the region doing who knows what when it happened. All I remember is the sight of coming home and seeing the place cleaned out, blood everywhere and not a living soul in sight."

"What did you do next?"

"I had made some friends during my ... outbursts. I had nowhere else to go, and with my father gone I could not depend on his good word to balance out the negative reputation I had earned for myself. I think a small part of me also hoped that I'd be able to really take to the lifestyle, maybe become an infamous, powerful bandit leader. If I could find the ones responsible for their death, I could get revenge."

"Did you ever find out who did it?"

"No. And worse, I proved to not be particularly good at living a life of crime. Some years passed and I grew comfortable living in shadows, slinking through alleyways, and stealing whatever minor things I felt I needed to keep myself sustained."

Cynkz felt stuck. He couldn't think of anything to say, and certainly didn't want to come across as insincere by forcing out anything. He let out a mild huff of air and looked back at the parade. It was much easier to take in the wild view now that his mind was on something weightier.

Kadd continued. "It's also weird, in that I can't remember how I died."

"Really?" Cynkz nearly fell over as he readjusted his posture to signal that Kadd had his full attention once more.

"Yes. I vaguely remember being inside. I think I was resting, maybe eating something. Perhaps I was poisoned? I'm not sure. I just remember feeling light as a feather as I descended into darkness, and then a great stone weight pushed into me as I awoke on a cold, desolate, rumbling mountain in Horgafell."

"That sounds awful. I was fortunate enough to wake up on soft soil in Dulrot, though I felt just as lost."

"In a way, I can understand the frustration you feel of not being able to remember who you were. I often deeply wish that I could remember how it was that I perished. Maybe I could make something of it. Instead, I was stuck with the feeling of a lingering, unfinished thread weighing down my mind for what felt like eons. It's like being lost in your own mind, and as you desperately grope at the darkness, you realize that there should be a light, maybe a memory, some sign of a soul, yet there's nothing but dread and frustration. Though hearing me whine about this must seem silly, considering your near total amnesia?"

Cynkz leaned forward to rest his arms on his legs, hardly paying attention to the vibrant displays below. "After a while, I tried to not think about it too much. I felt as if there would be no use in running my mind in circles trying to remember things. It seemed much easier to live in the present, and sometimes I'd even forget that I had a life on Peara. And yet…"

"Hmm?"

"And yet, the weight of my long-forgotten life came crashing back once I got a hold of the thread."

"I remember!" Kadd pulled himself forward, nearly falling off the building's ledge in his excitement, "That thread… a piece of an apostle. Do you still have it?"

"I do," Cynkz replied, lightly patting his chest pocket just above his heart. "I always keep it close."

"That's good, and amazing you didn't lose it in the ocean! You didn't even lose your hat, for that matter. I wonder how that works?"

"Add it to the list of things I try best to not think about too much," Cynkz said with a playful shrug.

Cynkz couldn't help but smile. Kadd chuckled, as he usually did. Kadd's merriment was immediately interrupted by the sight of something peculiar. Before he could point it out, Cynkz had already turned to try and see the odd sight for himself. The many sounds below them seemed to be reaching a boisterous crescendo. A rising, harmonic flair suggested an approaching audible climax.

"Is the parade almost over?" Cynkz asked. "What's going on?"

"I should have known he'd be the one orchestrating yet *another* parade so soon."

"Who?"

Kadd lifted his arm and pointed toward an oncoming platform. It had far too many wheels and just as many peach-coated steeds draped in colorful cloth and saddles. Several rows of dancers moved around the sides of the float in perfect unison, each side forming waves of plumage that bounced around as they performed.

It was difficult to see what exactly was on the float itself through the countless feathers flying off of the headdresses and tassels worn by everyone in the parade. Cynkz finally saw a tall, thin figure waving on top of the attraction. It was a man, perhaps as tall as Cynkz himself, in a pearl-white suit adorned with several nonsensical accessories mimicking the flamboyance of the other performers. A deep crimson vest poked out from beneath his white coat, and where buttons and threading would normally sit were rows of small golden tassels that exaggerated his every movement as he pranced and waved to the crowd.

What stood out most was his top hat. It was long and thin, reminding Cynkz of the crown the priest in the church wore. This hat, however, held many short golden threads hanging off of its wide brim, and as he turned his head back and forth, it formed glittering waves that brushed away the wind like the skirt of a skilled dancer. He too wore a mask, though it merely covered the upper half of his face and half of his mouth. The mask possessed a uniquely distorted expression, partially showing a gleaming smile, and partially showing an intense scowl. Protruding from everything was an abnormally long hooked nose that was perhaps reminiscent of what a goblin or imp would have, yet was clearly exhibiting the same artistic flair that one does not often find in nature. Its tip looked sharp enough to carve diamond.

"That's Harquin," Kadd said, leaning in so Cynkz could hear him through the increasingly loud orchestra following the march.

"Who is he?" Cynkz asked, giving Kadd his ear, while keeping his attention on the subject of their discussion.

"Harquin the Ringmaster, also known as the Lord of Festivals, is a self-proclaimed 'munagerist' since rumors have spread of him taming muns. Which is funny, because muns cannot exist in Potarium, yet he uses the name all the same to draw attention to his performances."

"Those are quite the titles."

"Indeed, and well-deserved. He hosts the biggest, most extravagant plays and circuses in all of Potarium. He constantly works to orchestrate regular festivals. There are many rumors about him, with some saying he has made dark pacts in order to find the time and energy to do what he does."

"I figured time was just as meaningless here as it is in Munderworld. It does not seem like such a big deal."

"Exactly!" Kadd's arms flailed out, and his excitement was loud enough to pierce the fog of boisterous instruments blaring ahead of them.

The so-called 'Lord of Festivals' seemed to take notice, and for a split moment looked over in their direction. Kadd waved and smiled, though Cynkz found himself staring curiously. He could feel the masked man's glare even from beneath his elaborate mask. Harquin seemed to take note of the newcomer in an instant, and quickly returned to addressing the crowd as his float slowly drifted through the street.

Cynkz kept his eye on the man, taking note of several things: his energy, his forcefulness, the way he aggressively threw out every action. Everything about him seemed sharp and aggressive, as if he were trying desperately to hide his attempt to break loose of something. It was not unlike watching an angry beast barely able to hold itself back while in captivity.

"And the best part—" Kadd continued.

"Huh?" Cynkz said, finally coming back to his senses.

"I said the best part is that he often hosts a full-blown circus at the end of each of his parades!"

"A circus? Even after all of this? There's more?"

"Of course there's more! Potarium is not one to half-ass things, you know—Oops."

"What's wrong?"

"Well," Kadd reached back to scratch his head, the elongated sleeves of his robe waving back and forth as he bashfully expressed his anxiety. "As a holy man, I'm not supposed to be using such crass language."

"It makes no difference to me, you know. You can relax."

"I know, I know, but I do wish to live up to the good example the po of our city see me as." Kadd brought his hands back together and brushed them off before putting them back into the large open ends of his sleeves. "Anyways, if you're feeling up for it, we can follow the tail end of the parade. It'll end at the circus tent where Harquin will most likely host a grand show."

Cynkz looked back to the parade to see that most of the extravagant attractions had left, leaving only a street covered in colorful feathers and glistening ribbons and tassels in their wake. A huge crowd of po had also gathered and were following close behind the parade. Despite their extravagantly lined and threaded clothing, their mass was far less vibrant in comparison to what had come before. It was a nice change of pace, and much easier on the eyes, giving Cynkz a moment to rest his mind after the excitement. As the music faded into the distance, the rumbling murmurs of countless po shuffling past one another took its place as the horde pressed forward.

"Seems like a fun time," Cynkz said. "I would love to see a good circus performance."

"Splendid!" Kadd quickly revealed his hands to clap them together. He seemed to forget that the music was gone, and he didn't need to be as loud anymore.

"We can follow behind the crowd," Kadd continued. "I can get us great seats, reserved for the nobility and other such important, religious folk. This is gonna be fun!"

CHAPTER 7

A SHINING POINT BEGAN TO POKE through the horizon formed by the flowing rows of bodies shuffling in front of Cynkz. From a distance he couldn't make out much more than a fierce glint reflecting off of the world around it. As they grew closer, the object grew larger, and Cynkz's eyes adjusted. He was able to discern the overwhelming silhouette of a massive structure. It was a tent! The largest, shiniest, most elaborate tent he had ever seen.

Cynkz had not committed much of Potarium's streets to memory but felt such a structure would have stood out to him when Kadd showed him around. The tent itself was like a large circular dome with a pointed top and a sizable flag waving above its center. The flag matched the striped colors of the tent, crimson and gold interlacing to make a mesmerizing pattern.

Of course, no part of the structure was simple. Where simple yellows would do, bright golden streams reflected the heavenly light above. Where ordered, straight stripes would do, instead curved streams of color covered each surface, giving the structure a "wave-like" effect that Cynkz swore was moving. Perhaps it was just an optical illusion caused by his own movement messing with his vision of a stationary pattern. Where a simple straight wooden pole would have sufficed, instead a white, gleaming, ornamental spear with curves and ridges outlined its edges as it reached up toward where the flag was tied. Where a simple, clean cloth would have done well enough, a glossy stream of silk billowed in the wind, complete with thin, golden threading that danced in the light. Even the posts surrounding the tent, which were presumably tying down the entire structure, were silvery arches of some unknown metal.

Cynkz was no blacksmith, but he could recognize that whatever metallurgy Potarium was capable of was far more advanced than anything he had ever seen. He wondered how simple po hands could manage so many delicate series of interlacing loops and waves in hardened minerals. Even the ropes tied to them consisted of finely twined gold, presumably made of the same material as all the other golden threading, the so-called 'tinsel weed' that the po were so fond of.

A huge, dark split in the fabric of the great tent seemed to be swallowing up the mass of po as they entered excitedly. If not for the general cheer flowing through the crowd, it would have appeared ominous. Kadd's own pleasant expression as he marched confidently forward also put Cynkz's mind at ease as the dark veil of shadow ran over them upon entering the tent.

The sheer size of the tent made itself fully known at the last moment as Cynkz looked up only to see that nearly the entire sky seemed to be hiding behind towers of red and gold stripes. Once his eyes adjusted, he was awestruck that the space within the tent appeared to be larger than one would anticipate from merely glancing in from the outside. A massive, sand-covered ring sat in the center, and countless rows of immaculate seats lined the circular edge of the arena. The poles and ledges were just as ornamental and ostentatious as the ones outside. Even the sand seemed special. It was an off-white color with enough of a beige tint to make it pleasing to look at and helped to draw out pleasing rows of shade within each ridge and crevice. Cynkz wondered about the 'great desert' Kadd had mentioned sitting beyond the borders of Potarium, and he wondered if this sand belonged to that obstacle.

Speaking of Kadd, Cynkz noticed he was nowhere in sight. He had seemingly lost him again in the raucous sea of po shifting as they walked up to fill the seats. Cynkz looked around worriedly, though he kept his cool so as to not appear like a lost child looking for his parents. The sharp gesturing of a robed po caught his eye, revealing Kadd sitting by himself in a rather ornate looking bench near the top of the seats, and a fair bit away from the ring. Only Kadd and a few other noble-looking po were seated up there, and they were spread out quite far from one another. Cynkz smiled and waved before making his way up a winding series of steps leading up to Kadd's perch.

"These types of seats are often reserved for the nobility and other notable figures," Kadd said as he slid over to make room for Cynkz.

"You are awfully good at finding the perfect place to get a good view of things," Cynkz said.

"It helps to explore and get a handle on these sorts of things ahead of time, just in case."

"I could not agree more."

"You know," Kadd looked around at the empty seats around them. "There's usually at least a few stuck up types here. Guess it's a slow day for the great Lord of Festivals."

"If there is one thing I know, it is that the whims of the royalty move to their own beat and cannot be challenged."

"That is most certainly true. They're probably sleeping off a hard night of drinking in some chamber high-up in the tower. Can you imagine having to be one of the servants tasked with cleaning up after them?"

"Are stains caused by bodily fluids as difficult to get rid of in Potarium as they are everywhere else?"

"Pfft, even more so! Everything is so bright and clean, a simple brown splotch of vomit sticks out like a sore thumb. Sheesh, imagine being the one having to hold their hair back as they let their innards loose into a latrine?"

Cynkz laughed.

Kadd puffed up his chest and held out a dainty finger from one hand while holding a stiff gesture in front of his mouth with the other. "Ahem, ahem! I dare say, dear maid, this is–this is a—*bleerrgghh*... Ugh, be sure to cle—*urp*—clean that up.'"

Cynkz finally broke and had to rest his head in his hand as he laughed. He couldn't remember the last time someone had gotten to him in such a way. Perhaps Fiddle had done so some while ago, before their harrowing trek through Munderworld. He could feel Kadd patting him on the shoulder as he laughed with him. The only thing that stopped their merriment was a quick shifting of light within the tent, and the rising beat of drums and other unseen instruments coming from the now darkened ring. The show was about to begin.

A few mumblings could be heard throughout the crowd:

"Apparently, Ringmaster Harquin has found a method to put his performers in real danger."

"That would explain why his shows are so thrilling."

Danger? Cynkz thought to himself. *Just what type of show does this 'Harquin' conduct?*

Several spotlights swirled around the ring of sand, matching the tempo of drums rumbling out of sight. At once, all the lights collided onto a single point, revealing the same masked figure that had guided the parade, now seemingly alone in the center of the giant ring.

"Hello my fellow po! Who's ready for a good show?!"

Harquin's booming voice was refined and had the pitch honed like a finely cut diamond. It hit the ear with as much impact as one would expect from a hard material. The crowd followed his question with a roar and rounds of clapping. The show hadn't begun yet, and fervor had overtaken the arena.

Another booming sound followed as the ground began to rumble, and rounds of whimsical jingles and sharp chords accentuated the reveal of countless performers hiding in plain sight. As the music ebbed and flowed, so too did the many po as they moved past each other on all sorts of strange devices. Many rode on unicycles, others danced on impossibly long stilts. Several flew by one another as they juggled colorful orbs and baubles, going so far as to toss these items to one another, and never dropping the act for even a moment. It was mesmerizing to witness such chaotic athleticism circling around in impeccable order. Cynkz noticed that every single performer was multitasking, every available limb was being put to use, and all with easygoing smiles that stood at odds with the surrounding mayhem.

The spotlights spread out, illuminating most of the arena as they followed the performers around, though parts of the arena remained in shadow. It was from this darkness that a loud, almost ear-shattering horn blasted through the crowd. The sound seemed to roll in echoes, like a trumpet blowing in waves. The many spotlights followed the sea of colorful performers as they circled toward the center of the sandy ring like a whirlpool of bodies, only to reveal the source of the frightening sound—an elephant!

The beast was just as decorated as everything else, bearing a shining velvet blanket on its back, lined with countless golden tassels that swayed back and forth as it trudged forth. The lights flew up to reveal Harquin standing on its back as he had ridden his float in the parade. In one hand, he held onto a pair of glistening reins to guide the creature, and with his other hand, he commanded an impossibly long gold and crimson whip. Flinging his tool through the air, he guided the audience's attention with each crack and snap, revealing a horde of other exotic animals following close behind, each bearing their own costumes and riders.

Patterns began to arise with each of the animals as they presented themselves. The elephant held a large brass horn at the end of its trunk. Several bears stood upright as they pulled and squeezed accordions. Even many birds of several species, not just hummingbirds, flew around above each animal holding a single ribbon that whistled as they were dragged through the air. Following the marching and flying animals were a number of cream and peach-coated equines from the parade with po riding on their backs playing sharp notes through long brass and silver flutes. Each line and button on the flutes flung bright beads that glistened in the light, the way beads of water might on a field of dew-covered grass.

As the variegated mass of po and beast bodies made their way around the ring, the elephants were revealed to have been dragging something behind them the whole time. Great, thick ropes had been tied to them, and could be seen flowing just beneath the uppermost layer of sand. Their slack tightened, and the elephants began to pull with all their strength. As they tugged, many thick poles were slowly pulled up and out of the sand. Upright, coils of twisted fabric let loose as the ropes carrying the poles snapped, freeing the elephants to spread out as they continued to circle the perimeter of the ring. Once all of the fabric loosened and settled, a large, crimson tent stood in the middle of the ring.

Amazing! Cynkz thought. *Where did all of that come from? How much time does it take for one to invent such a trick?*

Before the crowd's focus could settle for too long on the new addition to the ring, rolls of weighty drums slowly rose from the edges of the stage, and the many performers and beasts began to slow as they made way for the lights to twirl unobstructed. The pace of the percussive barrels picked up and grew louder, the many spotlights tightened their focus and center at a single point above the mysterious new tent. Just as the drums reached an electrifying crescendo, the familiar thin form of the ringmaster lowered himself on a rope. Even from the far reaches of the stands, his beaming smile poked out from beneath his mask. The beat of the drums, the spotlights, and the rope from which Harquin playfully hung from stopped abruptly, giving him the audience's full attention.

"I have quite the surprise for you, good po of Potarium!"

Harquin, still hanging just above the tent, quickly kicked the top of the structure, and all the cloth and beams immediately collapsed, revealing yet another blood-red cloth covering something organic. The hidden object was not much smaller than the large tent itself. Whatever was inside seemed to be breathing, indicated by the edges of its covering expanding and shrinking at the appropriate rhythm.

"You see, my dear Potarium," Harquin continued. "Here we have a—"

Before he could finish, a world-shattering roar shot forth, burrowing its way into the ears and hearts of everyone in the crowd, shooting through each po, only to bounce off of the tent's walls and back again, creating a lingering echo that trailed into a soft growl. A few gasps could be heard following the frightening sound. Harquin put a curious hand to his chin as he looked down at the source of the beastly call.

"Hmm, I could have sworn we taught the beast better manners than that. Whoops!"

His hand slipped. All that could be seen was a thin pale body falling beneath the covering below. The unknown monstrosity snarled and lashed out, seemingly taking the opportunity to tear its unwitting prey to pieces. A series of shrieks followed, and more gasps flowed through the crowd. As the screams of agony simmered, the rotating spotlights twirled and focused at the side of the flailing cloth, only to reveal Harquin casually walking to the side, mimicking his calls for help with a humorous flair. The crowd sighed in relief and fell into laughter. Harquin multitasked, calming the beast beneath the covers with one hand and quelling the audience with the other.

"Well, that was a close one. But wait…" Harquin reached up and felt around the top of his black, coiffed hair. "Has anyone seen my hat? Ugh, how rude!"

He stomped and propped his hands on his hips, imitating the mild tantrums of a child. More laughter followed as he deliberately trudged to an opening in the red cloth. He stood and stared for a moment, before waving his hand and inserting it inside, rummaging for his hat the way one would reach underneath a bed for something just out of reach. A bone-shattering snap quieted the crowd, and Harquin recoiled and revealed a stump where his hand used to be. More gasps ran through the crowd as the ringmaster seemed to writhe in agony, only to slowly turn his cries to laughter once again. With a final, aggressive shake of his arm, his hand poked out from his sleeve, completely unharmed and immaculate. Even his glove remained unsullied. The crowd joined him in his hysterics and gave a steady round of applause.

Harquin brushed himself off and took a deep breath before addressing the crowd. "I may need some assistance retrieving my hat. Do we … have any volunteers?"

A short breath fell over the crowd, and immediately gave way to rounds of cheers and hollers. A masterful sleight of hand had Harquin pulling out his trusted whip from seemingly thin air, and he used the golden tip of its handle to point to the audience, directing the many spotlights as they danced frantically. The weighty drums picked up, rolling steady beats to accent the rising anticipation as the lights slowed and gathered as they dragged across the scene. It didn't take long for everything to eventually settle on the noble's perch. It seemed like an odd choice, considering how few po were seated in that section.

It was then that Cynkz noticed it had gotten uncomfortably bright. As if on cue, Cynkz lowered his head to shade his eyes from the burning light, the drums stopped, and everything went quiet.

"And we have a winner!" Harquin's booming voice broke the silence. "You there, the dark stranger! Come on down, if you don't mind?"

A round of applause rose, and even Kadd joined in as he looked gleefully at his friend. Cynkz was struck dumb. Yet again, he found himself the center of unwanted attention. It seemed as if Potarium was making it their mission to initiate new souls in the most extravagant way possible, and at every opportunity possible.

Cynkz leaned over, desperately accosting his guide for assistance. "Kadd!" he whispered. "What do I do?!"

"Just go with the flow!" Kadd said through a series of claps. At least he had the courtesy to lean toward Cynkz and hold his hands away from their faces. "Who knows? Maybe he'll take a liking to you and help us with your mission?"

Everything in Cynkz's body wanted to reject the show, yet he couldn't deny Kadd's logic. His worried expression softened as he pondered the possibility. Perhaps 'going with the flow' was the right thing to do. He gathered himself, took a deep breath, stood, and began making his way down the stands.

"There we go!" Harquin shouted to the crowd. "Let's give our newest soul a hearty welcome!"

The once steady applause grew into a deafening roar. Countless collisions harmonized into an almost soothing sea of noise that seemed to recede to the back of Cynkz's mind. The burning lights still followed him, and he had to keep his head tipped down, using the pointed tip of his cap to shade his eyes. As he looked at the ground, he focused on his tall, sharp shadow cutting the sea of blinding light. He couldn't help but liken it to a dark claw piercing heaven's veil. Why did he feel as if he were invading a place he did not belong?

Cynkz finally made his way into the ring, and the tireless applause simmered into silence as Harquin took control of the world's attention.

"Hello, newcomer! I mean, you *are* new, right? I'm fairly certain I've never seen you before."

"That I am, sir."

"Ah! So polite!" he addressed the crowd. "Have you ever met a po fresh from the abyss and the dark ocean, still capable of such good manners?"

The crowd chuckled. Cynkz, unsure of what to do, merely smiled as he looked around.

Harquin continued. "Tell us, what's your name, stranger? Hopefully, it rolls off the tongue better than, well, 'stranger?'"

"I am Cynkz. A pleasure to meet you all." Cynkz instinctually bowed ever so slightly, remembering the feelings of playing the court jester in a lifelong past.

"Cynkz? Cynkz?! What a name!" Harquin's voice boomed as he stretched his arms out to the crowd as if trying to give the world a hug. "I'm sure you've heard a thousand jokes about it during your time in the afterlife?"

"Indeed," Cynkz replied. "The sailors who pulled me from the sea mentioned how ironic it was that I did not merely 'sink' into the dark ocean."

More laughs rolled through the crowd. Cynkz couldn't help but smile. *Perhaps this was Fiddle's secret to handling these sorts of situations? A bit of jesting melts the ice quicker than the sun, it seems.*

"That's the spirit!" Harquin continued, "I think you're gonna fit in well here. But first, I'd like to ask you a favor—"

A swing of his long arms pulled the great tarp to the side, revealing the terrifying silhouette of something neither Cynkz nor the rest of Potarium were prepared for.

"This here is our newest pet. I call it a Calican, and it seems to have a hold of my precious hat." Harquin's elaborate mask did little to conceal his crooked, mischievous smile. "Would you be so kind as to retrieve it for me?"

The crowd let loose their usual gasps and weighty breaths of astonishment, yet Cynkz remained completely silent. He had seen many creatures before—Munderworld was filled with odd things—though this particular specimen was different from anything he had come across before.

It was a towering, brutish animal, top heavy and muscular. It possessed the detailed anatomy of a honed cat, yet its posture and bulk resembled that of an oversized bull. Its coarse, finely threaded coat of fur was a refined combination of dark browns, vibrant crimson spots, and an almost golden undercoat. Countless soft spikes outlined the body as if merely touching the thing would draw blood. It possessed a large, wide head, with a stout, pugnacious nose that drew its face into a perpetual scowl. Its broad skull and jaw alluded to a bite meant specifically for crushing its prey, looking strong enough to pummel even stone.

As Cynkz glanced around the beast's figure, his eyes were drawn to its legs, their width greater than his own body. Heavy paws dug deep into the sand. Around each ankle Cynkz could see the dull glimmer of metal shackles hiding beneath its fur, their chains disappearing into the ground. As confident as Harquin seemed, he felt it necessary to take at least *some* precautions, instilling doubt in Cynkz's mind of the beast's supposed 'training.' The creatures of Munderworld were adapted for pure brutality, their forms often crude and unrefined. This creature, however, was clearly designed, possessing the type of sleek, streamlined form of something built to make an impression above all else.

Harquin leaned in to whisper to Cynkz, "It's alright. Remember the protective huum! Just play along, if you will."

The same 'great huum' that could not save my forehead twice this morning, Cynkz thought. Still, he remembered Kadd's logic of 'going with the flow,' and he already stood out badly enough. It seemed better to try and keep things going at a good pace. The last thing Cynkz wanted was to be disruptive or awkward.

The beast sat with its giant maw opened wide. As expected, an impressive row of jagged, sharp teeth lined the top and bottom of its mouth. Their unnaturally white sheen made them oddly reflective inside of the otherwise dark and cavernous opening. It breathed softly, and yet the heat and moisture it exhumed was immense. Whatever dental care the beast was receiving must have been exhausting, as it gave off no smell.

Everything about the situation gave the impression of a trap waiting to spring on him, but Cynkz felt equally compelled to play along with the festivities. Slowly, he reached inside, attempting to move as little as possible. One wrong move and the thing could catch a taste of his flesh, a most off-putting scenario if there ever was one. The further his hand delved, the heavier the creature's breath seemed to feel. He wasn't sure if he was just paranoid, or perhaps over-thinking the situation, but Cynkz swore something shifted within the creature. A quick glance up and he could see the minute twitching of muscles along its mouth, perhaps the curling of its nostril as it examined him. The way these movements occurred seemed to mimic something pulling back, a fierce tensing of energy in preparation for a burst of action. Finally, his fingertips touched the hat, and the moment it began to move along the beast's tongue, its mouth convulsed. Something clicked, and his instincts took hold of him.

Snap!

Cynkz recoiled so quickly his senses escaped him, and the world became a blur. He only came to as he hit the ground.

He was safe, it appeared, but became worried when he saw the perplexed twisting of Harquin's face peering out from beneath his strange, elaborate mask. He could feel the shock of countless eyes staring at him, the tense energy of po sitting on the edge of their seats, just as unsure of what was going on as him. The silence may have continued for an eternity, if not for the quick intervention of the ringmaster.

"W-well, well! Look at that? He did it! How about a few rounds for the quick, brave po who saved my favorite hat, eh?"

A worrying, slow clap began to rise from the stands. Fortunately, it didn't take long for an energetic rhythm to take hold and put everyone at ease.

Harquin stepped over and reached out to help Cynkz stand. As he did, he performed another sleight of hand to retrieve his hat in a single, sweeping motion, adding a flamboyant flourish to the otherwise simple action. It seemed to have a positive effect on the crowd, and an electrifying chorus of claps and cheers drowned the entire tent.

Harquin continued waving to the audience, placing a firm hand on Cynkz's shoulder as he leaned in to whisper, "Come see me after the show. I'll try to make amends for the unnecessary scare."

Cynkz, for a moment, was without a response. Something about the man's grip caught him off guard. It was an unusually firm grip, barely restrained and on the verge of letting loose an energy similar to the beast's snapping jaw. Cynkz could feel his brows pressing together as he tried to make sense of it but quickly caught himself and nodded. Harquin gave a smile and gestured for his guest to return to the stands.

The walk up the stairs was much quicker than the descent. Cynkz wasn't sure if it was due to him being familiar with the journey, or if he was merely in a rush to return to the comfort of his seat. As he finally sat himself back down, the applause softened, and Kadd greeted him with a warm smile and a friendly squeeze of his shoulder.

Kadd's grip was softer and more preferable to whatever was going on with Harquin. Cynkz was well aware of his odd proclivity for noticing details, but even now, he wondered if he was overthinking. He decided to rest in the knowledge that, for the time being, he was back in good company. He took his first relaxed breath and cleared his thoughts, ready to enjoy the rest of the show.

CHAPTER 8

"**A**ND THAT'S A WRAP!"

Harquin's voice bellowed across the stadium. It was impressive how he was able to maintain his vocals effortlessly through the entire show.

"With that, I bid you all a farewell. Until next time!"

Harquin reached out, and the performers lined up beside him. Everyone bowed together. Though it was a simple act, it was impressive to see so many bodies moving in perfect sync with one another, even if it was to merely bow their heads.

The shuffling of loose bodies filled the air as po began to stand and march out of the tent. Despite everyone else seeming to be more than ready to get up and stretch their legs, Kadd remained seated. He appeared to have tired himself out laughing and cheering and clapping so heartily along with the crowd. Cynkz didn't mind and waited alongside him in silence. At least, it would have been silent, if Kadd hadn't immediately leaned over to begin conversing with Cynkz.

"I saw Harquin whisper something to you while you were down there," Kadd said. "What'd he say?"

"Well," Cynkz rubbed his hands together, sliding his palms across his knuckles, going so far as to stop a finger or two to run along the crude ring the Sisters gave him. "He said to wait after the show, something about making up for the scare-"

"That's great!" Kadd's voice was loud, still adjusted to the raucous cheering during the show. It caught the attention of a few po, but not much else, thankfully for Cynkz, who preferred to not be the center of attention.

"I mean, I was almost eaten." Cynkz said, "I would not necessarily say it was 'great.'"

"Nonsense, nonsense!" Kadd said with a dismissive wave. "I am most certain that the great ringmaster had it all under control. No one is ever truly in danger in Potarium."

A young woman made her way up to their seats and stood only a few feet away from them. She was one of the many performers from the show, it seemed. Her outfit had so many tassels and accessories hanging off of it that she had to constantly brush them aside as she moved.

"Excuse me, gentleman," she said, pawing away several golden slivers hanging from her headdress. "Master Harquin would like to speak with you, if you're ready?"

The woman rolled her 'r's' aggressively as she spoke. Cynkz racked his mind trying to decipher the accent, but alas, no answers came to mind. He had little to no knowledge of any specific accents, or regions, or other cultures outside of Munderworld. It was safe to assume that Potarium was the ultimate 'melting pot' of sorts, and that if he wanted to learn anything specific, he'd have to devote time to reading when he was able.

Kadd lifted himself up with a newfound energy, excited as a child going out to play.

"Splendid! Let's go, Cynkz. We shouldn't keep the 'master' waiting."

As the two began their way ahead, Cynkz couldn't help but notice some of the woman's hair poking out from beneath her costume. It was the same intense auburn hue he noticed from his mysterious suitor during the parade! Though not much could be done to inquire about the likeness, so he gave himself to fate once more, and quietly followed close behind.

✿

The trio slowly made their way around the outside of the massive tent. It was so large that Cynkz worried how long it would take for them to circumnavigate the structure, considering the woman briefly mentioned that Harquin was residing at the big top's rear. Fortunately, it was relatively quiet away from the tent's entrance and exit, giving Cynkz time to observe the surrounding cityscape. It looked as if a huge open space had been sanctioned deep in the city to make room for the circus, but not far beyond the flat brickwork, the usual cream-coated buildings and stalls began to show up. To his left, he could see rows of smaller structures flowing down the side of the great mountain. The po did not seem to build particularly high, so it was easy to peer over any distant structures. The view on his right was taken up completely by the massive tent, its height once again being such that it nearly swallowed the sky. Cynkz craned his head back as far as he reasonably could in an attempt to see where the structure ended.

"Cynkz?"

"Huh?" Cynkz was snapped out of his trance by nearly bumping into the woman guiding them.

"Your name," the woman said staring at him. "Cynkz? That's a nice name."

"Oh, uh, thank you. Most people find it strange."

"How is it spelled?"

"C-Y-N-K-Z!" Kadd interjected, relishing the moment in a mischievous, almost childish way.

"Really?" she said. "That is so interesting. I never would have thought there'd be a 'z' in it."

"But how rude of me," Cynkz said, bowing slightly toward the young woman. "Please, what is your name?"

"My name is Pairne. Pairne A'Byrne."

"That's a lovely name, Miss A'Byrne," Cynkz said. "It sounds nice through your accent, as well."

Her pale cheeks began to flush into a growing sea of red, enough so that her many freckles were hardly noticeable. It was only then that Cynkz noticed she had removed her mask, revealing her youthful, rounded features. She could hardly maintain eye contact with him as she tipped her face into her hands.

"Ah, you can just call me Pairne. Are you really from Munderworld?" she asked. "Most new arrivals have very little in the way of restraint or charm."

"He's always been like that," Kadd said. "Even in the deepest, darkest crevices of the abyss he kept good manners."

"I knew you were different, you certainly stand out in the crowd."

"Well," Cynkz said, trying to keep up with her fast moving, accented manner of speech. "I try not to—"

"And everything about you seems so interesting! I've heard rumors of you assisting Father Kadd and others down there in Munderworld. I never thought you'd look so … refined. And when we bumped our heads, that was… I have not felt any sort of pain in so long."

"Oh, I forgot to apologize for that. Truly, I am—"

"It was so exciting! Feeling a new sensation, after so long—It was intoxicating. If you can somehow do that on accident, I have to wonder what else you could do, what other sensations you could—"

"Ahem." Kadd came to the rescue.

Cynkz could only feel the rush of blood going to his head, drowning out any attempt to think or say anything in response to the woman's advances.

"Oh, I'm so sorry," Pairne lifted a delicate hand up to her mouth, doing her best to remain decent. "How inappropriate of me. Please, just this way, we're almost there."

Pairne turned quickly and the countless accessories hanging off of her outfit flung to the side, rustling together before settling. Kadd chuckled and shook his head. Cynkz didn't know what to think of it all. Ever since coming to Potarium, he had been presented with one new experience after another. The great city of po was overwhelming in more ways than he had ever figured.

A number of smaller tents revealed themselves as they made their way around the corner of the big top. Most were hardly tall enough for Cynkz to walk into without having to bow his head. They were also haphazardly scattered, and much more practical in their design and color, mostly consisting of muted browns and faded blues, all easy to overlook at a wide glance. A number of performers and assistants could be seen making their way back and forth through the makeshift shantytown. Without their elaborate masks and towering headdresses, they seemed much less impressive, approachable even. Cynkz almost forgot about the wild acts they had performed moments ago.

One tent in particular caught his attention as Pairne led them straight toward its entrance. She was quick to prance ahead and lean inside. Just as Cynkz and Kadd caught up, she leaned back out to address them.

"Master Harquin is ready. He will see you now."

She stepped to the side, bringing with her one of the loose flaps operating as a door. Kadd, as usual, went in first, his curiosity getting the better of him as he rushed forward. Cynkz looked at Pairne, and the two shared a quick smile and a nod before he himself entered.

Once his eyes adjusted to the shift in lighting, Cynkz began to take note of whatever he could see lying about. Nothing stood out, just a plethora of shiny, though clearly used tools and props, large orbs and striped hoops and thick ropes, all sorts of things one would have expected to play a role in a circus performance.

At the end of the tent was a thin man sitting in a chair, tending to his whip. It was definitely the same man who had guided the parade and managed the circus, yet seeing him without his mask, hat, or even his elaborate coat, made him appear almost mundane. Indeed, underneath the glitz and glamor, he was a man like any other. He appeared a bit older, at that delicate time in one's life just before the onset of the many tells of old age such as wrinkles or drooping skin. His skin was light, though it had clearly faced the elements, maintaining the slight peachy tan one would expect from someone who had spent many years outdoors. He possessed poofy black hair that came down to his shoulders and was perfectly coiffed in bundles of dark fluff that made for a pleasing contrast to the rest of his bright attire, as well highlighting his grayish-green eyes.

Next to him was a large container with dozens of ropes sticking out of it, replacements for his tool of choice. He was carefully rubbing a thick, glossy substance over the whip he had used during the show.

"Ah, you're finally here," Harquin said.

Cynkz had grown so used to seeing the man smile and shout that his calm, noble demeanor caught him off guard. "Thank you for having us," he replied.

"I'm surprised you're so calm and polite. Considering the fright my antics must have given you during the show, you'd have every right to barge in screaming slurs at me."

"I have found that it is more productive to conduct oneself amicably, regardless of the circumstance."

"Huh…" Harquin leaned forward in his seat, rubbing his chin as he quizzically looked the jester up and down. "Are you truly new here? Fresh from Munderworld? Most new souls are a tad bit more … uncourtly."

"It's interesting, right?" Kadd said, "You'd hardly believe this was the brave soul who traveled the realms and led myself and others on a path forward."

"So this is the one you spoke of? The strange man who came swooping down from the layers above and helped several po find their way to Potarium?"

"Well, you two make it sound as if I had some grand plan or knew what I was doing," Cynkz said.

"It's the intent that matters," Kadd said. "You had no reason to try to help us. You put yourselves in harm's way, and it eventually led to salvation for a number of us. Even after Harla spoke so unkindly to the both of you—"

"'Both of you?'" Harquin leaned back, his brow twisting tight lines into his forehead.

"Ah, yes, Cynkz did not travel alone," Kadd continued. "He was aided by a small, quippy imp."

"An imp? A mun, essentially? A creature of the dark?"

"That is right," Cynkz replied.

"And it… He? They? They helped you?"

"Yes. Fiddle and I have been friends for as long as I can remember. He was my companion for as long as I was in Munderworld."

"A helpful mun with a name? How odd…" Harquin leaned back hard enough for his wooden seat to creak, his arms crossed, and his eyes looking about in disbelief. "You wear many hats it seems."

"Excuse me?"

"A realm traveler, po savior, mun befriender. Anything else?"

"He was also a jester!" Kadd exclaimed, letting his excited energy get the best of him once again. "And a courtier. And he grew up on a horse farm in Hirlwe, if I remember correctly."

"That is… hmm…" Harquin went quiet and looked Cynkz up and down.

"I am sorry," Cynkz said. "It is really not as impressive as it sounds. I merely try to do what I can to help."

"That mindset has served you well it seems," Harquin said. "My show could very well use a multi-talented hand such as yours. I mean no offense when I say this, but most new po have very little to show on their resumes."

"You're telling me," Kadd said. "The most I had to my name was a sketchy history of banditry."

"And look how far you've come!" Harquin sat upright to formally address Kadd. "In the relatively short time you've been here, you've gotten along well with nearly everyone, working your way into the church, quickly attaining deaconship, rubbing shoulders with the Royal Court. Many have taken to referring to you as 'Father Kadd,' as well they should."

"Much like Cynkz, I merely wish to do whatever I can to help. It's the least I can do to show my gratitude for having been given salvation."

"You know, 'Father Kadd,'" Harquin's eyes began to level into a slight squint, "I always wondered why you decided to stay down near the docks. With how well you've taken to the church and the city—and of course the Royal Court—you could very well be a bishop by now, relaxing in the great golden tower, perhaps with a stature above my own."

"Well, I dare not appear too ambitious," Kadd said. "The last thing I wished to do was come across as an ungrateful child, only looking to work my way up some hierarchy after arriving in heaven. Besides—" Kadd stepped over and placed a warm hand on Cynkz's sharp shoulder. "I wanted to make sure I was available to properly thank the po who helped me."

"What a lovely confluence of fates, then." Harquin continued, "Unfortunately I have little in the way of stories preceding my time here in Potarium. I've never been to Munderworld myself."

"Consider yourself lucky," Kadd said, giving a playful shrug. "Much of it is wet, unsanitary, and dark. Hardly any accommodations."

"I can only imagine," Harquin said. "But enough of all that. How can I help make things up to you, Cynkz? You are already in good hands with Father Kadd, but surely there's something an influential man such as myself can do to make your time in Potarium that much better?"

Without hesitation, Cynkz made his request: "I need help finding someone very important. I'd like an audience with the Royal Court, to ask for assistance."

Harquin's once relaxed demeanor stiffened. His eyes shot wide and his mouth shut into a harsh, flat line. Kadd's feet could be heard shuffling just behind Cynkz.

"That is quite the bold request…" Harquin said, his voice quiet, his mind seemingly pondering the possibility.

"You said it yourself, Cynkz seems quite capable," Kadd said, stepping forward. "It would perhaps be fortuitous to arrange such a meeting. Perhaps he could help the court with 'that' little problem they've been having?"

Harquin scoffed, going so far as to throw his hands up as he leaned back in his chair. "Ugh, not you, too?"

"What is it?" Cynkz asked.

"Apparently," Harquin continued, "there have been growing rumors of shadowy, hooded figures sneaking through the night. As the years go on, more and more complaints have inundated the guards, and by proxy the court, with these supposed sightings. Yet in all this time, nothing conclusive has come up. If you ask me, it's the result of bored po looking for ways to get themselves involved in something more interesting, even if they have to go so far as to make things up."

"Yet the rumors and sightings continue?" Kadd said. "I know that, despite the city's size, word gets around quickly in Potarium. Surely you know better than anyone how fickle po can be? For such rumors to persist for such a length of time, there must be some validity to—"

"Pah!" Harquin waved his hand dismissively through the air. "It is little more than the ravings of bored po, as far as I care. They can take their minds off of such unsavory things by attending my shows, if they so please. Not that they have anything to worry about, anyway, considering the oppressive huum working eternally to protect us all."

"'Oppressive?'" Kadd's tone grew heavy, and he stepped forward to assert himself. "That is an odd way to regard one of Paithos' greatest blessings."

"Oh, excuse me, Father, I meant no offense. A poor choice of words on my part, certainly." Harquin broke eye contact for the first time as he lowered his head. Cynkz noticed the man's deference and wondered what kind of pull the church held over Potarium. "Back to you, Cynkz. Why do you wish to go to the Royal Court specifically?"

Cynkz said, "I need help finding someone very important, and Potarium is massive. What better method to get the word out than through the highest authority in the land?"

"That makes sense. Get the nobility to send word rippling down through the city. If this person is truly so important, then the po will certainly be intrigued to hear about them, straight from the mouth of the strange new soul making waves in our peaceful city."

"Wait," Kadd said, "so you'll do it? You'll get us an audience?"

"I'll see what I can do. I think Potarium will be talking about this most recent show for a while, and I can relax for a bit. It'll give me something to do during my time off." Harquin took a deep breath, then looked at Kadd. "I presume Cynkz is staying with you for the time being?"

"That's correct," Kadd said.

"Hmm. It's a tad embarrassing that we don't have more free housing available for new arrivals." Harquin sighed. "Even in the afterlife, managing real estate is a chore."

Cynkz took a short bow before interjecting, "Thank you, Lord Harquin. You have no idea how helpful this all is."

"Of course," Harquin said. "It should be very interesting. It also gives me an excuse to see the court and give them a hard time for missing today's show. I'll send someone to your estate bearing news within the week, Father Kadd."

"Perfect!" Kadd exclaimed. "Everything is going so wonderfully! Paithos has truly blessed us."

"Indeed," Harquin replied.

"Well, with all that out of the way, we should begin making our way back," Kadd said. "It's a fair walk back, and I could use some sleep. I always get so drowsy when the day's light begins to dim."

"Fair trip to you both then," Harquin said, "and may Paithos guide you."

Kadd bowed. "May Paithos bless you."

Cynkz followed suit with a bow of his own, and the two made their way out of the tent and back into the dimming light. Cynkz could hear Harquin turning back in his chair and rubbing more of the glossy solution on his tools as they left.

⟡

The duo made their way to Kadd's humble estate. Time seemed to fly by rather quickly in Potarium, as dusk was fast approaching well before they reached their destination. Kadd continued doing most of the talking as they made their way through the streets, shuffling past the many po cleaning up the excesses of the day's festivities.

It was interesting seeing the once white roads littered with colorful feathers and tassels and other party favors. The ground was more colorful as a result. Not even the hummingbirds, their rainbow feathers filling the clear air, were anywhere to be seen. They were most likely settling in to rest for the night, and soon their trill snoring would lull the city to sleep as it did the night before. Cynkz actually found himself looking forward to it. As much enjoyment as he gained from stargazing in Dulrot, there was never much ambience to accompany his hobby. The dead silence of the violet-hazed nightly realm was not particularly stimulating. Fortunately, he had depended on Fiddle to keep things from getting too stagnant. The chorus of snoring birds, while not as interesting, was a calming replacement if nothing else.

Another oddity Cynkz finally noticed was that there was no sun, yet Potarium still experienced the usual cycle of day and night. He could remember this cycle from vague memories of his life back on Peara and figured Dulrot was stuck in perpetual night due to having no sun of its own. It seemed as if the shining orbed sky mimicked this cycle, slowly phasing through different types of light as the day progressed to maintain the circadian rhythm. It made sense, as this would be what those who had lived their days in the living world were accustomed to. It took some getting used to for Cynkz, however. In Potarium it was impossible to fly away in the middle of the day without drawing all sorts of unwanted attention. Having to maintain appearances during the day instilled within him a deep yearning for the night's cover.

"Ah, we're almost home," Kadd said. Cynkz could hear the slight scuffs of the man's sandals dragging against the pavement.

"You do not mind if I go up top and relax on the roof, do you?" Cynkz asked.

"Of course not! Do whatever you need to do. Get comfortable. Though I still find it odd that you don't seem to like being inside."

"My apologies. I am sure that, with enough time, I will grow more accustomed to everything here."

"Well, there's no rush! Time is as meaningless here as it was in Munderworld. You can take as long as you need."

"That is comforting."

"You know, if you really wanted to, you could probably fly to the tower yourself and—"

Cynkz raised his hand to Kadd, smiling before interrupting, "I highly doubt that they would appreciate an odd stranger flying up to their doorstep, bringing demands."

"True, but imagine how exciting that would be!"

"Too exciting for my tastes. I'd like to match the good first impression this city has made upon me by returning the favor."

"I can't argue with that notion."

Cynkz smiled, then went quiet, and looked back out on the city. The orange haze of oncoming twilight seemed to paint the otherwise cream-coated architecture with a cozy hue. The setting light homogenized the otherwise varied colors and shapes of the city, as if a warm, transparent blanket were being set upon Potarium. The only structures that stood out were the giant flags billowing in the slow wind at different corners of the city.

"Is something wrong?" Kadd asked.

"This 'great huum' you told me about earlier," Cynkz said, turning his attention back to his friend, "the one being projected by those giant flags? Are they meant to protect everyone?"

"Yes. It is one of the greatest things about Potarium. Because of it, we never have to worry about facing any harm."

"I believe I may be immune to its effect."

"Yes, I figured much the same."

"You noticed it as well?"

"The incident with Vicar Reindall, the young dancer, the circus beast…None of that should have been possible. Any sort of harm, both intended or accidental, is negated by the constant huum projected from those very flags. Did it really seem as if the circus beast would have done harm to you?"

"Yes. Without a doubt."

"How bizarre…"

Cynkz shrugged and gave a huff. "Even in heaven, I suppose I am not granted such a luxury… It is a shame that I am not deemed worthy enough for His protection here. I wish I could just relax and be myself, without having to worry about such things."

"I wouldn't think of it that way, Cynkz."

"How should I interpret it, then?"

"Paithos has a plan set for all of us. But you, Cynkz? It's very difficult to tell. You seem to be both blessed and cursed to find your own way through the wilds of the universe. In a sense, you are completely free."

Cynkz found himself speechless. He always appreciated wonderful bits of prose, not unlike his favorite poem about the stars. Kadd's insight seemed to cut deep, forcing Cynkz to take his words to heart as he looked into the man's soft eyes. Kadd, doing what he always did, merely smiled and placed a soft hand on Cynkz's shoulder.

"We will figure this all out, Cynkz, worry not. And no matter what, you're always welcome in my home. Or on top of it, whatever floats your boat," Kadd said.

"Thank you, Kadd," Cynkz said, returning the smile. He looked up at the sky, then over to the shingles on Kadd's roof. "I think I'll go up and rest for now. I would like to watch the stars again."

"Of course, of course. You know there are stairs in the back, right? You don't need to fly or climb or anything silly like that."

"Oh, I had not noticed…"

Kadd released his grip and began to turn toward the short bricked pathway leading to his front door. "I'll see you in the morning, then. Good night, Cynkz."

"Good night."

CHAPTER 9

CYNKZ HAD LOOKED FORWARD TO AN easy night's sleep. He had to force any thoughts of the great huum, or his place in Potarium, or Yla and the sisters, or what Fiddle may have been doing to the back of his mind. Thoughts of the Royal Court—their appearance, their demeanor, how he would or should address them—also had to be pushed aside. He was determined, for the moment, to clear his mind and relax. He missed the many long stretches of darkness in Dulrot that nearly put him into a trance as he soaked in the calming night sky.

Before he could realize it, he was lulled into a deep sleep, and had nothing to look forward to but the sweet, tranquil embrace of the night.

This peaceful state was soon interrupted by the noise and bustle of po carrying themselves through the street. Cynkz was used to not having dreams, but he could remember the sensation of rest that came from his slumber. For once, he had merely closed his eyes, and not even a moment later, he opened them to find himself bathed in the morning light, his ears swarmed by not-too-distant noise and gossip.

I wonder what's going on? Cynkz thought to himself.

The creak of a heavy wooden door caught his ear, and Cynkz quickly made his way over the roof's slanted ledge to hop down and greet his friend.

"Good morning, Cynkz," Kadd said.

"Good morning, Kadd." Once Cynkz landed softly on the bricked pathway, both he and Kadd looked to the road before his curiosity got the best of him. "Is there another parade today? The streets seem awfully busy this morning."

"Not that I know of. Even the good po of Potarium need to rest between festivities, ya know?"

Cynkz turned his head and could just barely make out some of the mumblings being carried through the crowd:

Have you heard?

Heard what?

Some puppeteer is causing trouble, apparently.

Trouble? A puppeteer? Is it such a big deal that—

She's been screaming at the guards all morning to come to her aid.

Screaming? How odd…

The voices trailed off as the two speaking made their way into the distance.

How odd indeed, Cynkz thought.

"Well, guess there's no reason for us to not go check it out," Kadd said.

"I agree. I have yet to witness a proper puppet show since arriving," Cynkz said.

"It's settled then! Let's hurry, maybe we can squeeze into a good spot and get a nice view of the drama."

Something was different about the crowd. Without the energy and excitement of a looming show, the bodies of po moved uniformly. It was significantly easier for Cynkz to keep track of Kadd and move ahead. Still, he worried about accidentally bumping into anyone. There was no telling how much trouble his supposed 'immunity' to the great huum would cause if he were careless.

It wasn't long before the mass of bodies began to slow and bunch together. Po seemed to be gathering on the side of a particularly large street. Cynkz, being at least a half-inch taller than most of the other bodies around him, was able to press up onto the tip of his toes and get a decent look around. He could see a number of stalls and booths that were empty, their many wares still freshly laid upon their counters. It was reassuring that po trusted each other well enough to leave their goods unattended, but that brought Cynkz right back to his original question. What was getting everyone's attention?

They were still a ways back from the front of the crowd. The collective murmurs of the po around them were loud enough to drown out the commotion occurring at the center of the stalls. Kadd seemed to be getting frustrated and began to push his way through as politely as he could manage, taking full advantage of the great huum's protection. As he pushed and shoved, most of the bodies merely seemed to be brushed aside, as if some invisible force were intervening. The effect was subtle, but uncanny and unnatural enough to draw attention. The action would have made Cynkz anxious if not for the comical assertions Kadd was shouting as he moved forward.

"Excuse me, coming through!"

"Man of the church, official church business!"

"Pardon your Father, my child."

Other than a few odd looks, no one seemed to mind. Perhaps it was merely one of the perks of being a prominent member of the church. Cynkz had to restrain himself from laughing as he followed close behind.

As they neared the edge, Cynkz could see the tall, bright cherry-red tower of feathers poking out from a knight's helmet. It was whipping around aggressively. The shouting he heard coming from the scene matched the manic energy of the flailing headdress. Cynkz tried to focus and listen on the nearing drama.

"There's nothing there! Quit your—"

"I swear to you! I swear on my soul! I saw it! I saw one!"

"You've riled up several of the guards over nothing, woman! Just go back to your puppet show and—"

"No! No! I already told you! It was one of them that was possessed! It blinked at me! It did!"

Possessed? Cynkz thought. *I have not heard of any sort of possession since Peara was still around.*

They made their way to the front. Kadd nearly disappeared to the side of the opening he created through the crowd. Cynkz slipped through just as the mass began to close in on itself and stood next to his friend to watch the commotion. One of the guards, dressed in the usual ornate collection of shining silver layers hugging his form was stressing as he addressed a po woman grabbing at his legs. The guard was holding a spear of some kind, though it had a rounded, decorative blade on its end and reminded Cynkz of the sentinels and their pikes in Munderworld.

The woman was trying, and succeeding, in hindering the guard's movements as he tried to push her off.

"I'm telling you, we couldn't find anything!" the guard yelled.

"Because you didn't try!" the woman screamed back, her dark, frazzled hair bouncing around, accentuating her movements and cries for help.

"Whatever it was, it's gone. Now stop bothering the other citizens and my fellow guards—"

"No, you lazy, wannabe knight! They're still—"

"And clean up this mess. This pile of puppets and trinkets behind your stall looks awful."

"No! It'll catch me! It'll wake back up and—"

Clink!

The sound of light wood hitting pavement echoed through the air. Everyone immediately went quiet, with nothing more than the rustles of a few turning heads to break the silence. The sound seemed to come from behind the pile of puppets laid chaotically behind the woman's stall.

Unlike most of the architecture in Potarium, most of the stalls were made of much darker and more vibrant materials, and the puppeteer's stand was no different. It held the usual lengths of deep crimson silk, held loosely over the front and sides of the oak construction like curtains, their golden threads following their ends as they just barely draped along the ground. On the ground were a number of elaborate wooden puppets that had been carelessly strewn about in small piles around the stand. The puppets themselves came in all sorts of shapes and sizes, though they had one thing in common. Each possessed a long thin piece of wood coming out of its head, and many held a feather or two sticking out, mimicking the many headdresses the po were so fond of. It seemed to be where the strings for the puppets entered their hulls. It was an odd design, but a clever one. One could only wonder how intricate these things must be on the inside to perform. They also possessed an odd variety of expressions on their exaggerated faces. Caricatures of sleeping, sad, happy, and even nonsensical half-expressions made the sea of lifeless, humanoid bodies on the ground uncomfortable to look at. It was an oddly messy scene for such an otherwise tidy and immaculate city.

Clink!

The sound shot forth once again, prompting a few of the witnessing po to gasp. The clank of light wood began to slowly rise from behind the pile of timber bodies. The woman, the guard, Cynkz, and Kadd all held their breath. The overwhelming quiet among such a large group made the air tense, almost thick enough to cut with a knife. The tapping and clanking continued, as if following the footsteps of a drunk po. The otherworldly sounds seemed to be making their way closer to the crowd. No one had the courage to break the silence.

Clink! Clack! Clink!

As the unknown sounds continued, the world seemed to hold still. The tense aura that seemed to have its grip on the world reached its apex as a small, blocky hand edged its way around the corner of the stall. Following it was the large circular head of a small puppet, its bobbled eyes moving independently, and its wooden mouth flap easing up and down as if to mimic breathing. It would have been cute, if not for the eerie truth that was its unnatural existence. All eyes were wide and focused on the anomaly. And then … it spoke!

"Woo! What a ride. Hey, it worked! I'm really here! And… Uh oh…"

Something about the puppet's voice immediately stood out to Cynkz. It was a small rattly voice, a pleasantly bizarre combination of a high, cordial tone mixed with the gruff of something long-lived. It reminded him of Fiddle, but it was distinctly different. Cynkz was so lost in ponderings that it took him a moment to realize that chaos had erupted around him.

Groups of po screamed and pushed past one another, desperately trying to get away from the adorable monstrosity. Kadd tried to stay close to Cynkz, but the mass of bodies flushing around them separated the two. It was interesting to see the invisible hand of the great huum keeping everyone far away enough from one another to prevent harm. Bodies flew and ran a hair's width around one another, as if some unseen, omnipotent force were intervening between every potential interaction.

It was mesmerizing, but Cynkz was more interested in the puppet, and why it reminded him of Fiddle. He looked back to see the puppet flying! It cackled in glee as it escaped the clutches of the guard as he dove and jumped toward him. The puppet seemed to throw itself through the air in a childlike manner, not too dissimilar to how Fiddle often would.

A cursory glance revealed that more of the puppets—once lifeless bodies laid out like the deceased—were picking themselves up and joining in the chaos. As most of the po dispersed, more guards ran toward the scene. The harsh clank of metal followed their footsteps, alerting the impish puppets to their presence. Most of them laughed and giggled like children, perhaps not fully aware of what they had wrought upon the once peaceful city.

Cynkz had no idea what to do and tried to avoid bumping into anyone as he made his way toward a nearby alleyway, out of the line of action. Just before he could reach the secluded shadow of the alley, a familiar voice pierced the fog of chaos, one that he had not heard in a long time.

"Cynkz! There you are!" the voice said. "You stick out like a sore thumb, as usual!"

Now *that* was a voice Cynkz recognized. He would recognize the husky, cordial tone anywhere. Once in shadow, he turned and was greeted with the visage of a short marionette with long dangling limbs that cracked and clunked as the creature flailed in excitement.

"Fiddle?" Cynkz said, for a moment unsure of himself. "Is… is that you?!"

"Yep! The one and only! It's great to see you again—"

"What in munder is going on?!"

"Oh, well, uh…"

Fiddle seemed caught off guard by his friend's directness. The imp attempted to reach back and scratch his head, his usual nervous tick, but his loose limbs did not allow it. Cynkz thought there was something oddly calming about the puppet's stiff joints clicking together, their rhythms forming what could be described as what one would hear from a simple wooden instrument, perhaps a maraca, or some other beaded tool.

"I am sorry, Fiddle," Cynkz said, relaxing his shoulders and his sharp expression. "It truly is good to see you again, of course, but what is happening?"

"You were gone for a really long time, and dad was getting annoyed because me and a bunch of my brothers and sisters were hanging out and asking a bunch of questions and he got fed up and—"

"Fiddle! Calm down and breathe. Or, breathe if you can in that form. How did you get here? Are those all your siblings?"

"Yes! Pops figured it wouldn't hurt to send some of us ahead to possess some dolls and check up on you."

"'Pops'? Ugh, did he really have to do this?" Cynkz rubbed at one of his temples. "I was trying to keep a low profile and maintain some level of peace."

"Well, pops said it couldn't hurt if he enabled us to check things out. Apparently, it takes a lot of work for him to do it, but he was getting so angry at us for hanging around and annoying him with questions and such. Also, apparently, there was a parade? That got everyone excited and they demanded to come ASAP."

"The parade was yesterday."

"I tried to tell the other idiots that time is weird between the realms and we wouldn't get here in time for anything! They never listen to me, try as I might—"

Their conversation was interrupted by the harsh thud of a small wooden body flying into a nearby wall. The lump of wood and feathers and string fell unceremoniously to the ground at Cynkz's feet.

"Hey Coda, you doing alright?" Fiddle said.

"Yeah, I'm good—Oooohhhh! You!" Coda picked himself up and leaned against the wall, keeping the puppet's beady, bobbing eyes on Cynkz. "You're the jester! Cynkz! The Lord of Imps!"

"The what?" Cynkz said, his brow twisting in confusion.

"Ah, yeah, I may have told them stories about you," Fiddle said, once again trying to reach back to scratch his head, to no avail.

"Yes! You led Fiddle through Munderworld, allowing him to finally convince dad to help us out! You're a legend!"

"Come on, he wasn't gone for that long. Though I suppose our adventure could be called legendary," Fiddle said.

"It is not over yet, Fiddle," Cynkz said.

"Oh! More adventure! The other sister, Yla? Have you found her yet? The old ladies are worried."

"Eww, they're so old and boring," Coda said.

"Hey! Be nice! They were helpful!" Fiddle said, nearly yelling through his fluttering, wooden mouth flap.

"I know, I know, but still," Coda looked back at the crowd. "This is boring. I'm going back out to play with everyone else. See ya!"

"Wait!" Cynkz said, reaching out to the odd puppet just in time for it to fly off, cackling into the distance.

"They're impossible to control, I swear…" Fiddle said, this time merely resorting to a light shrug, something that even his limp form could manage.

"They seem to be easily distracted," Cynkz said. "How can we calm them down?"

"Heck if I know!" Fiddle said.

"Fiddle, please think. You know them better than I do."

"Hmmm, maybe you could do what you always do! Turn into something big, and I don't know, lead them away!"

"Something big…"

Cynkz looked around and observed the chaos unfolding before him. The massive road seemed cramped as countless bodies pushed past one another, diving and ducking out of the way of the many dangling marionettes that flew through the air. Despite the po clearly being scared for their lives, calling out to one another and even for mercy, none of the possessed puppets were trying to harm anyone. They seemed to revel in the loud noise and the jaunty screams and wild movements. Their childlike laughs and giggles, while innocent sounding in their tone, only made their presence all the more unsettling to the unsuspecting citizens of Potarium. Whatever tranquility that once defined the world was lost in a sea of giggles and clicks and clacks and screams. Songs, whether organized or

disordered, natural or unnatural, seemed to domi-
nate the mood.

That's it! Cynkz thought, a wild idea snapping
within his mind akin to the flicker of a light in the dark.

Fiddle, in his stiff puppet form, turned his expression to the jester, and it was clear to see his own
deep curiosity about his friend's epiphany in the flat
wooden face.

"Fiddle, try to clear out the area just ahead of the
alleyway," Cynkz said.

"Aye, aye!" Fiddle said, swinging one of his dangling,
multi-jointed arms into a failed salute.

The puppet turned and slowly drifted toward the
panicked crowd, herding several nearby bodies away in
fear. Cynkz receded into the dark shadow of the alley.
Not a moment later, a gust of ashen smoke billowed
out from between the two buildings, and a new, massive form emerged.

A gigantic, towering marionette began to step forward from the dark alley. It was taller than the nearby
buildings, and its rounded body and long limbs nearly
betrayed its humanoid form. It wore a pointed hat, with
massive bells hanging loosely off of each end in great
pieces of spherical metal that reflected the harsh, heavenly light, and met with an equally impressive jingle
of hard bearings colliding against their interior walls.

The sharp points of the red and violet harlequin-pat-
terned hat led down to a cartoonish face bearing a wide
grin and pointy eyes that mimicked cheeks pressing up.
A long spiked nose made it easy to tell which direction
the unnaturally flat face was looking at any given time.
As the head bobbled, the nose pointed down toward a

simple cloak that appeared too small for the puppet's body, adding the subtlest flare to its eccentric movements as it brought its long arms back and forth to clap.

In place of proper hands were two large, circular brass plates that crashed into joyous bronze rings and drowned out everything nearby. Around its waist was a simple thick twisted rope from which countless silver chimes hung. The thin pieces of metal swayed back and forth in a smooth, wavelike motion complimenting the twinkling bells and the harsh cymbals with a soft undercurrent of pings that maintained the one-man symphony.

Its body was a tawny shade before merging with the last notable feature of the entity, the pointed, curling leather slippers. These coverings possessed the same flare and coloring as the hat, but were noticeably padded on their bottom, allowing each step to end with a soft brush of cushions pressing against concrete.

The jaunty mass of bells and percussive claps forced the crowd to stop and stare in awe. Even the wild, possessed puppets inexplicably stood in place as they looked on.

As the new jester puppet began to march forward, Fiddle was the first to break the tension with a simple cheer.

"Woohoo! Puppet parade! Puppet parade! March of the imps! March of the imps!"

Other voices could be heard mumbling throughout the street. Cackles and giggles gave way to a focused cheer as they followed the new puppet.

"Puppet parade! Puppet parade! March of the imps! March of the imps!"

Fortunately, Cynkz remembered the general direction of the desert, and the streets appeared large enough for him to make his way forward and lead the troublemakers away from the city and out of danger. Crowds of po merely sat and stared in awe at the performance unfurling before them, though they were cognizant enough to shuffle and move out of the way as the giant jester puppet stomped forward.

Cynkz took a quick peek below him to make sure his mighty footsteps weren't causing any damage. From his perspective he could barely make out the tip of his shadow, once again reminding him of a dark tendril cutting through the light. Something about this world of light only seemed to make the shadows within more intense. It was a bit unsettling that his own shadow reminded him of this contrast, but for the time being he thought he was doing good.

Fiddle flew to the front, swaying back and forth through the air as if trying to dance or "lead" the march. Cynkz could also hear rows of joyfully clicking joints and sharp cackles and giggles staying near him.

His plan seemed to be working, and the edge of the city was in view.

So close! Cynkz thought.

The possessed puppets grew quieter, perhaps tired of the one-note display, and a few could even be seen from the corner of Cynkz's eye attempting to drift off toward the side, distracted by po huddled against the buildings. Cynkz was unsure of what more he could do with his current form.

Fiddle noticed this as well and looked around for a quick solution. Something appeared to catch his eye, and he quickly dashed out of sight. The moment felt like an eternity to the jester, and an intense anxiety began to swell within him as he wondered if he was marching by himself, afraid to stop and look behind him to see what the puppets were doing.

Fiddle returned, holding several flaming wooden batons.

"Hey everybody! Check this out—*Ouch!*"

Fiddle could hardly hold on to the bundles of fire and ended up singing the edges of his wooden body as he wildly attempted to juggle the torches.

It seemed to be working, as hordes of raucous, impish laughter emerged behind the giant puppet as they made their way to the border of the city.

There were a few sparse wooden shacks and cabins dotting the edge of Potarium. Even the once immaculate bricked roads faded away into hard bleached sand. Cynkz could feel himself growing bolder and more confident in his movement as he was granted open space to operate. The imp's fervor grew as Cynkz nearly jumped from one foot to the other as he danced ahead. He noticed many po coming out of the shacks around them, with one familiar face looking more wrinkled and shocked than the rest, a pair of beady eyes peering from beneath a curtain of barely kept dreads of grayish-blonde hair—

It was Harla!

I wonder if she remembers me, Cynkz thought. *Seems like Kadd indeed helped her out of Munderworld. That's good to know.*

For once, Potarium stayed silent as it observed the odd collection of thumping footsteps, jingling bells and chimes, and the childish laughter and cheering trailing off into the arid horizon.

CHAPTER 10

LATE DAY FADED INTO NIGHT. THE glistening of the many golden accents and windows of the city was now far enough away that it blended in with the stars in the night sky. The possessed puppets were just as energetic, and probably would have been capable of cheering and playing to the ends of the eternal desert, if not for the abrupt stomp and stopping of the giant marionette leading them forward.

While the others appeared confused, Fiddle gave a look of relief as he finally dropped his utensils to take a moment to breathe. Cynkz slowly turned around, and some of the imps could be heard chatting among themselves:

What's going on?

Hey! Why'd we stop!

Imp parade! Imp parade! Let's keep going! Then go back to the city and back out again!

Yeah! Again! Again! Again!

Their cheering was interrupted by a sudden burst of colorless smoke and a gust nearly powerful enough to blow nearby puppets away. Once the dust and sand settled, a familiar jester emerged from the cloud, and Fiddle drifted close by. A quiet gasp rolled across the massive collection of puppets, and they too flew to the ground and settled on the sparkling sand. For a moment, all was quiet, and it took quite a bit of effort for Cynkz to refrain from chuckling at the sight of the countless little beady eyes looking up at him in awe.

"It's him!" one of the puppets cried out.

"It's the dark jester! The one Fiddle told us about!" another said.

"It's the Lord of Imps!" another exclaimed.

"The Realm Walker!" cried out several of the puppets.

"The Dark Leaver!"

"The Munder Vassal!"

"Ooooohhhhh…"

Cynkz shared a quick glance with Fiddle, the floating puppet dangling at shoulder-height next to him. Fiddle tried to shrug and failed, though Cynkz could tell what he was doing. He looked back at the crowd in order to address them.

"Well," Cynkz said. "It is a pleasure to meet all of you, but … who are you?"

"Remember me?! I'm Coda!" one puppet exclaimed.

"I'm Aria!" another puppet called out.

"I'm Viola!" another said. "And that's Beat, and he's Flat, and she's Clef, and that's—"

"I don't have a name yet…"

"Ugh, I can only come up with so many names for you guys," Fiddle huffed.

"You all are Fiddle's siblings?" Cynkz asked.

"Yes!" one puppet said, forcing her way through the crowd.

"Why are you always so pushy, Viola?" Fiddle asked as he looked down at the thin bell-shaped marionette.

"I'm not pushy, I'm just helping!" she said.

"You just like to come in at the end and act like you helped!"

"Nuh-uh!"

"Yes-uh."

"I mean, he's got a point," Coda said, rolling his short form, joints still out of place from his crash in the alleyway.

"I do help! I'm helping right now," Viola said.

"How so?" Fiddle asked.

"I'm up here talking and keeping everyone focused on the important stuff," she said.

Fiddle huffed and threw himself forward. "Important?! 'Important' my ass—"

"Your names are quite lovely," Cynkz said.

"Aww, no, they're just, you know," Viola said, half-turning away from Cynkz's gaze. He wondered if she was blushing? Or mimicking the motion? It was difficult for him to read the emotions on the cartoonish painted and carved faces of the puppets.

"Well, I came up with the names," Fiddle said. "It makes it easier to keep track of everyone."

"Indeed, but what are you all doing here?" Cynkz asked the crowd.

What would have been dead air was filled with the clicks and clacks of wooden joints colliding as many in the crowd looked to one another as if the group were searching for an answer, or more likely, a good excuse.

"We thought you might need help," Viola said. "You were gone for a long time, and then papa said there was a parade or something, and he could feel danger in the thread, and—"

"The thread?" Cynkz interrupted.

"Yeah, that. Papa said he could feel you ducking out of danger, or something like that. And Fiddle convinced him to help us come here and check on you."

A small wooden hand rose up from deep within the crowd. "Hey, Mr. Cynkz, do you know who our moms are?"

"Ask dad," Fiddle said.

"I tried! And he—"

"Shush!" Viola cried out, "We have more important things to talk about now!"

"I agree," Fiddle said, barely able to hide the bitter disdain in his voice.

"You all should have thought this through a bit better," Cynkz said. "I was trying to maintain a low profile. I would prefer to keep whatever peace I can."

"We're sorry, Mr. Cynkz," Viola said.

"You can just call me Cynkz," Cynkz said.

"Gosh, that's so informal, I don't know if I—"

"Viola! Quit trying to butter him up! You're not his type!" Fiddle shouted.

"Ugh, so loud and annoying," Viola said, mumbling under her breath.

"As much fun as you are, I need every one of you to go back to Munderworld," Cynkz said.

"What!?" the crowd shrieked in unison. "Noooooo!"

"Munderworld has been so boring lately," Coda said.

"Oh yeah, you're still here," Viola said.

"You don't have to be rude…" Coda mumbled.

Fiddle drifted toward Cynkz and whispered, "Try as I might, these guys are hard to keep control of. Even pops struggles to keep them in line. I think they're gonna need an, uh, incentive or something, to go back."

An idea immediately popped into the jester's mind. It came so quickly, and so effortlessly, that even he was proud of it. He reached into a pocket in his shirt and addressed the crowd once more, going so far as to mimic the same posture Harquin held during his show to help project his voice to the audience.

"My beloved imps," Cynkz said. "I need you to return to Munderworld for me and undertake an important quest."

"A quest?" Viola said.

"Ooh, neat," Coda added.

"A quest? An adventure of our own?" another voice echoed from the crowd.

"The Lord of Imps has need of us! Let's listen!" a final voice exclaimed before the sea of wooden puppets settled and watched, their focus set intently on Cynkz, and particularly his hand hiding beneath his cloak. From a distance, it looked as if he merely had his hand resting on his chest, the way a general might hold themselves as they nobly address their soldiers.

Fiddle, seeing an opportunity to help, sat himself on the ground ahead of Viola and Coda, and bowed to Cynkz.

"What do you need of us, mi'lord?" Fiddle said.

"I require you to relay a message directly to the Sisters of Elm," Cynkz said.

A voice from deep within the crowd rang out. "Eww, not those old hags…"

"I need you to tell them Cynkz is hot on the trail of their long lost sister, Yla," Cynkz said. "I will be having an audience with the highest authorities in Potarium within the week and should have a solid lead with their assistance."

"We have to go flying through, like, five different realms to get to them," someone said in the crowd.

"No, you don't! It's only, maybe, three at most," Fiddle said, nearly yelling his response.

"We were all long lost brothers and sisters once," another voice said, their tone uncharacteristically heavy and somber.

"What's in it for us?" Viola asked.

Cynkz continued. "If you can do this task quietly, and without causing disruption, I will allow each and every one of you to hold *this!*"

Cynkz quickly pulled his hand from beneath his cloak and held up between his fingers the divine thread. The radiant light pierced the dark desert night, drowning out the stars themselves.

A single, rumbling sound rolled over the mass of puppets: "Ooooooooooohhhhhhh!"

"I wanna hold it!" an anonymous voice called out.

"Me too!" another one added.

"Does it taste good?" a third one asked.

"It tastes like a sweet carrot!" Fiddle exclaimed.

"But you said when you held it you couldn't feel anything," Viola said.

Murmurs washed over the crowd, doubt filling the air like an unwanted miasma. Fiddle flinched, and quickly fired back, "I lied."

The crowd instantly stopped, then a sea of clicking wood and clapping puppet hands rang out as they cheered.

"Woooaaaaahhhh!"

"What are we waiting for?!" said yet another voice in the horde.

Each one that called out so far was unique. Cynkz began to wonder just how many of these creatures there were.

"Yeah, let's hurry back! Then when we're done we'll have an excuse to come back again!" a final voice said.

Cynkz, feeling his grip on the imps slipping, attempted to interject, "Wait, you can't just—"

Before he could finish, the mass of puppets focused and shook, and their bodies fell limp. There was a final thud, and a slight brush of wood falling into sand, followed by total silence.

Cynkz wondered if his scheme would be sufficient. He pondered for a moment before Fiddle spoke up, knocking the jester out of his endless ruminations.

"You see what I have to deal with?" Fiddle said. "I can hardly control these buffoons."

"It must be hard," Cynkz said as he returned the burning sliver of light to his coat pocket. "It must have been a lot of work to find them all, and it is probably even harder to keep track of them."

"Tell me about it," Fiddle said through a shrug and a motion that seemed to mimic a sigh. "Not even pops wants much to do with them. He thought it was fine helping us find them all, but he said he'd only do it if I promised to look after them myself."

"The Munder King seems reluctant to put much effort into anything, huh?" Cynkz said.

"Yes! I tell him that all the time, but then he tells me to hush and leave him alone. He sleeps a lot."

"Does he need to sleep?"

"I doubt it. He just uses it as an excuse to make us go away so he can 'relish the peaceful solitude of the dark' or something dumb like that."

"So far, nothing has turned out as I would have expected it."

Something caught Cynkz's sharp eye in the distance. A lone figure was walking toward them. They appeared to be alone, but who would be willing to follow the chaotic march out into the wasteland?

"Kadd!" Fiddle cried out.

Cynkz recognized the shimmer of deep violet robes and the dancing of golden edges as they waved back and forth with each step. It was more than a relief to Cynkz, as he worried about what he possibly might have needed to do or say to explain himself.

Fiddle flew ahead, and Cynkz followed behind. He took great care not to step on any of the lifeless puppets strewn about the desert floor. Fiddle met Kadd near the edge of the mass of bodies.

"Hey! You remember me?" Fiddle said.

"I think I do," Kadd said, huffing ever so slightly from oncoming exhaustion. "I remember the voice at least. You are the little imp that accompanied Cynkz, right?"

"Yep! The one and only Fiddle!"

"It's a great pleasure to see you again, little one! But what happened? Who were all those other puppets? And actually," Kadd crossed his arms and looked Fiddle directly in his beady, puppet eyes, "how did you manage to get here?"

"Dad helped us. He gave me and my siblings a little boost and guidance. The puppets looked like a perfect medium for us to inhabit, so we—"

"So you decided for yourselves to take a bunch of our puppets, things many of us po worked hard to create, for your own amusement?"

"Well, I mean, when you put it like that…"

"Wait, did you say 'dad?' So, it's true then…"

"Yep! The great, magnificent, all-powerful ruler and creator of Munderworld—The Munder King himself—is my dad. Well, he's our dad," Fiddle waved one of his dangling limbs around the sea of wooden bodies.

"I can't believe it's true…"

"Indeed," Cynkz said, finally catching up to the two.

"Cynkz! I'm impressed, though I guess it should come as no surprise," Kadd said.

"Hmm?" Cynkz raised an eyebrow at the man.

"You were able to come up with a plan on the spot to quell the chaos! Once you and the other puppets made it out of Potarium, things quieted down, well, at least a little bit."

"I was the one who gave him the idea," Fiddle said. "I just told him to turn into something big and fix it."

"Well, I'm glad it worked, either way," Kadd said.

"Is everyone fine?" Cynkz asked. "I did my best to avoid causing damage. Who knows if the imps destroyed anything or hurt anyone?"

"Nonsense!" Kadd replied, nearly throwing his arms in front of him as if to dismiss any worry. "A few folks said they took a few bumps to the head, and some stalls got turned over, but there was no serious harm."

"That is a relief," Cynkz said, letting out a sigh.

"We didn't want to hurt anyone," Fiddle said. "We just wanted to check up on Cynkz. Also, I think they were all bored."

"They?" Kadd said, his eyes pressed into a stern squint as he looked the odd puppet up and down. "Your siblings? All of whom are direct children of this … Munder King?"

"Yep. When pops isn't sleeping or acting grumpy, he's actually more than willing to help out if I ask nicely."

"Grumpy? The Munder King gets 'grumpy?'"

"Yep. He's basically a tired, cranky old man."

"By Paithos…"

"Who?"

"Paithos? The Creator?"

"Never heard of Paithos. Even dad's never called The Creator anything other than, well, 'The Creator.'"

"It is what we call him here. It is from an ancient dialect predating all modern po. 'Paith' is an ancient word that roughly translates to 'maker' or 'creator' and 'thos' is an old formal word for 'The,' as if addressing someone nobly."

"I should begin reading while I am here," Cynkz said. "I would love to learn more about that."

"Of course!" Kadd said, "It's been tough trying to tell you everything there is to know about Potarium in the short time you've been here."

"Short time?" Fiddle said, "It's been ages since any of us have heard from Cynkz."

"Well, I may have a theory for what has happened," Kadd said. "How did it feel when you were drifting through the dark ocean, Cynkz?"

"I felt as if I was lost in a haze," Cynkz said, "trapped between being conscious and unconscious. I could hardly tell if I was dreaming or awake."

"The dark waters are meant to heal those who have been dropped in it. Physical, spiritual, even emotional trauma, it is a sort of elaborate baptism meant to get one ready for their arrival in Potarium. It can go so far as to reduce one's age to a point where they are at their peak."

"Why are you still so old looking, then?" Fiddle shook his loose limb at the man, as if trying to point and demand.

"W-well, I wouldn't say I look *that* old—"

"It takes a different amount of time for each po to be healed? Some need more time than others?" Cynkz asked.

"Yes," Kadd replied.

"Well, if anyone's got a few screws that need tightening, it's this guy," Fiddle remarked, elbowing Cynkz as best as his loose limb would allow him. "What with his mopey poems and his missing arm—*Wait!* Your arm! You got it back!"

"You finally noticed?" Cynkz said through a warm smile.

"How in munder... Well, I guess Kadd explained it."

"Your arm?" Kadd said.

"Yeah, Cynkz lost his arm saving me in a gross pink mist place," Fiddle said.

"What in creation did you two go through after we were separated?" Kadd said.

"Quite a lot," Fiddle replied. "Cynkz got me and Orla out of a swamp, we fought a bunch of muns in a black desert, some idiot trapped me in a bottle and tried to kill us, Cynkz seduced a giant snake, and we got to reunite with Orla and meet the Sisters of Elm—"

"What in the world..." Kadd's eyes darted around as he rubbed his chin and the sides of his face trying to take in everything the imp was saying.

"That's not all!" Fiddle continued, "We met the first sentinel, or at least that's what he called himself. He was a shrimp, barely bigger than me. Then we broke through his dingy cave made out of po and fell into a giant evil eyeball spirit thing that was also made of po—I think—and then we talked with The Munder King down at the bottom of Munderworld. It was a scary ride."

All three of them stood quiet for what felt like an eternity. Even the desert seemed stunned, with not a single brush of wind or rolling sand to ease the mood. Cynkz looked on with concern at Kadd, who held a twisted, confused look on his face as he stared motionless at the unassuming puppet in front of him. Once again, it took Fiddle chiming in to break the silence.

"What did I say?"

"T-that is quite the adventure you two must have had," Kadd finally said.

"You're telling me," Fiddle said. "It's 'cuz Cynkz wanted to find out about the visions the thread was giving him. If I had known what we were signing up for, well… I still probably would have done it, but you know what I mean."

"And yet you two made it through! You did so well that here we are, reunited in heaven—in one form or another—having a wonderful conversation beneath the most beautiful night sky Potarium has to offer."

"We did worry about you, you know," Fiddle said, his voice taking on an uncharacteristically calm tone. "We kept barreling forward through Munderworld and things got crazier and crazier and—"

"It's fine, little one," Kadd said, raising up a thin hand from one of his sleeves. "All po souls are destined for Potarium's shores."

"Even the ones stuck in the giant evil eyeball?" Fiddle asked.

"I believe Cynkz mentioned him, the one called Eshra'Tel? Though I've never heard of a 'giant eyeball,'" Kadd said. "The deepest realm anyone in Potarium has witnessed seems to be the maze-like forest the Sisters of Elm reside in."

"Yeah, it's huge!" Fiddle exclaimed. "It's almost as big as that giant shiny orb in the sky above your city."

"Truly? Is it that vast? Our sky here is seen as a sort of lens, a heavenly window for Paithos himself to watch over us," Kadd said.

"Pops uses Eshra'Tel to watch over Munderworld. He doesn't really need it, but he says it makes it easier for him," Fiddle said. "Still, how eerily similar the two things are, if that's true…"

"There is naught but darkness and despair beneath the sisters' realm," Cynkz said. "The poor souls trapped in the cave below the sisters' home is the last bit of land or structure before an infinite black void, one that The Munder King seems somehow bound to."

"Who bound him there?" Kadd asked.

"The Creator, or Paithos, as you call Him," Cynkz replied.

"It's so peculiar, as we have no records or scripture detailing a Munder King or any 'giant evil eyeball,' or anything really beyond the uppermost layer of the abyss."

"You mean Dulrot?" Fiddle said.

"Yes. Apparently, the deeper realms did not exist, perhaps not before the arrival of The Munder King."

"What of Peara?" Cynkz asked. "I have heard multiple times of its disappearance, but no one has concrete information on the phenomenon."

"That too is a mystery," Kadd said through a shrug. "All we have are a few scriptures describing the world being engulfed in a 'glorious rapture of His light.'"

"Dad doesn't like talking about that kind of stuff," Fiddle said. "He always gets super angry whenever I try to get him to open up about the past. But, well…"

"But what?" Kadd said, kneeling down to give the puppet his full attention.

"But … it's not his usual kind of anger, like when me or one of my brothers or sisters annoys him. It's a sort of deep, sad kind of anger, like he feels guilty or something."

"Guilty?!" Kadd said, springing back to his feet. "The lord of darkness? The king of the abyss? He who supposedly created the deeper, torturous layers of Munderworld? He feels guilty?"

Fiddle pulled in his still dangling arms, almost recoiling into himself. "Maybe, I don't know. He's not the easiest guy to talk to. Honestly, he was nicest when we first met him, when Cynkz was there."

"I see, I suppose our jester friend has a way of bringing out the good in people, even great lords of darkness!"

"He gave Cynkz a one-way ticket to this place! Talk about privilege…"

"It feels a bit strange to be talked about as if I were not here," Cynkz said, smiling all the while.

"It's just so weird!" Fiddle said. "I'm his kid, and yet I gotta pull teeth just to get a good reaction. He doesn't even like my jokes!"

"What kind of jokes does one dare to tell a lord of darkness?" Kadd asked.

"I like simple ones, such as asking him if he's keeping an eye on Eshra'Tel, and he doesn't chuckle."

"Where I come from, we call that a 'dad joke,'" Kadd said.

"Well, he's a dad, and he didn't laugh, so I guess it's not a good one," Fiddle said, straightening his slack posture as best he could and attempting to throw his arms into a crossed position.

"He sounds difficult, and yet here you are, and your siblings were reunited too. Perhaps he does really care for you deep down."

"Yeah, I guess. He never actually hurts anyone. He just scares us and tells us to shut up and go away."

"Even someone as far removed from a normal po as him shares in the struggle of properly expressing himself to his children, it seems."

"Maybe so," Fiddle tried to shrug, but his loose limbs and joints wouldn't allow it. Despite his flailing form, it was easy to read the energetic imp's body language. "What are you guys gonna do now?"

"We may have been granted a personal audience with the Royal Court," Cynkz said. "They are the highest authorities in Potarium. If anyone can lead us in the right direction, it will be them."

"What's a Royal Court?" Fiddle asked.

"To put it simply," Kadd said, taking in a quick breath, "it is a collection of kings and queens of old who dedicate themselves to maintaining order in the afterlife."

"Ugh!" Fiddle scoffed. "Everywhere we go there's kings and rulers or whatever. Munder King, po kings— Why isn't there an imp king?!"

"Isn't that what The Munder King is, in essence, considering he is your father?" Kadd said.

"Oh yeah, I guess you're right," Fiddle said. "But why does there have to be some high and mighty figure sitting somewhere calling himself the boss."

"It is the way of things, I'm afraid," Kadd said. "Peace demands order, which demands organization, which often needs titles and ranks for delineation. Titles are the words we use to more easily describe those whose actions have warranted them."

"I have no idea what all that means," Fiddle said, "but pops must be a terrible king if his 'kingdom' can't manage to be half as neat and orderly as this place."

Cynkz couldn't help but chuckle, and Kadd followed suit. The puppet merely looked back and forth, swinging his loose form around as he tried to determine what was so amusing.

"What?" Fiddle said, his voice stern, showing his frustration at feeling left out. "What's so funny?"

"I can see why your 'pops' may be prone to vexation!" Kadd said.

"I don't know what that means," Fiddle said.

"I believe it is a fancy way of saying someone is annoyed or irritated," Cynkz replied.

"You know, Kadd," Fiddle lifted himself off the ground and motioned toward the robed po in front of him. "I've talked with a lot of supposed scholars and philosophers and other smart po folks who ended up in Dulrot. Most of them used simpler words than you do!"

"I'm sorry, little one, I'm not trying to confuse you," Kadd said.

"No, it's neat! It's how I learn about stuff. Maybe if Cynkz spent less time staring at the night sky and more time talking to smart folks he'd have something else to mope over than his lost memories!"

"Fiddle…" Kadd said, his stern voice reflecting the harsh tone of a parent scolding their child. "You shouldn't tease your best friend about such things!"

"It's fine," Fiddle said, his own voice seemingly dismissive. "He knows I don't mean any harm, plus he's said my joking helps to keep him in a good mood."

Kadd looked to Cynkz, a raised eyebrow the only thing sticking out in his otherwise flat expression.

"It is true," Cynkz said. "Joking and quipping are about all we had to keep ourselves entertained in Dulrot. It has led to many a good time."

"I wish we could go back to those good times…" Fiddle said, his large, wooden head now bobbed toward the ground.

"We will, Fiddle, worry not," Cynkz said.

"Speaking of which, we should head back to the city," Kadd said. "We could help clean up, and our summons to the Royal Court could arrive any day now."

"That sounds exciting," Fiddle said. "Even all the way out here you're still having adventures, Cynkz."

Cynkz shared a smile with the puppet, or at least, he thought that was what he was doing. The puppet's face couldn't do much beyond flapping its mouth and turning its head.

"If I may be so bold," Kadd said, stepping forward as he raised a hand toward the two. "I may have exhausted myself sneaking out to follow you two. Would it be alright if—"

Cynkz raised his own hand toward Kadd and smiled. "Say no more, friend. I will ferry you back."

"Pfft, just like old times, huh?" Fiddle said.

Cynkz smiled once more, then stepped back into a burst of colorless smoke, from which an elegant steed emerged.

"Ah, a Hirlwen steed. You mentioned you had a history with the creatures."

"I figured he'd turn into a giant snake or bird or something," Fiddle said. "Though that might scare everyone…"

Cynkz knelt on his forelimbs which dug several inches into the sand. He was low enough that Kadd was able to easily climb up and get himself situated. As the steed rose, Fiddle flew over, the clanking of his wooden joints expressing his excitement.

"Allow me to escort you two fine folks back to the city," Fiddle said.

Kadd smiled and gave a slight bow before they began to make their way through the night. The thin line dividing the bleached sands and the dark sky above made them easy to track, though Cynkz's light-colored form almost blended into the sand itself. From afar, it must have looked as if a robed figure were riding the waves of the desert across the bottom of the cosmos.

Whatever soft tranquility the scene presented was interrupted by an impish voice.

"So, what happened to you, anyway?" Fiddle asked Kadd. "How did you find your way to Potarium after we got separated?"

"Well," Kadd said. "Seeing as we have some time before we make it back to the city, let me tell you a story…"

CHAPTER 11

I REMEMBER LEAVING BEHIND THE CRUM-
bling walls of the cave in Horgafell. The dull grays and
moonlit blues of the cavern descended into a flash of darkness. I couldn't see or hear anything, yet I could feel my
body phasing through… something. The hard, cold air of
the mountains seemed to melt into a dreamy haze as I
descended further into the abyss. My nose soon grew numb
to the oncoming stench of a swamp, and I awoke in what
appeared to be a dewy marsh beneath a foggy yellow sky.

"W-where are we?" I mumbled, my voice dragging
nearly as slowly as my own body as I tried to sit up. "Harla!
Cynkz! Fiddle! Where are—"

*I looked around and realized that my vision was
impaired. Clouds of invisible, noxious fumes nearly
drowned out my senses, and the solid structures of the trees
and foliage around me swayed with the wind. It took
everything I had to keep myself upright. The dissonance
between the shifting of the world clashing against my still*

body induced a potent nausea. My head felt light as a cloud, and my stomach and chest felt as though they were filling up with thick, odious fluid.

It seemed only natural that I would turn my gaze to the ground, hoping to find some sort of balance within the disorienting miasma of the swamp. Here I noticed solid objects pressing into the soft, dew-covered grass next to me—It was someone's hand! My eyes followed the appendage to see a familiar body lying near me in a state not too dissimilar to my own. The wrinkled skin, and her fierce, bitter expression barely hid beneath a curtain of unkempt, graying dreads.

"Harla!" I cried out.

Something in me snapped, and I became lucid enough to focus. It was difficult, yet something spurred me forward as I crawled closer to her. I noticed she was still breathing, and I shook her arms and shoulders in a desperate attempt to get a proper reaction.

"Harla, wake up!" I said, "Wake up! We made it! We—*huff!*"

The thick, noxious air was beginning to get to me. Whatever focus I had gained was beginning to drain as I coughed and wheezed above my friend.

A sharp, trailing hiss flowed out from her in that moment. "Sssssssssshu—"

"H-harla? Are you awake?" I mumbled.

"Ssshush," she whispered, her eyes closed and her body still motionless. "I'd like to get some sleep, just once…"

I almost laughed, taking solace at least a couple of us had made it through unharmed. It was then that the sound of something being pushed aside in the forest caught my ear. Strange, otherworldly chatters and odd gusts of pink smoke began to make their way in our direction. I couldn't tell what was coming for us, and I had no intention of finding out.

"Harla, we have to go. Get up!"

She merely let out a sound that was trapped between a belch and a groan. "Uuurrggghhhh…"

I remember being so frustrated, so unwilling to potentially waste the chance we had been given, that I somehow managed to force myself up, and picked Harla up with me. She wasn't terribly heavy, but I could feel the oppressive weight of the swamp doing everything in its power to push me back into the ground. With a deep breath, and a puff of my chest, I dragged us forward and away from our pursuers.

I couldn't tell you how quickly I managed to move or how far we traveled. I was once again lost in a toxic haze, pushing us through vague hallucinations of swirling colors and shapes that barely represented the world around us. It took the shock of a new scene to snap me back into some sort of sense. It was the end of our pocket of the forest. An infinite, flat expanse of shining black mud lay before us.

For a moment I was stunned, and completely lucid once again, yet I could still hear faint trails of something dragging through the brush behind us. It sounded like a collection of small, almost alien feet digging their heels into the soft soil of the marsh. With nowhere else to go, I continued to drag us into the flat plane of sludge. Strangely, it was not very deep, but it was thick and cold, and constantly reminded me of the scratches and sores on my feet with each step.

For a time, everything went quiet. My arm and shoulder had grown numb from carrying my companion for so long, yet I couldn't bring myself to stop. Without the constant variety of stimuli that the woods provided, along with the growing pain of exhaustion, I seemed somewhat able to fend off the mind-altering haze of the swamp. All that I could recall was stepping through a black sea against a flat yellow sky.

Then I saw it—A shape far off in the distance stood out from the otherwise flat horizon. It was sharp, something flowing, and seemed to glide effortlessly just above the surface of the mud. It moved elegantly along the desolate plane, occasionally disappearing into brief flashes of light.

A sister of Elm! I thought to myself. *It has to be one of them! If only...*

"*Ack!* Put me... put me down you... you idiot... I need to rest," Harla whispered.

"Harla, please," I pleaded. "We might have found a way—"

"Never should have... should have followed that dumb jester, that dumb imp. All of you are just—"

"Harla, quiet! We just need to keep moving."

"Shush! It's your fault I'm even in this mess—"

"Harla!"

Something in me snapped again. I suppose the most patient among us have their limits. Perhaps it was the result of frustrations grown over who-knows-how-long, but for the first time, I screamed at Harla. I screamed so loud that my chest hurt, and I could hear my voice echoing against the murky air around us. It was loud enough that Harla seemed to snap out of her usual bitter mood and looked at me with the only soft expression I have ever seen on her, an expression of worry. I stared at her for a moment, took another deep breath, and noticed the hooded figure had stopped. They were far enough away that I couldn't make out any of their features, but I could tell that their head was turned in our direction.

Even though I had made it my goal to approach them, seeing them watching us in the distance instilled an intense fear within me. I braced myself and stood my ground. Harla didn't seem to notice and relaxed herself in my arm as she looked back down at the ground. I was afraid to take my eyes off the figure but felt compelled to give a quick glance at Harla to see if she was alright.

The pointed figure appeared to grow in size. In fact, they were headed straight for us! Fear took hold of me again, and I tried to turn around, perhaps in a vain attempt to flee. I tripped and fell into the mud. Harla fell from my grip, and my senses were reduced to total darkness. Exhaustion had taken its toll on me, and I finally began to lose consciousness.

The same lost feeling I had experienced upon first entering the realm returned. For a time, everything was dark, and if I'm being honest, I couldn't tell you what exactly happened next. I think I was unconscious, though I'm not entirely sure. I couldn't feel my body but could sense I was being moved… somewhere. It took a while before I finally came back to my senses.

I remember waking up deep underground. I was in some sort of shanty, and the only light came from a ghostly emerald glow from outside. Speaking of the outside, I could hear many light footsteps making their way across wooden boards. By all accounts, I should have been terrified, yet something about the place put me at ease. I suppose if my captors had anything nefarious planned they would have done it already.

A faint shadow blocked out some of the light peeking from beneath the door, and my savior slowly made her way inside. It appeared to be the same hooded figure whom Harla and I had seen out in the swamp, though her head was uncovered. She looked like a normal po woman, save for a single detail: her skin reflected a subtle gray tint against the green light. Her hair was also unnaturally gray, she seemed far too young for its color to be fading, but then again, it's impossible to tell how old anyone truly is in the afterlife.

"Ah, good. You're finally awake," the woman said.

"That I am," I replied. "Um, where am I, exactly?"

"You are in the great Sisters' abode, far below the woods of Porin and the final safe haven before the infinite darkness that holds The Munder King."

"That's … quite the mouthful. I assume I have you to thank for getting me out of that swamp?"

"Yes. Though normally we would not speak with you. In fact, the woman you were carrying, as well as a few others nearby, are already in Dulrot awaiting ascension."

"I… I can't believe it…"

I leaned back into a deep sigh, so relieved that I almost fell over. I couldn't remember the last time I had experienced true comfort and was but a moment from throwing myself back to rest. I would have done so, if not for the woman speaking up again.

"You may rest for a moment," she continued, "but the reason I was instructed to bring you here was to ask a favor of you, on behalf of the Sisters of Elm."

"S-surely! Anything I can do to help."

"The Sisters, they personally met with an odd jester and his imp friend. I believe you know whom I speak of?"

"Ah, Cynkz and Fiddle. Are they okay?"

"They are fine. The Sisters have given them a task that will see them through the remaining layers of the abyss. They also believe the jester will get along well with The Munder King and be granted passage to Potarium—"

"Potarium?" I said. I didn't mean to interrupt or be rude, but my curiosity was piqued.

"Yes," she continued. "It is where saved souls go, where the apostles in Dulrot take those chosen to ascend. It is your heaven."

"Why haven't you ascended, yet? You all seem more than capable of going up there yourselves."

"The Sisters of Elm are duty-bound and choose to aid those lost in The Munder King's machinations. We lesser maidens choose to help, and after providing sufficient service, we may recruit others into our ranks, replacing ourselves, and go forth, though it comes at a cost."

"What is that?"

"We lose our memories of our time here."

"Why is that?"

"In becoming a sister, maiden or otherwise, we make a pact granting us empowered huums. It is how we channel the many staves through which we travel. But in doing so, we sacrifice one of the few benefits of the afterlife—the comfortable stasis of immortality."

"I see…but how do you end up losing your memories?"

"The city of Potarium is set before an infinite, dark ocean. The apostle will drop ascended souls into it, and its healing waters rejuvenate you as you make your way to the city's shores."

"D-does it hurt? Is it uncomfortable?"

"Not necessarily, but you will feel exhausted and vulnerable to the whims of the ocean. Fear not, however, for all waters lead to Potarium. You will be enraptured in a deep slumber and eventually wash upon its shores."

"When you say rejuvenate, does the ocean de-age you? Perhaps it returns you to your youth?"

"Yes. That is why we lose much of ourselves when we sisters finally ascend."

"I suppose it's a small price to pay for salvation."

"Indeed. But that is where our favor comes into play."

"Oh, of course." As exhausted as I was, I made an attempt to lean forward and appear presentable and attentive. "What do you need me to do?"

"When you get to Potarium, do try to keep an eye out for the jester, would you? He is no normal po, and we do not know what effect the waters will have on him. Be his guide when he finally arrives in the great city."

"Well, that sounds like a noble task! I accept your offer!"

"Good. The Sisters will be pleased."

She began to turn away, ready to close the door on her way out.

"W-wait, what should I do now?" I asked.

"For now, just rest. When you next awake, you will be with the others up in Dulrot. Eventually, an apostle will happen upon the land, and you will have an opportunity to ascend."

Kadd couldn't refrain from letting out his frustration. "Sheesh, is everything in Munderworld so cryptic?"

I swear she chuckled, but she did her best to conceal it, trying her best to maintain her stately presence.

"Not everything, Kadd. Not everything."

She finally made her leave, and once the door closed, I surrendered myself to the shack's accommodations. I tried to stay awake and soak up the comfort for as long as I could, but alas, I was out like a light in no time. I next awoke in Dulrot and saw a gathering of familiar bright lights slowly walking across the desert as they followed what I presume was an apostle hovering above. I quickly made my way to the group and followed their lead. The celestial's radiance blinded me, and I found myself whisked away by the dark ocean.

❧

"Lucky you," Fiddle said. "You got a nice, comfy express ticket to heaven! Cynkz and I had to go the hard way."

"Well," Kadd continued. "I presume the Sisters knew you two would be capable of making your way to The Munder King."

"They have a funny way of working with others, don't they?"

"I'd have to agree. I suppose they have been cooped up in that hole in the ground for eons. They're perhaps not the most socially adjusted individuals."

"I don't know, they seemed alright. I think they act all spooky in order to make themselves seem more intimidating."

"A shrewd thought, my friend."

The sky began to glow with waves of soft light spreading out from the great orb above Potarium. The many stars faded behind rays of morning radiance, and the bleached sands, for a moment, were almost blinding for the trio. Soon their eyes adjusted, and the city itself was within reach.

Several pillars of billowing smoke revealed themselves as they approached. Nothing else appeared to be in any sort of disarray, yet the sight brought on a mutual curiosity between the three desert walkers.

"What's that all about?" Fiddle asked.

"I'm not sure," Kadd said. "Everything seems quiet. The po must be burning something, perhaps some trash from yesterday's chaotic outbreak?"

"Fire seems kind of dangerous for a place like this."

"The great huum protects us anyhow. It's not as if it could or would do any serious damage to us."

"That's amazing!" Fiddle's wooden head clicked as it turned, his excited energy overtaking his dangling form. "So, if you *really* wanted to, you could literally dance in a firepit and it wouldn't do anything?"

"I mean, the great huum would intervene and the po would be unharmed, but I doubt anyone would want to throw themselves into a flame to test it out."

"What about me? Could I do it? Would the huum protect me?"

"I am not sure, to be honest, little one. Huums are meant for po, not imps or muns."

"That's awfully lame."

"This should be far enough, Cynkz. I can walk the rest of the way."

Cynkz stopped and knelt down. Kadd promptly slid off of the steed's back. Cynkz took a quick glance around, and with a quick puff of colorless smoke, was returned to his original form.

"Don't you get tired of being a pack mule?" Fiddle asked.

"I only wish to help, Fiddle," Cynkz said. "I have no issue with lending a helping hand, no matter the form."

"Besides, he was a beautiful steed, not a mule!" Kadd said.

"Eh," Fiddle shrugged. "Anything that walks around on four legs and carries things is a beast of burden if you ask me."

"Wait... Listen," Kadd whispered as he crept behind a nearby shack on the city's edge. Other than a handful of nearly decrepit bundles of wood that comprised the shantytown, there wasn't much to get in the way of one's view into the city. Further in, a collection of wooden puppets could be seen stacked high into a pile, as well as many po carrying torches. Some could even be seen picking up and tossing more puppets into the pile.

"Ah, so that's what they're doing," Kadd whispered.

"It doesn't look good," Fiddle said.

"Fiddle, it may be time for you to head back to Munderworld," Cynkz said.

"What?!" Fiddle cried out.

"Shush!" Kadd said. "You're gonna cause another riot if anyone sees you like this."

"But I just got here!" Fiddle said, trying to stay quiet, but failing. "I want to hang out with you some more!"

"Fiddle, I promise we will catch up soon." Cynkz continued, "Once I find Yla, and we can establish a means of contacting the Sisters—"

"Like before with the ring, right?" Fiddle asked.

"Yes, see? I still have it." Cynkz held out his hand, revealing the crude twisting of simple metal wrapping his middle finger.

"That's nice, but… Ugh, how long is that gonna take?" Fiddle asked.

"I'm not sure, Fiddle, but I promise—"

"I could bring my siblings back—"

"Fiddle…"

"We will form an army! Stronger than ever!"

"Fiddle!"

"We will conquer the land of po! With you leading the charge, the Lord of Imps, with me at your side, the High Mun Commander!"

"You wouldn't dare—"

"I'll do it!"

"Fiddle!"

"Ugh…" Fiddle slouched, his loose, wooden limbs cackling against each other as he sulked.

It was impressive how expressive the marionette was. Its face was static, save for its mouth flap opening and closing to allow the imp possessing it to speak, yet Cynkz could decipher quite a bit from body language and tone alone.

"Fine!" Fiddle said in a huff. "Fine, fine, fine. But you better not take so long this time! Munderworld is so boring with you gone."

"Thank you," Cynkz said. "Until we meet again, old friend."

The puppet set itself on the ground, gave a final click of its heels and a salute, or at least, he tried to salute. His loose limbs did little to allow for such a stable gesture. Fiddle took in a final, deep breath, and the body shook and fell to the ground in a small bundle of wooden joints and string. Despite being well away from the more developed parts of the city, the ground was firmer than what the desert offered, and didn't budge when the marionette fell upon it.

Cynkz wondered if he was focusing on these things to get his mind off of the fact that his best friend was, for the time being, gone again.

Kadd noticed Cynkz's forlorn expression and stepped over to comfort him. "It'll be alright, Cynkz. I'm sure it won't be long before—"

Footsteps approached from around the corner. Immediately, Cynkz and Kadd went quiet, only to see one of the po who had been tossing puppets into piles, stop and greet them, a lit torch still in his hand.

"Ah, it's just a couple of po," the man said. "Oh, and Father Kadd! How do you do, sir?"

"Hello, how are you faring this morning?" Kadd replied.

"'Tis all well and good now, I'd wager. We've been up all night and morn trying to gather as many of these wretched puppets as we can."

"Seems like the creatures left quite the mess."

"Indeed, but we'll manage. But I have to ask, Father…"

"Yes?"

"What are you doing out here? It looks as if you were in the desert, coming from the same direction as that giant—"

"He came to my aid," Cynkz said. "Being new here, I did not know where to run and headed into the desert. My good friend found me and made sure I did not get lost during the mayhem."

"I see…" The po looked a bit puzzled, but he seemed to buy the story. As he looked around, rubbing his chin with his free hand, he ended up looking down and noticed the puppet sitting just beside Kadd.

"Ah! Another one," the po said. "I'd be glad to take that foul mun husk off of your hands. I'll add it to the pile."

Kadd gave a bow and moved aside, giving the man room to drag the puppet over to the mound.

"Well, I think I've had enough excitement for one day," Kadd said. He gave a hearty stretch, and the sounds of his silk robes sliding around were quite pleasing to the ear. "Let's go home."

Cynkz nodded, and Kadd began to walk ahead. Cynkz couldn't help but stop to take notice of the puppets one last time. It was odd to see so many humanoid forms thrown about so unceremoniously. Though this particular pile had yet to be burned, his nose caught whiffs of singed wood carried by the wind. He looked back at the puppet Fiddle had possessed. It was surreal, how just moments ago they were joking about the imp and po dancing in fire, and now his form was about to be sacrificed to flame.

It would do him no good to remain lost in melancholy. With a deep breath, Cynkz moved along, stepping quickly to catch up with his friend.

CHAPTER 12

NOT MUCH HAPPENED IN THE COMING days. It wasn't long before the streets were cleaned up and peace returned to Potarium. Of course, many stories and rumors spread about the incident, though surprisingly few were present to witness Cynkz's intervention. Many did not seem to believe it happened, which was fine as far as he was concerned. He still preferred to fit in as best as he could. So far, the good po of Potarium had given him a wonderful impression, so much so that he began to think of what he would do to settle in.

Cynkz also began to spend more time inside, though he still couldn't bring himself to sleep in a room just yet. During the past days he had often found himself sitting in at home, speaking with Kadd about various things and trying out the many types of teas he liked to brew up. Apparently, Kadd liked to experiment and create new flavors of brew during his free time.

Even now, as Cynkz sat in the living room with several piles of old books stacked around him like castle walls, he was being presented with cups of steaming beverages. He couldn't remember all of the names Kadd had come up with, though a few stood out.

There was a deep, earthy-red mixture called "dragonberry," another bright, almost clear-lemon liquid Kadd called "tinsel juice," and a bright concoction with little swirls of emerald and cobalt with no name. Kadd said he was trying to think of something appropriate for that one. Cynkz worried that his palate had somehow been ruined, as he could hardly tell the difference between any of them. The smells were quite distinct, however.

The 'downtime' was perfect for Cynkz to finally get in some reading. Kadd had shown him a room tucked away in his home with countless rows of dusty tomes. It was terribly disorganized but seemed to possess a wide array of knowledge for Cynkz to delve into. A handful of books held titles such as *A Beginner's Guide to Paithos* and *Where the Light Comes From*. They were heavier than most of the others and strangely dull in their appearance.

Most of the books he saw, once the layers of dust had been blown away, revealed the usual golden edges and rich colors that defined most things in Potarium. Yet these two had simple blank covers with the tiniest bit of faded embroidery on their spines. They didn't even have author names on them. Unlike most of the other books, they appeared to be handwritten. Cynkz had seen some of the printing presses the po used to manufacture large quantities of volumes. He wondered who would take the time to meticulously craft hand-written books and for what reason.

It was as good a reason as any to begin reading them, and he took to deciphering *Where the Light Comes From.*

Once sat down, Cynkz began to parse the texts, spreading the pages apart with his nails and skimming through whatever bits of information stood out to him. He began to notice a pattern in the many passages as he read. The words "light" and "dark" were constantly brought up. It almost appeared as a concerted effort to literally balance the two words, to ensure that each page and verse had the two terms in equal measure.

Many passages spoke of accepting the "balance" of two elements within the soul. Others discussed "light piercing the dark, and dark piercing the light." One chapter discussed huums, and how their "light and airy effect indeed must come from the depths of one's person first and foremost." As he looked deeper into the chapter, he noted how huums were described as being the "source of one's po-hood." As nice as it sounded, Cynkz did not feel any closer to understanding how to huum, or if it was possible for him to do so.

As he flipped through more and more of the book, filled from top to bottom in cursive text, one page in particular caught his eye. It was nearly empty, save for a single phrase displayed at its center:

Light guides, Darkness compels.

The phrase must have been important, considering it had an entire page to itself, in what was otherwise a messy, glorified notebook. The next page revealed nothing. Cynkz looked further and realized the book must have been incomplete, as the remaining handful of pages were completely empty. He didn't necessarily mean to skip to the end of the book, yet here he was. Perhaps Kadd would have a better understanding of what it all meant.

A sharp knock at the door caught Cynkz off guard. He almost fell out of his seat, catching the leaning tower of books next to him as they began to tip over. He could hear Kadd's footsteps beating quickly against the floor as he rushed to the door.

The familiar heavy creaking of wood filled the room, as well as light from the outside, and revealed a single, well-dressed woman in a green and silver dress with intense red hair giving her bow and greetings.

"Hello, Father," she said. "Master Harquin has come to visit you and—Cynkz! Hello again!"

Cynkz stared, recognizing the bouncy young woman from earlier in the week. He smiled and waved from behind a small tower of books.

"It's lovely to see you again, Pairne," Kadd said. "I see Harquin came along in his nicest carriage."

"Well, he said it was the first one available," Pairne said. "Between you and me, he's as excited about all this, and meeting The Royal Court, as anyone else. Though he'll never admit it."

"Who can blame him? It's a good excuse for all of us to have a good time with the nobility. Cynkz?" Kadd gestured for him to come along. "If you're ready, we should get going. No reason to keep all the important folks waiting!"

"Of course," Cynkz said.

Once outside, Cynkz took note of their transportation sitting beyond the short walkway. It looked more like an elaborate, bell-shaped music box on wheels than a proper carriage. Each wheel was nearly as tall as Cynkz, and its rims consisted of interlacing streams of silver that then turned and flowed toward the center, forming the spokes. The carriage itself was a large dome-shaped container with countless swirls and lines forming symbols similar to the ones in the many flags depicting written huums. The base of the carriage reflected an odd pastel rainbow hue that shifted with the light. The top was pointed, its shape mimicking the ornate spear tip from the crest of the circus's big top. In front of the carriage, a silvery drape covered what was presumably the seating for the coachman, but Cynkz couldn't quite see what was underneath. Iconic Hirlwen steeds were attached to the carriage. Their accessories were surprisingly utilitarian, only consisting of the usual components—stirrups, reins, a harness, and so on.

Pairne pranced ahead and opened the side of the carriage. The structure was so ornate that Cynkz couldn't tell the difference between the door and the rest of the wagon. The inside appeared to be equally luxurious. Soft velvet cushions lined the seats on both sides with plenty of space for leg room. A pair of legs sporting finely tailored pants could be seen poking out from the side. More than likely, it was Harquin awaiting his guests.

"Right this way, gentlemen," Pairne said with one hand on the carriage's door and accentuated a polite bow with the other.

Kadd made his way in first, excited as usual. He made a quick nod as he greeted Harquin before taking a seat next to him. Cynkz pulled his cloak and his braid of hair into his arm before stepping in.

Everything looked so delicate and refined, it made him a bit anxious as he remembered to slightly hover with each step so as to not break anything with his weight. Despite finally growing accustomed to being inside, the carriage was far more confined than he was prepared for, and caught up in his own head, he almost forgot to greet Harquin upon entry. As quickly as Cynkz had seated himself, Pairne made her way into the carriage behind him. The thud of the door closing shook the carriage, and Harquin reached up giving two knocks on the wood behind him. The carriage shook again and the sound of large flat hooves clapping against the pavement carried them off.

Hardly a moment passed before Kadd spoke, sparking the conversation. "I presume you were able to get everything in order for us, Master Harquin?"

"Indeed," Harquin said. "It was rather easy, actually. Considering everything that's been going on lately, the nobility feels as if they're missing out."

"You know," Kadd leaned forward with a wry smile, "I was a bit worried, after that whole fiasco with the possessed puppets. I wondered if they'd be afraid of inviting more strangeness into their lives."

"You know how they are. Despite sitting up in their lofty tower, they are quite interested in the happenings of the po below. I swear, some of them wished they had been there to witness the event."

"I assure you, they did miss quite a show—"

"You were there?" Pairne asked, for the first time taking her eyes off of Cynkz.

"Yes! Both Cynkz and I had front row seats to everything," Kadd said, leaning back to rest on the lush cushion.

"So, you were there too!" Pairne turned back to Cynkz, curious as ever. "How was it? I heard it was a rare case of the po being in danger! It must have been exhilarating. I even heard about a giant—"

"Pairne, please," Harquin raised a hand, interrupting the young woman. "Cynkz is more than likely overwhelmed. Besides, we need to go over how this will go."

"Ah, yes. Please inform us of the upcoming proceedings," Kadd said.

"It's nothing too complicated." Harquin readjusted himself, crossing his legs before continuing, "Once we get to the tower, I will lead you in. Kadd and I will go ahead to greet the nobility and make sure they're in a good mood. Cynkz will briefly get spruced up with the perfumers. Once he's presentable, we'll escort him into the throne room, and the floor will be open to you both."

"Sounds exciting," Kadd said. "You know, I mentioned that Cynkz should see about getting his hair tended to."

"I didn't want to say anything," Harquin leaned back, crossing his arms as he pushed himself into his own seat. "His hair looks quite healthy and well-cared for, but it is certainly excessive."

"I love it!"

Pairne's outburst caught everyone's attention. Cynkz merely looked down as he touched the side of his head.

Pairne continued, "Truly, I'm a bit jealous. I wish I could grow my hair that long. Maybe if I washed it more in the rejuvenating ocean water..."

"I'm not sure that's quite how it works," Kadd said.

Harquin shrugged. "Either way, it is a suggestion, Cynkz. I'm sure the perfumers would be more than happy to give it a good bit of brushing and braiding."

"Thank you, Harquin," Cynkz said. "I've held on to this hair for as long as I can remember. It would not be so easy to part with it."

"Of course," Harquin said.

"You know, one of my favorite things about the Hirlwen steeds are their magnificent black manes," Pairne said, leaning ever so slightly toward the jester. "But I think your hair might actually be far more luxurious."

"You know, funny coincidence," Kadd said, giving his usual, mischievous smile. "Cynkz grew up in Hirlwe on a farm breeding Hirlwen steeds."

"Oh!" Pairne broke her intense focus as she took in the information. "I remember Master Harquin mentioning something about that the other day. Is it true? You seem awfully refined and stately for a farm boy."

"It is true," Cynkz said, maintaining eye contact with the young woman for the first time since their ride began.

"Cynkz here has quite the resume," Harquin said. "He's been a farmer, horse breeder, a courtier, a jester, even a sort of realm traveler and abyss walker. He is quite talented from what I hear."

"If only you knew!" Kadd's excitement seemed to get the best of him, his voice too loud for comfort in such a small enclosed space.

"I'd like to know more," Pairne added.

"We shouldn't badger the poor man with questions regarding the past," Harquin said. "We have a pleasant eternity to look forward to, after all."

Cynkz decided it was a good time to steer the conversation toward something productive. "What of the Royal Court? Is there anything more I should know about them? Are they truly comfortable meeting a stranger so soon after the puppet calamity?"

"Yes, they're very interested in meeting you," Harquin said. "Considering it's been so long since we last saw—"

Thump!

The entire carriage shook enough to jostle the passengers in their seats. Everyone, once readjusted, merely looked curious, save for Harquin, who was visibly annoyed by the interruption. He took a deep breath and pounded several times on the wooden backboard. A muffled voice sounded back from the driver's carriage.

"Sorry, mi'lord. Just a small bump in the road, sir."

Harquin sighed heavily. "As I was saying, it's been a long time since a new po arrived on our shores. That, along with many po talking about your involvement in the last circus, as well as the supposed possessed puppets creating chaos, and they feel as if they are missing out. They didn't hear about the puppet madness until the day after, and not until a day after that did they actually begin to believe it. They are so disconnected from the populace, I swear."

"That sounds about right," Kadd said. "What was the word you used to describe nobility? 'Lofty,' was it?"

"That is a perfect word for them, surely," Harquin said. "Though I would never tell them directly."

"Of course," Kadd said. "You possess more than enough tact to do such a thing."

"Speaking of which," Harquin crossed his legs the opposite way before bringing his hands together, "I only have one request of you two, especially you, Cynkz."

"Of course, what is it?" Cynkz replied.

"I would appreciate it if you kept talks of Munderworld to a minimum. Many po, even the nobility, carry deep trauma from their time in the abyss. I fear it may be unavoidable, considering the purpose of your wanting to meet with them."

"I can most certainly avoid the subject as much as possible if need be," Cynkz said. "I only need to find someone. Once I find her, then—"

"Her?" Pairne interrupted, her once beaming expression scrunched into a puzzled look.

"I am merely a returning of a favor to the po who helped me finish my quest in Munderworld—"

Pairne said, "Who is she? A sister? Not a lover, I hope?"

"No, no, nothing like that, I assure you," Cynkz said.

"I suppose there's no reason to be cryptic," Kadd said, inserting his arms into his billowing sleeves. "Cynkz seeks the fifth Sister of Elm. Her name was, um, what was it, again?"

"Yla." Cynkz put his hands together and couldn't help but rub the crude ring gifted to him. The more he thought about his mission, the more he wondered how exactly he would manage to re-establish contact with the sisters. Though if she were truly a Sister of Elm, she more than anyone would be capable of managing such a feat.

"The Sisters of Elm?" Pairne asked.

"How interesting…" Harquin finally separated his hands from one another to rub his chin. Strangely, he paused for a moment, running his eyes up and down Cynkz. He seemed to be putting a lot of thought into his next words. "I have heard stories, but never thought they could be real. Though I have heard and seen so many strange things that I wouldn't be surprised if they were real."

"They are!" Kadd said. "I actually had a lovely chat with one of the many maidens working under them. She told me of their meeting with Cynkz and instructed me to keep an eye out for him in Potarium."

"Hmmm…" Harquin continued to rub his chin, his expression flattened as he looked around, rummaging through countless unseen thoughts.

"I… I hope that is not a problem, Lord Harquin?" Cynkz asked.

"No, of course not. I believe the Royal Court will be more than happy to hear your story. It is far too interesting to pass up."

Cynkz couldn't help but smile, leading to Harquin and Kadd following suit. Cynkz swore he could see Pairne looking happy as well from the corner of his eye but felt it might be too much to look directly at her in that moment. Harquin's attention turned to Pairne, taking great notice of her interest in the jester.

"You know," Harquin said, "Pairne has been a most helpful part of my shows for some time now. She volunteered to personally gather the two of you at the circus and wanted to accompany us to the great tower."

"I only wish to be helpful," Pairne added.

"It truly is a wonderful thing witnessing a budding romance."

"M-master Harquin!" Pairne declared. "I wouldn't, I mean, I don't know if, it's just—"

"There's no shame in it, my dear. If we po are meant to spend an eternity together in this wondrous city, there is no harm in forming lasting relationships, but…"

Harquin's pause seemed to catch everyone off guard. Even Pairne looked curiously at the man.

Harquin continued, "I have to wonder if it's all pointless."

"Pointless?" Cynkz said. "In what way could such a thing be pointless?"

"Hmmm," Harquin paused once again. "Father Kadd, you haven't told Cynkz yet, have you?"

"Told him what?" Kadd asked.

"That po cannot birth children in the afterlife, even in Potarium," Harquin said.

"It's a fact of the afterlife, even in Munderworld," Kadd said.

"I suppose that's true. Still," Harquin said, "I often wonder how many po actually consider the implications of such a fact."

"I've thought about it a lot, actually." Pairne looked down, and for the first time her youthful cheer was gone, replaced with a noticeably solemn expression.

Cynkz could hardly make out her bright amber eyes from his perspective.

Pairne said, "I never got the chance to bear children. I passed away at quite a young age."

"I'm sorry, Pairne…" Cynkz said.

"It's alright. I'm more than grateful to be in Potarium, regardless. Though I have to wonder how things might have turned out, if I had not been forced to witness the end of Peara."

"Y-you were there?!" Kadd had to place both of his hands at his sides to brace himself, his pose wide enough to bump Harquin's elbow, though he didn't seem to notice.

"Yes, or at least, I think I was," Pairne said.

"If you don't mind my asking," Kadd said, "what was it like?"

"I'm afraid I can't relay much you probably don't know. It was as you have heard. One day I was outside, soaking up the sun's warmth. Then, it seemed to get brighter and brighter, so much so that it became uncomfortable. It felt as if the world stood still, and then—Poof! A wave of light engulfed everything, and we were all gone."

"That sounds frightening," Cynkz said.

"It was strangely painless," Pairne added. "It happened so quickly, that if it were not my last memory, I would probably struggle to remember it."

"How bizarre…" Kadd leaned back, resting one hand on his robed knee and his other on his chin. It was the first time he spoke quietly.

"Yes, this is why I sometimes worry for us po, even in Potarium," Harquin said. "Our numbers, while great, are ultimately limited. The city will continue to grow, and yet our population will stagnate. Is it possible for Potarium to become too big? Will we continue to build outward? Could we possibly reach a point where there are not enough of us to organize and manage this great land?"

The carriage went silent. For the first time no one was looking at anyone in particular. Cynkz himself noted the noticeably heavier air residing between them all. The odd thing about eternity was its effect on the future. Without the pressure of utilizing one's limited time, it was easy to spend it carelessly. With enough time, even the greatest traumas could be lifted. Though, as with all things, there was a cost. The weight of infinity stared down from afar.

Cynkz discovered a newfound sympathy for the po. The thought of raising his own family had never crossed his mind, but he could imagine the pain others must feel to have something so precious and core to the soul seemingly ripped away from them. He couldn't help but notice Pairne fidgeting with her hands beside him. Try as she might to hide it, Cynkz could see that the topic was one she had wrestled with before. It appeared there were scars that heaven itself could not heal.

"This is why I'd like to keep the conversation with the nobility light," Harquin said, finally breaking the silence. "It will do us no good to weigh down the great lords and ladies with such troublesome thoughts."

"I agree," Cynkz said.

"It is comforting, knowing that you possess such prudence, Cynkz," Harquin said. "If you were lacking tact, I'd have probably reconsidered this whole venture."

"Even in Munderworld, Cynkz carried himself politely and amicably," Kadd said. "I believe that we have nothing to worry about."

"Indeed," Harquin said. "But, we have a little ways left to go before we approach the tower. Let's return the conversation to something more blithesome."

"Of course," Kadd said.

Cynkz gave a nod but stayed quiet. He couldn't help but continue to think about everything he had learned thus far. Pairne seemed to notice his contemplation and calmed herself down to join the others in their conversation.

CHAPTER 13

"WHOOAAA-HA! WHOOAAA-HA!"
The coachmen's muffled calls could be heard through the thick layer of wood inside the carriage. After a bit of jostling about, the vehicle came to a stop. Cynkz had grown accustomed to the rocking cadence of his transport and felt a niggling sense of unease once it was gone. Perhaps without the constant movement, his mind was forced to focus on his confined surroundings.

"It appears we have arrived," Harquin said.

Pairne quickly stood and opened the door. The weighty thud of the brass handle and lock was soothing, as if reminding the listener of the material's quality. Of course, this only forced Cynkz to consider his own odd attributes. Remembering to constantly keep himself ever so slightly afloat was a tiring affair, and he was relieved to soon be rid of the need to worry over such a thing. Cynkz deliberately waited to be the last one to leave the carriage, making his ruse that much easier to maintain.

After he stepped back down onto solid ground, he was forced to confront the grand structure standing before him. It was the same tower he had ventured to a week prior, yet to him it may as well have been a never-before-seen part of an undiscovered realm.

The difference between the day and night's light on the world was undeniable. At night, it was no issue to simply gaze upon the simple, smooth rod of gold. In the day's early light, it almost assaulted the senses. No matter where one looked, or how one positioned themselves, every line and crevice and curve of the massive tower gleamed with bright beads of light that shimmered along the surface like drops of spring water. The structure was still simple in its shape, yet one would swear that they could find some new detail wherever they looked. Looking up and toward the sky, the once sharp, multi-pronged crown of the tower merely disappeared into a mist of blinding white radiance. It was as if the sun itself were reaching down into the mountain to hold it in place. Every few seconds Cynkz had to turn his eyes downward to rest his sight on the many comparatively darker, duller plants that concealed the exact seam where the tower met the ground. He tried to find the spot he ran into when he flew up to the tower's top but couldn't tell one grassy bush from another. A brief glance around showed a massive pavilion, with meticulously laid brickwork that was unlike anything he had seen before. Of course, where simple, straight-edged bricks would have sufficed, a series of interlacing, curved flat stones wove intricate swirling patterns in the ground. Cynkz actually began to wonder if the brickwork was forming huums of its own, though if it did, he could not recognize anything specific.

It took the sensation of the skin of Pairne's warm hand taking hold of his own to shake him out of his stupor.

"Cynkz, come along," Pairne said. "We shouldn't keep everyone waiting."

As Cynkz was pulled forward, he could see Harquin directing groups of po back and forth in front of a pair of towering pearl-white doors. They were cracked open just enough so Cynkz could catch a glimpse of what was inside: stairs. Lots and lots of stairs draped in crimson cloth seemed to extend upward forever. Kadd of course stood out in his usual, comparatively dull violet robes. The other po Harquin was barking orders at were all dressed exquisitely. They too wore robes, mostly consisting of bright silvers and shining emeralds, the usual golden threads revealing the lines of drooping sleeves and puffy coats. The common fashion seemed to be whatever would best reflect the heavenly light above. Kadd seemed none too bothered in his drab, humble robes, but Cynkz felt as if he were constantly being reminded of his own stark attire. He was beginning to understand Harquin's suggestion for getting a makeover prior to his final meeting.

Even as they approached the others, Pairne seemed to hold onto Cynkz for as long as she possibly could before it became noticeable. As they stopped just behind Harquin and Kadd, she gingerly released her grip, and in such a way that her fingers slid down the length of his hand. He worried that she might accidentally pull off the crude ring he still wore.

"Everything seems to be in order so far," Harquin noted. "Let's hurry along. I refuse to keep the court waiting any longer than necessary."

"This place is built like a maze," Kadd said, "but I think you'll have an easier time not losing sight of your guide here, eh, Cynkz?"

"Of course," Cynkz said through a soft smile.

Harquin began to lead the group up seemingly endless, impossibly winding steps. The interior was massive, and despite there being more than enough windows to allow sufficient light inside, it was hardly enough, only allowing enough brightness within to be considered comfortable.

Much of the interior consisted of a pleasingly dull marble that reflected a soothing blend of blue and grey against the light. Countless off-white swirls and near-emerald sparkles filled out much of the empty space in the material. Everything was muted, allowing the eye to glaze over everything without interruption. If not for the crimson carpets lining the path up the stairs, it may have been easy to miss them.

When Cynkz looked up, he could see many doors far off in the distance, most of which were appropriately elaborate. Their handles and bolts were the same golden hue as the thread lining much of the flags and clothing. As far as he could tell, everything was polished to a mirror shine. He had to wonder just how much work went into keeping everything presentable. Try as he might, he could not find a single speck of dust or dirt anywhere in view. The many prisms of chandeliers reflected and bent the fair light that peeked in from the far-off windows into spots of light that dotted the dull marble floor with bright beads. Cynkz was reminded of the many stars piercing the dark night sky, though none of their formations resembled any known constellations.

As they made their way upward, many of the robed figures following Harquin split off from the group, presumably heading off to attend to their duties.

"Apologies for making you walk so much," Harquin said, keeping his hands behind his back and his attention forward. "As you'd expect, the Royal Court resides at the very top."

"I would expect no less from Potarium's highest nobility," Cynkz said.

"Well, since we have a ways to go before reaching the top, you'll have plenty of time to consider whether or not a haircut is necessary," Kadd said, his body half-turned to smile at Cynkz.

"Come now, there's no need to tease the man about his hair," Harquin said. "A man's hair is his own business, and he should be allowed to handle his business as he sees fit. Besides, there's probably not enough time for that anyway."

"Ugh, now you sound just as stuffy as the nobility," Kadd said. "I'm not the only one noticing this, right? Pairne? Do you agree?"

"I dare not criticize Master Harquin for wishing to conduct himself as properly as he can manage when on royal grounds," Pairne said.

"I mean, that's understandable but... Cynkz?" Kadd looked back at Cynkz, never dropping his smile for a moment.

"I must agree with Pairne's assessment," Cynkz said.

Kadd merely huffed and shrugged, though he maintained his childish grin. Cynkz couldn't help but chuckle, and Pairne followed suit. Harquin remained stern and silent as he guided the group farther up the tower.

Despite being inside, there was more than enough room for Cynkz to feel comfortable. Many of the ceilings they walked under had a way of sloping up and away, giving the already spacious interiors the illusion of being larger than they really were. They never happened to go up any paths that brought them close to a window, but Cynkz was able to catch a glimpse of the outside every now and then. He could see the bleached horizon pulling back further and further as they traveled higher. Whenever they came to a new floor, there was always something new to look at. One floor possessed a massive wooden platform, perfect for dances and the like. Another held countless opulent seats and tables. Perhaps it was where influential po would gather to discuss important deals? Another appeared to merely be an art gallery, or more accurately, an entire art museum. As one would expect, most of the paintings consisted of portraits of well-dressed, noble looking po and their families, though he swore he could see one sculpture that merely depicted a diminutive dog, standing upright and holding a sword and shield, as well as a dramatic, billowing cape that framed the creature. Cynkz decided if he got the chance he would love to return to that floor specifically and soak in the many works.

Cynkz actually began to worry they would ever reach their destination. He had long lost count of how many stories they climbed. Pairne seemed to be just fine, maintaining the youthful spring in her step. Kadd, try as he might, began to loosen his gait as they moved farther up. The sharp, controlled movements he expressed on the lower floors gave way to wide, almost heaving steps. Harquin remained entirely unaffected. His nose remained held high and his precise regal stride was consistent throughout. Finally, they reached a floor that stretched out into an impossibly long hallway. It was a surprisingly functional layout that stood in stark contrast to everything that came before. There were not any windows to look out and gauge one's progress, and only rows of lanterns and small chandeliers holding countless glowing stones lit the space before them. An impossibly long crimson rug was the only thing that truly stood out.

Harquin led the group to one door in particular, though it did not seem any different from the others as far as Cynkz could tell. It possessed a smooth, deep oak texture that was shiny enough to ever so slightly reflect the rug sitting in front of it. Harquin, without hesitation, reached ahead and opened the door, revealing a horde of young, happy faces tending to a number of tasks within the room.

"Hello ladies," Harquin said, one hand behind his back and his nose held high.

"Ah! Lord Harquin!" one woman cried out. "We were beginning to wonder if you'd ever show."

"My apologies," Harquin replied. "I hope we did not keep you waiting."

"Of course not!" another woman said. "We were getting everything ready for our guest."

"Yes, I brought him as quickly as I could manage." Harquin stepped to the side, his hand still holding the door while he gestured toward Cynkz. "Make sure you take good care of him. Kadd and I will be back shortly to present him to the Royal Court."

Cynkz walked inside. He looked around to see a number of maidens spread about the room, each wearing a different combination of simple colored dress and shining ribbons tying back their hair, all in unique fashions, of course. They seemed ready for work.

"Hello everyone. I am Cynkz. A pleasure to—"

Just as Cynkz bowed and gave his greeting, he could hear the door quickly closing behind him. It was a bit of a shock to see that he had been left alone. Harquin, Kadd, even Pairne was nowhere to be seen.

A chorus of voices barely in sync with one another brought his attention back to the room.

"Hello, Cynkz!"

Cynkz felt the soft hands of two women taking hold of his arms, gently guiding him toward a seat in the middle of the room. It was quite large, and even lounged back, and sat in front of a giant mirror that nearly took up the entire wall.

"Right this way, young master," one of the women said.

"First, we need to decide what you'll wear," another said, "then we'll fashion your hair up nicely and… Oh my."

"W-what's wrong?" Cynkz asked as he looked nervously at the woman who was standing behind him.

"Lord Harquin was not kidding," she said.

"By Paithos, it's so long!" another cried out.

"It's even more amazing than he described," a third said.

"Let's hurry and get him outfitted," a fourth said. "We're going to need a lot of time to deal with all that."

Cynkz could sense that they knew each other well. It would have been nice to hear at least a few of their names, however, so he could keep better track of everything.

They quickly stood him in front of the giant mirror and began to fly back and forth as they dragged out articles of clothing from behind a large room divider. It was material similar in its makeup to what he had seen before—puffed blouses and smooth coats and tailored shirts, each possessing their own elaborate combination of golden buttons, threading, and buckles.

"I sort of like what he has on now," one woman said.

"I don't know," another added. "The dark, harlequin pattern is… different. It's like he's trying and failing to pass as a jester from a romance novel or something."

"The asymmetry is a bold choice," another said. "Not many po are willing to show off a half-cloak of all things."

"It's as if he's trying to hide something," another exclaimed.

"What would you have to hide, oh mysterious one?" a fifth woman said, playfully grinning and twisting her brow to feign suspicion.

"I, um…" Cynkz was overwhelmed. He could hardly keep up with the bodies shuffling around him and the glittering clothes and accessories being passed around and occasionally held up to him for sizing.

"I've heard rumors!" one woman said.

"Chantelly," another responded. "You really need to stop pushing your gossip into every conversation."

Finally, a name, Cynkz thought. It was something to ground him a bit, something concrete to hold on to in his mind.

"Ugh! Darnuelle! I thought we agreed we weren't going to give away our names—You know, to keep him guessing?"

Another name, Cynkz thought. He was beginning to feel more confident about his situation with each new bit of information.

"Well," a third woman came up and held a long coat striped from top to bottom with golden swirls and embroidery in front of Cynkz. "He'll never get to know *my* name—"

Several of the women looked at each other playfully before turning their attention back to call out in unison, "You wish, Sillen!"

"Pfft, I guess I brought that upon myself," Sillen remarked.

Cynkz couldn't help but chuckle at the bedlam unfolding before him.

"Here, Mr. Cynkz. Try this," another woman came up to his side with an entire outfit folded into a silky, neat square in her arms.

One of the women spoke up. "Ah, Head Mistress, that looks like a good fit for the man."

"Since we're all sharing names, you can just call me Vairhen."

"Is Lady Vairhen alright?" Cynkz said.

One of the women could be heard calling out from behind the screen. "Oh! So polite!"

"Well, I suppose that will do," Lady Vairhen said, turning her head ever so slightly to tug at the single golden ribbon holding her long twisted blonde braid in place. It reminded Cynkz of Foa's braid the more he thought about it. He sometimes wondered if it was just a coincidence that the leader of the Sisters of Elm kept such a simple style of hair for the same reason he did.

She continued. "You can go right behind the divider and try on the outfit. I promise none of the girls will peek. Right?" She gave a hard glare to the rest of the women, who merely huddled together and giggled.

Cynkz quickly stepped behind the panel, ready for a bit of cover and comfort away from prying eyes. Even as he began to change, questions began to pour in from the group.

"So, Mr. Cynkz," Chantelly said, "I heard that you're the son of a mysterious noble. Who is it?"

"What?! Where did you hear that?!" Sillen replied, her voice as sharp as a whip snapping.

"From somewhere..." Chantelly mumbled.

"I heard he's a dark prince from a long lost kingdom," another voice called out.

"Nonsense!" Darnuelle stepped forward, asserting herself to the group. "I heard that he traveled all across Munderworld, battling creatures and—"

"You're crazy. He's far too pretty to be doing any sort of fighting." Sillen's voice seemed to be the most restrained of the bunch.

"Well, why don't we just let him tell us?" Lady Vaihren's voice was weighty, projecting itself well above the others. "Where do you come from, if you don't mind me asking?"

"I am from Hirlwe, believe it or not—"

"Hirlwe?!" The single word echoed as it was called out by nearly everyone in the room.

"There's no way," Chantelly said. "What could someone as stately looking as yourself do in Hirlwe?"

"I grew up on a farm, tending to horses and the like," Cynkz replied.

"A farm boy?!" Again, several voices called out in unison. It was impressive how the chaotic bunch seemed to be on the same wavelength.

A moment of silence passed, with little else to fill the air other than the sound of fine silk and cloth being pulled over Cynkz's body as he finished dressing himself. He was grateful that they were considerate enough to give him something that appeared simple to put on.

"I don't buy it," Sillen noted.

"Me neither," Chantelly added.

"Come, come. We shouldn't be treating our guest like some kind of lowly liar," Lady Vaihren added.

A tug here, a pull of cloth there, and Cynkz was nearly finished. Then he remembered the thread! It'd perhaps be best to not leave it in his old clothes. He rummaged through old his coat, and once he found the pocket, he took great care to completely cover the thread in his grip before transferring it to a patch buried deep beneath his new coat. The women merely resumed their chatter, his surreptitious maneuver a success.

He took in a deep breath, brushed himself off, and emerged from behind the thin divider standing between him and the world. He was greeted by a round of elated gasps that trailed off into several giggles. He wasn't sure what exactly to make of the reaction, but it appeared to be positive overall.

"It's perfect!"

"It's surprisingly form-fitting."

"He has to be a prince of some kind. The look suits him too perfectly."

"Come! Look in the mirror, Cynkz!"

Cynkz obliged the young woman's request and stood squarely in front of his reflection. He looked down at a dark coat that reflected the faintest bit of lavender against the light. Dozens of golden seams crossed one another across the front of his top. His neck was mostly covered in a short, flared puff of frilled, white cloth, and as he moved his hands, he noticed the same material accenting his sleeves, right where his wrists would otherwise be visible. Draped softly over his left shoulder, where his once dark cloak used to sit was a shimmering cloth colored like plum wine that nearly reached his knee. The front of his coat was short, tapered into a lengthy coattail that reached further down than his hair. His trousers poofed into wide bell shapes bearing a subtle striped pattern of their own that sat around his thighs before snuggly closing in just above his knees. Dark stockings covered the rest of his legs and nearly blended in with his original shoes. It evoked the same dark mood as his old clothes, yet the shining material helped him to fit in with everything else he had thus far seen in Potarium.

"I don't know about the hat," Darnuelle stated, her delicate hand sitting in front of her mouth as she looked up toward the man's head.

"I like it, honestly," Chantelly said, "It rounds out the look, giving his otherwise streamlined silhouette just that extra bit of flair and edge to stand out."

"I suppose it can stay," Lady Vairhen added. "Please, Cynkz, if you'll have a seat we will tend to your hair and get you perfumed."

"Perfume?" Cynkz's puzzled look must have been amusing, as Lady Vairhen could hardly restrain a chuckle of her own.

"Why yes," Lady Vairhen said. "We are casually referred to as 'perfumers,' as I'm sure you've heard."

Cynkz was beginning to wonder just what he had gotten himself into. Unfortunately, over a dozen, wide open, gleeful irises peered into him expectantly. Perhaps it was best to follow Kadd's advice and just 'go with the flow.' He stepped over to the lengthy crimson cushioned seat and readied himself to sit. He had to take a moment to pull his braid out of the way before getting situated, which prompted a snappy response from the Head Mistress.

"Ah, Master Cynkz, let us help you with that. Ladies?"

Two of the women stepped over and attempted to lift the braid to the side. After Cynkz finally sat himself down, he could hear them struggling to heave the massive bundle of hair.

"By Paithos!" one woman cried out. "It's heavy!"

"Nonsense!" Lady Vairhen snapped. "This is no time for games—"

"No, really," the other woman said. "Come see for—oof! Come see for yourself."

Lady Vairhen gave a suspicious look but quickly motioned for a couple others to hurry over and assist. Cynkz, unsure of what to do, decided to slowly lean back and rest his neck on the headrest. A moment of struggle later, capped with a satisfying thud, and his braid was finally laid straight behind him. It was almost comical listening to the handful of women burdened with the laborious task nearly wheezing as they took a breath of relief.

All of the women gathered behind Cynkz. He felt as if he had become the subject of some strange, arcane experiment, and only realized it too late. Everyone seemed to stare with weighted anticipation as he heard the shuffling of his braid being pulled undone behind him. A soft, prolonged shusssh followed as his locks spread in all directions, covering a frightening portion of the floor with a sea of thick jet-black strands.

"Wow..." one woman muttered.

"It's so dark—darker than the night sky," another said.

"It hardly reflects any light," a third noted. "Is that weird?"

"Come on, girls," Lady Vairhen said, clapping her hands as she stepped forward. "We don't have much time. Get it brushed and braided as nicely as you can manage. I'll go get a couple of the fume sticks so we can finish with a nice spritz of fragrance."

"Fume sticks?" Cynkz pulled his head forward as he raised his brow. He could feel a couple of the women who were brushing his hair being pulled forward with him.

"Ah, yes," Lady Vairhen continued as she stepped out of sight and into a closet Cynkz had not noticed before. "We have these lovely little critters that exude a most intoxicating mist. Just a little tap on their cage and *poof!* Out comes a pink cloud."

Pink mist? Cynkz thought. *That seems… No, it must be a coincidence.*

Lady Vairhen could be heard rummaging through several things out of sight, still having enough focus left over to continue. "Yes, I believe their scientific name is, um… Chantelly, what was it, again?"

"I don't remember, ma'am," Chantelly said.

"I believe it was, um, 'fumer phantasm?'" Sillen said.

"No, no, it's 'fumer phasmotilis.'" Darnuelle said, her tone betraying her vexation.

"Well, regardless, the creatures are lovely." Lady Vairhen finally emerged holding a small, silver cage with something odd and still sitting inside. It was a long, thin insectoid standing on a number of impossibly thin legs. Its neck—or what could be deduced to be its neck—consisted of several overlapping layers of brown chitinous shells that tapered up to a fine, rounded point. Its tiny mandibles reflected the light as they twitched open and closed.

Cynkz's eyes shot wide open, and he nearly jolted out of his seat. *It can't be! It looks just like those creatures from the forest—*

"Good, everything is nearly finished," Lady Vairhen said, looking up and down at the women moving tirelessly to work the heavy strands into a neat braid. "If you'll remain still for but a moment longer, Master Cynkz."

Lady Vairhen lifted the cage a foot away from his head, and she readied her other hand to tap the cage. For a moment, Cynkz wasn't sure what to do. Was he worrying over nothing? Was it just a coincidence? The creatures were more than reminiscent of the colossal beasts patrolling the Sister's realm that emitted the same, acidic mist that took his arm. He worried about Kadd's deduction that Cynkz was seemingly not under whatever protection the realm offered. But it couldn't be so bad, could it?

Despite the countless worries running through his mind, none of it mattered. The second the woman tapped the cage, the creature's tiny mandibles stretched, and Cynkz ducked to the side as quickly as he could. He hardly noticed the shrieks of the women stumbling as they were pulled with him.

A faint, dissipating mist quickly faded into the air where his head once sat. It was at that moment that he noticed a burning sensation on the edge of his cheek. It was subtle, but unpleasant enough that he knew he had made the right move. It was then that he noticed the wide, almost scared looking eyes of Lady Vairhen looking into him like two bright green crystals peering into his mind. He had to avert his attention away from her and noticed a couple of the women who had fallen over being helped up by the others. Without a thought, he conjured up a way to salvage the situation.

"Ah, I am sorry, ma'am, but I have suffered from terrible allergies in the past. I know I am probably safe from such things in Potarium, yet the trauma of old experiences still lingers. Do we perchance have anything a bit … milder?"

"I, um, I'm not sure." Lady Vairhen sounded unsure for the first time. She held the cage close to her chest and cradled it, as if unsure of what to do with the object.

A sharp knock at the door shot through the room. Cynkz turned and gave a sigh of relief, perhaps the most satisfying one of its kind he had ever given in his life, or after life for that matter. The door opened, and a familiar face poked into the room.

"Cynkz, everything is ready. The court will see you now," Harquin said, paying no attention to anyone else in the room.

"Yes, very good…" Cynkz pulled at his collar and patted down his coat. He stepped forth as stately as he could manage, hurrying ahead without a single look back. The creak of the door closing made him feel as though he were leaving behind something he no longer wanted, as if locking away an uncomfortable memory.

Harquin quickly stepped ahead and addressed Cynkz once more. "We only have one more flight of stairs to ascend. All you have to do is follow my lead. I'll address the court, get things started, and the floor will be open to you. Are you ready?"

Cynkz stared for a moment, then took a deep breath. "Y-yes, as ready as I'll ever be…"

Harquin smiled and placed a soft hand on Cynkz's shoulder.

"There's nothing to worry about, truly," Harquin said. "You look good, by the way. The girls work quickly, don't they?"

"Yes, they're very efficient."

"Efficient, indeed." Harquin released his hand and turned away. "Right this way, then."

Once back down the hall, they came to a final set of stairs. They were surprisingly dark in tone as if intentionally designed to be moody in some way, an ominous foretelling of something grand approaching.

Fortunately, it was easy enough for Cynkz to keep track of Harquin as they made their way up the darkened stairway. At the top, he could see intense light poking through the crevices around a large door. Harquin approached, stiffened his shoulders, and gave a mighty push. A great, blinding light completely enveloped them. Harquin's faint silhouette could be seen stepping into the heavenly mist. Without a second thought, Cynkz pushed himself forward into the veil and disappeared with him.

CHAPTER 14

A POINT OF FRUSTRATION CYNKZ HAD come to terms with during his venture through Munderworld was the constant descent into darkness.

The darkness was like a warm, comforting blanket to those accustomed to its veil, yet even children of the abyss needed contrast from time to time. The heavy hand of gloom eventually grew wearisome for anyone trapped beneath it. Yet in Potarium, Cynkz was beginning to grow equally weary of being regularly blinded by glorious light. Perhaps it was not necessarily a matter of dark or light, but the dread of being robbed of his senses.

It was fortunate, then, that his eyes soon settled onto the most pleasing sight. It was difficult to truly grasp how large the golden Hand of Po was when traipsing through its many rooms and halls and while guided up its many orderly steps. This room—the throne of The Royal Court—was perhaps the first and only room to take full advantage of the tower's breadth.

The space between the far walls was completely open and huge windows allowed the radiance from outside to bathe the entire room in a milk-honey hue. The space was rounded, as if sitting inside a dome, and the circular perimeter defined the layout of everything within its border. A simple glance upward revealed the architecture tapering into a mist of warm, heavy light.

Split evenly along the windowed walls were a series of flags that shimmered as they settled. Cynkz wondered what air was causing them to waver, and closer inspection revealed tiny holes at the base of each flagpole that seemed to let in just enough air to ruffle the hanging cloth. From where the openings led or where their winds were coming from, Cynkz could only guess. Where most of the flags in the city below primarily displayed their darkly colored base, these were so reflective that the bright light completely covered them. They would have appeared as simple slivers of heavenly air if not for the subtle shadows around the edges of their golden threading. Matching their threading was the gold and silver filigree that separated much of the swirling, ornate design built into the structure of the room itself.

The room was so spacious it amplified every sound within. It reminded Cynkz of the first church Kadd had taken him to. Everything echoed clearly in the room, and Cynkz's ear caught wind of a number of po seated in an arced arrangement nearer to the room's center. A curved line of absurdly tall thrones poked harshly against the soft, warm light. Each one was uniquely crafted, though there were some notable similarities. Each one faced toward the front of the room and had a long drape of cloth that extended out from the seat and covered the few steps in front. These cloths, upon further viewing, possessed their own unique designs sewn into them. Instead of the usual golden lines and swirls that represented written huums, they bore regal symbols and embroidery.

Cynkz couldn't recognize any of the symbols, but he could make out what a few of the emblems were attempting to portray. For example, one depicted a lion bearing a crown and holding a scepter up to the sun. Another had a decorative image of a bird spreading its wings before a great mountainside. One even had what appeared to be several trees arranged in a square pattern, with an open hand sitting centered between them.

As far as one could tell, each one was a sort of heraldic emblem meant to represent a different nation. It seemed reasonable that they too represented different periods of time, considering the court consisted of a variety of rulers from times of old. Unfortunately, Cynkz did not recognize any of them in particular. He could remember his visions of his time in a kingdom on Peara, but no matter how hard he tried, he could not recall anything specific.

It was then that he finally noticed the po accompanying these many thrones. Each one was extravagantly dressed, each one fashioned just as distinctly as their thrones. Gold and silver lined the seams of their coats, shining tassels accented their many coattails. Furred edges stood out like small clouds wherever their clothing would allow it. As usual, where simple

colors would have sufficed, instead nearly every surface bore curving stripes and meticulous ornamen-
tation that bordered on being gaudy. There were so
many different tints and hues on display that Cynkz
made a quick game out of trying to deduce their specific names. Cobalt zippers, ivory buttons, eggshell fur
that seemed to literally absorb the honeyed light, lilac
waves covering vermillion leggings that led the eye
naturally toward umber slippers.

Surprisingly, none of them wore crowns, but their
elaborate headwear reminded Cynkz of the pointed
chapeau Vicar Reindall wore. It appeared they were
meant to be symbolic of crowns, rather than literal
ones. Perhaps it was meant to represent a more unified
form of governing—no one crown to bear its weight
on the ruling? Cynkz did not feel comfortable asking
such a question directly, and then thought fondly of
Fiddle, who surely would have no problem digging
into such matters.

What really caught Cynkz off guard was how casually the supposed royalty were behaving at that moment.
He expected them to at least be seated already, awaiting
their arrival. Though the more he thought about it, he
was perhaps not distinguished enough to elicit such an
impression. Still, they began making their way to their
seats, sharing bits of chatter as they moved that Cynkz
couldn't quite make out due to how far away they were.
It was amusing to watch the supposed greatest nobility
that history had to offer nearly stumble over their outfits as they went to their seats. Not every seat was being
occupied. From his count, Cynkz noted seventeen seats,
yet only five of them were filled.

I suppose not everyone could make it… Cynkz thought.

Several footsteps approached from behind. A quick turn of his head revealed the sight of his friend leaning in to speak with him.

"It's grand, isn't it?" Kadd said.

"Very much so," Cynkz said back, as quietly as he could manage. "But it's all a bit much, isn't it?"

"Well, would you expect anything less of an 'ultimate throne room?'"

"Perhaps not, but still… There's opulent, and then there's excessive."

"True, but just remember," Kadd leaned in even closer, "as fancy as all this is, they are merely po, no better than you or I or Pairne or any of these poor guardsmen that have to sit up here and stare at this all day."

Cynkz craned his head to look at the wall behind them. Nothing much stood out from a small assortment of knightly looking guards standing at attention near the door. They each carried the usual accessories, a tall plumage of vibrant feathers, and each held an ornamental spear in hand. Their formation would have been perfectly symmetrical, if not for a single woman standing among them, looking back at him with happy amber eyes. She gave a small wave, and Cynkz smiled and returned the gesture.

Harquin was already far ahead and centered before the royalty, ready to address the court. He adopted the same booming oration that he carried during the circus.

"Lords and ladies! I presume everyone is doing well on this lovely day?"

One of the kings spoke. He was a portly fellow, possessing darker skin and a loose posture giving off an open, comforting, and even nonchalant air. "Harquin! It's been too long, my good sir."

"Indeed, it has, Sir Galtheal," Harquin said.

Another name... Cynkz thought. *I will need to work doubly hard to keep track of them all.*

Harquin continued. "I do hope you all have been keeping yourselves adequately entertained?"

An older looking woman, constantly looking down her nose and past a stiff upper lip, leaned forward to speak. She was much thinner and quite fair in her look. She exuded such an air of dignity that even the few wrinkles she possessed appeared to lock themselves in formation as she spoke. "In truth, we have been keeping to ourselves as of late."

"That seems unacceptable, Lady Uthrine." Harquin bowed his head ever so slightly when he addressed her.

Lady Uthrine... another name...

Cynkz noticed some of the royalty were occasionally averting their gaze to get quick glances at him. Despite the makeover, he still stood out, though that came as no surprise.

Lady Uthrine continued. "You know, Harquin, I have been hearing the wildest rumors as of late, concerning your show and some madness with puppets. Flying puppets! Can you imagine?"

Another king leaned forward, pushing himself forward so quickly Cynkz thought he was about to throw himself out of his seat. He bore a lengthy, light-colored beard, braided not dissimilarly to Cynkz's hair. Its coloring appeared unable to decide between a shade of silver or sepia.

"I swear, if I have to listen to any more droll gossip and rumors Paithos himself will be in awe of the mess I'll leave after jumping out the nearest window."

"Ugh, uncouth as usual, Cerhnbal."

Cerhnbal... There were only three new names so far, but even Cynkz was beginning to worry how many he would have to remember.

Another woman could be seen from the corner of Cynkz's eye moving in her seat. She was so small that her feet could barely reach the floor as she sat. Her hair coiled upward into a great tower of shining, braided caramel. Just at the tip of this tower resided a single round gem. The small shining crimson orb acted as a proverbial cherry on top.

"It is more than mere 'rumors,' Cerhnbal. My youngest son was relaying to me the other day about having to hang up his own puppeteering shop after the chaos. He mentioned something about everyone below working tirelessly to burn down anything related to them."

"Ah, Lady Krine, you should have informed me," Harquin said. "If he has suffered any serious damages, I'd be more than happy to assist—"

"Oh, thank you, Harquin, but we will be fine. Your help won't be necessary."

Krine, Cerhnbal, Uthrine, Galtheal... Cynkz was beginning to feel as if he were watching a poorly refereed match of cricket as his mind darted back and forth, trying to catch each new name as if scoring points for a non-existent team.

"I'd very much like to get things underway," Harquin said, scanning the row of thrones. "I see that not everyone is here. Should we be expecting anyone else?"

"Ah, well, there may be one or two stragglers who happen in later," Lord Cerhnbal said. "Some of us are constantly mired in business, as you know. Please, do what you need to do."

"Splendid!" Harquin reached out, assuming an orator's stance. His talent for addressing a crowd was on full display. "Recently, you may have heard of a number of odd happenings occurring in our beloved city, from a mad stampede of puppets to a nail-biting encounter shocking the world at a circus. Preceding these events—the arrival of the first new soul Potarium has seen in decades. It did not take long for him to adjust to our city, and more impressively to begin getting in the good graces of notable figures, such as yours truly. And *more* interesting is that he brought with him a most important mission from his adventures in the abyss beyond."

"A mission?!" Sir Galtheal seemed to almost bark the words like a cough, restraining a gruff chuckle as he kicked in his seat. "What kind of mission could one possibly have coming from the abyss? There is naught but darkness and slime and beasts, as far as I've heard."

"How about I let the man speak for himself?" Harquin, with his arms still stretched out gestured toward Cynkz. "I present to you the realm traveler, a jester of old, the mun wrangler, and a savior of fellow po—Cynkz!"

All eyes immediately shot toward Cynkz. Time and time again his standing out brought him to the center of attention, though this was different. For the first time, he was grateful to be in such a position. Finally, he would be able to make some serious progress. It would not be long before he would find the final sister, surely.

Cynkz felt several soft pats on his back, Kadd himself showing his support with a wide grin, as he often did. Cynkz quickly smiled back and stepped to stand alongside Harquin. As he approached the center of the room, where the light above shined brightest, the tip of his shadow swept behind him. With it gone, he was free to focus on what lay ahead, and he felt as if a great weight were being slowly lifted off of his shoulders. He could feel himself finally fitting in and moving forward. For once, being at the center of things energized him, and it showed in his quick, assertive steps and his barely restrained smirk. Some deep part of him, perhaps once lost to his time on Peara, was coming back in full force. Nothing could stop him—not the light, not the dark, not even himself.

As Cynkz approached, Harquin moved to the side enough to give him breathing room at the center of the court. It was time to shine.

"Your royal highnesses and graces. It is a great honor to finally meet all of you." Cynkz gave a deep bow. He was not sure why, but the extra flair came naturally to him. His right arm crossed his chest, his left arm extended out, allowing his cloak to stretch out like a fanciful wing. He even slightly bent one knee and extended his other leg forward. As he returned to a normal stance, he could see many pleased eyes looking him up and down. Even Harquin was smiling, or at least, it seemed like he was from the corner of Cynkz's eye.

"How wonderful!" Lady Krine called out. "Most po who arrive are so lacking in manners."

"Indeed," Lord Cerhnbal added. "Many make the mistake of immediately addressing us casually, calling us 'sirs' or 'ma'ams' as if we share any rapport."

"I must say, he is an interesting looking specimen," Lady Uthrine said, almost mumbling as she lifted a dainty hand to her chin. "He seems to have made an impression on Father Kadd—"

A new voice interrupted the conversation. It was a sharp, quick tone accented by vexation. "He's certainly better mannered than the last slab Kadd brought to us."

Cynkz looked on at the woman with a bit of puzzlement. Her blonde hair was the only one fashioned in a way so as to not make use of its length. Two great bobs were pulled back behind a sharp face that seemed allergic to expression. Her robes were simple and elegant, merely a deep dark olive gown that only revealed its color in the light, that hugged her chest tightly before billowing out into a great skirt.

"Ah, Lady Lilithen," Harquin said. He stepped backward to share information with Cynkz. "When Kadd first arrived, one of the po with him was a… Let's just say, she was a troublesome woman with a sharp tongue. The first thing she did was—"

"She told me to 'stuff the pleasantries into that extra pocket you're hiding beneath that glorified curtain you call a dress.'"

Harquin continued. "*Ahem.* Yes, well, if not for Kadd's intervention and good word, she would very well be living out the rest of her eternal days in a cell somewhere in the desert."

"I hear you are ultimately the reason for her ascension," Lady Lilithen said, addressing Cynkz, "along with several others, such as Father Kadd."

"I apologize, your highness." Cynkz bowed once more, this time humbly leaning over a loose arm he held close to his chest. "I was only trying to help those I saw in need."

"You are quite noble, young Cynkz!" Sir Galtheal's boisterous tone echoed harshly throughout the domed room. "To selflessly aid someone so caustic, and in such a dire circumstance, it speaks volumes about your character."

Kadd's footsteps could be heard shuffling toward the center of the room. "If I may be so bold as to interject, your highnesses, this man's influence has spread throughout the entirety of the abyss! He ventured from top to bottom of that nonsensical world, helping other poor souls along the way. Tales of his befriending and charming muns still resonate within Munderworld's dark walls, I am certain."

Cynkz kept his attention forward, but he could see Harquin's expression quite clearly from the corner of his eye. The once light and smiling face was slowly resting into something flatter and more stern. He remembered the ringmaster's request to keep talk of the abyss to a minimum, but surely he should have anticipated Kadd would struggle to restrain himself? Still, things appeared to be going well. Almost too well.

"I have heard a plethora of tales concerning Harquin's circus beasts, with many even jokingly calling him a 'munagerist,'" Cerhnbal said and rested a firm hand on an arm rest, as if propping himself up. The contrast between his level of care next to Sir Galtheal was almost comical. He moved slowly enough that the countless tiny jewels lining his coat and sleeves were finally noticeable. Each one seemed to reflect a completely different hue.

Cerhnbal continued. "Perhaps you have greater experience with wrangling beasts than our own Lord of Festivals, eh?"

"Did any of the muns you charmed have names?" Sir Galtheal bellowed out his question the way a child might toward a half-attentive parent.

"Well, it was mostly Fiddle, the mouthy imp that accompanied him," Kadd said.

"An imp?" The echo of several voices speaking in unison rolled over the entire room.

Cynkz addressed the room. "Yes, his name is Fiddle—"

"Fiddle?!" Again multiple voices collided against one another, this time louder, taking full advantage of the room's acoustic properties.

"Ha! Haha!" Sir Galtheal finally leaned back in his seat, convulsing in his merriment. "W-where did–hehe–where did he get the name from?"

"In truth, I am not sure," Cynkz said. "He says he ended up giving himself the name. He spoke often of his time talking to other po who seemed capable of sharing interesting knowledge with him—"

"And he's an inquisitive one to boot? A bookworm imp?! Hahahar!" Sir Galtheal was enjoying himself far more than anyone else in the room, it appeared, though everyone seemed to be in good spirits.

It felt invigorating to be in the midst of shared cheer, and Cynkz began to think of outlandish ways to cap off the event. *Maybe I could show off the thread... No, no, that's too much...*

Cynkz merely smiled and took in a satisfying breath. There was no reason to push more than was necessary. This was as good a time as any to work his request into the conversation.

"I have to ask," Lady Lilithen said, hardly moving from her original, stately pose. "What could possibly motivate one to go through your trials?"

The heavy creak of polished wood slowly filled the air, and all eyes shifted their attention to behind Cynkz. New footsteps made their way hurriedly through the room.

"It is so good that you were able to make it, Lord Peltony," Lady Uthrine said, greeting the late arrival as her eyes followed the man's movements.

"Yes, yes, my apologies," Peltony said. "Just dealing with some permits and papers and the like. I wanted to get a little bit of work done before relaxing with you all."

As the new lord hurried past, Harquin was the first to bow. Kadd followed suit and Cynkz quickly after. He was able to catch a glimpse of the new kingly figure. He was rather short but walked in a clearly focused and assertive manner. Everything he wore was pitch black, with only the reflective lines of the light above revealing his attire's edges. He wore a distinct flat cap with several golden beads hanging from its rim. The cap nearly blended in with his equally dark hair, which was tied back and blended into the back of his dark coat. Each step forward revealed his puffed leggings and caused his lengthy coattails to wave gently from side to side like the feather of a noble bird mid-flight.

When he finally sat down Cynkz noted his distinct features. His sharp eyes and slightly tanned skin made him stand out from the others. Cynkz could only wonder what sort of empire he once ruled over.

Galtheal called out as soon as Peltony sat down, strangely a few seats away from everyone else. "We were discussing an imp named Fiddle."

"An imp? An actual imp? A mun with a name, no less?" Peltony's squinting eyes gave his skeptical tone a particularly potent flair.

"Yes, yes," Galtheal continued. "He was a good friend of our esteemed guest."

"Ah, I did not know we would be indulging the rumors surrounding Potarium's newest arrival," Peltony said, finally resting in his own seat.

Lady Lilithen chimed in, "Actually, I was about to ask the young man to inform us of a burning question I am sure we all have."

"Don't mind me then," Peltony said with a quick, dismissive wave. "Please continue."

Lady Lilithen continued. "As I was saying, Cynkz, what could have possibly spurred you forth on such a dangerous, laborious venture? You were presumably already in the upper most realm of the abyss, no? Why go through all that trouble? Why not just seek proper ascension like any other po?"

Whatever confidence Cynkz had garnered felt instantly shattered. He often wondered what pushed him ahead. The few po he happened across believed him to be a shapeshifting mun of some sort. Even after meeting Fiddle, he never once thought it would be possible for him to merely reach out for salvation from the apostles. There was the possibility of the many sentinels guarding the roving po to catch wind of his trickery, only complicating things more than he cared to deal with. Cynkz's eyes darted around, as if grasping for answers in the dark of his mind. He thought of the thread again, and once again concluded it may not be best to unveil it so soon. Then he remembered something that Kadd told him not too long ago. He liked him for his 'simple, straightforward and honest' nature. Perhaps that was the easiest path: simple, straightforward, and honest.

Cynkz took a deep breath, steeled his gaze, and projected forth. "I lost something important to me long before my time in the abyss. I sought answers and crossed paths with a number of other po along the way. I made my way to the depths of Munderworld, and only with the help of the Sisters of Elm, was able to move ahead. In return, they asked a single thing of me. To find their long lost sister, a woman of great import."

For the first time since the meeting began, the court went silent. All eyes were on him. He was thankful for the deep breath he had managed just before speaking, as it may have been the only thing grounding him under the scrutiny of sitting beneath heaven's light. Slowly, he read the many different expressions held across the room. Lady Krine pulled back into her seat, stretching out her small limbs as if to hold on to her throne, preparing for some sort of turbulence. Lord Cerhnbal was skeptical, an almost angry brow weighing heavy on his eyes. Lady Uthrine had her own brow raised, looking as if attempting to piece everything together. Sir Galtheal, for the first time, stiffened his posture, going so far as to sit himself up proper. Lady Lilithen, the once supremely stout and proper one, sat with her eyes wide, the first round expression she had held since the meeting began. Lord Peltony rested onto one of his arms, a curious hand on his chin and an even curiouser finger slightly raised in front of his thin lips.

From the corner of one eye, Cynkz could see Kadd nearby, still smiling, though more softly. From the other eye, Cynkz could see Harquin holding a much sterner expression, but not one of anger. It was almost as if he were examining Cynkz, as if he knew of something deeper in his story. Cynkz could only imagine what the guards or Pairne were thinking.

"W-well," Lady Lilithen stumbled ever so slightly over her words, the first true sign of something raw and natural in her speech. "That is a most interesting, um, what did you call it? Your 'mission?'"

Cerhnbal leaned forward, gesturing with a free hand to accentuate his tone. "So you came all this way to gain aid in finding this, er, woman of great import?"

"That is correct, your highness," Cynkz replied.

"Well, you may need to be more specific," Lady Lilithen said. "As I'm sure you know, Potarium possesses countless women of import."

Sir Galtheal smiled once again, pushing himself back before barking his thoughts. "Yes, though he can start by crossing you off the list of potential suspects!"

Everyone seated, save for the poor woman at the center of the jesting, gave a round of unchecked laughter. Harquin seemed unaffected, though Kadd needed to turn his head to hide his own giggling. Cynkz lifted a swift hand to politely cover his own grin.

"I must say, Sir Galtheal, if your judgment of women were reliable, you wouldn't be on your sixteenth marriage," Lady Lilithen said through the subtlest of sneers.

Lord Peltony felt the need to lower his head, hiding most of his face beneath the brim of his hat. Cynkz wondered if he should try on a larger hat himself, but then noticed the man's shaking shoulders clearly giving away his reaction. There was only so much one could do to hide their emotions, it seemed.

"Perhaps, but it is a bit strange coming from the woman who decided to be my eleventh," Galtheal barked out. "Did you believe that to be your lucky number?"

Cynkz couldn't help but look to Peltony, who was leaning forward, desperately trying to hide his reaction. Lady Krine had no such filter, going so far as to clap and kick her legs as she laughed. She was so short that her feet didn't touch the ground as she swung them back and forth. While Galtheal seemed to have to charm his way into affording his stridence, one got the impression that Lady Krine's tiny stature did most of the work for her, allowing her social flexibility.

"All right, all right, that's enough, you children," Cerhnbal said. "Let us focus on something more important."

A few deep breaths and pats of the chest, and everyone resumed a more presentable air.

Cerhnbal continued. "Cynkz, I must say, you have brought about a most interesting scenario. As you'll eventually learn, the afterlife can get quite droll. This leaves much room for all sorts of wild stories and rumors to ferment. If what has been said about you is correct, then perhaps you can aid us in dealing with a little issue we have been struggling with for some time."

"Ugh!" Harquin gave his first strong response. He was so disciplined and restrained, yet once again this particular subject was all it took to break his otherwise unbreakable persona. There had to have been more to the issue than just mere rumors competing with his shows. *But what could it be?* Cynkz thought.

"Is something the matter, Harquin?" Cerhnbal said, maintaining his authoritative tone.

"I find such persistent rumors to be a constant pain, my lord," Harquin said.

"Either way, Cynkz is the perfect man to investigate the matter!" Kadd said, his own filter seemingly giving way to his excitement.

"I do not think it to be productive in any way to have the newcomer, of all po, troubled with chasing supposed ghosts and shadows in the night—"

"Cynkz!"

A great, booming voice rattled the walls and windows of the dome, shaking everyone to their core. Everyone's eyes shot wide as they looked around.

Immediately, Cynkz noticed that the nobility had each settled their gaze on a single point behind him. Kadd and Harquin seemed to catch on first as they whipped around to see the source of the interruption. Cynkz followed suit and couldn't believe his eyes— It was him! The very same king that Cynkz saw in his visions!

The same regal figure he witnessed leaning against that palace balcony so long ago now stood before everyone. His clothing was more elaborate than before, not just the usual combination of cream-colored fur and shining crimson stripes. A bright pair of piercing blue eyes poked through the sharp frame of jet black hair that formed his short curled hair and respectable beard. For a moment, Cynkz was without words, unsure of how to take the reunion.

"Sir Burlowesque!" Galtheal called out. "So glad you could finally make it, my friend."

Burlowesque, Cynkz thought. *So that was his name, and hers… Orilay Burlowesque…*

The late arrival kept his eyes fixated on Cynkz. It was so intense and unflinching that it burned away whatever confidence Cynkz had maintained. Before he could respond, or consider the situation further, he began walking straight for Cynkz. What would have been a heavy silence was interrupted by the sharp strikes of Burlowesque's shoes hitting the marbled floor. With each step forward, his expression became more clear. Whatever fire and rage he was bringing with him, it was all focused on Cynkz.

Cynkz's mind drew a blank, and he was forced to merely stand and wait for whatever came his way. And then—

Crack!

A swift fist came across the jester's face. It was louder than Burlowesque's call, and the echo threatened to shatter the otherwise shining, pristine windowpanes lining the curved walls. It was difficult for Cynkz to tell if the resonating sound was causing the panes to shake, and with them the light reflecting inside, or if he were merely reeling from the shock of sitting on the ground. The familiar sound of Kadd's sandals and robes shuffling accompanied his efforts to help Cynkz sit up and gather his bearings.

"W-what is this?!" Cerhnbal called out.

"How did he..." Lady Lilithen mumbled.

"Burlowesque!" Galtheal nearly jumped out of his seat, his wide feet stamping against the topmost step leading to his throne. "Explain yourself! We were having a wonderful time before your—"

"Shut it, Galtheal." Burlowesque barked, keeping his gaze on Cynkz. "This man, this—this—traitor!" His teeth grit, and his palms clenched, both with enough force to cause the man to shake. "Allow me to tell you about our newest guest and how he ruined my beloved daughter's life!

I remember it as if it were moments ago. This snake of a man snuck into *my* kingdom, still in the midst of a multigenerational war. He came as a lowly jester from Hirlwe, but quickly worked his way up the ranks, charming everyone from peasants to courtiers, and managed to impress my closest advisors with ideas of how to handle the war—*My* war. I noticed my own daughter, my precious, naive Orilay, falling for his ruse. I supposed I too was fooled by a fool, because I allowed him within the ranks of my advisors. Yet that was not enough! He knew Orilay was meant to marry Duke Fraderiche! Instead of accepting his place, he took it upon himself to hire an assassin! And worse still, he outed his own assassin, just as he was making the kill, to make himself appear the hero!"

"T-that is… Burlowesque, that is quite the accusation!" Cerhnbal said. "We have seen nothing of Cynkz here that would—"

"Silence!" Burlowesque cried out. "I have known this man longer than any of you! I witnessed his treachery firsthand! Do you know what happens when you backstab a backstabber? You can only go out one way—a knife in your own back!"

Kadd interjected, "There is no conceivable way that Cynkz of all people would do something such as—"

Burlowesque stamped his foot, as if trying to purposely shatter the glass lining the room with a violent echo. Once the room returned to silence, his gaze found Cynkz with such fury that he seemed hardly capable of maintaining himself. He took several deep breaths, then continued.

"Do you want to know the worst part of it, Cynkz? It was not the shattered political relations, nor the embarrassing death of Duke Fraderiche, or even word of your treachery spreading. No… No, do you want to know the worst part of it all?"

Cynkz could not answer the man. His eyes tightened, his mind raced, and there was the tense pulling of skin twisting itself above his brow, but inside? Nothing. There was nothing he could do but watch and wait along with everyone else.

"My dearest daughter, whom you so selfishly loved, Orilay…" Burlowesque's lips tightened, and he broke his gaze for only a moment to recollect himself. "She couldn't take it. She fell into a deep depression, and ran away, never to be seen again. I ran myself and my forces raged for *years* trying to find her, but to no avail. After I died and came here, I hoped that Paithos may have been kind enough to show Orilay the path forward, so she could at least find peace here in heaven. And yet…"

No… Cynkz thought. *That means she is—*

"She is more than likely still suffering in Munderworld! As you soak up heaven's light she is more than likely trapped in some dark pit in the abyss! All because of your selfishness!"

Cynkz's visions rushed in to fill the void in his mind… Orilay, the poem, the king and the duke observing from on high. His lapses in memory were beginning to come together in the worst way imaginable. He had long since wondered what kind of person he had been before the end, and long did he grasp helplessly in the dark of his mind to try and piece something together. After eons of having nothing, he was finally granted what may as well have been shattered glass forced into his own hands, the blood from which could not be distinguished from the blood of the souls he betrayed, and the lives he ruined. He couldn't look into Burlowesque's eyes, though he could still feel the man's fiery gaze bearing down on him as Cynkz looked to the ground.

"I suppose it was foolish of me to think anything more of a mere jester and a snake," Burlowesque said.

Cynkz kept his eyes downward, but he could feel Kadd's grip loosening as he, for the first time, stepped away hesitantly. He could only imagine what must have been going through Kadd's mind. All that time waiting, hoping to help and guide someone he thought highly of, now reduced to something worse than a criminal or scoundrel or even a bandit.

"You have some gall," Burlowesque continued. "Thinking it appropriate to show yourself on my doorstep, or in Potarium at all. But we can fix that—Guards!"

A row of quickly shifting steel colliding with itself rang out. The sound-enhancing qualities of the domed room seemed to drown beneath the weight of Cynkz's thoughts.

"Take him away," Burlowesque shouted. "Drag him out to the farthest bunker we have in the desert! He can rot there for a millenia or two while I decide what to do with him."

Kadd cried out, "N-no! Wait!"

"Do you wish to join him, Father?"

Kadd merely looked at the man and decided to quiet down. He gave a final worried glare to Cynkz before hanging his own head.

The guards rushed to the center of the room. They formed a neat, circular wall around Cynkz, and forced him to stand. It took two of them to lift Cynkz to his feet, and it took another pair of hands from behind to push him out of the court. He could tell that the guards were not used to serious confrontation, which only made him feel worse. These people had grown so accustomed to long-lasting peace, and in an instant, he had ruined it. Perhaps it was indeed best for Cynkz to be taken far away, where he would not cause any more trouble.

As he was escorted out, dreading the long walk down the tower's countless stairs, he remembered the cryptic words of the first maiden of Elm he spoke with in Munderworld, "Remember that the po in Munderworld were put here for a reason as were you."

As was I... I suppose I did get the answer I wanted, Cynkz thought. *I finally found out why I deserve to rot in the abyss.*

He could hear a few final words being shared as he exited the court.

"I don't know whether I should curse you for reminding me of these traumas or thank you for allowing me some form of justice, Harquin," Burlowesque said.

"You highness," Harquin said. "I truly had no idea."

"It doesn't matter, Harquin. Just... Thank you, I suppose."

Once again, Cynkz found himself returning to darkness as the great heavy doors behind him closed, shutting out heaven's radiance.

CHAPTER 15

EVERYTHING THAT CAME NEXT WAS rendered to a slow, dragging blur in Cynkz's mind. He could vaguely remember the sensation of being continuously pushed from all sides as he was forced forward. He could remember the cold steel chains being clamped around his wrists. He could remember the mumbles and murmurs of the guards and eventually other po witnessing the endeavor. He could remember his long walk through the city, and the once bright, open and inviting streets that now appeared less comforting than the wasteland beyond Potarium. He could remember day slowly turning into night as they made their way across countless sandy hills and bleached rolling dunes.

He could remember the oddly smooth patch of sand in the middle of the desert revealing the roof of the bunker. Numerous pipes thrust up from its roof, and it had to be forcefully opened by several of the guards. He could remember not being able to see very far down into its depths. He could remember being forced down the many steps that led to a long dingy hallway that stood as a stark contrast to the rest of Potarium's furnishings. He could remember being led past countless empty cells. It made sense that there would not be too many ne'er-do-wells, and in fact he was glad to be granted some time alone. He didn't deserve company anyway, as far as he was concerned.

Everything was being forced to the back of his mind as he continued to think about the poem, about Orilay, about his visions, and his time in Munderworld. He wondered about the false hopes that the po had built up surrounding him throughout his venture, and he wondered about the kind of person he was back on Peara. Beneath the ballroom smiles and dances and whatever else he could recall, he knew now he was worse than a troublemaker, a derelict, a bum, or even a scoundrel. Worse than a snake, he was a betrayer and a murderer.

His accommodations were as paltry as one would expect. There was merely a hole in the ground, presumably for taking care of one's business, and a hole in the ceiling that allowed a small portion of night light to peer into the cell. Cynkz was so lost in thought, he hadn't even noticed the guards had already removed his cuffs and made their leave. He was alone once again, beneath the stars, and for the first time, he could not enjoy it.

As he slunk into a dark corner of the dimly lit cell, he noticed the cold, smooth texture of the floor. It reminded him of how Orilay's hand felt as it brushed across his cheek in his first vision. He tried to push thoughts of the once beloved poem out of his mind, but he couldn't help but think it over one last time:

Every star
Near and far
Waits for us
To just
Reach out
And accept them…

He wondered what it all meant, especially considering what he knew. He looked down at his pointed fingers and wondered what he could possibly be reaching toward. Rather than stretching out a kind hand, perhaps reaching—for him at least—was merely a chance to expose his fangs to turn something beautiful to his own selfish needs, the way a snake would its prey.

He thought about escaping, maybe sneaking around and taking his task upon himself. Yet Potarium was a massive city, and he would no doubt have the entire populace working against him. He even wondered if Kadd would want anything to do with him. He didn't know what else to do, and for the time being, decided to take the time to stew in anguish. It was the least he deserved, as far as he knew.

The morning came quickly. Cynkz hadn't moved a muscle since he sat down. If not for the changing color of the singular spotlight afforded by the hole in the ceiling, he would not have known that any time had passed. Everything remained completely silent. The tranquility was interrupted by the rustling of dusty cloth in a cell diagonal to Cynkz's. From beneath the coverings a disheveled, messy po arose. He gave the most strained, drawn-out yawn Cynkz had ever heard, and eventually a pair of eyes stared at him. They seemed caught between an amber and green mixture, an unusual trait as far as Cynkz could tell.

"Hey, hey!" the man said, his voice caught between a husky groan and a barely restrained whisper. "When did I get a new roommate?"

Cynkz remained unresponsive. He could barely muster the energy to look at the man and slowly returned his gaze to the sunlight spot on the ground.

"Well, you must have really messed up to be dragged all the way out here," the prisoner said through yet another prolonged stretch. "Since we're gonna be roomies, we may as we get to know each other, eh?"

Still, Cynkz kept his head hung low. The one thing he had to look forward to—time alone to think things over—was being taken away from him. They say it's the little things in life that make all the difference, Cynkz was learning that such a saying possessed both positive and negative interpretations.

"The 'strong, silent type,' huh? There's no use bein' 'cool' down here, mate." The man began to pace back and forth along the bars of his cell, still stretching and rubbing his shoulders. "I tell ya', nothin' humbles a man like havin' to relieve 'imself in a hole in front of someone else, yeah?"

Cynkz looked up, slowly, listlessly, and noticed the man scratching both his stomach and the side of his messy, dark curly hair. Numerous flakes and bits of sand flew out from the mass.

"Ah, but where are my manners?" the man continued. "My name's Tucorio! Tucorio Willin! But you can jus' call me Tuco."

Never before had Cynkz felt the slow sensation of frustration building from a mere conversation. Such small talks were usually a joy to him. Perhaps it was another beautiful thing he could no longer appreciate.

"Well," Tuco continued, "at the very leas' ya don't have to worry about goin' hungry. The guards bring round a few bowls of sludge—er, I mean oatmeal, and if you're good, they'll even bring you a blanket! I doubt them fancy dressin's you got on do much against the cold desert nights, eh?"

Cynkz could feel his brow, as if with a mind of its own, pressing down into his eyes. He had to let out a light huff to keep himself from scoffing at the man.

"Listen, mate." Tuco stepped forward and placed two sandy hands against the cold, steel bars, "We're gonna be here for a while. The best thing you can do is get over whatever's got your loins in a bunch and—"

Bam!

A great shockwave rattled every loose bar and crevice in the bunker. Tuco reeled nearly a half-foot as he stared at the noticeable crack in the wall where Cynkz had struck it to release his pent up fury.

"Sheesh! Alright, alright," Tuco said under his breath. As he shuffled over to his blanket in the corner, he looked over his shoulder at Cynkz. "If you ain't gonna do much but sulk, the leas' you could do is leave a few bowls of gruel out for me, eh?"

Cynkz could see the man smirking from the corner of his eye but couldn't gather the energy to care. The man shook his head before retreating beneath his covers in a shaded corner. If nothing else, it was quiet once again.

Over and over, Cynkz watched the spot on the ground change color. It shifted from a near-white burning circle to a soft dim blue. Every time his thoughts acted up, they were bombarded with images of Orilay, of Burlowesque, and of what sorts of schemes and lies he relied on to make his way through life. It was easier to just shut it all out and relax in total silence, once again surrendering to another sort of darkness, one found in his own mind.

Tuco's daily routine didn't consist of much, understandably. He would get up in the morning, walk around and stretch. Sometimes he would lean on the bars of his cell to catch a glimpse of the new inmate, then briefly return to his own activities. He would pace back and forth, sometimes even mumble things to himself. The only time he grew excited was when the guards came carrying a bowl of plain, splotchy brown gruel for the both of them. The gruel was dropped in front of their cells, and the guards would wait for them to finish eating.

Tuco ravaged his bowl the way a starving beast might eat a steak. Mere seconds was all it took for him to haphazardly devour the stuff. Cynkz, however, never looked up. Each time this happened, the guards would leave his bowl by the door, and it didn't take long before a small pile began to clutter the front of his cell. After a time, Cynkz noticed Tuco would walk over to leer a glazed eye at the small mountain of stale sustenance. Eventually, he grew so bold as to twist his blanket into a fine rope and throw it out to try and snag one of the bowls. It was always too far for Tuco to manage anything.

Cynkz caught himself taking a small amount of joy from watching the man struggle. Though all it did was confirm to Cynkz that he must have been a real snake underneath it all. Never before, as far as he could remember, did he ever take joy in someone else's struggle. The levity of his initial delight was immediately crushed beneath the dread of how far he must have fallen. It was easier to cast out all thoughts and merely sit in silence.

What he couldn't ignore was the heavy clang of metal doors being dragged open and closed whenever the guards came by. They never said anything, perhaps finding it vexing to have to perform such a thankless task. One day they seemed to come ahead of schedule for their routine feedings, and a guard stopped in front of Cynkz's cell.

"You've got a visitor," the steel-clad man said.

A familiar, violet-robed po stepped into view, his thin arms tucked neatly beneath his large, billowing sleeves.

"Hello, Cynkz," Kadd said. "It's been a little while, hasn't it?"

Cynkz couldn't look his friend in the eye. He took the time to look down at the man's robe and at his feet bearing the usual thick golden-laced sandals Kadd always wore.

Kadd turned his head and looked at the guard. "Please, can you give us a moment alone?"

Once the heavy metal doors creaked open and closed once more, a heavy silence sat between the two. Cynkz kept his eyes on the ground, and Kadd could only look solemnly at his friend. Eventually, Kadd took in a breath and sat himself down on the ground in front of the bars between them.

"Cynkz," Kadd said. "How have you been—"

"Cynkz!" a small voice ruptured from beneath a fold in Kadd's robe. It was enough to get the jester's attention, and he watched as something crawled around beneath the shining silk garb, desperately seeking an exit.

"H-hold on," Kadd said. He had to reach beneath his robe to pull the critter out. It was a miniature toy, fashioned similarly to the many puppets that once occupied many of the stalls in Potarium's streets. It too possessed loose dangling limbs and a wide tawny head with a cartoonish face carved into it. It also possessed a single, bright red feather stuck in its crown, acting as a crude plumage that moved wildly as the diminutive marionette shook itself free.

"Cynkz! It's me, Fiddle!"

For a moment, Cynkz couldn't believe it. Yet as quickly as his eyes shot wide to observe his friend in a new form, his brow brought his eyes back to the ground. It should not be such a surprise that a mun as capable as Fiddle, with help from the Munder King, would be able to return in any form he saw fit.

"Cynkz! What happened?!" Fiddle said, his little limbs and joints clicking against his body as he raved. He almost fell out of the platform Kadd's hand provided him as he excitedly spoke.

"Fiddle…" Cynkz mumbled. "I… I found out why I was sent to Munderworld."

"Well yeah, you died! Just like everyone else!" Fiddle cried out.

"No, Fiddle. I mean, the *reason* behind my banishment to the abyss."

Fiddle threw himself from Kadd's hand and entered through an opening between the rusted bars.

"I mean, I get that there's a reason," Fiddle said, "but why are—"

Fiddle stopped and stared, taking in the surroundings. He noticed a number of deep scratches in the sand beneath Cynkz's hands and the crack in the wall to his side.

"Cynkz," Fiddle muttered. "What happened?"

"The poem… Orilay… The woman from my visions, and her husband-to-be and her father! I… I ruined everything." Cynkz's fist tightened where it rested in the sand. He could feel the many hard grains being pressed into his palm.

"Kadd mentioned something about them, but…" Fiddle looked at Kadd, then back to Cynkz. "It couldn't have been *that* bad."

"I had Orilay's fiancé murdered… and worse! I murdered his assassin to make myself look favorable and have Orilay all to myself. And then, when I inevitably ended up with a knife in my own back, Orilay… She ran away, never to be seen again."

"Well, she's gotta be here, right?" Fiddle said, "I mean, considering—"

"No, Fiddle…" Cynkz couldn't look the puppet in the eye.

"Oh… Oh no… So all this time she's been—" Fiddle reeled back, or at least his actions seemed to resemble someone reeling back in shock. He did it with enough control that his limbs and joints didn't make noise.

"I mean, all is not lost, right?" Fiddle continued, "We can get the Sisters of Elm to help find her! And her husband too! No matter how long it may take, we can help—"

"Of course, Fiddle, but…" Cynkz paused, his mind still weighed down by guilt. "It does not change what I did… I cannot seek forgiveness for such a heinous act."

Kadd's robes ruffled against the dirt as he leaned forward, an elbow on each knee and his hands together in his lap. "No one is perfect, Cynkz. We have all sinned. What matters is that we work toward bettering ourselves, that we—"

Cynkz looked up and interrupted, "There are some traumas, some scars, not even heaven can heal, Kadd. I learned that from Pairne. Even now, she has to go on for an eternity, forever carrying the regret of never being granted a full life or having the opportunity to bear children. Countless bright futures she may have paved the way for, all ripped away from her. Just how many others are there like her, all carrying scars from their past, unable to move on? And what kind of scars have my own heinous actions left? On Orilay? On

Burlowesque? On the duke, even? Who knows how many more. What children may the two have had, that will never exist, thanks to me? What sort of damage did I inflict on Burlowesque's remaining years alive, only for him to arrive in Potarium and realize the dreadful truth that while he spends his time in the comfort of heaven's light, his own beloved daughter is suffering in a dark pit?!"

It was a rare moment where Cynkz left the others stunned. Not even Fiddle knew what to say at that moment. The imp shared another worried look with Kadd, or the closest thing to a worried look that a caricatured puppet would allow.

"Cynkz, you said it yourself," Kadd said. "You lost your memories long ago. You may as well be a completely different person now. I know it's hard, but it does no good to blame yourself eternally for—"

"Blame?" Cynkz interrupted his friend, for the first time furrowing his brow at him. "Blame is too light a sentence. I feel nothing but complete and utter shame. How dare I think of myself as anything good? Who am I to force my way into heaven, barreling past countless other souls who suffer in the abyss below? This stupid adventure, and that stupid thread, all thanks to a stupid bit of whimsy—a prank on a celestial being—doing far more good for the po than I ever could."

Fiddle couldn't help but look at the ground. He was so used to doing the talking for his friend, and always having something sharp to aid the conversation, yet he had nothing. His best friend seemed more distant than ever, despite sitting mere feet away.

"Do… Do you still have the thread?" Fiddle asked, sheepishly rubbing the wooden knobs he held in place of hands.

"Yes," Cynkz muttered.

"That's good, at least," Fiddle mumbled.

"I mean, if it helps any," Kadd said, leaning back to cross his arms, "your 'stupid adventure' helped me and others find a way forward. Even Harla was saved! You got to meet the Sisters of Elm and whip them back into activity. You braved the deepest darkness and the infinite ocean in order to provide further aid to the sisters."

"I can take no credit for what the sisters do," Cynkz said.

"It's not about taking credit," Kadd said. "This isn't a contest, Cynkz! Regardless of what may have happened in the past, you have proven to be capable of moving ahead and doing good!"

"Yeah! And think about it," Fiddle said, clicking and clacking his way toward the jester. "If not for what we did, my siblings would still be lost to the far corners of Munderworld! Think of all the cute little imp hearts and souls you helped—"

A raspy voice rang out from the cell diagonal to Cynkz's. "All right, I can't stay quiet no more."

"What in munder—" Fiddle cried out.

"Ah, excuse me, gents. The name's Tucorio Willin! But you can just call me—"

"Nobody asked for your name, bozo!" Fiddle's limbs shook violently as he gestured toward the man. Kadd merely looked over his shoulder, just as surprised but remaining quiet for the time.

"An' what in Paithos are *you* supposed to be?!" Tuco cried out. "Are you a … mun? How are you possessing *anything* in Potarium? Maybe all that stale porridge 'as got me seein' things. Just what 'ave I missed during my time here…"

"None of your business, you bum!" Fiddle practically charged toward Tuco's cell in a fit. "Go back to your little corner and curl up! The adults are talking!"

"I can't believe I'm bein' scolded by a toy of all things. I may as well be talkin' to hats."

"What?" Fiddle uttered.

"Whaddya mean by 'adults'?" Tuco seemed barely able to restrain his laughter. "You soun' like a wee babe! I've 'eard baby calves with a deeper voice 'an you—"

"Shut up!"

Fiddle flew toward the man. Kadd nearly fell over as he tried to get up and rush over to the scuffle. The sounds of light wood banging against flesh could be heard amongst the noises of feet and hands dragging against the dirt. Fiddle worked his way to one of Tuco's dirtied hands and clamped his tiny mouth flap on the flesh as hard as he could.

"Argh! You little pest!" Tuco swiped the back of his other hand against the puppet, causing it to crash into the ground nearby.

Fiddle picked himself up and shook off the damage, though Tuco seemed quite puzzled.

"How is that possible?" Tuco mumbled. "I thought them fancy flags were supposed to protect everyone. I know we're far from the city, but we ain't *that* far."

"That's right!" Fiddle shouted. "There's nothin' protecting you from me! So watch it!"

Tuco, still rubbing his hand, looked at the puppet with an expression Cynkz couldn't decipher. It seemed to be stretched in all directions, caught between excitement, worry, and fear. He must have felt everything he understood of the world was being challenged.

"You know what, you don't mind me, I ain't seen anythin'." Tuco dusted himself off and retreated back to his corner, going so far as to wrap himself up in his cloth cocoon.

"That's right," Fiddle declared with a hollow stomp of his wooden foot. "And don't even think about tellin' anyone about—"

"Ah, shut it, you little ingrate. Ain't nobody believin' a word from me anyway. It's one o' the perks of bein' known for lyin'."

As the little marionette stamped its way back to Cynkz's cell, Kadd couldn't help but shrug and laugh. "Sheesh, things are always so interesting with you two around."

"So now what?" Fiddle asked. Again he overestimated his wooden form's capabilities by attempting to shrug. He did little more than shake his limbs and shoulders.

"I see no reason why we can't continue trying to find Yla," Kadd said. "I can try to speak with the Royal Court, maybe see about forgiving poor Cynkz, and we can continue looking for the lost sister."

Fiddle chimed in, "I suppose I could go back to the sisters and update them, and ask them to start searching for this Orilay and, erm, who else are we looking for?"

"His name is Duke Fraderiche, I believe," Kadd said. "I'll try asking his highness Burlowesque for more information."

"Sounds like a plan, but..." Fiddle turned and looked back at his friend. "What about you, Cynkz?"

"I think Cynkz should stay put for the time being," Kadd said. "We need to be very careful if we are to get back in the good graces of the court."

"Well, that's boring," Fiddle pouted.

"Perhaps," Kadd said as he rubbed his hands together in his lap. "But we must abide by Potarium's rules if we wish to get everyone to work together."

"I would very much like to get along," Cynkz said. "I never wanted to cause any trouble."

"I know, Cynkz. By all rights, you have the power to fly up and demand—Oops." Kadd caught himself, and peeked over his shoulder toward Tuco, who was still curled in a ball beneath his trusted blanket.

"It is fine, Kadd," Cynkz said with a soft gesture of his hand. "Word of all I have done and can do will come out eventually. I would very much like to be more honest and forthright from here on out."

"Well, if you say so, but who knows how the po will take such knowledge?"

"We'll have to see it through when the time comes."

Kadd smiled warmly, and Cynkz responded in kind.

"Thank you," Cynkz said. "Both of you."

The puppet reeled himself back, swinging a loose arm around to accentuate his response. "Ahhhh fuggedaboutit!"

Cynkz merely stared, his eyes pressed into a hard squint and his brow pushing down into his eyes. "What?"

"You'll have to excuse him," Kadd said. "Fiddle here has been hiding with me for a little bit, and he's been picking up on some of the 'lingo' the younger po like to sling around."

"That is an incorporeal, indubitable, intimation!" Fiddle cried out.

"Alright, shush," Kadd huffed. "You can't throw out interesting words you hear and expect anyone to get it."

"But it's fun."

"For you, maybe. I'm the one who always gets a headache trying to figure out what you mean and when you mean it."

Cynkz smiled for the first time in what felt like ages. After keeping his face placid and still for so long, it almost pained him to express such things. Fortunately, Kadd took notice and smiled as well, and even Fiddle managed a little chuckle of his own.

Kadd took a deep breath and pressed to his feet. He spent a good minute dusting off all of the dirt and dust that covered the lower half of his once pristine, silky robes.

"Well, then, let's get a move on, Fiddle," Kadd said. "We have work to do."

"For certainly," Fiddle said, taking the opportunity to climb up Kadd's leg and burrow beneath the first flap of cloth he could find.

Kadd turned but looked one last time down at Cynkz. "I promise we'll be back as soon as we can with news, alright, Cynkz?"

"Mrrf-mrrf."

"Fiddle, he can't—Ugh. Fiddle says goodbye."

Cynkz merely nodded and waved and watched them disappear before the unveiled light of the desert as the heavy metal doors opened and closed.

For a moment, tranquility returned, but was interrupted by the sound of Tuco pulling down his covers to peek around. He looked at Cynkz, quickly got himself up to press against the bars, and speak.

"I don't know what to make of half-a-that," Tuco said. "You know, you're awfully mopey for someone with friends still lookin' out fer 'em."

Cynkz let out a strained sigh and returned his attention to the ground.

Tuco continued. "Well, if all yer gonna do is sleep, think you could pass me a bowl or two of that uneaten gruel?"

Cynkz remained unresponsive. Tuco, realizing the futility, let out a loud huff and retreated to his covers. Once he settled in, he could hear what sounded like a puff of smoke blowing dirt and sand around outside his cell. Quickly, he shot himself up and looked over, only to see a small pile of messy bowls pressed up against the bars of his cell. Cynkz appeared to be in the exact same position that he last saw him.

"What? How did…" Tuco stopped himself and smiled. "Ya know, you're a strange one, but I gotta thank ya!"

The sounds of a hungry po chowing down, while not particularly glamorous, did much to lighten the load on Cynkz's mind. It was not enough to atone for his previous sins, but it was a start.

CHAPTER 16

THE COMING DAYS AND NIGHTS CAME quicker than expected. Breaking up the monotony with the occasional exchange with his 'roommate' did much to help pass the time. Unfortunately, Tuco was not very forthcoming, and Cynkz, with his own fractured memories, didn't allow much room for meaningful conversation. Still, he was able to pick up on a few things.

For one, Tuco had no shame—or he had learned to shed the burdensome weight that shame bore on a person. He had no trouble relieving himself in the hole in his cell. He also seemed to care little about the mess his meals left. Yet, despite his aloof, carefree nature, whenever a proper authority came around such as one of the guards tasked with delivering their meals, he would acquiesce to them completely. It seemed that much of his personality was an act. Cynkz often wondered what sorts of traumas led the man to become who he was but felt it indelicate to dig any deeper.

There was one trait Cynkz admired about him. He managed conversation with the same sort of 'mindless ease' that Fiddle often did. While Cynkz always held himself back, adopting a 'wait-and-see' approach, Fiddle and Tuco had no issue throwing themselves into the center of attention. Even if it was an act, there was something commendable about being able to wear one's heart on their sleeve. Though sleeves alone left Cynkz feeling a tad bare and vulnerable. He needed a cloak and a hat to feel complete. Even worse was the thought of cutting his hair. It may as well have been a tail, an extra limb to provide counterbalance as he moved throughout the world.

Such silly thoughts made the day go by incredibly quickly. Once again, Cynkz found himself awake and alone, staring at the one spot of light the late hours afforded his cell. Tuco was snoring in the corner of his cell, and for once Cynkz's mind was unburdened with troubled thoughts. Perhaps he could let himself get some rest.

Clang!

The sharp twang of metal on metal forced his attention into the waking world. Immediately, Cynkz's eyes focused on the light blue circle of night at the center of his cell, and in its center, something shiny twinkled. He stared for a moment, unsure of what to make of it. A glance showed Tuco was still fast asleep—he had mentioned that he was a notoriously heavy sleeper. Considering it was the first bit of real, new stimulation in a long time, Cynkz felt compelled to action.

He pushed himself up, brushed himself off as best as he could, and walked over to pick up the strange new object—

It was a key!

Before the implications could run their course through his mind, Cynkz could feel the odd, unexplainable sensation that someone was watching him. He looked up and met eyes with a hooded figure staring down at him. The stranger's face was covered entirely in shade, and he couldn't make out any specific features, save for the fierce glint of night light bouncing off of the stranger's eyes.

"You are Cynkz, I presume?"

The voice was decidedly feminine. It caught Cynkz off guard, though in truth, he wasn't sure what he was expecting a hooded night watcher to sound like.

"That I am," Cynkz responded. "With whom do I have the pleasure of speaking?"

"Heh," they chuckled again with a soft and disarming feminine flair. "It's true, then, what I've heard about you. You really are too polite for your own good."

"Excuse me?"

"There you go again."

"If you would like, I could be more boorish, perhaps scream up through this pipe?"

"That won't be necessary. I merely come to you with an offer."

An offer? Cynkz thought. *How strange. Is this the source of the strange rumors? I suppose I should hear them out.*

"Go on," Cynkz said, the key glistening in his hand.

"What you have in your hand is a copy of a master key, right from the golden tower itself. It'll unlock any cell door."

"That is quite the gift, but… what do you want in return?"

"You have a choice. You can mosey back to Potarium as a wanted man, or—" the hooded figure waved a thin, oddly pale hand in front of themselves "—you could join us and be given a second chance at a proper afterlife."

Their tone, while delicate, was as stern as one would expect from an authority figure. Whoever they were, they spoke as if they commanded respect. Even more curious was their offer. Cynkz thought it was hardly an offer at all. They spoke with the confidence that they knew the answer long before asking the question. They must have done this before, perhaps countless times. Such experience must come with contingencies of a sort.

Cynkz wondered what kind of trouble they might stir up if he were to refuse and stay put. He also wondered what the consequences would be for merely running off with the key. Would anyone back in Potarium believe him? What of Tuco? He wasn't close to the man, but surely leaving him here to fend off whatever force must lay in wait was not adequate.

"And who would I be joining?" Cynkz asked. "It is the afterlife, after all. Why should I take the risk of going with you when I could wait out my sentence here?"

"Ha!" The figure's sharp cackle caught Cynkz off guard. "If they went to the trouble of locking you up out here, well... I hate to be the bearer of bad news, but Potarium fully intends to leave you to rot. Surely, there is another worthless bum who has been festering in their own filth for decades?"

Cynkz looked over at Tuco, still completely unaware of anything beyond his slumber. He was never able to get a direct answer from the man regarding his time locked in the cell. The sort of thorough, relaxed and contented air he gave off spoke of one who had grown accustomed to his situation for *too* long.

While he was lost in thought, the stranger's voice called to him once again.

"Heaven isn't as nice as you hoped, is it?"

Cynkz took a deep breath and met eyes with the figure. "Potarium has been quite nice, actually. It was my own doing, my own actions, that led to my imprisonment."

"That is quite the noble attitude," they said. "Still, the choice remains. Freedom? Or Potarium?"

Cynkz looked back at the shining rod of gray metal in his hand, a thousand thoughts swimming through his mind. *Kadd said to stay put while he talked things out with the court, but who knows how long that will take. Who knows if he will be successful in convincing anyone to work with us. After everything, would they be willing, or able, to help us find Yla? This might be a prime opportunity to get a good look at these supposed 'hooded sneaks.' And, of course, I still have my powers, kept secret, as a trump card in case anything goes wrong—*

There it was, the realization that he was in fact capable of scheming.

Cynkz couldn't help but look one final time at the lit spot in the ground as he contemplated what he was doing. For all of his talk about wanting to be more forthright, more honest, he found himself reverting to his schemes. Despite his lost memories, his nature must not have changed much since his time on Peara. It was a troubling thought, but he found the logic irrefutable. A decision needed to be made.

"Fine," Cynkz said. "I will join you."

"Splendid!" she exclaimed. "Well, what are you waiting for? You have the key. Come meet me outside."

"I have but a single request."

"Huh… You're not exactly in a position to be making requests of anyone, but sure, let's hear it."

"I would like to bring Tuco with us. I would feel awful leaving him to rot any longer."

"Tuco?" She turned, as if looking around, or perhaps sharing a brief word with someone else accompanying her. "I suppose we could always use an extra hand. If he's willing to work, then—"

"Well color me shocked!" Tuco sprang from his sheet, his off-white smile beaming through the dark corner of his cell. "And I thought I'd never get a chance out of 'ere! Let's go, Cynkz!"

Cynkz squinted and turned his head toward the man. "Were you awake this whole time?"

"It depends on what ya consider awake." Tuco stretched mightily, as he always did after waking up. "In truth, I can never fully sleep on this 'ere cell floor. You wouldn't believe the number o' ways I've tried bunchin' up that blanket to make things more comfortable."

"Whatever you decide, Cynkz, make it quick," she continued. "We have a long way to go, and we need to be out of sight before dawn."

The figure faded from view, and numerous footsteps could be heard trailing off toward the front of the bunker. Cynkz stepped over and unlocked his cell before making his way out. Tuco watched expectantly, a great smile plastered across his face. It wasn't until Cynkz stood directly in front of the man, wrestling with the key to unlock his cell, that he noticed how malodorous his presence was. It was no surprise, of course, but it forced a harsh curling of Cynkz's nostrils. He dared not breathe through his mouth for fear of what he may invite into his body.

The moment Cynkz pulled the bars open, Tuco let out a hearty chortle and barreled toward the exit. The sounds of Tuco desperately trying to pull apart the large heavy steel squares echoed throughout the bunker.

"H-hey, buddy," Tuco said. "Think you could use that key o' yours to open this?"

Cynkz could only shake his head as he made his way down the hall of cold bars. Once again, he calmly unlocked the door, only for Tuco to attempt to rush forward.

In the hall, it took a moment for his eyes to settle on the new light bathing him but saw Tuco standing sheepishly before a group of hooded po. There were five of them from Cynkz's count. Their dour hoods were nearly the same color as the sand itself. The contrast between their faces covered entirely in shade against their much brighter cloaks was striking, if nothing else.

A brief glance at Tuco revealed him capitulating in the same way he often did with the guards.

A smaller, more svelte figure approached from the side. Their face remained shrouded in the shade of their hood, but the same disarming voice came through.

"Hmm, you're a bit taller than I imagined," she said.

"Sorry to disappoint you," Cynkz retorted.

"Heh, I don't blame you for being guarded. I suppose we look quite sinister in our hoods."

She reached up, revealing her pale hands to pull back her hood. Her escorts followed suit, but Cynkz kept his eyes on their leader. She appeared to be an ordinary woman, but something caught Cynkz's attention. Beneath a bundle of darkened, smoky dreads and mature, bony features was a woman who seemed to be too young for such features. Her eyes showed a chilling blue color, though faded enough that they appeared silver in the moonlight. They broadcasted a steely gaze that denoted untold experience. Her pale skin also stood out and appeared to reflect an ever so slightly gray tint against the light. Finally, as if acting as the last, most important touch in a work of art, a shining strand of hair hung in front of her face, as if defying the rest of her restrained coiffure. Her gaze was sharp enough to cut glass, and Cynkz could feel her peering into him without resistance.

"If you two are ready, we need to go," she said. Her expressionless manner reminded him of Lady Lilithen. She was faring much better than he at fending off Tuco's offensive odor, apparently.

"Of course, but—" Cynkz said, nearly stumbling over his words.

"Hmm?" The woman stopped and looked over her shoulder, already several steps ahead.

"May I have your name, if you do not mind me asking?" Cynkz said. "You have been addressing me all this time, and yet I know not how I should address you."

"You can call me Ynette."

Cynkz couldn't help but stare for a moment too long. Most of the po in Potarium possessed names with some kind of flair to them, yet hers came across as quite short and pragmatic. Though Kadd also had a simple name, it felt more inviting, as if trying to be something more. You even needed to open your mouth wider than normal just to pronounce it. Ynette seemed like the sort of name that you could shoot out with a quick hiss.

"Is something wrong?" Ynette said.

Cynkz caught himself and quickly raised a hand to gesture an apology. "Ah, no, of course. You'll have to excuse me."

"That ring…" Ynette's eyes fixed on the crude twisting of metal wrapped around Cynkz's finger. "Where did you get that?"

"Hmm? Oh, this," Cynkz lifted his hand and cradled the ring between his thumb and forefinger, spinning it around. "A good friend gave it to me after assisting me in Munderworld. It is funny, really. I wear it all the time, yet I often forget that it is even there."

"I see." Ynette turned around and began marching forward. "Let's go. We have a bit of traveling to do before we get to our base."

The other hooded po quickly followed behind her. Tuco was strangely quiet, but went along all the same, as did Cynkz.

The night seemed to drag on for longer than usual. Perhaps it was the course of questions and theories running through his mind, but he seemed completely caught in the moment. He was neither scared nor excited. Only deep curiosity remained. A quick glance behind revealed the shining mountain city to be exceptionally far away. It was so distant, in fact, that it could hardly be seen poking through the horizon. Strangely, no matter how far away they moved, the great, marbled orb blending into the sky above was clearly visible. It was comforting to have a stable beacon to reorient oneself in the infinite expanse of the desert, no matter how otherworldly or nonsensical it may be. He turned back around to see the group silently marching on. As he tried to think of a good way to begin asking questions, Tuco took care of that small issue for him.

"'Ey, I 'ave a question, for you, Cynkz."

Cynkz looked over to the man. Before he could say anything, Tuco continued. "How in munder 'ave you stayed so pretty? You was locked up for a while. It's really weird."

Cynkz opened his mouth but struggled to think of a proper answer. Fortunately, Ynette looked over her shoulder and quickly interjected. "I'd suggest you quiet down, Tuco. We still have a fair walk ahead of us."

"Where are we goin', anyway?" Tuco blurted out.

"You'll see soon enough," Ynette responded.

"I mean, yeah, obviously, but it'd be nice to have a heads up on what we should expect."

"What's wrong? You're not afraid of surprises, are you? Considering how long you must have been locked away, I'd imagine you of all po would be excited."

"Well, in truth," Tuco took in a thoughtful breath, "I quite enjoyed the peace imprisonment afforded."

"Then why come with us?"

"I don't know, I guess I acted without thinking."

"I'm guessing that's a regular problem for you."

"Okay, okay, ya got me."

"It's fine. A structured schedule and a good day's work should be more than enough to help out with such tendencies."

"Yeah, work… About that…" Tuco paused, going so far as to stop his walking. Ynette also stopped to look at the man, and the rest of her group did the same. A quick moment of silence weighed heavy on the desert night air.

"When you say 'work,'" Tuco continued, "what exactly does all that entail? What kinda work are we talkin' about, 'ere?"

"Well," Ynette said with a heavy breath. "We do a lot of mining and transporting of materials underground. If you're any good with tools that would definitely—"

"Ah!" Tuco interrupted. "I, uh, think I left something back in the cell—"

Immediately, Tuco twisted himself around and tried to run. In the blink of an eye, Ynette flashed a great whip and entangled the man's ankles. She moved with the same sharp, barely restrained energy that Harquin showcased. Without a single word, the other larger po dove on top of Tuco and restrained him. Cynkz never thought he would see a po being hogtied, and certainly not in heaven of all places, yet here he was. Even now, Potarium was surprising him with strange new sights.

He didn't know whom he should pity more—the man being tied up, or the unfortunate po who had to endure his odor as they restrained him. When they were done, after the expected round of lashing and screaming, Cynkz noticed a strange substance on all of the ropes. It was a dark, murky red, almost like a liquid rust. It appeared dry and crusty, as if having been set to settle into the material for some time.

Once he was bound and gagged, the largest of the escorts hoisted Tuco over their shoulder. Ynette walked over to him, eyeing their catch before addressing her assistant.

"Thank you, Nidan," she said. "You don't mind carrying him for the rest of our trip?"

"Of course not, boss," he said. His manner of speech was short and sweet, much like his buzzed, dark brown hair and stout square head. He stood nearly a foot taller than Ynette, and nearly half a foot taller than Cynkz. His top-heavy build reminded him of the circus beast.

"Let's continue, then," Ynette said, as usual in the midst of stepping ahead, as if trying to make up for lost time.

Perhaps I should save my questions for later... Cynkz thought to himself.

CHAPTER 17

J UST AS THE EARLY MORNING LIGHT broke through the glistening horizon, Ynette moved ahead and stopped at an unassuming pile of sand at the bottom of a sandy hill. The angle of the light cast a deep shadow over the dune.

"We've arrived." Ynette knelt, brushed away some of the sand, and pulled on a small rope handle embedded in the ground. The slow creaking of metal accompanied the raising of a small platform that opened up the ground. One by one, the hooded po made their way down. Nidan waited for the others before going in himself. Cynkz could see Tuco's displeasure as he dangled over the man's broad shoulder. Ynette, still holding the way open, looked at Cynkz curiously.

"Is something wrong?" she said. "I know how it must look, but as you can see, we merely prefer to live unbothered by the stuffy suits in Potarium."

"Ah, it is not that," Cynkz said. "It is just that … I am not fond of small cramped spaces."

"Hmm, that's understandable. But trust me, it's only a few short steps and hallways, then a short elevator ride down, before we reach the much larger underground city. I promise it gets better."

Elevator? City? Cynkz thought. *Just how big is this place? And how many po could be hiding out of sight?*

Cynkz groaned—internally, of course, so as to not appear rude—and descended into darkness once more. He could hear the heavy steel being pulled shut not long after he entered. A bright light was soon raised ahead as the po in front held up a sophisticated-looking torch. It was a simple rod with a small metal bowl on its top–perfect for safely cradling what appeared to be a small fire that didn't flicker. As the group began to make their way down, it seemed to be the perfect time to inquire further.

"So, do you often recruit ne'er-do-wells?" Cynkz asked.

"Heh, no, not often, and certainly not these days," Ynette responded. "It is not often that a po misbehaves to the point of needing to be incarcerated. And considering that you are the first new soul to arrive in decades…" Ynette let out a tired sigh. "Those hags must have gotten lazy."

"You know them? The Sisters of Elm?" Cynkz asked.

"I know of them, yes."

"This ring was given to me by one of the sisters."

"I know. I would recognize their crude craftsmanship anywhere."

"Crude… Yes, I can see that. The many staves they used to mark the lands of Munderworld could definitely be described as such."

"They always struggled to advance. Absolutely no appreciation for refinement, I swear. They were always so short-sighted, too."

"Just how well do you know the sisters? Were you a maiden working for them, perchance?"

"Ha!" Once again, her sharp cackle caught Cynkz off guard. It was so jarring that he nearly lost his footing on one of the many dark steps.

"I'd never waste my time on such inefficient methods," she continued. "But enough about the sisters. Is there anything else you'd like to know before we arrive?"

"Other than criminals, why would anyone want to live away from the city? It's too lovely a place to merely leave behind."

"Well, po are po, and they don't always get along. Also," Ynette readjusted her shoulders, and let out a hearty breath, "there is something to be said about freedom. Potarium is quite rigid and stodgy, and certainly stuck in its ways. No doubt you've experienced some of the many circuses they use to keep themselves content, no?"

"I have."

"I heard of the little incident at the circus. Apparently, you nearly had your head bitten off, from what I gather."

"Well, surely the great huum would have protected me, but…" Cynkz paused, forcing himself to recount the incident. He had had many close calls before, but something about the presentation of that encounter, practically serving himself up on a platter for an audience, no less, made it all the more unsettling.

"Yes, the 'great huum,'" Ynette's tone flattened, as if speaking of something for which she held unbridled disdain. "For such a wondrous 'blessing,' it sure is awfully oppressive, isn't it?"

Oppressive... Cynkz thought. *That was precisely how Harquin described it. Knowing my luck, next she will describe our meeting as a 'confluence of fates,' or something similarly sentimental.*

"We're nearly there," Ynette said.

"Where?" Cynkz looked around but could see nothing beyond a great dark pit, seemingly unending, perhaps deep enough to reach Munderworld.

The frontmost assistant jumped into the pit. Cynkz recoiled in shock, but before he could say anything, the others joined him. Even Tuco let out a muffled cry as he was dragged into the darkness. For a moment, Cynkz was alone.

"Are you coming?" Ynette's sharp feminine voice pierced the darkness, as if she were right beside him.

"W-what? Where are—"

The woman's face poked through the dark. She could hardly keep herself from smirking.

"It's just an illusion," she said. "Just hop down and you'll see for yourself."

Again, before Cynkz could get in a word, Ynette disappeared beneath the blanket of darkness. He stared for a moment, having to go so far as to remind himself that he could still fly, and he jumped.

A moment later he found himself in an adequately lit room. It was quite wide and circular in its dimensions. Nothing stood out other than a few bright odd-looking stones embedded evenly across the dull painted walls. The floor came so quickly, and as such a surprise, Cynkz didn't need to pretend that he was actually falling in order to keep his abilities hidden. He was, in fact, falling and was caught off guard. Once he gathered himself, he could see the others walking ahead, save for Ynette who stood, still smiling at him.

"No doubt you've seen at least one medium being used?" she said, pointing leisurely toward one of the sharpened stones in the wall.

"I have," Cynkz said. "It was only used to show off some lights."

"Of course," Ynette shook her head. "There are plenty of neat things you can do, if you know how to channel the right huums through the right material."

"I suppose paranoia is a most potent fuel for creativity."

"Heh," Ynette's scoff was drenched with a sharp, bitter tone. "There's a fine line between paranoia and caution, Cynkz, and I am well aware of precisely where that line is."

"I meant no disrespect," Cynkz said. He looked about and at the stones in the walls in an attempt to lighten the conversation. "How does one figure out such things?"

"We have nothing but time, at the end of the day," Ynette turned and walked toward the rest of the group, who were waiting patiently. "There's plenty of room in the afterlife for performing all sorts of experiments. With enough time you can learn how anything works."

Cynkz had to pick up his step, as everyone else began to walk quite briskly through a pair of simple double-sided doors and into a short hallway.

"I remember Kadd mentioning that mediums could potentially possess many applications. I believe we even spoke of the possibility of long-distance communication and teleportation."

"Ha!"

Her sharp cackle got to him, though this time he was able to maintain himself fully. He wasn't sure if it was necessarily a good thing that he was so quickly adjusting to the woman's outbursts.

"In a way, you're not far off the mark. I wouldn't say you could 'teleport' anything through a medium, but communication and summoning is certainly feasible."

As they approached the end of the dim hall, Cynkz could see that the others had stopped in front of an odd-looking doorway—it appeared like a gate more than anything.

"We're finally at the elevator," Ynette said. "I swear, I've never gotten used to the long walk from here to Potarium and back."

"What is an 'elevator?'" Cynkz asked.

Ynette stopped and had to turn around to look at the jester with an oddly open expression. Whether it was shock, or amusement, or something else, Cynkz could not tell.

"I suppose I never considered what time period you were from," Ynette said. "I guess most po are used to merely being carried around on horseback and going up and down stairs."

"I know of carriages and boats, at least, if that helps any," Cynkz said.

"Some of what we have may be a shock to you then," Ynette continued. "An elevator is like a lift. With the pull of a switch, a few simple gears and mechanisms are activated, and a platform can be raised or lowered as needed."

"It sounds complicated."

"It's really not. Come and experience it for yourself."

Cynkz couldn't help but feel uneasy. He was already worming his way underground, moving through small cramped spaces, and now being led onto some new, advanced device he did not fully understand. If it was similar to a lift, then he would have to put in that much extra effort to make sure he didn't weigh it down.

The gate leading inside was lifted, and rows of light metal could be heard climbing past each other. Ynette moved forward, and the group huddled together in the small, square space of the platform. Cynkz entered and was able to find a nice spot in the rear of the group to reside. Being in the back always made it easier for him to float ever so slightly off the ground. The only one who could see him was Tuco, still gagged, and his eyes seemed to be darting around to focus on anything but the jester.

Ynette reached over and pulled on a conspicuous rod of brass jutting out from the wall. The elevator jostled. Cynkz could feel his center of gravity being knocked around as well, yet before he could brace himself, the gated door closed and the entire platform began to descend. It moved rather quickly, and Cynkz found himself on the tips of his toes before he pushed himself down to simulate a resting stance on the platform.

The constant whir of metal and stone passing by buzzed in his ear. The only thing that kept him calm was the occasional passing of bright stones that lit the interior, and everyone else's calm demeanor. Even Tuco seemed rather unphased, though perhaps still annoyed at his current predicament. The odd quiet in the small space made every passing moment feel longer than the last. Cynkz fidgeted with his hands a bit, trying to calm his mind. He wondered if he should ask if everything would be alright.

Before he could act on such a thought, however, the world opened up to them.

The rocky walls vanished as they descended, revealing that they were being lowered in what appeared like a gated tower. Cynkz looked out and could see a massive open space large enough to rival Potarium in sheer size.

It was an open underground settlement, not unlike the Sisters' abode, although much larger. There were numerous great pillars reaching from the ceiling to the floor and looked as if they were merely parts of the ground that had been left untouched, acting as crude support beams. Further down were countless rows of simple square buildings. Unlike the lavish architecture in Potarium, these structures were utilitarian in every way. Even their coloring seemed to be simple shades of rusty browns and dull grays, matching the surrounding rock that framed the entire space.

Many different lights poked through the many openings acting as rudimentary windows and doors.

The only thing elaborate about it all was the overall layout of the buildings. They were meticulously planned to form arches that seamlessly interlinked, with the many pathways between the structures creating nice shapes from above.

One detail that stood out was just how tall some of the buildings were. It seemed that in order to make the best use of the space given, many of the structures made use of height, unlike Potarium, where everything was kept quite short so as to not obstruct one's view down the mountainside or the great golden tower above it all. The residents even went so far as to make use of the empty space between buildings. There were simple sturdy bridges linking almost every building together.

From above, everything appeared like an artificial web. It was not so different from the impression Cynkz had of the Sisters' home as he looked down from on high, seeing the many maidens walking across the many bridges connecting the walls together. The only thing missing was the eerie, yet soothing green light emanating from below.

The closer they moved to the city below, the more Cynkz could make out a number of steel rails that stretched all throughout the city. Even more interesting, there were metal carts zipping along them! Most of them contained some combination of po sitting within them and piles of materials, what looked to be minerals and scrap of all sorts, being transported all around the city at wondrous speed.

Cynkz had a deep passion for the Hirlwen steeds, yet he wondered what use such creatures would be in the face of such technology. The sounds of their wheels turning mimicked the whir of the steel elevator passing down. Even from so far away it was quite loud, though not necessarily enough to mask Tuco's muffled excitement as he looked around. What would have been a peaceful trip was soon interrupted by an unexpected voice.

"Holy hells, what is this place?!" Tuco exclaimed, the cloth gagging him sitting halfway down his neck.

Nidan looked over his shoulder. "I coulda sworn we tied you up better than that."

"Hey! I think you guys did alright," Tuco said. "But the jaw is a wondrous thing, it's quite flexible ya know—*Oow!*"

"Shut. Up." Once again, Nidan was short and sweet. Ynette didn't have to look to see what the commotion was all about. She seemed to have complete trust in her assistant.

"Ugh, fine," Tuco muttered. "Guess I'll jus' stare at the ground... Hey, Cynkz—Man, are ya standin' on your tippy toes? *Oow!*"

"I ain't telling you again, bum. Shut it, or I'm throwing you out right here an' now."

Tuco, still bound at the hands, shrugged. "Lotta good that'll do. The great huum'll jus' soften the—"

"There are plenty of deep pits around here that seemingly go on forever," Ynette interrupted. "I'll even let you choose which one we'll drop you in, if you'd like?"

Tuco tried to look over, but merely sighed and relaxed over Nidan's shoulder.

"Good," Ynette said.

Finally, their descent slowed. Despite slowing down, Cynkz could feel his own sense of gravity messing with him. He was used to flying about of his own free will, but something about the lift made the sensation feel artificial, and oddly disconnected. Even outside of Potarium, he yearned for the freedom to go about as naturally as he pleased. Even in exile, he had to hold himself back.

The lift stopped, and the metal grates shifted out of view. The group began to file out of the device. There were a few other po that were waiting for them. Ynette stepped ahead and began barking out orders.

"Nidan, if you don't mind, take my coat, and take our smelly guest here to one of the cells down below. I'll stop by later and have a chat with him."

"So, ah, will I at leas' get some real food?" Tuco asked, sheepishly as ever.

"Food? Maybe. Eventually," Ynette said. "I believe another month of solitary confinement would do much to help you with your attitude problem."

"What?!" Tuco screamed, "Tha's unfair! You're an absolutely cold bi—*Oow!*"

Nidan shifted his shoulder, harder than usual, enough to nearly knock the wind out of Tuco. Without a word, he carried the man off and down some steps leading to who knows where below.

"Also," Ynette continued, completely ignoring the screaming man trailing off into the distance, "one of you should inform Harquin that I have returned. Tell him to meet me in my office as soon as he is able. I want to begin making preparations for a night run tomorrow."

"Harquin?!" Cynkz blurted out. A few of the others looked at him surprised. Ynette, as usual, did not seem phased by the outburst.

"Yes, I work closely with Harquin," Ynette said. "He manages his time like no other. He's been quite helpful—"

"I do not know whether I should thank him or curse him, considering all that has happened," Cynkz said.

"You would have been imprisoned eventually. Imagine how awkward it would have been if you met the spiteful king out in the street? At least you had a bit of privacy when everything went down, no?"

"I… I suppose."

"He truly did not know about Burlowesque, or his past traumas," Ynette continued. "Harquin is a very careful man. If he had known, he probably would have gone about things differently, or might not have allowed the meeting to occur."

The sound of the king's name caused Cynkz to stare wide-eyed but only for a moment. He looked away and let out a heavy breath. It did no use to hold a grudge for someone who more than likely did not deserve it.

"So, what now?" Cynkz asked.

"Come with me. We can talk more about things in private."

Cynkz's curiosity was piqued, then instantly dashed with dread. He could recall Fiddle bringing up a funny detail about Cynkz's trouble with women. Try as he might, Cynkz could not get a good read of the strange woman. She seemed to know quite a lot, perhaps more than any normal po should. He remembered her reaction to his asking if she were a maiden, but what other explanation could there be for her? Then again, if Kadd's story was to be believed, maidens apparently lost much of themselves upon arriving in Potarium, so perhaps she was telling the truth. And her name—Ynette? She never said the name with any real assertiveness, as if unsure of its meaning. Could she be Yla? Perhaps she knew Yla? Regardless, how did she arrive in Potarium, and how and why did she manage an entire city of supposed exiles?

Questions upon questions upon questions, Cynkz thought.

When Cynkz finally rested his mind, he noticed that Ynette was already several steps ahead, walking along a railed balcony. He hurried forward and matched his step with hers.

"You're not going to starve the poor fool Tuco, are you?" Why this was his first question or concern, not even Cynkz knew. Perhaps he was merely looking for an easy way to start talking again.

Ynette looked through the side of her eye, then quickly returned her focus forward. "Of course not, but we are not inexperienced with unruly sorts such as him. In time, he will be grateful and ready to help. A po who has been starved of both body and future will learn to love the opportunity this place has to offer him. You're awfully empathetic. I doubt a smelly scoundrel such as Tuco would express much care for you if your situations were reversed."

"Perhaps, but—" Cynkz stopped and turned his eyes toward the ground, the tip of his pointed hat providing an adequate shield for him to look around. "Everyone has their traumas and issues. I believe the only thing separating a flawed po and a better one is merely time to grow."

Ynette stopped to turn and look at him, knowing precisely where to rest her eyes in order to meet his own when he inevitably looked up.

"That sounds nice—almost platitudinous—but do you truly believe that? Does the thought apply to you as well? What heinous act were you imprisoned for, again? Are you merely extending sympathy thoughtlessly in order to appear kind?"

Cynkz stared puzzlingly at the woman. More and more he struggled to understand her. Despite her attempt at making herself, and everything she did, as pragmatic and efficient as possible, the way she spoke to him reminded him of Potarium.

Nothing could be simple, and everything she revealed seemed to add more murky layers over her possible intentions. It always struck him when he found himself speechless. Ynette seemed to catch on, recognizing that he couldn't think of a response, and smiled before continuing on their path. Cynkz could see the corner of her lips curling up into a noticeable smirk. Despite her sharp, boney features, there was more than enough to accentuate her expressions.

"Well, if nothing else, you appear to be a good person," she continued, "and I'm sure you'll be a good partner to us."

"Partner?"

"Yes, I've heard you're quite capable. Wild rumors about battling muns and traversing the abyss. Even acting as a savior of po."

"Silly rumors seem to spread far too quickly in Potarium," Cynkz scoffed.

"And so humble, as well! You're much easier to talk to than most, Cynkz. I think you will be the perfect aid for helping me with something extremely important, but we can talk about that later."

More murky layers, more cryptic speech... Cynkz couldn't help but feel a tad on edge. If not for his powers, he would think he was in a dire situation. Still, curiosity reigned supreme in his mind, and spurred him forward, so much so that he refused to let simple silence waste an opportunity that could be used to ask a burning question.

"What is this place called, anyway?" Cynkz asked.

"Heh, well, I never cared to give it a fancy name or anything. Such a flourish is useless if you ask me."

"I suppose I will merely refer to this place as the Underground, then."

"That will work, Cynkz."

CHAPTER 18

LITTLE OF NOTE OCCURRED FOR MUCH of the remainder of their walk through the winding streets of the underground city. It was interesting to look around and compare things to Potarium. Where every corner and edge needed an extra bit of flair in the shining city above, below everything seemed stubbornly simple.

Every wall was simple, every window was practical. Many of the buildings were much taller as well, lining the streets and alleys with great walls of brick and stone. Despite the sheer scale of the cavern, with the ceiling almost disappearing into darkness due to its sheer height, Cynkz felt cramped. It was odd, then, that he sort of appreciated the perpetually dark cozy space above. The Underground was a nice change of pace from the constant bright light of Potarium. In a way, it reminded him of the endless dark nights of Dulrot.

Another detail that, while noticeable from above, only became truly apparent as they weaved their way through the many simple stone paths. Everything was layered. Buildings upon buildings, ledges upon ledges, stairs upon stairs and bridges overlapping bridges to connect everything together. There were countless po in simple garb—plain shirts and dusty trousers, of course completely lacking the golden threads that accentuated everything in the city above. Everyone was dressed purely for function, as if always ready for a hard day's work. It reminded Cynkz that he still wore the shining, elaborate outfit the perfumers had given him in the golden tower. Even down here he felt out of place. As usual, it was impossible for him to fit in entirely.

Something rumbling in the distance caught Cynkz's ear. He looked up and out as far as he could into the distance, only for his sight to be met with the dark rocky interior of the vast underground. Ynette took note and stopped, waiting for the distant echoes to simmer away into silence.

"Don't mind the noise," she said. "That is merely a few miners doing their work on the edges of our city."

"Doing what, exactly?" Cynkz asked.

"Using explosives to break away the tough bedrock."

"Explosives?"

"Yes. Surely, they at least had explosives in your time?"

"Yes, but… Well, I am not sure what I was expecting, in truth. Though if Potarium can have fire, then explosives should not be too surprising."

"Explosives are just another tool. In fact, I'll give you a minor demonstration."

"Demonstration?! Is that safe?"

"Of course, it is. The great huum protects all, remember?"

"Ah, yes, true…"

"You really are new here. Though it's been a long time since we've had someone new come along. I've forgotten that it often takes a while before new souls adjust to it all."

They were making their way toward the edge of the underground settlement. The many po shuffling back and forth as they conducted their business faded away in the distance. Still, there were more structures ahead, though their purpose, or what they housed, remained a mystery to Cynkz.

More rumbles and the violent cracking of rock could be heard bouncing off the far walls. In the distant dark, he swore he could see portions of the bedrock collapsing. He was so focused on trying to pick out any details of the excavation that he hardly noticed Ynette walking right up to what appeared to be a large trolley.

"We're almost there," Ynette said. "We can take this the rest of the way."

"How does this device work?" Cynkz raised a light finger to his chin and leaned over a bit to squint at the mechanism.

"Come inside and I'll show you. It's quite interesting, actually."

Ynette disappeared through an opening in the vehicle's side. Cynkz stared at the dull steel rim acting as the door's frame. Much like everything else in the underground, it was very utilitarian and simple in its design. It was nearly as tall as a short building. It had wheels like a carriage—large, steel circles embedded in the metal railings—but no seats of any kind. With no furnishings, Cynkz got the impression these devices were meant for practical and efficient work, much like everything else underground.

Cynkz noticed the potentially precarious balance of the trolley as it sat on the railing. It was good that he saw this, as it reminded him to adjust his weight accordingly so as to not obstruct the vehicle's operation, whatever it may be.

Once inside, he saw Ynette waiting for him by a series of levers and other arcane studs and buttons. He took his place behind her and waited as she began to work the mechanism into action. A few clinks of brass rods being pulled, and after countless presses of the many buttons, Cynkz was already lost. Just as his eyes began to glaze over, Ynette reached up to open a container hanging above the controls. She clicked open its bottom rim, and several tiny capsules fell out. They were the same dried, rustic color as whatever was coating the ropes they used to subdue Tuco. It seemed as good a time as any to finally ask about the substance.

"What is that, exactly?" Cynkz asked.

"This is dried beast blood," Ynette responded as she rolled the pellets through her thin fingers. "When mixed with a little sand from the desert, it has a number of unusual effects on other compounds. In fact, the explosions you can hear in the distance are coming from a special mixture of these pellets and tinsel soil."

"Ah! The golden grass," Cynkz exclaimed. "I remember Kadd saying the substance could have a number of uses. I even remember seeing barrels filled with the compound one night when I, uh, when I was out exploring, you could say."

"Making trouble in the night, huh? How cute."

Ynette reached over and flipped open another capsule, this time one embedded in the panel of buttons and levers. She quickly dropped each pellet in, one at a time and closed the lid. Rumbling from below began to shake the entire vehicle. Not a moment later, the trolley was propelled forward. The sound of the wheels grinding against the metal rail created a whirring buzz not too dissimilar to the elevator.

Ynette kept her hand on a lever that acted as a throttle. As she slowly pushed the throttle forward, the trolley increased its speed. There was something calming about seeing the many buildings and pathways beside them whizzing by. The sound of the wind brushing past drowned out the grinding wheels. It made Cynkz miss his days carelessly flying about.

"This specific combination of the compound is particularly potent," Ynette exclaimed. She had to nearly yell for Cynkz to hear her. "With just a few pellets inserted into the ignition, they compress and mix with a fluid inside the engine, and the combustion mechanism forces a number of pistons that—"

"I, uh, I have no idea what any of that means." Cynkz found himself stuck between having to nearly scream to be heard and feeling almost ashamed at his ignorance."

"Ah, my mistake. I helped to invent these things, so I often forget that most won't catch on to how it all works."

"I always wanted to do more reading, and learn more, but quite a few incidents got in the way of it."

"It's admirable, at least, that you wish to learn. Most po are entirely content to waste the afterlife away on games and drink. I'm sure you've seen plenty of that in Potarium."

The farther out they traveled, the sparser the buildings became. Similar to the pit that first led them underground, there were countless glowing stones lining the railway. For a time, it was the only thing Cynkz could see in the distance, other than the rusty colored stone walls forming the interior of the cavern.

"Well, it's quite amazing regardless," Cynkz said. "I can only imagine what sort of effect such advances would have on Potarium."

"Like I said, the po in Potarium are lazy and complacent. Because of this, they are remarkably slow to progress. It's difficult for me to care much for them."

Cynkz stepped forward. "They're good people, Ynette. I do not think such a harsh assessment of them is fair."

Ynette remained quiet, keeping her attention on the way forward as she gently managed the throttle in her hand.

"They were awfully quick to cast you out, weren't they?" Ynette said, peering from the side of her eye toward Cynkz. "No trial? No justice? Just the word of an angry king and that was it?"

"That, well…" Cynkz took in a deep breath, only for him to wonder how fresh the air was down here. It seemed fine at first, but something about being confined, even in such a large space, spoiled what should have been a refreshing action. "That was merely the result of a mistake I had made long ago coming back to bite me, like a serpent lying in wait for centuries, ready to strike its prey at just the right time."

A large building, out in the middle of nowhere in the dark, began to shift into view. Ynette slowly pulled back on the throttle, and the trolley began to follow suit. As it slowed to a crawl, nearing the large building, the vehicle shook violently as its many metal parts grinded against one another. Everything screeched uncomfortably but it was over soon enough.

Cynkz saw a wide stone pathway leveling out the ground in front of and around the structure. It was a large, possibly four or five-story structure consisting of the same dull gray and rusty colors as many of the other buildings down below. Ynette finally let go of the controls and turned to address Cynkz properly.

"I can sympathize with how you feel. I too hold a number of old regrets, ancient pains that eat away at me from time to time."

Once again, she moved briskly, already several steps ahead as she walked across the flat plane of level stone.

"Hurry along," Ynette said over her shoulder. "We have much to discuss."

The building they entered was in fact a warehouse. Much of the inside was empty, though a number of items were strewn about. Odd metal trinkets and other scrap, a wheel and some tools. In the corner, Cynkz thought he noticed a half-built cart of some kind.

Unfortunately, he couldn't make out anything else specifically. It seemed to be a space sanctioned away for crafting inventions and the like. The stale air and oil and grime made it clear that it was a productive space.

Ynette led Cynkz to an incredibly tall metal stairway attached to the wall. He was so used to seeing stairs made of stone or wood that he wondered how sturdy they would be. Still, just to be safe, he did what he always did, and hovered himself ever so slightly to save the structure from bearing the full brunt of his weight.

The two slipped through a door at the top and walked down another sterile hallway before Ynette opened a door.

"Right this way, Cynkz," she said.

Cynkz nodded and made his way in. The room was well-lit and well-furnished. There were several chairs, a wide desk, and a handsome bookcase that stood prominently in the corner. He could feel his feet sinking into the thick maroon carpet.

The door closing behind him, and the sound of a lock clicking into place caught his ear. He turned around quickly to see Ynette sitting herself down in a chair beside her desk. She crossed her legs and looked directly at Cynkz.

"You seem pretty smart, so you might have already put two and two together, but…" She closed her eyes and drew a deep breath, as if summoning the strength to pull out an ancient heavy memory.

"I am Yla. Yla Fron Ilde, the fifth Sister of Elm."

CHAPTER 19

PART OF HIM WAS SHOCKED, AND YET, paradoxically, another part of him expected the revelation. He took a moment to observe the woman, as if holding on to some stubborn amount of incredulity. He couldn't help himself from raising an eyebrow at Yla.

Foa did mention that she was different from the other sisters, but he never expected someone so cryptic. She spoke plainly, and clearly, yet it was never clear as to what precisely she meant at any given moment. Everything was buried beneath dark and murky layers, purposeful obfuscation acting as a barrier between her and the rest of the world. Part of him, perhaps naively, expected her to be excited at the prospect of re-establishing some sort of connection with her sisters, yet it seemed to be the last thing on her mind. She also possessed an unnerving level of confidence. She had no trouble ordering others around, or venturing out into the desert to recruit criminals, and even now she dragged him, a stranger, all the way out to a dark corner of the underground to lock *him* in a room with *her.*

Even with others around, she seemed to operate entirely alone.

He looked her over once again, this time putting in great effort to take in who exactly sat before him. Her dark gray dreads resembled the same texture and coloring of the other sisters. Without the cloak she wore in the desert, he could see the full length and abundance of her hair as it bunched together like loose threads around her waist. She did not appear young nor necessarily old; she was caught in the same strange in-between that defined a mature individual. She was thin and possessed a normal posture and height, unlike the other sisters in Munderworld. Her features were sharp and refined. Even when resting, her cheeks and eyes looked as if they could cut glass. Yet her piercing gaze seemed to cut both ways, as it revealed a clear thoughtful glint in her cold eyes, the sort of eyes that had spent far too much time thinking about the past. In a sense, she possessed the same look in her eyes as The Munder King.

Here before him was yet another who stood in stark opposition to the old adage of time healing all wounds. A quick glance revealed a characteristically utilitarian, yet detailed outfit. There was nothing loose or hanging, and plenty of pockets to stow away all sorts of items. She almost seemed like she was geared up for an adventure. When he turned his eyes back up to hers, he noticed a simple faded bandana that barely held back her locs, and the same stubborn strand of hair shining in defiance across her face that seemed to not bother her one bit.

Cynkz realized he had been holding his breath during his entire examination. He quickly drew in a much needed bit of stale cavern air and spoke.

"I suspected as much. But, of course, I could not know for certain. You look …very different from the other sisters."

"Yes, even I was caught off guard when I first emerged out of the dark ocean eons ago." Yla continued, "The healing… No, I would say regenerative properties of the dark ocean are extremely potent. Unfortunately, it is also quite slow acting, making it difficult to observe and study."

She loosened her hands from one another to lean forward. Her eyes shifted around, as if searching for answers in the dark, all while she curiously scratched her bony chin. As she turned her head ever so slightly downwards, the soft lighting cast sharp shadows on her face.

"I've tried countless times to experiment with the water," she continued, "but I can't get any consistent results out of it. Tell me, do the sisters use their water portals?"

"Yes. It's a very interesting way to travel."

"I see. I have not been able to replicate the spell in Potarium, unfortunately…"

She paused for a moment, then continued, "Superficially, the water in the ocean seems to restore matter to its physical peak, but I believe it goes deeper than that."

"Deeper?" Cynkz asked. "How? What does that mean?"

"It attempts to mend spiritual traumas as well. No doubt you experienced a dreamy haze as you were lost in the dark ocean? It's as if you're caught between a soft dream and the harsh reality that you are, by all accounts, stranded in the middle of a vast ocean."

"Yes, it was somehow unsettling and calming at the same time. I felt as if I had no choice but to let myself go and let the waters take me where they may."

"Exactly!" Yla shot back into her seat. No matter how many times he experienced it, he could never get used to these out-of-nowhere bursts of excitement from her. "Unfortunately, how precisely it determines what a po's particular 'peak' is, I do not know. I retained my memories, for example, but much of my huumming prowess was lost. It was as if centuries of practicing the arcane art had been ripped away from me."

"Arcane?" Cynkz decided to raise his other eyebrow this time. If he was going to give himself wrinkles trying to piece everything together, he may as well go for an even spread.

"You've seen the sisters doing their 'magic,' correct?"

Yla crossed her arms and her legs. Cynkz could see that Yla was quite guarded, despite her occasional attempts to appear open and cordial in conversation.

"Of course," he said. "Though, I never put much thought into it. Munderworld is filled with so many oddities that a few magic spells did not seem worth much worry."

"That's understandable. But those 'magic spells' are what allow the sisters to do much of anything down there."

"So, they're huums? The most I have seen huums do is enhance light and warm up nearby po."

"Heh, yes. Po are so simple and shortsighted. Few are willing, or able, to attempt experimenting with the art. I swear, they only discovered the enhancing properties of mediums by accident, and worse, they were content to leave the discovery as is. Once they became a religious tool, no one dared to try and do more with them."

"What more can they do?"

"Well," Yla began to speak with her hands. "You can, in fact, communicate between two mediums over a long distance. There seems to be no limit, in terms of distance."

Cynkz took note of the fact that any sort of technical discussion seemed to excite her. Unfortunately, such subjects were beyond him, but he was more than used to operating beyond his comfort zone.

"However, the huums inscribed on the mediums have to be perfectly matched, in every way. Even the makeup of the stones have to be practically identical, right down to their internal structure."

"That makes it seem nearly impossible."

"Yes! Nearly impossible but not *actually* impossible. You spend enough time mining and carving stone, and you will come across at least a handful of materials that will fulfill all of the necessary criteria."

"That reminds me." Cynkz flared open his cloak to open his arms in preparation for his request. "The

Sisters of Elm assisted me in my journey through Munderworld. In return, they asked me to find you and ask if you would re-establish a connection with them. They all miss you dearly."

The excitement on Yla's face slowly faded into a scowl. She crossed her arms once again and leaned back, looking up and away from the jester. The light seemed to flatten her features, yet her sharp gaze remained. Even the glint in her eye appeared harsh as it bounced off of her eyes and into his.

"I see… So that is what motivated you to do all this, to come all this way."

"I sense something deeper here," Cynkz said. "Surely you have thought about reuniting with your sisters at least a few times during your countless years here?"

Yla took in a deep breath and let out a painful sigh. She returned her gaze to the fluffy maroon carpet below, and hung her head in silence for what seemed to be an eternity.

"I don't think I can ever speak with them again. We have … too many differences. I'm sure they were very nice to you when you visited but trust me, we have had our spats and our arguments. And after so much time, I don't think that—"

"Nonsense!"

Yla quickly jolted her head toward him and stared with wide eyes.

Cynkz continued, "They love you dearly, and they miss you even more so. I comforted Foa as she held her head in agony, letting out tears of age-old pain and regret as she whimpered for the opportunity to see you again! Whatever happened, it does not matter anymore.

You have moved on. Time can heal any wound, but only if you let it."

It was difficult to hold eye contact with Yla. Even with her eyes wide she maintained the same piercing look. Still, Cynkz held his ground and stared back. It was long enough that he began to think over what he just said and wondered if he could have worded things better. Perhaps this was the risk one took when speaking from the heart. Yla broke eye contact first, and returned to looking around in the dark of her mind as she held her head down.

"I… Hmm…" Yla stood up for the first time and walked behind her desk. It was wide enough to allow her ample time to think over her next words carefully. "The sisters didn't tell you about how we came to be, did they?"

"No, they did not," Cynkz replied.

"I won't bore you with an entire history lesson." Yla finally reached the large cushioned seat behind her desk. She dropped into it, as if she had finally been given the chance to release something heavy that had been burdening her for years. "Long before the lower levels of Munderworld existed, me and the others— the Sisters of Elm—were normal po girls. It was our mother who first learned to huum, and more still, she learned how to channel her huums into mediums, such as stones, or staves, or what have you. She was able to peer into the afterlife, into Munderworld, and it frightened her. Before the lower levels existed, every-thing existed in Dulrot. It was a much more chaotic and dangerous realm before things naturally spread out among the lower layers. In fact, it was an ancient responsibility of the sentinels to protect po however they could, allowing them to venture out and seek ascension."

"That explains a lot about the brutes," Cynkz said.

"I'm sure you've had more than a few run-ins with them, then?" Yla asked.

"Yes, you could say that…"

"Heh. Anyway, our mother, she worried greatly for all of us, and wanted to give us the means to protect ourselves even in death. It was so long ago I hardly have any memories of the ritual, but we took part in an ancient pact of our mother's creation that instilled us with the knowledge and prowess needed to channel huums as greatly as she did. This came at a cost, however. The afterlife, in a way, is stagnant, and it does everything it can to maintain things as they are. This is why dead po never grow any older. It is, perhaps in some small way, a benefit of the afterlife, never having to contend with the pains of aging. We, the sisters, sacrificed that, however. We made our very essence, our very souls, vulnerable, in order to maintain and expand our talent with huums. Unfortunately for our mother…"

"What was her name, if I may be so bold as to ask?"

"Ira Cain Ilde." Yla leaned forward, rubbing her hands together as they rested on top of her otherwise bare desk. "She was the first to experience accelerated aging. She literally turned to dust only a few years after the ritual. Devastated as we were, we decided to use the opportunity to try and do some good, taking it upon ourselves to assist other po, even in the afterlife. We promised to forgo having any children of our own, for fear of what effect our ritual—or curse, to put it more bluntly—may have on any offspring."

"Did you happen to see the end of Peara?"

"No, no. That came long after us. But it was not too long before Peara was destroyed that I met someone…"

Cynkz perked up, raising another eyebrow toward the woman. Yla did not come across as the romantic type, but far be it from him to make assumptions.

She continued. "I remember it as if it were mere moments ago. I remember the exact look on my face as I stared into my reflection in his dark eyes. I still remember the deep, resonant tone in his voice as he promised me a child. I can even remember this exact annoying strand of hair dropping down in front of my face as I turned my head to gaze more deeply into him. This stupid hair—Do you know how many times I've tried cutting and plucking this strand? Yet it always grows back, fiercer than ever. Anytime I pull my hair back, or braid it in any way, it is always the first to fall out of place. It's like a constant itching reminder of what I lost. If only we could cut away our regrets like loose hairs, things would be so much easier."

Pairne was the first thing that popped into Cynkz's mind. Then came Harquin's words regarding Potarium's growth outpacing them. The ramifications of such a curse seemed so far off, yet, in a realm where time meant nothing, perhaps the space between then and now was just an illusion. Without the need or responsibility to birth and raise new po, it seemed more understandable that they would spend so much of their time on circuses and shows. Perhaps it was just a means of avoiding the painful realization that this was it.

Nothing more, nothing less. As grand as Potarium was, it was limited, as were the po residing within.

"It seems that some wounds cut so deep that heaven itself cannot heal them," Cynkz said.

"Perhaps…" Yla continued looking away, still wrestling with whatever was eating at her mind.

Cynkz broke the silence. "There must be something I can do to change your mind? Even now the sisters await some news of your well-being."

"Aside from my own trepidation," Yla interrupted, "and as amazing as long-distance communication via mediums can be, not even I know to perform such a feat. There needs to be a strong connection and likeness between the two objects being used as mediums in order for it to be possible. And, I said a moment ago that the distance appears to be limitless, yet I don't know how that would fare when trying to communicate between two entirely different realms of existence."

For a moment, Cynkz was stumped. He had never considered the logistics of his task. *There must be a way,* Cynkz thought, raising his hand to rub his chin. He did it so thoroughly, in fact, that he noticed the crude metal of Foa's ring dragging against his skin. Instantly, like a light in the dark, he remembered.

"Wait! This ring!"

"Hmm?" Yla raised her own brow.

"When we finally met The Munder King, all he had to do was merely tap the ring with his nail, and we were able to speak with the Sisters!"

"Wait. We?" Yla, with her brow still raised, leaned back in her seat.

The creaking of her chair caught him off guard as he remembered that he never properly introduced his companion. Cynkz said, "Ah, yes, I did not travel alone."

"Indeed. I do remember hearing something about an imp assisting you?"

"Yes. His name is Fiddle, and he has been my greatest friend for as long as I resided in Munderworld."

"An imp… a mun with a name…" Yla seemed to be lost in thought. When Cynkz least expected it, she returned her eyes to him. "I know that The Munder King had many children early on, all imps and children of darkness, but… He never *named* any of them. In fact, he seemed to care little for them, allowing them to be lost to the many far off corners of the abyss to fend for themselves."

"Yes, even The Munder King was surprised to hear that Fiddle had a name. Believe it or not, both Fiddle and The Munder King have recovered most of the imps. I got to meet them, actually."

"What?! How?" This outburst was different from the others, as she threw her hands to her desk, filling the room with a satisfying thud.

"It was during the chaos with the puppets," Cynkz continued. "The Munder King helped Fiddle and the others possess the things in order to find me and check up on my progress."

"That is…" Once again, Yla retreated to her mind.

Try as he might to be as candid as possible, he could feel that she was struggling to believe what he was saying.

"I heard that a giant puppet popped up out of nowhere and led the creatures out of the city," Yla said. "You didn't have anything to do with that, did you?"

Of course... Just as he took note of his attempts to be honest, he was forced into a position where he had to choose between perhaps being *too* forthright, and maintaining some sort of boundary for himself. He could tell that the woman was being guarded herself, so it only made sense that he should maintain a few secrets of his own.

"No, of course not," Cynkz said. "I nearly lost myself as I ran toward the desert trying to escape the chaos. Father Kadd, fortunately, came to the rescue."

"I see..."

Cynkz could only wonder if his ruse worked. He thought he was good at reading people, yet Yla completely escaped him. He also figured that Yla herself was experienced at reading people and wondered what she thought of him. He could remember the sentinel guard Rackel's criticism of his supposed 'acting ability,' which gnawed away at what little confidence he had. Perhaps his issue was overthinking things?

"The imps seemed more than ecstatic to be reunited. I'm sure your sisters would feel the same to hear from you once more. If there is one thing that Fiddle has taught me, it is that most things are not as scary as they seem, especially social fears. No matter what, it is often best to reach out and accept our loved ones. There must be a way to make it work. I will assist you in any way if it means fulfilling my task and reuniting you."

Yla remained still. Even her eyes remained fixed on a specific, nondescript location on the ground. Then, she thoughtfully tapped a thin finger on the top of her desk several times, seemingly struggling with something in her mind. Finally, she turned her eyes upward toward Cynkz, first at the crude ring on his hand, and then toward his face. She was plotting something, but as to what, Cynkz had no idea. His mind remained blank as he awaited her response.

Eventually, she pushed herself back from her desk. Despite the carpet's fluffed texture, her steps seemed to stand out sharply as she made her way toward him. She finally stopped and stood uncomfortably close to him. Before he could consider the thought that he had no idea what to do, she reached up and pinched his cheek. She pinched so hard that his overthinking mind was interrupted with a single, appropriate response:

Oww... Thank goodness Fiddle is not here. I can only imagine how much merriment he would be having at my expense.

"I think I may have figured out a way to make everyone happy." Something about her tone was odd. She was practically mumbling, as if, for the first time since they had known each other, she seemed unsure. Still, Cynkz couldn't help but feel excited at the prospect that he had won her over in some way.

"You have?" Cynkz said, barely able to maintain his joy. "You'll speak with the sisters again? You will—"

"I can't make any promises," Yla said, "but I have an idea. We will need a few things to make this work."

"What do we need? I'll do anything, just ask."

Yla leaned against her desk before continuing. "I, too, used to have a ring just like yours. But I lost it on a run one night while exploring one of the temples. You know the ones, with the massive flags and all?"

"The ones covering Potarium in the protective huum? Yes, I have seen them."

"Have you been inside one?"

"No, not yet. Father Kadd mentioned taking me to one, but I suppose we never got around to it."

"Well, the protective huum is stronger the closer one gets to the flags. It is nearly impossible for a normal po to get within several hundred feet of one without their entire body being forced to the ground. Unfortunately—"

"You lost the ring near one of these flags? And now you cannot retrieve it?"

"Heh, you catch on quick. Normally, if a wandering po, or some item gets lost within the flag's range, you can get one of the guardsmen to retrieve it with a net or something."

"I imagine you cannot merely go in and ask nicely?"

"Exactly. So we need to go back and get it ourselves. The ring should be clearly visible, as all the ground near the flags is also compressed, perfectly flat with clean bright sand."

"Wait, 'we?'" Cynkz said curiously.

"Yes. I want you to accompany me on this run. From what I have gathered, you may be strangely resistant to the great huum. If this is true, then you may also be able to provide the perfect material for the mediums to initiate contact."

"Material? And what mediums?"

"The rings," Yla said, lifting a hand to point at Cynkz's ring finger. "I believe with your ring and mine, as well as, um, maybe your hair acting as an enhancer, we can finally—"

"My hair?!" Cynkz exclaimed.

"Yes. You have plenty of it. I figured it would make for the perfect material to enhance the rings. If you are resistant to this realm's protection, you may very well be a most potent amplifier. And with your strong connection to Munderworld..."

"I, um, I do not know if I can so easily part with my hair." Cynkz instinctively reached around to hold his long braid the way one might a limb. "But... I suppose it would merely grow back, given enough time. And if it would help you reach out to the sisters once more..."

Yla crossed her arms but couldn't help but curl up the edge of her thin lip. "Ultimately, the choice is yours, Cynkz. I won't force you to do anything you don't want to do."

Cynkz stared at the stream of thick black threads. Something about parting ways with his hair in any capacity felt wrong, but he had said he was willing to do anything to help the sisters. Once he came to terms with the prospect, he let go of the braid and turned his attention back to Yla.

"Well, Father Kadd always joked about me needing a haircut, anyway," Cynkz said, "I suppose I can take solace in knowing that he, if no one else, would respond positively to the change."

"Perfect!" Yla said, going so far as to clap her hands together as she smiled wider than ever before. "You have no idea how helpful this will—"

A knock at the door cut her off. Her smile immediately disappeared as she rested her hands on the desk and turned her attention toward the door.

"Come in, Harquin," Yla said.

The door opened, and the familiar ringmaster stepped through.

I could have sworn she locked that door, Cynkz thought.

"Ah, Cynkz. It is good to see you here and doing well," Harquin said.

"Yes. I presume it was you who put in a good word for me with these kind folk?"

"Heh, well, perhaps," Harquin said, reaching up to rub his chin as he chuckled. "I figured Lady Yla would be interested in you, considering your unique talents and the situation. Also, I do apologize for taking so long to reach you. You know how it is between conflicting schedules, logistics, keeping up appearances and all that. We are busy po, indeed."

"No need to apologize. Everything worked out in the end," Cynkz said.

Yla stepped forward. "It's a good thing you're here, Harquin. I believe we need to prepare for another night run. I need Cynkz's help retrieving something from one of the temples of Paithos."

"Ugh, I cannot stand it," Harquin scoffed. "Skulking around in the night like a common rat. I don't know how the rest of you can put up with it."

"It is pretty fun, actually—" Cynkz caught himself mid-sentence. He only realized too late that it was perhaps not the best idea to allude to his own sneaking abilities.

"Oh? Confident, are we? Though, if you truly have traveled through the many realms of Munderworld, I suppose it should be no surprise." Yla's tone was lighter than usual. She finally seemed to be enjoying herself, in her own cryptic way.

She turned back to Harquin and continued. "Harquin, please take Cynkz downstairs. Gather Nidan and the others and get him briefed. I will personally be leading a small group to the temple tomorrow night."

"As you wish, Lady Yla," Harquin said through a courteous bow. "Come along, Cynkz. We have much to go over and I need to see if we have better attire for you. We can't have you sneaking around in a shining courtier's wardrobe."

CHAPTER 20

ANOTHER PEACEFUL NIGHT WASHED over the pearly mountain city. There wasn't much to fill the otherwise silent air save for the rolling sea of snoring hummingbirds lulling the world to sleep. As one ventured away from the heart of the city and closer to the handful of temples on the perimeter, a new sound slowly took over.

The great heavy cloth with arcane scripture sewn into the fabric billowed in the wind, loud enough to drown out most of the other soft sounds of the night. It was soothing in its own way, like the occasional touch of a protective hand brushing over one's ear.

It was the perfect setting for one to go unnoticed. If anyone but the guards employed to lazily watch over the temple's entrance watched, they might have seen several flashes of faint shadows slithering their way toward the structure's rear. If one had also been inclined to investigate further, and at the right time, they may have witnessed those same shadows disappearing behind loose brickwork that stood out from the rest of the structure's immaculate form. Finally, if one were truly brave, they may have been able to sneak up to those stones, place an ear near them, and listen in on the shadows as they spoke to one another in hushed voices.

"Alright, we're finally here," Yla whispered.

Cynkz was beginning to notice Yla's proclivity for announcing their arrival to places. He felt as if she was assuring herself more than those traveling with her. He was in no position to be ungrateful for having a leader who chose to be clear and concise. Cynkz had little idea of where he was, other than near a temple at the edge of the city. The temple itself seemed to be particularly old, not necessarily due to its physical condition, but due to its design. It certainly stood out as a relic from a different time period, if such things were still noted in the afterlife.

Between the countless pillars lining the building's perimeter, the layered ridges connecting everything together, and the sheer size of the structure, everything appeared to be made specifically to imprint a wondrous image on the observer, rather than to serve any functional purpose. Though it seemed to be in line with everything else in the city.

"Was it really a good idea to bring the new guy along?" Nidan whispered, his tone so harsh and bitter it could hardly be considered a whisper.

"Yes," Yla snapped back, with a similarly quiet, though harsh tone.

"It seems risky, if ya ask me," another one said. He was considerably smaller than Nidan but wore his dark cloak as well as anyone else there.

Cynkz himself didn't know what to think of their attire. He was glad to finally be out of the stuffy coat and trousers the perfumers had given him, but it felt unnatural to depend on something so fickle as a dark cloak and padded clothing to sneak around in. Perhaps it was easy to take his powers for granted. Sneaking was an effortless affair for him normally, but having to traipse around in the dark, tiptoeing between shadows, gave him a new appreciation for the skill normal po needed to exhibit to do anything stealthily.

"Most of you know the drill, but I'll quickly reiterate for Cynkz." Yla wasted no time in getting to business. Whatever objections the others wished to bring up, she was clearly not going to waste time indulging them.

"The architecture in these old temples is quite primitive. Rather than proper air ducts, everything adheres to an open design. Case in point—" Yla pointed a thin finger toward the ceiling of the empty room they had snuck into. It was exceedingly tall, and the old brickwork left many deep grooves in the walls, but not much else could be said about it, save for a clear ledge that sat prominently in place of a proper seam.

"From there, we make our way onto the joist beams above the main hall. The beams will lead us directly to the inner hall, then to the flag yard. We will need to be exceptionally quiet, as the main hall is one big open corridor, and any sounds will be amplified. In truth, the true obstacle we face is the sheer size of the place.

We will need to make our way slowly along a rather long rafter."

"Just remember, newcomer," Nidan interjected, "move lowly and slowly an' we won't have any troubles." He gave Cynkz a mighty pat on the back, enough to knock him. Most were caught off guard by Cynkz's heavy nature, but Nidan's mighty palm seemed to have no issue with it. Cynkz nodded and returned his attention to Yla.

"The guards, as inept as they are, make the occasional rounds through the building. Though we should hear their clumsy steel-ridden footsteps from a mile away. Just follow my lead, as you have been doing so far, and everything will be fine."

Cynkz gave another quiet nod.

"Good," Yla said. "Let's get going, then."

She moved quickly, climbed the wall, and disappeared over its ledge as quietly as a mouse and as traceless as a ghost. The others followed suit, and all Cynkz could think about was that it was surprising, and a little frightening, seeing someone as burly as Nidan creep over the wall in such nimble fashion. He waited for the last body to disappear before he drifted over and up the wall himself.

As Cynkz peered over the ledge, he could see Yla far ahead, leading the group. She remained low, practically slithering along the darkened surface of the thick support beam high above the marble flooring. As expected, the others were mimicking her movements, and Cynkz did the same. It felt awkward to 'slither' without transforming, but it was strangely fun.

The scale of the temple began to set in as they moved along. The beam itself was wide enough that they couldn't see anything past its edges. Out of curiosity, Cynkz raised his head to get a quick peek of what was beneath them. It was difficult to tell, but he figured they were at least fifty feet above the ground. Po seemed to love their high, grand ceilings wherever they could afford them.

The beam itself appeared to stretch forward in a similar length, yet they only made it halfway before the light taps of steel on marble began to approach from the far end of the hall. Yla and the others immediately froze. Cynkz followed suit but couldn't keep himself from turning an ear toward the oncoming guard. Another set of feet sluggishly traipsing along came in from the opposite direction. He imagined at least two guards coming to meet each other.

"Another dull night, it seems," a hoarse voice rang out.

"When is it ever *not* a dull night?" another, slightly raspier voice said.

"I feel as though we should be grateful."

"Why's that?"

"Well, what with the usual rumors of hooded sneaks spooking the po, as well as that nonsense with the puppets and talk of the first new soul in ages being imprisoned... I mean, it'd be nice if *something* interesting could happen here, no?"

"I got to experience a bit of a story myself the other night, believe it or not."

"Really? Do tell."

Yla shifted a bit. It looked as if she were sighing, silently, of course. Cynkz couldn't help but chuckle at her impatience. Silently, of course.

The guard continued. "I had the privilege of chasing a young couple off one of the royal's properties."

"A young couple, eh?" A moment of silence passed, and Cynkz imagined the guard rubbing his chin and giving a wry look to his associate. "What were they up to?"

"Some new trend, or at least, I think it's a trend. They called it 'skinny skimming.'"

"What in Paithos' name is that supposed to be?"

"Apparently, you find a big body of water…"

"Right."

"And then you strip down, butt naked and all."

"Uh-huh."

"And then you try to belly flop into said water from on high, even angling your body in a real dangerous way."

"Seems like it'd normally hurt, if not for the great huum."

"No, see, that's the interesting part. The great huum intervenes and tries to lift your body upward, but you push yourself down real hard into the water as you fall."

"Well, what does that do?"

"Lemme finish—"

Yla was clenching her fist so hard Cynkz worried she would slam it down and break the concrete beam that supported them all.

The guard continued. "The huum's effect will bowl up underneath you, and your body keeps flying ahead, just along the surface of the water."

"Oh!"

The other guard's exclamation was loud enough to sharply echo. Yla and the others nearly jumped in response.

He continued. "So it's like skipping stones?"

"Exactly!"

"But with your body, right?"

"That's right."

"But…Why do you have to be naked to do it?"

"Apparently—and this is their words, not mine— the effect is more potent the more 'vulnerable' you are."

"Honestly, it just sounds like an excuse to take off your clothes."

"That's what I said!"

Cynkz couldn't help but look at Yla. She seemed to be accepting defeat and hung her head low as she waited for what must have been the most inane, useless, time-wasting conversation she had ever been subjected to in her afterlife.

"Well, I suppose we should continue with our patrol, huh?"

"If you see any hooded shadow ghosts or what have you, be sure to alert me so I have something to do."

"Yeah, yeah, right."

Cynkz, curious as ever and near the beam's edge, shifted himself over to get a peek below. Just as he noticed the flash of bright red plumage from a guard's helmet coming into view, he rested a hand and a knee on the beam, and for a moment completely forgot to manage his weight. His attention was broken by the dissonant crumbling of ancient concrete beneath him. He instantly recoiled, but it was too late.

Several large chunks of slightly gray, slightly yellowed rock tumbled down below. Cynkz looked ahead only to notice all eyes were on him, the whites clearly visible from beneath their hoods. Cynkz wanted to shrug, but a loud, ear-shattering clang stopped him, followed by the quick running of metaled feet.

"Horik? Horik!"

More footsteps tapped their way from both ends of the hall and settled below.

"What happened to Horik?"

"I-I don't know! Horik and I were just talking, and as soon as we parted ways to continue our patrol, something fell from above and landed on him!"

Something waving ahead caught the corner of Cynkz's eye. Yla motioned for him to hurry ahead and join them at the far end of the beam. It was smart to use the commotion as cover to mask their steps, and Cynkz scurried along, listening for more of the conversation unfolding below.

"Commander Prayus! It's Horik."

"What happened here?!" Prayus' voice was distinct and possessed an authoritative weight.

"I swear, commander, we weren't up to any funny business!"

"Just calm down and tell me what happened."

"We were talking and about to go back on patrol when a piece of that beam fell on Horik's head and knocked him out clean!"

"That shouldn't be possible. Neither the building crumbling, nor the physical harm done to Horik…"

"Do you think it's maybe the work of the hooded sneaks? Maybe the rumors were true."

"Silence. I've grown tired of the rumors. Besides," Prayus' heavy steps could be heard shuffling ahead, presumably toward his fallen comrade, "I doubt anything in Potarium could defy the great huum in this way."

"What're ya thinking, commander?" A new voice joined in, sounding considerably younger and less assured.

"These temples are some of the oldest buildings in Potarium, but they're not *that* old, at least, not so much that they should be falling apart. I've spoken personally with many of the architects that maintain these buildings tirelessly to make sure they're in good shape."

"Do ya think the protective huum is falterin'? Maybe we've been lackin' faith an' Paithos is lookin' ta correct—"

"Quiet, you fool! Leave such concerns to the holy men. You two, carry Horik outside and get him upright. And you two? Clean up this rubble and go outside with the others and wait for me. I don't want anyone else suffering from an embarrassing accident."

"Surely, there's a doctor we can—"

"At this time of night?" Prayus interrupted, sounding more annoyed than anything. "Between the protective huum and the healing ocean, we have had little need for doctors. Horik will be conscious and fully recovered before we could find one and even knock on their door."

"If he's truly hurt, we coul' jus' dunk his head in the ocean, anyhows."

"Commander?"

"Just get him outside and clean this up. I'm going to make a final sweep of the place. Once settled, all of you wait for me out front."

"Yessir!"

The mess of clunky steeled feet shuffling across the temple floor provided more than enough cover for Cynkz to hurry his way ahead and down the ledge where the others were waiting. They were now in a much smaller and much darker hallway that appeared to line the main hall. It was so dark, in fact, that Cynkz could hardly see Yla and the others. If it weren't for the sparse night light reflecting off of them from the sizable window panes lining the hall, they could be considered invisible.

"Alright," Yla whispered, quieter than before. "Cynkz and I will go into the flag yard. The rest of you spread out and keep watch. The foliage and trees decorating the perimeter of the flag yard should cover us well enough but hide yourselves well and signal us if you see anything coming out toward the inner hall."

The shift of the soft blue light reflecting off of the others' hoods indicated their nodding. Quickly, everyone save for Yla dashed aside and hid themselves among the shadows. Yla carefully unlocked and pressed open the nearest window enough for her thin form to slip outside. After she ducked and crawled ahead into the nearby brush, Cynkz did the same.

The shrubbery and trees were similarly lush and vibrant as the foliage that lined the outer edge of the golden tower but were far less maintained. There was no time to consider any of that however, as Cynkz quickly found himself reunited with Yla. There was a clear line differentiating the naturalistic decor of the indistinct shrubs and small trees and the flat expanse of bleached sand.

In the distance was the great flag. It had a massive trunk of smooth oak that reached all the way up to the sky, and at its top was an equally massive cloth of a deep, murky blue lined with golden threads. The sounds of the flag waving in the wind seemed to tread the line between soothing billows and violent thrashing.

Cynkz finally noticed Yla had stopped, and when he looked at her, he noticed something was wrong. It must have been the effects of the great huum supposedly weighing her down. Strangely, or perhaps not so strangely, he didn't notice anything.

"Yla, are you alright?" Cynkz whispered.

"I-I'm fine. I can keep going," she responded.

"Keep going where? There's nothing but flat sand and the flagpole out there."

"I told you already that we need to find the ring. How are you feeling?"

"I'm feeling fine."

"So am I, so let's go and search, as quickly as we can."

Yla hurried forward, noticeably more sluggishly. The way she stumbled made it seem as if she were bearing a great weight on her back. Cynkz wondered why she was so stubborn—What was she trying to prove?

Cynkz stayed close behind her. He knew he was supposed to be looking for the ring, but he couldn't help but keep his eyes on Yla. He feared how angry she might get if he were to touch her, even if it was to help her move about, but as things were going, she might not have a choice in the matter. Even more peculiar, she didn't appear to be searching for anything. She kept her eyes focused on the flagpole as she pushed ahead.

The sand seemed strange, unlike the natural bumps and waves that the desert provided. Here it seemed to be pressed down, and as they moved closer to the flagpole, it seemed to become more level.

Just as he felt good for finally looking in the sand, even if he were only indirectly looking for the trinket, a soft thud caught his ear. Yla seemed to collapse and could hardly move. Even her cloak seemed to be dragging her down into the sand. Still, she struggled to move forward, as if desperately attempting to defy a greater power.

"Yla, I'll go ahead and look. Just try to—"

"No!" Yla's tone was loud, but not loud enough to surpass the billowing cloth flapping above. She didn't turn her head to look at him, or perhaps she merely couldn't. "I can… Just… Ugh…"

Yla reached forward, her body pressed into the otherwise flat sand leaving deep grooves around her.

"This… stupid huum… I hate being trapped beneath the… Ugh… The oppressive heel of this wretched place…"

Growing tired of her stubbornness, Cynkz flattened his expression, drew in a deep breath, and dashed ahead. He could hear his heavy footsteps leaving deep imprints in the sand but didn't care. He wanted nothing more than to hurry up and get this little excursion over with.

It was surreal, being so close to the flagpole. Its true size became apparent once one was close to it. In terms of sheer mass, perhaps only the golden tower itself could eclipse it. He scurried around the perimeter of the pole, his eyes darting around furiously for the ring. He wondered how anyone could lose something like it in such a place. Still, the thought of finally completing his mission was more than enough motivation for him to put his all into the current task.

Cynkz figured he must have been nearly sprinting and had to circumvent the entire pole several times before growing frustrated enough to finally look up at Yla. The look on her face shook him to his core. He had seen her express a few emotions, try as she might to present herself as cold and in control. Still, something seemed to break within her as she held her mouth slightly agape, and her eyes wide enough to push several wrinkles into her otherwise flat brow. Cynkz caught himself staring, before he snapped himself out of his stupor to ask Yla if she knew anything that could help.

"Yla!" he called out in a half-whisper. "I don't see anything. Where exactly—"

"You… Cynkz…" Yla muttered to herself. She seemed to be deeply lost in her own mind.

"Yla!" It took everything he had to not scream, causing his hushed call to come across like a sharp hiss. This seemed to be enough to snap her out of her trance.

"Cynkz, hurry back," she said, clearly for once. "We should stop and go back. We can figure something else out."

"What?!" Not even Fiddle had aggravated him this much. "We came all the way out here to find this stupid—"

"Cynkz, it's fine. We need to go back *now*."

"Why?! What was the point of—"

The low chirp of a hummingbird shot out from behind the brush. Yla mustered all of her strength to look behind her.

"That's the signal," Yla said. "We need to go."

Cynkz could only shake his head and huff. He almost felt like a child stamping their feet as he pressed into the sand. He assumed a low profile and nearly flew across the ground hurrying over to Yla, lifting her off the ground, and diving into the brush.

As Yla put a hand to her chest and caught her breath, a set of familiar, steel footsteps could be heard just beyond them. They both froze and stayed low, pressing themselves deep into the bundle of smooth green leaves and other prickly limbs as they stared back toward the large window panes of the inner hall. The harsh edges of armor crept slowly back and forth behind the glass. It appeared to be Commander Prayus, though Cynkz could hardly tell any of the guards apart when in their armor. It was odd, considering that, all things considered, Cynkz was in no real trouble, yet he felt the cool trickle of a sweat bead rolling down the side of his face. Perhaps he was more concerned for Yla and the others than himself, yet when he glanced over he noticed Yla was as expressionless as ever. The only thing more frustrating to him than his failure to find her ring was his inability to read this woman to any degree. Just what was going through her mind? What was the point of all this?

Yla caught on to the guard's exit before he did, and she pushed herself away to crawl forward. Cynkz merely stared for a moment, perplexed as ever, but followed her as she opened one of the many dimly lit panes of glass. Once inside again, the others emerged from the shadows like dark spirits, grouping together around their leader.

"What in munder happened, Yla?" Nidan whispered.

"I've seen everything I need to," she responded. Yla looked over and smiled at Cynkz. "Let's hurry back. We have much to discuss."

Before Cynkz could get in a word of his own, she climbed a nearby wall. She disappeared over the ledge, and the others followed suit. For a moment he was struck dumb. He had a million questions, and he was beginning to grow tired of the cloak and dagger—all of the murky layers and unnecessary obfuscation. Though standing alone to huff in the dark would do nothing. For the time being, he had little choice but to climb over the wall and join the others for the long walk back.

CHAPTER 21

IT WAS RARE THAT CYNKZ'S PATIENCE was tested. He had no issue waiting for anything before, yet during the long walk back, after creeping through shadows and trekking over sand dunes, he felt ready to burst.

During the entire trip back Yla moved swiftly, nearly stumbling over herself as she hurried ahead. Any time Cynkz tried to speak to her, she ignored him. As the morning light began to ignite the desert once more, he could see Yla smiling beneath her hood. The deep grooves being pressed into her cheeks seemed sharp, almost unrestrained. Whatever she was trying to hold back, she was hardly succeeding.

The rest of the way through the underground went by quickly enough. The descent down the dark stairs, the lift, even the trolley, went by in the blink of an eye. The only stumble in the otherwise smooth venture was when she pulled Nidan aside to hand over their cloaks and to give him orders just out of earshot.

Yla led Cynkz to the distant warehouse and into her office, just as she had before. This time she didn't bother pretending to lock the door behind them, instead merely hurrying to her desk to lean against its top.

"Am I finally allowed an explanation of some sort now?" Cynkz said.

Yla perked up and smiled. "You should really cheer up, Cynkz. I got everything I needed from our little excursion."

"But we never found your ring. The whole thing seemed like a waste of time."

"Nonsense!"

Once again, her outburst seemed to come out of nowhere. It was a bit disconcerting that Cynkz was growing so accustomed to them.

"What do you mean?" Cynkz asked, his brow pushing his sharp eyes into an even sharper squint.

She leaned back and crossed her arms, and finally her odd smirk began to settle into a more comfortable expression. "I figured that you may be resistant to the great huum, but you exceeded my expectations."

"How so?" Cynkz relaxed his own expression. He had apparently been holding in a heavy breath, and it felt good to let it loose through a mild sigh.

"The other night when I was explaining the need for a potent material to conduct the sort of long-distance communication through a medium, I needed to see proof that you would be capable of providing something substantial enough for what we would need. You truly do seem to be of the abyss. Whatever connection you have with Munderworld seems to be even stronger than the great huum itself!"

"What does that mean?"

"It means that it will be easier than I thought to put together a proper medium to bypass the great huum! Think of the experiments. Think of the tools we could make and the things we could finally do without having to bear the weight of that burdensome spell! I heard rumors, Harquin even noted how his beast from the circus seemed capable of attacking you, and that king effortlessly struck you. I didn't believe it, but now that I've seen it…"

"So, you can make something to communicate with the sisters? Will you finally do it?"

"Of course, provided that you are willing to give me material, such as your hair, as we spoke about before."

Cynkz's eyes lit up. As he smiled, he drew in a deep breath, and then let it loose, slowly and smoothly. It was as if a great weight had been lifted from his shoulders. If nothing else, it was nice to know that he had finally accomplished something of importance. For a moment, he wondered what he would do next but was so overcome with joy that for once he cared little about the future. The thought of hearing the sisters again, and their voices as they reveled in their long-awaited reunion, was too much for him to contain.

"Finally…" Cynkz muttered. "Of course. You can take as much hair as you need, Yla."

"Well, I won't take all of it. I'll leave you with a nice, normal braid, if that works."

"Of course," Cynkz said with a slight nod.

"Splendid! Here, have a seat in this chair. I may need a moment to find a pair of shears big enough to cut into that tree trunk of a braid."

Cynkz couldn't help but notice how things had come full circle. Here he was, getting his hair tended to, yet again, and being guided along by a sister of Elm, yet again. It was a relief to not have the pressure of meeting royalty right after. It was amusing to listen to Yla behind him, shuffling back and forth as she struggled to heave his braid of hair around. It was impressive that she did it all by herself when it taken three perfumers to do the same.

He had kept his hair for so long that he considered it just as much a part of him as one would an arm or a leg. Considering he was able to keep moving after losing an actual limb, he figured it was an easy short-term sacrifice to make if it meant reuniting the sisters, even if it were only for a short call. Whatever excitement Yla had shown earlier seemed to be settling as she returned to her usual cold and calculating pace. She also remained strangely quiet. There wasn't much to fill the air between them, other than the rhythmic snipping of metal shears swaying back and forth. As he felt the soft pull and brush of hair tugging lightly at his head, Yla finally began a conversation.

"So, what do you think of Munderworld? It's a strange place, isn't it?"

"Yes, very much so," Cynkz said. "But you get used to it, once you spend enough time there."

"Of course, though I haven't been there in many, many years. How much of Munderworld did you see?"

"We traveled through every realm, believe it or not. I initially woke up in Dulrot, where I spent the vast majority of my time."

"You should consider yourself fortunate, then. Dulrot is quite peaceful compared to the other layers. And you had a little friend, right? An imp, of all things."

"Yes, Fiddle. I would not have made it without his aid."

"And you met The Munder King as well, I presume?"

"Yes."

"It's interesting that you seem so capable of befriending entities of the dark."

Cynkz had to pause for a moment. He thought about what Yla was saying, and the way she was saying it. Her approach seemed more calculated than usual as she meticulously waited between even brushes of his hair to speak. She also waited patiently for his responses. With his hair in her hands, he felt as if he was being restrained in a sense. She had full control of the situation and seemed intent on digging as deep as she could manage to learn something important. What that was, well, there was only one way for him to find out.

"I never thought of it that way," Cynkz said. "So long as they are good at heart, I take no issue with anyone."

"Hmm…" Yla paused and continued to undo and brush his hair. After several measured strokes, she finally responded. "What do you define as 'good?'"

Another question that forced him to pause. It was not a question that he ever considered before. Who was he to determine something so broad and abstract?

He and Fiddle had no issue helping others, whenever they could, but he never thought about why. There were certainly those who did not deserve their help, but he struggled to determine why he, if anyone, should get to be the judge of something such as that. To go further, how was anyone determined to be worthy of quick access to Potarium? Who got to determine who must stay in Munderworld, perhaps eternally trapped beneath its lower layers?

Cynkz could only be honest in his response. "I do not know."

"Well," Yla responded quickly, the first curt reply thus far. "What does 'good' mean to *you*, specifically?"

Her response didn't help him much. Rather than get caught up in anything too large and abstract again, he merely answered back quickly and honestly. "I suppose it comes down to a willingness to aid those in need, in whatever way I can, big or small."

"To those in need," Yla muttered. "Does that mean only po? Or do you include muns as well?"

"Yes," Cynkz snapped back with his quickest answer. "Fiddle, for example, has proven to be a great friend. I would do anything for him, as he has done for me."

He could feel the pull at the back of his head growing lighter as Yla began to cut his hair away. He wondered if she were merely concentrating on the task at hand, or if she were carefully ruminating over her next words.

"Do you consider the Sisters of Elm to be good?"

"Of course. They assist po in reaching Dulrot, giving them an opportunity for ascension. Even if they are not perfect, and even if they do not reach everyone in a timely manner, they still give po who may be trapped hope. That is certainly something I would consider worthwhile."

It was difficult to tell, but he swore he heard Yla chuckle. It was so faint however that it nearly blended in with the sound of brushing of hair.

"Imagine going through all that trouble just to end up in a prison cell in heaven," Yla said. Her tone seemed bitter, nearly as sharp as the shears in her hand.

"Yes, but," Cynkz said, taking a moment to think over his response, "it is certainly better than drowning in a swamp for all eternity, or being regularly crushed under mountains."

"Ah, Horgafell, I remember that realm in particular," Yla said. "The sisters rarely, if ever, visit that wretched place. There is not much hope for those unfortunate enough to be trapped there."

Before Cynkz could say anything more, Yla continued. "Both you and the imp must have had a run-in with Eshra'Tel, then? There's no other way to reach The Munder King."

"Yes, unfortunately…"

Yla's grip seemed to tighten. Cynkz wasn't sure if she was struggling to manage his hair or if something deeper was getting to her.

"What did you think of Eshra'Tel?" she asked. "How did you manage to get through?"

"I believe we only made it through thanks to The Munder King pulling us out. Fiddle seemed momentarily traumatized by the incident, and I have had the occasional nightmare because of it. It may very well be one of the most terrifying things I have experienced.

Having your entire being wrenched out of your own control, as countless hands… Each being forced beyond their will pressing into you, pulling and thrashing about as they drag your very soul into a sharp, malicious light… It was as if I were being forced to witness my own existential annihilation in slow motion. I hope I never have to experience anything such as that again."

"Did he speak to you? Eshra'Tel, I mean?"

"Yes…"

Yla stepped aside, a bundle of jet black hair in her hand, to get a good look at Cynkz.

"What did he say to you?"

Yla spoke with an icy tone and had an even colder expression on her face, at least from what Cynkz could gather from the corner of his eye. He remembered the thread but didn't feel comfortable unveiling it just yet. He wasn't quite sure what caused him to hold back so much. He wanted to be more honest and open, yet something deep within him, an instinct perhaps, forced him to remain guarded. For some reason, he was reminded of the tense feeling he had when he reached inside the maw of the circus beast.

"He wanted something," Cynkz said. "What, I do not know. I presume he merely wanted my soul, and perhaps even Fiddle's as well—"

"I doubt he would care so much about another soul falling into him," Yla said as she finally slithered behind Cynkz to continue dealing with his hair. "If he spoke to you directly, then there was something more he was after."

"You seem to understand the dark entity quite well." Cynkz felt awkward, forcing himself to interrupt someone else. It was not something he did often, but he felt it a fitting response to Yla's conduct. She paused yet again. Cynkz was beginning to find every moment of silence to be nearly unbearable. He never figured a simple haircut would be so taxing.

"Being one of the sisters, we have learned a lot about the abyss in our time," Yla said, "and the many entities residing within it."

"That makes sense…" Cynkz worried his response sounded half-hearted. Once again, she was being vague, going so far as to not address his question directly.

"What do you think the sisters could do to help those poor souls trapped in Eshra'Tel?" Yla asked. Whatever progress she had been making with Cynkz's hair appeared to be slowing down.

He wanted nothing more than for the conversation to end and to get on with things.

"In truth," Cynkz said, "I would have no idea of how to even broach the issue. Perhaps they could ask The Munder King to—"

"Ha!" Another outburst. This one seemed to be particularly harsh, as if on the verge of turning into a shriek. "What a foolish idea. How did you make your way through Munderworld while being so naive?"

Cynkz couldn't help but chuckle, as the perfect answer shot through his mind and out of his mouth, "Just barely."

The unbearable silence returned, but only for a short while. It was a welcome reprieve from what felt like an interrogation. Strangely, he didn't feel all that different, despite literally shedding who knows how many pounds in hair. He caught glimpses of the shining strands on the floor from the corner of his eye.

"Nearly finished," Yla said. "I left you with a small braid, it reaches just past your shoulders, if that's fine."

"Of course," Cynkz said.

Just as he reached around to feel the full length of his new look, a new thought flickered in his mind.

"Oh, I completely forgot to ask. How is Tuco doing?" Cynkz asked.

"He's … alright, I suppose," Yla said. "Why do you ask?"

"In a way, I feel responsible for him. He may be a bit of a scoundrel, but he deserves to be treated humanely, like anyone else."

Cynkz finally stood up, feeling out his new braid as he turned to face Yla. The look on her face said that she still had a question or two left for him.

"What will you do after all of this?" she asked. "What is your next move?"

Cynkz said as he finally lowered his arm and rested it beneath his cloak, "Have you heard about what lies beyond the big orb in the sky?"

"You plan to try going to Omundisia, don't you?"

"Y-you know about that? Is it true, then? That the land of Omun and Paithos is out there, just beyond the orbed sky?"

"Yes. It is true, though I doubt I know much more than you do."

"I see…"

"How badly do you want to go to Omundisia?" Yla asked, her head turned and a slight squint in her eye.

"I am not sure."

"I only ask because, well…" Yla drew a soft breath and crossed her arms, though she still kept her eyes on Cynkz. "Any goal worth pursuing requires sacrifice. Especially if you want anything done in a timely manner."

"Ah, I am in no rush." He didn't mean to cut her off again, but his response nearly leapt out of him. "I am more than willing to stay in Potarium for the foreseeable future. Perhaps after some time has passed, and things have cleared up with the Royal Court, I could do good there—"

"Just a hypothetical," Yla interrupted Cynkz, though she broke eye contact and rubbed her chin. "What if you had to sacrifice Potarium? Would you be willing to give up Potarium to reach Omundisia? To achieve a greater good?"

I guess the interrogation is not over yet…

"No, of course not," Cynkz said. "I see no reason to sacrifice anything or anyone in the name of my own goals."

She continued to rub her sharp chin, yet her eyes remained locked on Cynkz. Somehow, the more he spoke with her the less he understood about her. He could only think back to Foa's words about their sister being different, odd even, yet he was ill-prepared for this. The thought of speaking with the sisters all together eased his worries a bit. Surely they could enlighten him on some things and open Yla up a bit.

"Well then," Yla said, brushing herself off. "If you wouldn't mind waiting here a moment, I'm going to go get someone to help me carry all of this hair. It is dreadfully heavy."

"I could help you," Cynkz said. He stepped forward, about to kneel down and pick up some of the dark strands, but Yla stopped him.

"No, Cynkz, that is quite alright," she said. "I think you've done more than enough. Just rest for the time being."

"Oh, alright then," Cynkz said. He stood up and looked back at Yla. "And thank you, Yla, for getting me out of that cell and accepting me here. You picked me up at a particularly low point in my afterlife."

"Think nothing of it, Cynkz," Yla said. She promptly moved past Cynkz and walked through the door, shutting it quickly behind her.

He thought about their conversation, and how odd she was, but couldn't make sense of any of it. He looked down at the sea of glistening dark strands as they laid loosely on top of the maroon carpet. His head felt light, not just physically, but as the surreal image of his long-standing braid sitting lifelessly on the floor burned into his mind. It still bothered him to have to part with his hair but focused on what forms he could take to replace it until it grew back. A bit of shape-shifting—before presenting himself to others—could be fun. Though he did wish for a mirror to look into, so he could see the extent of his new style. Alas, he would just have to wait for Yla's.

Finally, he heard footsteps approaching from outside. *That must be her,* he thought.

Cynkz stepped carefully over the hair on the floor and walked briskly to the door, figuring it would be good manners to greet Yla and whoever else she brought to assist. Before he could reach the brass handle, the door flung open!

A flash of something heavy came for his head, and Cynkz was out cold. He had returned to darkness, once again.

CHAPTER 22

EVEN AFTER HIS MIND RETURNED, THE darkness maintained its hold of his senses. He could feel that he was being restrained. Each wrist was clasped within a dusty, cold bracelet. He tried to move, only to be met with the jostling of chain links clinking against one another. He could feel that he was kneeling, or perhaps had been pushed down in some way. His head hung low, and his chest lurched forward. The chill of stale cavern air brushed past his exposed body. He had been stripped of much of his clothing, and his hair draped loosely over his neck like an itching threaded curtain.

Something within his gut felt heavy, unsettled, as if a caustic liquid were constantly trying to worm its way out. He took in his first breath, and all that followed was pain. The air seemed to only push whatever was inside him back to the center of his gut and stirred the substance into a frenzy. Coughing made it worse, yet whenever he could feel something coming up and into his throat, it stopped, and quickly slunk back into him.

All of this, and yet he remained in darkness. He could feel his eyes were open but couldn't feel anything obstructing them. He tried to lash out, but the chains stopped him. The movement caused the noxious fluids within him to grind against his innards, forcing him to cough, pushing the substance up, before settling back at his core, and thus the process would repeat. The cycle continued several times before the bustling of feet against the floor caught his ear. It was enough to get him to focus on something other than his infected state of being. Several voices grew closer. He tried to focus but couldn't recognize any of them, except for one.

"Ah, Lady Yla, he's finally awake," Harquin said.

"How interesting," Yla said. "I didn't think much of you, Cynkz, when you were so easily knocked unconscious, but then we started pumping you with poison and sedatives. Do you have any idea how much of the stuff we had to waste before it started having any effect on you at all?"

Cynkz was unresponsive. In truth, he couldn't do much beyond painfully and weakly cough as he struggled to breathe.

Yla continued. "A mere flask of the concoction would put down the mightiest of beasts. A few drops would have driven a normal po blind and mad, and their insides would have spilled out on the floor before them within minutes. I don't know who or what you are, but I'm impressed."

"Yla," Harquin said, his footsteps ringing out as he walked over to her. "There's little time for this. You need to get moving. The others are waiting in position for your command."

"I know, Harquin," Yla said.

He couldn't see her, but he could feel her looking down her nose at him with the sort of disdain one would hold for a pest.

"I suppose I could inform you about Tuco, or 'Tucorio,' as the idiot liked to call himself. It only took a bit of coaxing to get him talking. He mentioned your strange conversation with the priest and a puppet. He also mentioned you performing some sort of 'magic' behind his back to give him gruel, and of course, there was talk about a certain thread…"

Cynkz grit his teeth. He tried to lift his head to look Yla in the eye, a pointless gesture, as he had neither the strength nor the vision to do so.

She continued. "Ah, that got a reaction out of you, did it? Well, don't worry about Tuco telling anyone. Once we got what we needed from him, we tossed him into the nearest pit. He's probably still falling as we speak. But the thread… I can see why my love would want such a thing. It seems powerful, ephemeral. I dare not touch it myself. I saw what it did to the others who tried to handle it. Even Nidan went mad the moment he grasped it. The stubborn mule. For now, it will have to sit on that desk over there looking pretty. If it's that important, we can come back for it later—"

"Yla," Harquin said, interrupting her. "He doesn't need to know…"

A tense moment of silence sat heavily between the two. Cynkz could only imagine what kind of glare Yla must have given Harquin.

She said to Cynkz, "I suppose I could tell you who it was that I lost, considering it is your material that will finally allow me to tear down those wretched flags and allow us to summon him. Finally, after literal eons, I'll be reunited with my true love, Eshra'Tel! We will finally be together again, and I will bear many powerful, dark children for him, and the universe will be ours. We will be free, once and for all, and we will finally be able to make something of this poor mess of an existence. And it's all thanks to you, Cynkz. Maybe he'll leave a few poor souls behind, so you won't be entirely alone once we're gone."

Cynkz struggled, pulling in vain at the chains holding him. He was acting almost purely on emotion. He couldn't even think or focus well enough to transform. His blindness, and the fact that he was sure they were underground, only made the prospect that much more difficult to consider. He felt just as powerless as he did when he fell into Eshra'Tel.

"I'd have thrown you into the nearest pit as well," Yla said, "but I don't fully know what it is you're capable of. For all I know, you'd merely fly out of it, or something like that. You mentioned before, about having nightmares about Eshra'Tel? Well, I too have dreamed of him. Every now and then he speaks to me in a dream and will share important information with me. He warned me of a strange newcomer, and of something amazing in their possession. I had hoped you would be more honest with me, Cynkz. But… I suppose we all have things we'd prefer to hide. Not that it matters now. Harquin will see to it that the rest of your stay in Potarium does not conflict with us."

"I'm looking forward to the rest of our time together," Harquin said. "I haven't had a good outlet in too long."

"Good, good," Yla muttered. "Keep him sedated and secured. Once we break open that gaudy orb in the sky, we'll stop by for you and the thread, Harquin."

"Of course, Lady Yla. What about Nidan and the others who went mad touching the thread?"

"We'll round them up as well. Eshra'Tel will take care of everything once he's here, don't worry."

Her light footsteps receded out of earshot. Harquin's heavier steps began to move around. It was hard to tell what he was doing, but Cynkz could make out the occasional sounds of leather and metal trinkets being gathered and moved around. He didn't want to imagine the tools, if they were tools, Harquin needed for his current task. After a time, he heard his footsteps approaching. The sharp screech of rusted metal being pulled and turned filled the room. It finished with a mighty thump. The footsteps were now unbearably close. He could feel Harquin moving to his side, and then behind him, and the sound of metal trinkets and leather being placed down tickled his ear.

"I owe you a lot, Cynkz. Truly I do. We all do, in a way," Harquin said over his shoulder as he continued digging through his tools. "This place—Potarium—it is dreadful. If it's not the heavy hand of the oppressive huum 'protecting' us, it's having to constantly keep up appearances for the simple, good po of the city."

The rustling of unknown materials stopped. Cynkz felt the sharp sensation of Harquin's hand lifting his head up to look at him.

"The poison's effect still seems to be going strong. Good, good."

Harquin let go of Cynkz's head and returned to his tools. Cynkz tried to exert himself, to breathe in more deeply, perhaps to muster enough strength to transform into something, anything, that would help him escape. All that greeted him was the same sensation of his insides and his throat filling with what felt like a burning acid.

Harquin continued. "It was odd. I could feel something was off the first time I placed my hand on your shoulder. It was during the show you almost made a mockery of. For a brief moment, I could feel... freedom. I could, in a small way, let go, and grip something unrestrained, and I was allowed to squeeze something so tightly it hurt."

Harquin could be heard moving again, though the silence between his footsteps was filled with something heavy being dragged alongside him.

"And here we are, once again—"

Snap!

A biting sting dragged across Cynkz's exposed back. The pain was enough to move him, but only for a moment, and just as quickly he was forced to return to his state of torpor.

"My whip is made from beast hair, and its tip possesses some of the same poison we injected into you. A bit of beast blood, sand from the desert, and a few nightshades we grow specifically here in the underground, for just such an occasion—"

Snap!

"Those idiots in Potarium... None of them bothered to ask how or why I kept so many beasts. I suppose as long as they were entertained—" *Snap!* "—they didn't care. Mindless. Worthless, the lot of them. 'Ynette' was the only po I met with true ambition! The fire of a living soul!"

Snap!

"She too couldn't stand the idea of just sitting here, wasting away an eternity keeping ourselves distracted—"

Snap!

"No goals!"

Snap!

"No purpose!"

Snap!

"Nothing to look forward to!"

Snap!

"Nothing but a constant reminder that we are all, in fact, dead..."

Harquin finally paused. Cynkz could hear him breathing heavily not too far behind him. Between the acid in his throat, and his back feeling as though it were on fire in great lines singeing deep marks into his flesh, he felt as though he couldn't take advantage of the moment of reprieve.

"Our world is gone. We have been rendered infertile, yet few care, because they get to sit comfortably in this glorified playpen and watch someone like me dance like a fool for their amusement."

Cynkz struggled, but eventually caught his breath. Harquin waited patiently for his heavy panting to settle.

"It's funny, really," Harquin continued. "I'm often asked how I am so proficient at conjuring new forms of entertainment. The dark truth is it's incredibly easy, once you realize that most po are stupid, simple things, hardly above the very beasts they clamor for during my shows! Case in point—"

Snap!

"How simple and naive you are. You thoughtlessly attempted to ingratiate yourself to your betters, and where did it get you?"

Snap!

"Locked away like a rat."

The rustling of leather being dragged along the grimy floor and into the air stopped. For a moment, Cynkz could hear Harquin breathing, finally exhausting himself. He tried to lean forward in an attempt to rest himself just a bit, yet the action was in vain as his gut acted up again. It felt as if a knife had been thrust into his core, and his back shot up straight.

Harquin continued. "I figured something was different about you. I figured you may eventually be useful in some way. As soon as I was able to break away from the nobility and inform Yla about you, she was more than intrigued."

Snap!

"She started getting her hopes up, wanting desperately for you to be the key to finally breaking free."

Snap!

"We figured you would be desperate for freedom, after rotting in a cell in heaven for a while, but she was surprised once she realized how obedient you were—"

Snap!

"Like a dog! Just as simple and mindless as the worthless hordes I have been forced to dance for!"

Snap!

"Yet… You hardly needed to do much of anything to make waves. You wash up on our shores, immediately get the red carpet treatment from a most beloved holy man—"

Snap!

"You manage to get *my* attention, Potarium's attention, the Royal Court's attention. Even Yla's attention."

Snap!

Snap!

Snap!

"Despite everything, your body is proving to be… frustratingly resilient. No matter how many times I strike you, you hardly bleed. That, combined with how much poison we've pumped into you… There was hardly enough of the stuff left for me to coat my whip! The beast blood used as a base for the concoction doesn't come cheap, you know."

The ground shook, and heavy tremors lumbered against the far walls of the underground cavern. They sounded impossibly distant, yet the handful of metal trinkets Harquin brought with him trembled, clinking against one another discordantly.

"This is it, then. The end is almost upon us. And a new beginning is but a stone's throw away, no doubt. Finally, we'll be free, and the few po among us who are worth a damn will finally be able to determine their own path. No longer will I have to dance and cheer like a show monkey for worthless po!"

Cynkz braced himself for another strike, but nothing came. He could feel Harquin waiting, leering at him from the dark.

"You were apparently a jester, once upon a time, no?" Harquin asked. "So you at least have some understanding of the pain of being forced to galivant around on command. But what are you, really? A farm boy? A horse tamer? A courtier? A spy? A realm traveler? A... heh, a munder conqueror? A friend for mun and po alike? Or... are you merely a fool?"

The sharp squeeze of Harquin gripping his whip's handle tightly, perhaps too tightly, stood out among the low, soft sounds of cave walls trembling below distant explosions. Cynkz could hear Harquin breathing again. He was trying to hide his waning endurance, it seemed.

"Whatever you are," Harquin continued, "you are truly unique, Cynkz. You of all po should know the pain of standing out. To be alone in the crowd, surrounded by other supposedly kindred souls, yet without a true, relatable kinship to rest upon. To be so painfully ripped apart from the audience whilst being tied to it, dependent on it! It's torture, isn't it?!"

Cynkz could hear Harquin slowly moving toward him as he spoke. The time between each step seemed to grow, and each step seemed to be more deliberate than the last.

"To be a jester is to court the attention of everyone around you. To play the fool, to be the life of the party! Even when you would rather be doing anything else. Even for those you despise... I can relate to that pain, but there is one significant difference between us: I understand the relationship in full. I know better and as such, I am capable of achieving better! But you? A naive, bumbling po traipsing through the world like a lost puppy? You merely exist to work for your better, to dance beneath your king, whomever they may be at any given time. That is where the mindless, such as you, belong—and that is where you shall remain—forever!"

The rumbling walls began to quake. Loose stone could be heard cracking and clashing against itself. The bars of the prison cell shook with each violent rupture. For a time, they happened so frequently Harquin didn't have the space to speak fully. Eventually, the tremors settled, allowing an uneasy silence between the two.

"It's strange," Harquin said. "I finally have a real outlet, and yet it feels oddly unsatisfying. Perhaps it's no fun having a one-sided conversation."

Cynkz interrupted, as he spit out a meager cough. Harquin took notice and was intrigued it seemed, considering that he took the opportunity to quickly move forward and lend an ear to his victim.

"Hmm?" Harquin hummed.

Cynkz mustered all of his strength, lifting his head and parting his lips, both of which felt like great anchors weighing him down. He finally drew in a pale breath, and whispered, "You … ungrateful … child…"

He couldn't see it, of course, but he could sense Harquin's pent up rage overflow. He could hear him shaking, gritting his teeth, and gripping his whip impossibly tight.

"You *dare* to call *me* a child?!" Harquin screamed. "I'll show *you* who the child is! You worthless—"

Cynkz heard Harquin pulling back his thin arm to prepare another strike, yet the blow didn't come. Something felt wrong, as an instant warm wind rushed between the two. Harquin was taken aback, enough so that he took several anxious steps away once he realized his trusted whip was gone.

"What?" Harquin muttered. "But how—"

The shadows began to giggle and cackle. Warm winds trickled from the dark corners of the room, and dozens of tiny footsteps began to move forward. They were surrounded by none other than a group of short scruffy imps!

One imp in particular pushed his way forward, practically drooling warm fire. It burned so hot even Cynkz could feel it singeing the tips of the tiny hairs on his exposed body.

The heat receded, only for a moment, long enough for a familiar husky voice to call out.

"Who… are you?!" Fiddle screamed. "What are you doing to Cynkz?! You know what, screw it! Hold him down so I can burn him!"

"Agh!" Harquin recoiled, trying desperately to push past the small warm bodies filling the room. The air filled with countless little bodies laughing and cackling as they grouped together and swarmed Harquin. He cried out in agony as they clawed and scratched. Finally, Harquin was forced to the ground with a mighty thump. He could be heard desperately dragging his limbs across the grainy dungeon floor as he tried to break free, but it was in vain.

The giggling settled, and Fiddle heaved himself into the air to draw in a great breath. The heat was immense enough that the other imps whimpered a bit, perhaps worrying for their own safety.

"No! No!" Harquin shrieked.

Cynkz was finally able to collect himself and took his first unhindered breath. Slowly the darkness gave way to blurred vision, and he could just barely make out the shapes of those moving around him. He witnessed as Fiddle finally spit out a great fireball that hurled itself toward the restrained po. In a final effort, Harquin kicked as hard as he could and pushed himself to the side and away from the imps holding him. A few childish cries and shrieks followed as the flaming orb collided with the ground. Harquin's cries blended with the violent rush of flames dispersing against the ground. He could be heard whimpering just to the side of the blast, now curled and writhing in pain.

"Ugh, I missed," Fiddle said. "Hold him again."

"No! Get away from me, you stupid muns!" Harquin kicked himself up and swiped a mangled, charred hand in front of him. Countless bits of blood and blackened flesh flew out, coating much of the room. Several of the imps recoiled as they tried to deflect the substance. Even Fiddle caught some of the debris as it splattered against his body and face. This gave the frightened man enough space to barrel his way forward past the small horde of imps. His frantic steps could be heard trailing off beyond a door and down a hall, along with the cackles and screeches of the dozens of imps that flew after him. Instead of giving chase, Fiddle quickly lowered himself and took hold of his friend, grasping at the chains on Cynkz's wrists.

"Cynkz, hold on! I'll get you free in just a second," Fiddle said as he hurried about. He looked at a short stand with dozens of shining trinkets laid messily on its top. He darted over and rustled through them and found a heavy key ring. He moved in such a hurry that he struggled to place each key into the steel clamp as he attempted to find the correct one. Finally, a weighty clink snapped the air and Cynkz's arm could fall and rest. Fiddle rushed to the other side and repeated the gesture, moving quickly enough to catch Cynkz before he fell over.

"Cynkz, what happened?!" Fiddle cried out. "I leave for five minutes and everything starts falling apart, and I find you like this. Can you move? How are you feeling?"

"Feeling… better…" Cynkz muttered through a pained half-smile.

"Geez, they took your hair, and—Wait!" Fiddle caught himself mid-sentence, nearly dropping his friend to the floor. "The thread! Where is it? Pops said he noticed a bunch of weird po were touching it."

Cynkz merely groaned and curled forward, leaning on the imp's tiny arms.

"Cynkz? Are you alri—"

The onslaught of fluid and bile cooled the warm charred floor. Fiddle recoiled up and back, giving his friend space to let loose his innards.

"Ugh! Gross… You know," Fiddle continued, "normally you're so noble and uptight looking. It's kinda nice to see you're not so different from the rest of us!"

After the immediate rush of blood to his head, Cynkz's senses settled onto something one could consider tolerable. He still couldn't see, but he could move at least, even if minimally.

"Fiddle…" Cynkz mumbled. "The thread, is it here?"

"Yep! Hold on, I'll go grab it."

Fiddle rushed past the cell door and brought back the shining sliver of light. He put a small, clawed hand on the jester's shoulder, and with the other placed the thread into Cynkz's hand. Cynkz's darkened vision was slowly taken up by a growing light. His head grew light, and a new, invigorating surge of energy coursed through him. He could see traces of faint images coming into view. Before they could come into full focus however–

"Bleurgh!"

Cynkz began to vomit once again. It was the first time a vision had been interrupted. He didn't know whether to be annoyed or amused at the notion. His eyesight finally returned, though hazed. He was just happy to be able to see again. As he continued to relieve himself, Fiddle looked on, shaking his head.

"Ugh, I don't know what color to call that stuff coming out of you," Fiddle said. "It's like a weird, shimmering yellowy-emerald. Then when it hits the ground it's all like—"

"That'll do, Fiddle," Cynkz said, breathing heavily, but smoothly, for the first time in what felt like an eternity.

"Hey! You sound alright now. Can you move? Everything is rumbling and exploding. I'd rather not stay underground."

"Y-yes. Just… Give me a second…"

Cynkz looked around and found the thread, half-covered in bile. He picked it up, then himself, as he leaned against a nearby wall, breathing as deeply and thoroughly as he could manage. The stale cavern air was not ideal, but it was good enough for the time being.

"Eww, you got spittle on the thread!" Fiddle cried out. "I'm not touching that thing ever again."

Cynkz's deliberate breathing was interrupted by several harsh chuckles. Once fully upright, he waved his hand and covered himself in colorless smoke, only to emerge in his cloak and hat of old.

"Going back to the old look, huh?" Fiddle said. "It looks kinda weird without the giant braid flapping around behind you."

"Fiddle... I found Yla..."

"What?!" Fiddle was so taken aback he nearly threw himself to the ground. "W-where is she?! Can she help? Maybe she knows what—"

"No, Fiddle. She was the one who locked me in here. She used me, and then betrayed me. And now—"

The ground and walls shook. The two looked up and waited for the trembling to settle.

"Yla... She was looking for a method to bypass the great huum," Cynkz continued. "She used me as a means to weaken the protective barrier shielding Potarium."

"But... why?" Fiddle asked.

"She wants to summon her lover ... Eshra'Tel."

"What?! There's no way!" Fiddle, once again shocked beyond belief, this time nearly threw himself into a wall as he reacted. "Pops would never let that happen! How would she do such a thing?! Though, we didn't need help from pops to get here this time, me and the other imps, I mean. Maybe she really does have the means to do it."

"I do not know, but we need to return to the surface, and get help wherever we can."

"Wait," Fiddle drifted over, placing a small claw on Cynkz's arm. "You're in no condition to be doing anything. You just got finished vomiting all over the floor, and you still look sickly."

"I am fine, Fiddle." Cynkz shrugged his shoulders and drew in a much needed breath. His gut still felt wrought with fire and heavy fluid, but he could move. "We need to go. Once outside, I can lead us to the surface. We have no time to lose."

CHAPTER 23

D EEP WITHIN THE DESERT, A SMALL mound of bleached white sand began to shift. After a few bangs of a hand against metal, a dark hatch emerged, and two souls emerged from the sterile opening. The dark forms flew out and up into the sky. What was normally a burning bright blue now resembling a muddled, overcast dark gray, though not a single cloud could be seen.

"It wasn't this dark the last time I was here," Fiddle said. "It looks weird. It's the middle of the day! And there are no clouds! What gives?"

"It feels good to get some fresh air," Cynkz said.

A distant echo boomed through the air. The two jolted toward the source but not much could be seen from where they were beyond the marble in the sky reflecting countless pillars of smoke. Under the gray light, both the sands and the sky blended together into a messy haze. Without a second thought, Cynkz leaned himself forward and began to dash through the air toward the city. Fiddle followed behind.

"I mean, it's just a bunch of po causing trouble, right?" Fiddle said. "It shouldn't be that difficult to handle—"

Another explosion nearly shattered the air around them, harsh enough that Cynkz and Fiddle paused. As the echo settled, the ground itself began to rumble and shake. The shifting sands appeared like waves in the ocean as they were forced to ebb and flow unnaturally. The once windless desert seemed intent on blowing the two souls away, whipping itself into a powerful frenzy. The overcast gray in the sky grew nearly black. Whatever light the orb in the sky reflected drained into darkness. These same lights appeared to drip and swirl below into a singular point. The energy quickly collapsed into itself, and with a final ear-piercing crack of the air, a new form appeared beneath the orb.

A new, impossibly dark sphere sat in front of the once glistening marble in the sky. Its size was such that it nearly consumed the horizon, and its presence defied logic in a way similar to the apostles in Dulrot. Threads of smoke and light appeared to listlessly sway around the orb, as if the twisting of physics disallowed anything nearby to hinder it. Speckles of faint lights drug slowly through the air and into the dark orb.

It took a moment of thought and squinting for the two to realize what it was.

"Po! Those are po souls being pulled into Eshra'Tel!" Fiddle shrieked. "Cynkz, we have to go! Dad can't leave Munderworld! There's nothing we can do here."

"No!"

POTARIUM

Cynkz's response caught the imp off-guard, enough so that he staggered.

Fiddle grit his sharp teeth, then snapped back. "W-what do you plan on doing? What can you do against Eshra'Tel, of all things?! Only my dad is powerful enough to deal with him, and he's bound to the bottom of Munderworld, thanks to this place's 'Creator.'"

"And where exactly will we run to, Fiddle?" Cynkz said, his own frustration coming through a furrowed brow. "There is naught but sand and desert out here. They could chase us for an eternity, if they so chose."

"Well, they might not! Maybe Eshra'Tel will get what he wants from Potarium and leave. This city is not our responsibility, anyway. Running head-first into oblivion won't solve anything!"

"It *is* my responsibility, Fiddle! This is in large part my own fault. Once again, my thoughtless whims are causing trouble. The po showed me kindness and had no issue accepting me—"

"And where did that get you? Locked away in a cell, *twice!!*"

Cynkz looked away, then returned to look directly into his companion's beady, tearful eyes. "My mistakes are my own, Fiddle. I moved forward, hoping to find answers regarding my past, and in a small way, I did. I committed an atrocity back in life, and its effects have followed me all the way here. But I have learned that we all have past traumas and regrets and sins. What defines us now, more than anything, is what we choose to do moving forward.

"If I merely run away, and let my mistakes ravage Potarium, what would that make me? I would be no better than Yla, who abandoned her sisters, abandoned her duties in Munderworld, and is willing to sacrifice heaven itself for her own selfish gains! I refuse to run, and I refuse to allow myself the easy way out. We sat about aimlessly for eons, only to be led forward by our whims. We cannot do that anymore, Fiddle. We have to take responsibility, if not for ourselves, then for those we share this existence with. The imps need you to stand strong, and the po need me to help stave off the chaos I unfortunately helped bring to Potarium. I *am* going to Potarium, and I *will* confront Eshra'Tel. I do not know what will happen, but I must try."

A heavy silence sat between the two, heavier than the frenzied dark winds surrounding them. Cynkz remained resolute, and Fiddle sat speechless, a rare thing for him. Finally, Fiddle chuckled and smirked, a good enough excuse as any to break eye contact.

"I know that look." Fiddle shrugged. "You've made up your mind, and nothing's gonna stop it. Welp, I may not like it, but I know that you're right, Cynkz. Besides, if I could follow you through Munderworld, then this should be nothing, right?"

Cynkz's expression softened into a smile of his own. He couldn't help but relax his shoulders and shrug back. "What's an adventure without a little risk, eh?"

The two took a deep breath and began to fly toward the crumbling mountain. As they drew close, they could see more of the chaos being wrought upon Potarium.

The great flags had been toppled, countless souls and debris filled the air, and the dark eye of Eshra'Tel nearly eclipsed the sky itself.

"So, how are we gonna do this?" Fiddle said.

"In truth," Cynkz said, hesitating a moment as his mind pondered the oncoming reality, "I have no idea. I just have to come up with something."

"Well, you're pretty good at coming up with plans on the fly! Perhaps our victory is assured!"

"I do not know, Fiddle... A simple 'plan' or idea may not be enough this time."

CHAPTER 24

DARKNESS REIGNED SUPREME FOR the first time in heaven. Great winds pushed violent waves back and forth into the dark ocean, which inevitably and constantly crashed back into Potarium's shore. The city, once a shining, cream-coated beacon that formed a harsh line against the dark water seemed to be blending in with its borders.

The once pristine and meticulously bricked streets cracked and crumbled, loud enough to nearly overcome the noise of the fierce winds colliding against every exposed surface. Every golden arch, silver lacing of fence, dark oak and shining flag post whipped about to the point of breaking, or if it had already broken, was being dragged into the air to swirl around and be sucked into the black orb that consumed the sky.

The smooth edges of Potarium's many homes, the towering points of its many cathedrals were all broken, jagged, and every finely crafted end and piece of architecture turned to rough and uneven edges revealing the coarse innards of their construction. Bright-coated horses and frenzied canines and felines scurried in all directions, desperate to find cover from the calamity. The po were just as disorganized. Those who had not yet been pulled into a maelstrom were diving into whatever open shop or building or crevice they could find for refuge. Perhaps odder, the po were quiet. Rather than constant screams and cries many were shocked, unsure of how precisely to process the chaos before them. Pure instinct seemed to be the only thing moving anyone forward.

Another oddity was the stream of feathers filling the air. Most of the hummingbirds were nowhere to be seen, presumably absorbed into the dark orb or having fled. Their colors were muted as they were over-whelmed by Eshra'Tel's great shadow swallowing the world below.

As more debris crumbled and was flung about, the cries and screams of imps could be heard, similar to a chorus beneath a dark symphony. They seemed to be the only entities capable of fully resisting Eshra'Tel's influence, but only barely. Every now and then a partic-ularly large piece of debris would fall and roll down the mountain, tearing apart everything in its path. These were the only moments the imps would go quiet as they desperately looked on in awe, making sure to avoid being crushed.

Despite the destruction, one structure stood tall. As if it were a final, defiant symbol against the onslaught, the golden tower, the great Hand of Po was starkly unimpressive without the overwhelming heavenly light of the great orb to expand its edges with an oth-erwordly burning radiance. The dark sphere slowly inched toward the tower, and the world around it shook, the air rumbling as Eshra'Tel pushed the world out of its way as it continued on its single-minded mis-sion toward the barrier in the sky.

The great eye finally stopped several hundred feet from the tower. It was close enough to put some sort of ethereal weight on the structure. Deep cracks began to slither their way up the dim golden form. The air felt as if it were quaking. Prolonged rumbling gave way to stumbling booms as chunks of the golden tower col-lapsed into itself. Before any glittering pieces of the once mighty structure could fall to the ground, the wind picked up, and forced the debris to split apart and roll away from Eshra'Tel to be flung down the mountain, crushing everything in its path. The sound of golden boulders digging deep paths into the crum-bling city drowned out the screams of the remaining po and imps that dashed about in fear.

Two small shadows made their way across the shaded sky just in time to witness the chaos.

"It's so loud!" Fiddle screamed. "All this wind and—"

"Kadd!" Cynkz cried out.

"Huh?!"

"We have to find Kadd! Now!"

"Sounds like as good a place to start—"

Before the imp could finish his sentence, Cynkz was in a mad dash through the air just above the city. It was difficult to discern any one part of Potarium from the next. The only thing that stood out were the golden boulders slowly making their way haphazardly down the mountain.

One particularly large and jagged piece settled not too far from a familiar cathedral in the distance. Cynkz immediately recognized it as the same one Kadd took him to when he first arrived. That was a good enough landmark for Cynkz to find the rest of the way to Kadd's home. Unfortunately, as he neared the area, all that sat before him were massive pieces of rock and broken concrete. He eventually found piles of the familiar dark red shingles that once formed Kadd's roof sitting in front of what was once his friend's humble home. Cynkz paused long enough for Fiddle to catch up.

"Cynkz!" Fiddle called out.

Cynkz remained unresponsive, keeping his attention on the destroyed home.

"Cynkz," Fiddle continued. "Is he… Is he here?"

"I do not see any bodies," Cynkz said.

"Well, Kadd once told me the temples are supposed to be safe havens. Maybe he's—"

A new voice broke through the air. It sounded like a po woman crying for help. Cynkz whipped his head toward the sound and instinctively flew toward it. Fiddle could hardly keep up, and he had to resort to flapping his little arms forward and back to give himself an extra boost, though it hardly helped.

Cynkz soon happened upon a half-dozen cloaked po breaking into a ruined home. They bore the same sand-colored hoods as Yla's assistant. Stranger still was that they were attempting to pull the helpless po out so they would be vulnerable to Eshra'Tel's winds!

The woman struggled and pulled and fought frantically, screaming all the while to yank herself free and back into the home. Without a second thought, Cynkz thrust himself down, and with all of his weight, bowled over the hooded figures. A couple of the hooded po were knocked out cold, and the remaining ones quickly picked themselves up and stared in fear. Before they could say anything, Fiddle drifted down, and that was enough to cause them to run away into the distant chaos. The woman ran back inside and wrapped her arms around another woman, an unconscious man, and three younger po who were all crying out. Their glowing bodies stood out brilliantly in the shade.

"What do we do?" Fiddle asked.

"Let's get them to a temple," Cynkz responded. "We can try to help however many po we can reach the temples and keep an eye out for Kadd."

"Alright then. I'll hang back a bit and let you do the guiding. They might be too scared to let an imp like me get too close, ya know?"

Cynkz drifted over to the po and spoke with them. Heads nodded, and finally Cynkz lifted the unconscious man to carry him out. He stayed low enough to the ground to lead the others forward. Fiddle stayed back and eventually followed behind, doing his best to appear benign. The two still conscious women seemed too worried and scared to even notice him, but surprisingly, the younger po looked at him more curiously than anything. Their pure, unaware expressions reminded him of his imp siblings, in a strange way.

Cynkz seemed to have enough presence to fend off fleeing animals as he essentially carved a way through the chaos. It was not long before the jagged tip of a massive fallen flag post could be seen jutting above the line of destroyed buildings. The po following Cynkz could be heard sighing in relief but were soon interrupted by more screams. It sounded as if someone was fighting. Cynkz immediately returned to the group to hand off the unconscious man to the two women. Again, Fiddle was too far away to hear anything, but soon enough Cynkz came over to speak with him.

"Fiddle! Watch them and lead them to the temple ahead. I'm going to go see what's going on," Cynkz said.

Fiddle merely nodded, and his friend flew off into the distance.

It only took Cynkz a moment to reach the front of the temple. It was merely a pile of crumbling stone, and many of its tall gleaming pillars were strewn about in the street. Hundreds of loose threads from the torn and fallen great flag filled the air. More shrieks echoed from within, prompting Cynkz to fly through the mess and into the flag yard.

There was a large group of po, most of whom seemed to be clinging to the edges of the yard in desperation. Two dozen hooded po scrambled about as they grabbed and held fleeing po. Further in, another small group tried to subdue a man in deep purple robes who flung a splintered piece of wood wildly, trying and failing to keep the others back.

Just as the hooded po descended on the man, Cynkz caught a glimpse of who it was.

"Kadd!" Cynkz cried out.

His scream was so loud that it broke past the howling winds and flying rocks. By the time all eyes were on him, Cynkz was flying to the center of the skirmish at full speed, his cloak whistling through the air like a feathered arrow. A massive burst of colorless smoke crashed into the ground, and from it emerged a giant, iridescent serpent. The serpent swirled around Kadd, its leathery hide forming a protective barrier for the man. The hooded po shrieked in fear and began to flee. The serpent whipped the full length of its body around and flung itself toward the fleeing henchmen.

He couldn't bring himself to eat anyone, of course, but Cynkz snapped his jaws loudly, and even scratched and bit a few of their legs to force them to leave. Before long, all that was left was the serpent, and several thin trails of blood burning crimson lines into the bleached sand. The serpent watched to ensure the coast was clear, and he slithered back into another cloud of smoke. The jester ran out of the smoke and toward his friend.

"Kadd!" Cynkz cried out again.

"Cynkz!" Kadd replied. "It's a pleasure to see you—*Unf!*"

Kadd nearly fell back, but Cynkz caught him just in time. The other helpless po who were hiding in the brush nearby emerged and slowly walked toward them.

"T-thanks, Cynkz," Kadd said. "I could have taken them, but thanks."

The two shared a warm smile. Just as Kadd gathered himself, Cynkz began to cough violently. Before Kadd could come over to try and comfort his friend, Cynkz let loose acidic fluid onto the ground.

Cynkz was finally able to calm himself down as he wiped his mouth the best he could.

"Sorry, Kadd," Cynkz said. "Just a little… poison…"

"What?!" Kadd cried out. "Poison?! How? Who would—"

"It was Yla. I found her. She tricked and betrayed me and started all of this."

"No... Why? I don't... After all that..."

Kadd was interrupted by the sight of a horde of imps slowly drifting into view. They were coming from the same direction as Fiddle and the group of po.

"By Paithos!" Kadd cried out.

"I think they are following Fiddle," Cynkz said.

"Ah... His siblings, I presume."

"Yes."

"They look quite scary when together like that."

Cynkz chuckled, then turned a shoulder toward Kadd. "Once you hear them speaking, you realize they're about as threatening as mischievous children—"

"Cynkz!" Fiddle called out, taking it upon himself to carry the unconscious man, with the help of a few other imps.

"Good work, Fiddle," Cynkz said. "I see you found others to help us."

"Of course!" Fiddle said, finally letting go of the man to rush ahead and greet Cynkz properly. "I saw some of 'em scrambling around and all I had to do was yell at 'em to come help. And Kadd! You're alright!"

Fiddle dove into Kadd's arms to give him the biggest hug his tiny arms would allow.

"Hey, Fiddle," Kadd said. "It's good to see you both are well. Or, well enough..."

"Cynkz figured it would be good to find you, and maybe we could think of a way to fix all of this."

"I appreciate it, I really do, but..." Kadd looked up at the sky; what was once a gleaming sheet of heavenly light was now reduced to malice and shadow. "I have no idea what we can do. Has Paithos abandoned us?"

Cynkz could feel the fluids within him building again. In an attempt to distract from the pain, he moved ahead and forced himself to speak.

"They managed to blow up the great flags," Cynkz said.

"Yes, but... That shouldn't be possible," Kadd replied.

"It... It's my fault..." Cynkz muttered.

"What? How?"

"Yla... She said she'd use my hair to form a medium to find a way to reconnect with the sisters. Instead, she used it for ... this..."

Kadd looked at Cynkz's back and was shocked when he noticed his massive braid was gone. He looked back to the remains of the wooden flag post, and then back to Cynkz.

"They were able to do all of this with just your hair?" Kadd said.

"Yes. The rumors of the hooded po sneaking about was true. They were exiles being led by Yla in a big settlement underground. They have access to a number of technologies beyond Potarium."

"Unbelievable..." Kadd muttered to himself. "But how did they bring about *that?*" Kadd threw up a thin arm to point at the calamity in the sky.

"Even pops was surprised," Fiddle said, drifting in beside the two. "One minute everything was peaceful and boring, then the next—*boom!* In a flash of dark light, Eshra'Tel was gone!"

"Yla mentioned she had been experimenting with mediums for ages," Cynkz continued, "and even said they could be used for summoning."

"This is unbelievable." Kadd rested his head in his hands and shook. "I don't even know what to think of any of this."

Cynkz looked ahead at the base of the destroyed flagpole. In between a mountain of jagged splintered wood and dull explosive powder, something sharp and shiny stood out. He squinted his sharp eyes and hastily walked toward it. He had to breathe heavily to keep himself upright as the harsh poisons coursing through him did their best to bring him down. Still, he managed to keep ahead of Fiddle and Kadd as they followed not too far behind him.

Cynkz let out a sigh of relief as he knelt down and began to dig through the broken pieces of oak, and finally lifted a meticulously carved, black stone. The medium seemed to defy logic, as dark as night yet somehow reflecting what little light it could beneath Eshra'Tel's shadow. It possessed a number of swirling, arcane symbols etched into each of its sides. A single thread of jet-black hair seemed to weave between several openings carved into the stone.

"A medium!" Kadd called out.

"It looks weird," Fiddle said.

"Look, there's more of them," Cynkz pointed down and pulled out several more of the hand-sized stones sticking out of the debris.

"They have huums carved into them, though I don't recognize any of those particular symbols," Kadd said as he lightly shrugged. "Is that your hair inside of them?"

"This whole thing is a mess," Fiddle said. "What are we supposed to—"

"Fiddle!" Another sharp, slightly husky voice called out from behind. More imps began to ask Fiddle for guidance. There wasn't much he could do beyond stammering over his words and scratching his head. He was just as lost as everyone else.

Fiddle quickly looked over to Cynkz for help, but the jester seemed lost in thought, staring at the dark mediums. He seemed to look at them for too long, prompting Fiddle to place a small claw on his friend's shoulder. They stared at the odd stones in Cynkz's hands.

"What are you thinking?" Fiddle asked. "Oh! Please tell me you have an idea!"

For a moment, Cynkz was unresponsive. He could hardly think, as the thread was furiously pulling down inside his pocket coat. The tickling sensation of the thread's twitching made him think of The Munder King, and how it helped guide him through Munderworld. The divine object had been unresponsive until now. What was it trying to tell him?

"I... I might..." Cynkz finally responded, though his voice seemed to lack any resolution as it tapered into a meek mumble.

"Great! What is it?"

Cynkz stood up and turned toward Kadd, the stones rustling around harshly in his pale palms. "What if... What if *we* used these?"

"What!?" Both Kadd and Fiddle seemed to recoil in unison, two minds reacting as one.

Cynkz continued. "What if we used these mediums ourselves? Perhaps we could open up a pathway long enough for The Munder King to reach through."

"I cannot believe this!" Kadd said, stamping his foot down, his fists clenched and his face pressed into a stern expression. "We huum for Him, and *only* Him, as in Paithos! The Creator himself! Our great Lord! To huum for anything less is-is-is heresy!"

"I mean..." Fiddle chimed in, scratching his tiny pointed chin with a tiny sharp finger as if he hadn't heard Kadd. "It might be possible. Pops can't leave Munderworld, but if we could open up some sort of connection, or at least start an opening, he could probably do the rest."

"No! I will not have it!" Kadd screamed. "It goes against every one of my teachings! It goes against Potarium's teachings! It goes against Paithos himself!"

Fiddle snapped, "Well, what else are we supposed to do?!"

"I don't know!" Kadd replied just as loudly. "But this can't be the way to do it! How blasphemous it is to chant holy huums f-for the dark lord himself?! I cannot imagine a greater insult to—"

Huff!

Cynkz keeled over in pain. The more still and silent he sat, the more the poison within him stirred. Fiddle immediately flew to rest a hand on his friend's sharp shoulder, and Kadd looked on, unsure of what to think.

The holy man turned around to see the many eyes of cowering po clinging to the remaining, broken walls and a horde of imps fluttering about, their faces looking as lost as that of unaccounted-for children.

Kadd looked up at the swirling mass of wind and rock and darkness, then to the many deep lines and debris embedded in the bleached sand that once marked Potarium's holiest ground. He rummaged through his mind, doing everything he could to think of another way, and yet he couldn't. He couldn't deny the imp's logic, and he couldn't deny that, if nothing else, Cynkz had a method of dealing with the calamity, and he did not.

Rage swelling from within nearly burst through Kadd's face, twisting his expression in harsh ways. Yet, before any emotions could break through, Kadd held himself back, and let loose a calm, if frustrated breath. His shoulders softened, and his eyes could be seen looking back and forth, as if searching for another answer, a justification, anything to make things easier on himself. Silence stood between them for only a moment before an answer finally did break through.

"Alright..." Kadd said. "Alright. We'll try it."

"Awesome!" Fiddle exclaimed, his newfound glee causing him to fling his small limbs in all directions. "So, how are we gonna do it?! Oh-ho-ho, this is gonna be cool!"

"We should..." Cynkz raised a hand to his chest, and patted it so a few more coughs could escape.

"Cynkz... You're still in terrible shape," Fiddle said. "You should go hide somewhere and rest."

"No!" Cynkz threw out an arm and pounded his fist into the sand. "I will not run! This is all my fault! I will assist, any way I can."

A harsh, bitter crackling in the wind tickled his ear. For a moment, the world was still. Everyone, po and imp alike, instinctively looked toward the sky, where the great marbled orb was hardly visible behind the dark eye. A soul-splintering shattering of glass ruptured through Potarium. The sound was so potent that those listening swore that their very hearts and minds were being ripped in two. The thunderous trickling of ethereal marble crumbling slowly settled back into the comparatively soft howling of mighty wind.

"That thing is really going to do it," Kadd mumbled. "It's going to break into Omundisia, dragging every poor soul with it…"

"I can… keep him distracted," Cynkz coughed.

"You can't do anything!" Fiddle cried out. "You're just gonna get yourself hurt, or worse, get dragged helplessly into Eshra'Tel."

Kadd shuffled over and knelt down, placing a hand on Cynkz's shoulder.

"Cynkz, what do you plan to do?" Kadd asked.

"I will confront… Eshra'Tel," Cynkz muttered. "I will keep him distracted with the thread… long enough for you and Fiddle to—"

Cynkz gripped his chest as he nearly expelled his heart from the excessive coughing.

"Cynkz, if you can, get to the ocean," Kadd said. "I don't know how long it will take, or what effect it may have on you, but it should heal you and get you in decent condition."

"I will," Cynkz said.

"The question I have is," Kadd continued, "who will be willing to huum into these… these dark mediums? Is it safe for po to do this…"

"Get the imps to do it," Cynkz said.

"What?! Imps?! Using his holy tongue? Madness! Do they even know how to huum?!"

"You're a good teacher, Kadd," Cynkz smiled, or at least he smirked. He was afraid to let out a chuckle, for fear that it would turn into coughing.

Fiddle finally released his hand to place both of them on his hips as he turned to Kadd. "We're really not so bad you know! Imps are quite nice once you get to know us."

"I see..." Kadd couldn't hold eye contact with Fiddle. He had grown fond of the creature, yet here he was chastising him like a child. He felt the slight tinge of shame in his chest as he held his head down low before Fiddle.

"Fiddle," Cynkz continued. "Lead the imps and keep Kadd and any other po you find safe. I'll hurry and heal up as soon as possible. I will do everything I can to keep Eshra'Tel in place. If you see the thread shining above..."

"Yeah, yeah, I know you've got this," Fiddle said through a thick, smarmy tone. "Just be careful, Cynkz, please."

"I'll be fine, Fiddle," Cynkz said. "Kadd can lead you to the temples. Try to get set up at each of them, get everyone you can to chant huums. Do not stop, no matter what. This may be our only chance."

"Of course," Fiddle said.

The two shared a nod, then Cynkz looked up to see Kadd smiling and nodding as well. With all of his strength, the jester pushed himself up. He drew a deep breath, and flung himself into the air, disappearing into the sky.

"This is crazy," Kadd whispered.

"Indeed, but what's an adventure without a little risk, eh?" Fiddle quipped.

"An adventure… Right."

CHAPTER 25

I T SEEMED THAT NO MATTER WHAT
Cynkz did, he couldn't settle into a tolerable state.
Staying still only brought on the stirring of poisonous
fluids, yet flying seemed more laborious than usual. He
could feel the full weight of his body dragging sluggishly through the air. His flight stuttered whenever he
coughed and wheezed, but a deep breath and a grit of
his teeth kept him elevated.

Cynkz was high enough above the many torn
buildings to catch a glimpse of the ocean in the distance. It was sufficient enough to lift his spirits, which
felt as heavy as stones in the ocean. Something else
he noticed as he made his way forward was an undercurrent of rumbling shaking the ground. The sound
was constant and instilled the feeling of having his
head constantly squeezed at the temples. Everything
else seemed to blend into noise: the howling wind,
the clacking of hooves, the barking and hissing and

desperate chirping, the crumbling of concrete and bending of metal, and the wild flapping of torn cloth. It was little more than a hellish cacophony.

At least, it was until he heard a shrill scream piercing the wind. It wasn't ideal, but it was enough to get his mind off of the pain of his internal affliction. He whipped his head down and could see the faint aura of a young po woman running through the street, with a single hooded figure chasing after her. Cynkz's insides felt as if they were burning, everything was telling him to hurry to the ocean, yet he couldn't. Something deeper compelled him to grit his teeth once more and dive toward the po in need.

The woman ran past several of the many large stones littering the street. She tripped over a deep crack in the road and fell to the ground with a weighty thump. She merely covered her head, fearing the oncoming steps of the hooded po reaching her. To her surprise, the clicking of footsteps immediately stopped, and a deep thud against a nearby wall caused her to raise her head and look behind her. She could see a sharp-hatted, cloaked man standing tall above the unconscious body of her assailant.

Cynkz walked over and offered a hand to the woman. Between a thick layer of tears that nearly covered her bright green eyes, she nodded, thanked him, and reached out. Cynkz quickly picked her up and flew off.

The woman shut her eyes tight and gripped.

Before she could process what was going on, she found herself being gently lowered at the once grand entrance of a dilapidated temple. She lightly tapped her feet to the ground and let go, giving herself room to catch her breath. Before she could turn around and thank her mysterious savior, he was gone.

For the first time in eons, Cynkz dreaded the thought of flight. It was as natural as walking to him, yet it felt as if he bore the weight of a massive jagged boulder on his back as he desperately tried to regain altitude. He wasn't coughing as much, though he had to keep his hands to his chest and breathe more deeply to stay focused. When a wave of pain hit him, he was forced to stop a moment to rest, and he nearly curled into a ball in midair. The sound of glass shattering and wood splintering beneath him caught his ear, and he was compelled to investigate. The sound seemed to garner the attention of a handful of imps wandering nearby. They looked lost, but they recognized Cynkz, and immediately flew over to him.

A half-dozen hooded po were gathered in front of a small shop that had been boarded up. Two of the hooded figures broke through the barrier of wooden boards and chairs that barricaded the front of the shop housing a small crowd of po. Their collective light burned intensely against the dark corner. Just as Yla's followers finally broke through the barricade, a massive burst of ashen colored smoke covered everything, and the weighty thumps of a sentinel's footsteps immediately settled behind them.

A quick gasp and several screams followed wind-shattering swipes of the tall, lanky, stone-like beast covered by the rags of a loose bleached robe. Hoods flew and bodies fell in a whirlwind of blows. Another gust of colorless smoke burst out, and Cynkz sat in the street as he clutched his chest. The little red and brown imps finally caught up and surrounded him, trying to help him up and comfort him.

"Hey, that was cool!" one said.

"Do it again! Do it again!" another cried out.

"Are you okay? Is that shapeshifting stuff really that hard for you?" a third muttered.

Cynkz took in another pained breath and stood straight.

"I need you guys to do me a favor," Cynkz said.

"Ooh! The imp lord has need of us!" one of them said.

Cynkz continued. "Look after the po in that shop. If the coast is clear, guide them to a temple, one of the buildings with a great big flag near it. Await further instruction from Fiddle if they happen by."

The imps gathered together and saluted, out of sync, of course. "Aye aye, mi'lord!"

Cynkz took a quick look inside the shop and greeted eyes with a crowd of frightened po staring back at him. He smiled, then turned and nodded to the imps, and flew off.

Flying wasn't getting any easier, but Cynkz took solace in the fact that he was finally nearing the dark ocean. What was once a thin, dark sliver of ocean on the horizon was taking up much of his view. From above, the many docks and piers stretching into the ocean appeared as thin spindly twigs, their splintered edges like frayed hairs on a limb. The dark waters were crashing with unforeseen force. A few of them broke off and drifted beneath the water.

The glint of collective light caught the corner of Cynkz's eye. He saw a small group of po hanging on to the edges of one of the piers, and they were slowly backing toward the water. The familiar hoods of Yla's men could be seen slithering their way up the pier toward the helpless po.

Cynkz couldn't tell if his growing anger was out of frustration from the seemingly constant interruptions, or if he was truly that bothered by seeing innocent souls being preyed upon, but either way, he didn't fight the urge this time. There was no other option in his mind.

Before the hooded henchmen could reach the po cowering at the end of the wooden dock, a great burst of ashen smoke blinded the group. From the smoke's center emerged a magnificent cat-beast, its fur like black needles, a form that represented a bull more than a feline, and a great, wide maw perfectly built for crushing its prey. A soul-piercing snarl emitted from the beast, and the frightened expressions of the hooded ones could be seen peeking out from the shade of their cloaks.

Yet, instead of running, they steeled themselves and, for the first time, brandished weapons. Long curved blades and knives shook ever so slightly in their grip. Cynkz took a slow step forward, hoping to deter the assailants. The hooded po followed suit, and took several small steps back, but they did not turn and run.

Why are they so hellbent on reaching these po? Cynkz thought to himself. *Is Yla truly that convincing? Are they so inspired that they would risk everything for her?*

A crack in the wooden boards broke the silence, and several hooded figures rushed forward, their dirtied blades glistening in the dim light of the realm. There was no time to think, only act and this reminded Cynkz why he hated fighting. Being forced out of the comfort of his own mind to thrash around was a horrible feeling to him. Still, he could not stand by and let these dangerous po prey on the weak.

Another crack of the wooden boards beneath them followed the extension of long beautifully curved claws. He was lost in the chaos as he threw his dark nails every which way, the dim lines of blood trails shining brilliantly against the shade. One by one, the hooded po were torn and tossed aside like debris into the water. The adrenaline was such that Cynkz couldn't tell if they were putting up much of a fight, or if they were managing to get any hits during the encounter.

That was until a frightened screech followed the cool sensation of metal being dragged across his bulky hind leg. The beast cried out with another ear-shattering roar, but again, Cynkz had no time to think. He whipped around and into another burst of gray smoke.

Immediately, rows of heavy thumps in the wooden boards followed the emergence of a massive wine-colored bull barreling forward. The po who had cut him, so frightened by the sight, dropped his blade and tried to turn and run, though there was literally nowhere for him to go but the ocean. Cynkz decided to oblige the fellow, and rammed his bulky, square head into the man. He couldn't tell if the shattering sound he heard was from the pier breaking beneath his weight or bones shattering within the victim. All that Cynkz noticed was the cloaked figure flying helplessly into the dark ocean, only to be dragged away by the raging waters.

For a brief moment, Cynkz felt triumphant. If his form would have allowed it, he would have smiled, if not for the immediate sensation of pain worming its way up his back leg. The beast cried out, then knelt into a final burst of smoke, leaving only the jester to grasp at his new wound.

Cynkz looked up and met eyes with a number of po still clinging to the split railing of the dock. His vision was beginning to grow hazy, and he couldn't make out any distinct features, save for their usual bright auras and the whites of their eyes revealing worried expressions. Cynkz smiled, taking solace in the fact that he at least did some good.

The winds began to pick up, and one particularly thin po woman could be seen flying up into the air and over the railing.

Before she could let out a shriek, Cynkz found himself lunging forward and grabbing the woman's hand. He was acting without thought, and only noticed he had successfully held onto the woman when he noticed the warm smudges of his own blood covering parts of her otherwise bright arm. Cynkz mustered all of his strength and dragged her back down, allowing her to get a good hold of the rails. Cynkz could feel himself collapsing. He would have fallen unconscious if not for the sharp pain of his head hitting the ground.

A single thought entered his otherwise blank mind in that moment: *Oww…*

The other po clawed their way over, desperately holding on to whatever they could as they huddled near Cynkz. The way they were holding onto each other made it look as if they were hugging.

"W-who are you?" one young man asked.

"I think I heard of him, he's that new guy who was…" another woman chimed in but stopped herself midsentence.

"It's… It's all my fault…" Cynkz muttered, hoping that the howling winds above would mask his meek utterances.

"What? How?" another asked. "You just saved us from those goons!"

"They are only here because… I messed up…" Cynkz responded.

"Even in all of this, you're helping us, and for that we thank you, stranger," another po added.

"I may be able… to… to fix all of this… But I do not know for sure…" Cynkz said.

The po looked at each other in disbelief, then back at Cynkz.

"C-can we help?" one meekly asked. "If we can do anything, just tell us."

"I can't… move very well…" Cynkz uttered. "I need to get to… the water… to heal, so I can fly up and confront… Eshra'Tel…"

He couldn't see it, but Cynkz could sense a fierce furrowing of brows above him.

"Eshra'Tel?" one po asked. "Who is that? Is it that … the thing in the sky?"

Cynkz felt drained and couldn't gather the strength to speak anymore. He could feel the poison within him thrashing about, not unlike the raging waters of the ocean, but he didn't feel ill. Perhaps he was growing delirious, through the poison and the blood loss and constantly exerting himself to transform. It seemed to finally be taking its toll.

Everything went dark. It was a similar feeling he had when he was stranded in the ocean. Yet, he could recall the warm hands grabbing onto him and lifting him up. He could also feel himself being dragged across a wooden surface, like the crew of the ship that first fished him out of the sea. He could hear the po he had just met yelling, and their feet scrambling about as they shifted their grip on the impossibly heavy stranger to push him along. The pain in his leg was the worst part. It felt as if his skin and bone and muscle were being pulled apart like clay. With every heave, his body felt heavier, and heavier, until—nothing.

Cynkz felt weightless, and in that brief moment, he parted his lids just enough to catch a glimpse of the world around him. His eyes met those of the po on the pier, the whites of their eyes revealing strange expressions of worry, of fright, but also hope. As his back hit the water, the world went dark again, but this time only in a hazy sense. The water beneath the surface felt surprisingly calm, enough so that he could fully focus on the faint lights of the souls who had helped him digging through the murky layer above him. One by one, he witnessed their lights being swept away into nothing. For a moment, he could take a much needed rest in the all-encompassing darkness.

Cynkz couldn't tell if he was awake or if he was sleeping. His body felt detached, as if he was looking at his form from a far-off corner of the abyss. Yet, he could see nothing in front of him. Thoughts slowly began to seep into his mind as he tried to remember things, desperately grasping in the dark for something to hold on to, to remind him that he still existed.

His mind returned to the poem. He was so used to reciting it nearly every night, that only now did he realize it had been far too long since he went over the cryptic verse:

> *Every star*
> *Near and far*
> *Waits for us*
> *To just*
> *Reach out*
> *And accept them…*

Thoughts of the poem forced images of the woman who first shared it with him into his mind. He could distinctly remember the cool brush of soft skin running along the side of his face as she gazed into him. Two bright blue piercing lights cut into his soul like daggers.

Orilay…

But now he had a fuller name! Something greater to add to his memory.

Orilay Burlowesque…

The king, someone who had, according to his memories, once seen great things in him, rightfully hated him. What damage he must have caused this poor family, and who knows how many other people, because of his selfish actions.

For eons, King Burlowesque must have held onto sadness and sorrow, the loss of his only daughter. Whatever children she may have had, whatever lineage they could have given the future, all gone in an instant, thanks to his own selfish desire. Even now, the thought of Orilay suffering somewhere in Munderworld must be weighing heavy on the king's mind. Even now, half-dead and sinking into the ocean, she was on Cynkz's mind as well. He was beginning to understand the king's pain.

As he tried to help others, he could do little for the po that were being swept away into Eshra'Tel, a living calamity brought upon heaven because of his involvement. No matter what he did, it only seemed to cause trouble.

Thoughts of trouble always made him think of Fiddle. Thoughts of the imp's sharp yellowed smile always warmed his heart, no matter the situation. He seemed to be getting along well with Kadd. This too warmed his heart and lightened his mind.

Lightening of the mind... Cynkz thought.

He remembered his early visions in the ocean, of the sisters and their shadows forming soft silhouettes against the light. Their names slowly came back to him:

Una...

Tia...

Lea...

Foa...

Yla...

Orla...

Orla came back into memory, the young girl he helped escape the shifting gray mountains in Horgafell. She was perhaps doing more good for the po in Munderworld than he ever could. At least, she was in a position to help po ascend and reach a better place, a place he unfortunately only brought ruin.

All of that, everything the Sisters of Elm did for me, the trouble I put Kadd and Fiddle through, even the warm and loving welcome Potarium gave me—

Everything only led to ruin. Thanks to the thoughtless intervention of a schemer, a selfish conniver, a treacherous murderer... Even The Munder King saw something in me and helped me through the abyss and showed me the way forward...

And for what...

Cynkz remembered his conversation with Kadd in the cell in the bunker. It was difficult to not ponder his undying belief in moving forward and doing better.

Kadd did say that we have the capacity to move ahead and make amends. Perhaps the benefit of having an eternity to look forward to is that no matter how great your past mistakes are, there is always time to heal, to grow, to learn, to move forward... Perhaps this calamity is just another step toward growth, paving the way for something greater... As long as we breathe, we can move forward!

All I have to do to keep my past from holding me back is to let go...

Fine, then. I will be held back no longer! I am still capable! I can help! All that I have to do is let go and push forward!

He couldn't help but draw in a triumphant breath. When nothing but healing water entered his lungs, he felt strangely invigorated. Whatever the waters needed to do, it was done.

As he twisted himself upward and burst from the water at great speed, he shot a straight line through the air toward the giant dark orb eclipsing heaven's sky.

CHAPTER 26

I T WASN'T LONG BEFORE THE DARK sphere's size completely took over the world below. Cynkz flew as fast as he could around Eshra'Tel's round form, speeding across the still glistening marbled sky where the golden tower once stood. It provided an odd visual, as he was once again approaching a harsh, ethereal line between the light and the dark. This clean line was broken by a massive crack in the sky. A huge shattered gash rumbled in the sky's center. The rumbling seemed to grow louder as he approached.

Crack!

The sound of fractured, incorporeal glass shot through the air, and the wound in the sky grew larger. Eshra'Tel must have been putting his entire focus on breaking into Omundisia. Cynkz tried to push aside thoughts of what the poor souls trapped inside must be going through. He needed to get the entity's attention somehow.

That was when he saw it: a humanoid form half-submerged within Eshra'Tel. It appeared to be a woman reaching up toward the sky, her loose dreads undone and flowing eerily like dark tendrils behind her. It was Yla!

That seems to be as good a place as any to begin, Cynkz thought.

He didn't know what he would do, or what may happen, but that didn't stop the jester from hurling himself forward at frightening speed toward Yla.

She noticed his approach and turned around to meet eyes with him. Eshra'Tel's influence appeared like dark mist reaching up and digging into her skin and bathing her in darkness. She was completely calm, and almost seemed to look past Cynkz, rather than directly at him, all the while bearing the most disturbed, calm smile he had ever seen on the woman.

Cynkz wanted nothing more than to run away, but he knew he couldn't. He had to do whatever he could to keep Eshra'Tel in place long enough for their plan to kick into action, however long that may be.

In mere seconds, Cynkz was a few hundred feet away from her, when something burst out from beneath Eshra'Tel's dark layer. A large blobby mass of inky black fog flew at an even greater speed. It crashed into him and carried him a ways into the sky before he finally twisted himself around and let loose a cloud of gray smoke. He took the form of a large serpent, whipping his body around to push the strange mass away.

Returning to his original form, he caught a good look at the mass and felt something unnerving radiating from within it. Malice and rage manifested into an unseen aura that somehow peered directly at Cynkz. The blob began to shake and collapse into itself, dripping its unknown fluids before taking the vague form of a man with a sharp unkempt beard, a rotund hearty body, and limbs that seemed too small. It went so far as to mimic a billowing sash wrapped around its torso. The form finally settled and a familiar voice called out.

"We meet again, little jester."

That voice! "Tall! The minstrel!"

Tall reared his head back and cackled. "Ha! So you remember me! Even after all this time."

"Strange, it has hardly felt like a fortnight to me," Cynkz said.

"Seems as though you've been taking it easy, then. Regardless," Tall puffed his chest and leered beneath the rim of his ragged button cap of old. "I've been hoping—no, praying—for the chance to see you again."

"How nice of you to finally come out of that cocoon," Yla said, her voice raspy and rattling against the air as it wormed its way into Cynkz's ear.

"Yla!" Cynkz screamed.

"I don't know how you escaped, but it matters not," Yla said. "That fool Harquin couldn't do something so simple... Pah! It makes no difference. He's all yours, Tall. Make Eshra'Tel happy, maybe see if he has the thread, and retrieve it for us. The universe will be just as much yours as it is ours."

Maybe if I can keep this conversation going...

"How in munder did you get here, Tall?" Cynkz said, snapping his attention back to the minstrel.

"That's easy," Tall replied through a half-chuckle. "The Munder King is a lazy architect. In truth, the many realms of Munderworld have little separating them. They may as well be one single place. There's no real rhyme or reason to any of it. I was trapped by those blasted witches in the pink, misty mountains of Hemin for so long… Who knew? Who knew! Who knew that all one had to do was submerge themselves deep enough within the supposedly 'infinite' pink fog, and you would eventually reach the actual, eternal, infinite darkness at the bottom of the abyss!"

"I presume you fell through agonizing pain for some time before reaching the bottom?"

"You… You have no idea…"

Tall grit his teeth. His fists clenched so hard that Cynkz swore he could hear it from dozens of feet away. Tall was completely covered in the dark substance from Eshra'Tel, yet the fierce glint in his eye shone brighter than the stars.

"Well, spit it out then," Cynkz said, imitating Fiddle's mocking tone. "It seems to me you are making a large deal out of nothing."

"Shut it, you childish fool!" Tall's voice boomed like an explosive blast focused through a barrel. "For years I fell through that mist! For years I writhed in agony as my body, my essence, was torn apart, melted and reformed and melted and reformed again and again! The only thing that kept me going was that stupid look on your face when I forced you to relinquish the thread, and I tossed your little rat friend into the mists! Nothing but searing pain, and anger, and an insatiable yearning for revenge! It was enough to hold my mind together long enough for me to reach the bottom of the abyss and fall into the invigorating embrace of Eshra'Tel."

Another part of my past, coming back to haunt me...

Cynkz noticed that the crackling of the sky had slowed, and he also had Yla's attention. She seemed to be enjoying the show, at least for now.

"What happened next?" Cynkz continued, "Did Eshra'Tel clean you up? Give you a nice bath? You feel better now, do you not?"

Tall looked away, as if reminiscing. "When I fell into Eshra'Tel's grasp... It was like heaven. Finally getting to rest, being healed, he even granted me some of his power! He told me to incubate within him and wait. The time would come when we would get to leave the abyss and have our chance to move forward! I've heard that we actually have you to thank for this, Cynkz."

"You're welcome," Cynkz scoffed.

"Speaking of which," Yla interrupted, "my beloved needs a little more time to crack open the garish barrier in the sky. Yet I would like to have this little problem taken care of posthaste." Yla turned her attention to Tall and stretched out a dainty arm, as if she was royalty gesturing to a beloved servant. "Tall, if you would be so kind as to deal with this—"

"My pleasure!"

The minstrel twisted and shot his body directly at Cynkz. He was fast, too fast, in fact, for Cynkz to even think.

Cynkz instinctively pulled himself back and down, and the dark mass flew over him. The inky blob screeched against the wind as it whipped itself around, preparing to fly in for another strike. Cynkz watched carefully and drew in a breath as he flung himself toward Eshra'Tel.

As Tall hurled himself forward, Cynkz descended into a burst of ashen smoke, and from its top, a massive bat-like creature with sharp wings that shimmered in what little light remained barely evaded his attacker. Before Cynkz could flap his new wings a single time, Tall used his movement as misdirection, baiting Cynkz into moving in a certain way to grab hold of his leg.

Tall pulled the bat creature down and immediately tried to wrap his hands around Cynkz's neck, only protected by a ring of prickly fur. Just as his intense grip began to set in, Cynkz drew his wings in to create a loose chamber around Tall, and he shrieked.

Tall's ears began to bleed. Where glistening red blood should have been, a black, viscous ink spurted out. This was enough to force Tall to release a hand, but this too was misdirection, as he only pretended to reach up and grab his head in pain. Instead, he formed a tight fist and pummeled the bat.

Spinning through the air, and after several blows, Cynkz was able to twist his neck enough for a strike to miss, giving him an opportunity to dig his fangs deep into Tall's forearm. Tall screamed, genuinely this time, and had to release his other hand's grip to grab some of the creature's loose skin and fling Cynkz away.

It took a moment for Cynkz to gather himself, but he soon realized he was hurtling toward Eshra'Tel! He threw out his arms to catch the wind and break his descent, but it was not enough. Just before hitting the surface of the dark mass, a burst of smoke erupted around him, and Cynkz emerged in an even larger form.

A great bird of prey, whose black wings fluttered anxiously, stopped just above the surface of the giant eye. The tips of his featured wings glistened as they grazed the edge of the calamitous orb.

The harsh whip-like cracking of the wind caught the fowl's ear, and on instinct, he flapped his wings to thrust himself out of the way and into another cloud of smoke to hide his movements.

Tall's form instantly dove into Eshra'Tel with a wet smack hitting the air like a stone being thrown into thick dirty water.

Cynkz emerged in his original form and slowly backed away from Eshra'Tel, watching carefully for signs of another attack. Despite having a moment of calm to think, he could not. He feared having his reactions slowed by rumination and decided to let intuition take over. This was interrupted, however, by the ghastly echo of a hoarse voice calling out from the orb.

"Hahaha! You are the same as I remember. Nothing more than a scared boy!"

Cynkz couldn't make out whatever sounds the man made next. It was something caught between a wet snarl and a chortle.

Tall continued, "What are you afraid of, Cynkz? Why don't you come into the darkness with me!"

Everything went quiet. Cynkz was so focused, so tense, he could no longer hear the raging winds or the slow fracturing of ethereal glass. He kept his eyes fixed on the sea of darkness. The glimmer of something bubbling out of the surface caught the corner of Cynkz's eye, and immediately he threw himself back, barely avoiding Tall.

Just as before, the blob whipped itself around and came flying back, only to submerge itself beneath Eshra'Tel. With each attempt Cynkz could feel Tall's fierce grip inching nearer and nearer to his throat. It was smart. Tall must have figured that if he could get a good stranglehold of Cynkz's neck, he could suffocate him, perhaps stop him from transforming. Cynkz wasn't sure if that would work, but he certainly was not willing to find out.

Tall flung himself into Eshra'Tel once again. His onslaught was constant and relentless, and he moved so quickly that Cynkz swore the man was teleporting. The only thing that allowed him to keep track of Tall was the dim light on his inky form as he flew through the air at unimaginable speed. He was getting predictable, however. Tall only came directly at Cynkz, doing little to alter or feint his trajectory. It was an opportunity to try something new.

Tall flew out once more, and predictably right for Cynkz. The jester flung his cloak back, and instead of moving out of the way, burst into smoke, a cloud so massive that it rivaled Eshra'Tel in size if looked at from the right angle. A tremendous winged-serpent emerged, revealing its open hinged jaw as it awaited the flying blob.

Tall, already moving too fast to stop, flung himself into the wet, venom-laden maw of the serpent. There was an ear-shattering snap that caused light ripples to echo over Eshra'Tel's surface. The serpent did not stop there, as it immediately opened its mouth wide again

POTARIUM

and snapped down on its prey, over and over again. The frightening sounds were akin to a titan beating against heaven's door.

A final snap led into an eerie silence. Something was wrong, and the serpent had an almost vacant look in its glaring eye as it waited. Harsh knocks trembled against bone, forcing the serpent to recoil into opening its mouth. A trailing hiss followed as the serpent flung itself back and burst into another cloud of gray smoke.

Cynkz, having returned to his original form, couldn't help but rub his jaw, though it did little to lessen the pain rattling against his teeth. He looked up and noticed Tall laughing at him in the distance.

"Now you're getting it!" Tall called out. "Go ahead. Eat me! I'd love to get a hold of that sensitive heart of yours!"

A piercing cackle rang from the side. The two looked over to see Yla's silhouette shaking against the marbled sky as she laughed maniacally.

"It's like watching children fight over a toy!" she cried, her voice possessing a slight quiver as it was half-caught in laughter.

"It doesn't matter, not really," Yla whispered. She bent over to embrace Eshra'Tel as best as her body would allow. "I am now free… Free to bear as many children as I want… Dark children who will also be free from the all-seeing eye of The Creator…"

Tall scoffed. "You're a madwoman, an ambitious fiend."

"Leave us be, Tall," Yla replied. "Hurry up and finish what you started…"

Tall drew in a deep breath and puffed his chest before charging at Cynkz once more. Cynkz threw himself into another burst of smoke, one that strangely lingered for longer than usual.

"This is getting old," Tall huffed. "You need a new trick."

Something was wrong. Tall had flown straight into the cloud, his hands stretched out and ready to grab Cynkz's throat, but there was nothing there. The smoke lingered longer and seemed to be growing. Tall tried to emerge from the mist, only to hear violent bursts of smoke popping all around and then above him. Before long, everything was concealed in pale smog.

Tall coughed and tried to look around for a way out. The prickling sensation of something clawing through his back caught him off guard. Before he could scream, another shining blurred form dashed ahead of him. The cutting sensation returned, this time across his chest. He tried to watch where the creature went, only to be blindsided by another quick burst of smoke that dulled his hearing, and the swipe of unknown claws searing deep lines into him.

Every time Tall tried to catch or strike whatever was in the fog, he was met with more cuts and scratches on his opposite side. He even tried to predict the strikes, throwing a feint in one direction and readying himself to catch whatever would appear on the other side. His movements were frantic, however, and his form was sloppy.

The creature in the mist blew more smoke into Tall's face as it transformed into something else and clawed him from a seemingly random angle. Bits of flesh and dark ink and what should have been blood began to fly through the fog, painting the misty walls with drops of Tall's essence.

Tall, now caught in a panic, hurled in all directions to escape, only for a quickening trail of bursting smoke clouds to follow him, and even surpass him, keeping him shrouded. Dark blurs flew from every corner of the mist. There were so many clawed strikes coming from so many angles that Tall wondered if there were multiple entities attacking him. He curled himself into a ball, his knees up and his head tucked into his forearms as he tried to defend himself against the onslaught. It did little to fend off the blows, but it provided him time to catch his thoughts and to notice a small break in the clouds. Nothing but the dark sheen of Eshra'Tel's massive body met his eyes, and Tall saw an out. With a quick shift of his marked forearm, he shifted his guard to deflect a final blow, and used the momentum to spin around and dive into his master's body.

The smoke finally began to settle, and Cynkz emerged. He tried to keep his eyes fixated on Eshra'Tel, anticipating another attack, only to have his attention caught by another shattering of glass in the sky. The massive, dark gash in the once bright orb melding into the sky had grown, its sharp end reaching above like a dark tendril into the cosmos. A familiar chill air emitted from the opening, but nothing could be seen through it. Heaven itself appeared to be ripping in two.

Something heavy flew into Cynkz, knocking him away. Tall held on to Cynkz's cloak, and quickly pulled him in. The two spun violently through the air as Cynkz desperately threw himself about, doing everything in his power to keep Tall's burly hands from reaching his neck.

Tall's frustration seemed to reach its peak, and he lifted a knee between them, thrusting a heavy foot into Cynkz's abdomen. The kick was enough to knock the wind out of Cynkz, so much so that he hardly noticed he was hurtling toward the mass of rock and debris that defined Potarium's streets. He caught himself just in time to twist around and slow his fall with his cloak. There was no time to rest, as Tall's dense form could be heard whistling through the air just above.

Cynkz turned around and burst into smoke once again, filling the open littered street with excess. Tall crashed into the crumbling pavement, only to be greeted with a furious primate. A short round of boxing played itself out before Tall shifted down on a knee and spring-loaded his body upward, both hands clasped into a single, rock hard ball to knock the beast on its jaw.

The beast caught itself, flying up into another burst of smoke, and from its center emerged a flightless raptor propelling itself back, throwing out furious swipes with extended talons. Tall followed suit, ignoring any damage to push away the flailing limbs to get in on the creature, only to be met with another cloud of empty gray smoke.

Something heavy met the ground with a heart-shaking thump, and an impossibly large bull cried out, its form hardly fitting between the rows of torn buildings and rubble. Tall remained unphased and dove straight for the bull. A clash of horn and fist wet the air as flesh and blood and dark fluid splattered the once cream-coated city streets.

Several imps caught wind of the action and, out of curiosity, came to witness. The diminutive creatures occasionally caught glimpses of their imp lord emerging from and descending into smoke as the strange, malicious entity chased after him. They had never seen so many different creatures and beasts in succession. Every clash was met by a twirling of dark cloaks whipping through the air. The dark assailant always dove in without fear, meeting whatever creature confronted him from the constant bursts of ashen colored smoke.

A great bear swiped from the mist, then descended into the form of an even larger black crocodile. The reptile rose into the form of a scorpion, and after exchanging blows, descended into a massive agile wolf. A violent pulling and tearing of fur and flesh led the canine to jump back into the form of a larger and more nimble cat-like beast whose powerful legs cracked the stone as it leapt forth, massive claws extended and ready to meet its foe.

The beast nearly had the upper hand, but immediately found itself pushed to the side after a heavy blow against its ribcage. Another gust of smoke, and the cycle continued as the two rampaged through what remained of the city streets.

Again and again, clouds of smoke revealed new creatures, new claws and talons and pointed tails and hooked tusks and impossibly long horns flailing out to meet the dark assailant who wormed his way past the defenses of every frightening beast before him.

Finally, a greater burst of smoke revealed the towering stone-like visage of a gargoyle sentinel rising up to immediately clasp its gnarled hands together on the fiend chasing it. Despite having no weapon, and its iconic robe getting in the way, the sentinel put up a good fight, cracking the streets and nearby buildings apart as it ducked and jumped and weaved between strikes.

An unfortunate miss left the sentinel open to a bone-shattering headbutt, knocking him back. Before the towering brute hit the ground, it burst into smoke, revealing the jester as he nearly fell over, his hands on his nose as he tried to stop the bleeding.

Tall stopped a moment to catch his breath, but the observing imps did not allow it. One by one, they flew headfirst toward the minstrel, giving their best war cry. The minstrel threw his burly arms to and fro, one by one knocking the creatures away like insects, huffing and screaming as he took out his frustration on every scruffy imp that flew at him.

Cynkz took the opportunity to catch his breath. Quickly, he pushed himself into another cloud of smoke, and from it, a giant serpent, bearing the iconic iridescent scales that hardly looked as such in the dim light, slithered forward and up a nearby wall before leaping at Tall. In the blink of an eye, the serpent wrapped its body around the portly minstrel, completely restraining him. The imps saw their moment to shine and couldn't help but cackle with glee as they took turns flying back and forth, their own tiny claws and fists extended and ready to swipe out.

Tall squirmed and struggled but could not muster the strength to break free. Eventually, all he could do was scream in agony, before throwing the full weight of his body into his writhing. He was able to force Cynkz to move and rammed their bodies into every available surface. With every wall and boulder and fence and pole they collided with, at least one imp was caught and crushed beneath them. This only enraged the creatures, turning their laughter into hisses and growls as they continued their assault.

Cynkz's grip tightened, and Tall's efforts grew more furious. He was more the wild animal than Cynkz was as he flung them into the ground and nearby walls, their dance only adding to the destruction. Eventually Tall was able to shift his weight in such a way that he could drag Cynkz high into the air, using the momentum to carry them down into a small shop with enough force to level the entire building.

Cynkz lay in the rubble in his original form and was unresponsive. The remaining imps caught in the blast lay broken and unconscious next to their lord.

Tall merely sat above them, huffing and breathing more heavily than ever. Each breath and scowl seemed to echo against his ribcage, the sound resembling an angered lion grumbling after a fight.

Just as Cynkz began to recover, a swift, heavy hand caught his exposed neck and squeezed. Before he could reach up to pry himself free, another hand, just as heavy and just as quick, joined the first. In between desperate gasps and gargles, he could vaguely see the eyes of the man holding onto him through his own squint. Tall's expression was flat, not a sneer or a grimace lifting his ragged beard. The torn brim of his cap did little to hide the fierce, diamond-like glint in his eyes as he stared at his prey.

Cynkz could feel his body being lifted, though the vice on his neck remained. It was not long before the two were alone once again, hovering far above Potarium and the great dark sphere. Cynkz continued to struggle, his legs flailing and his nails digging deep marks into Tall's hands.

"Just as I remember," Tall muttered. "Weak as ever. It is surreal. After so long, I finally, finally get my hands on you, and get my vengeance for sending me on that torturous journey."

Cynkz couldn't breathe, and he couldn't think. The dim light of the realm seemed to grow darker with every passing second.

Tall continued. "What you're feeling now—the painful, suffocating feeling of every sense in your body growing numb as your mind focuses on the pain—that is but a taste of what I had to endure. But endure it I did, because unlike you, I am strong! Strong enough that even Eshra'Tel noticed."

Cynkz could feel his limbs growing numb, and his body trembling. Whatever strength he had to flail his legs was draining. All he could focus on were his nails digging into Tall's grip. Several of them were pressing so hard into Tall's hands that they actually began to worm their way past Tall's fingers.

"I should thank you, Cynkz," Tall continued. "You showed me a way forward. I suppose I can return the favor by finally killing you now! Enjoy the pain, and enjoy whatever crumbs are left in this damned city!"

Cynkz slipped the edge of a sharp finger past Tall's grip! It allowed enough room for Cynkz to draw in a quick breath and to gather his thoughts.

Tall leaned forward, ready to press into his victim's throat a final time, but instead was met with an instant burst of smoke. A flash of shining light jutted forth, revealing a massive, golden-yellow beak piercing through Tall's vision! Before he could scream, the sharp spear of a beak split apart, and him along with it.

Tall, now floating in the air as little more than several torn pieces of inky muck, began to pull himself back together. The man's face and form slowly peered through the shifting blob, and the minstrel frantically tried to meld the seams of his different, torn parts back together when a strange trickling sound echoed from the mist.

The shining layered shell of an impossibly large and long crustacean curled and twisted its way through the smoke. The sound of its many rainbow scales clicking past one another as the creature torqued was like a spring readying itself. Countless, insect-like legs waved in beautiful rows, propelling the creature through the air, its form turning over and revealing a massive claw, larger than Tall's body.

A flash of dim light against a rainbow shell concealed a decisive strike. The full force of the shelled piston colliding at lightning speed met Tall's torn body and drowned out the world with an earth-shattering crack. The impact was thorough, and powerful enough that it reduced Tall's body to countless scattered drops of black ink that flew out and back into Eshra'Tel's spherical form, hitting the surface like heavy raindrops.

As Cynkz gathered himself, a bright orange flare caught the corner of his eye. He peered past the curved edge of the dark sphere to see Fiddle leading Kadd and a group of imps and po through the streets and toward another temple. Fiddle's fire seemed to be doing a good enough job of paving their way, but they needed more time.

Cynkz could see more po souls being dragged helplessly into Eshra'Tel. He wanted to dive forward and help, but it was too late. Before he could shift his body to dash ahead, they were submerged into the dark body. His attention was interrupted by another soul-shattering crack of ethereal glass. Cynkz whipped his head around to see Yla stretching out her arms toward the tear in the sky. She seemed to be ignoring everything else and could be heard laughing and cackling in the distance.

"Ha! Haha! We are so close! Just a little more, my love! We are so close to true freedom!"

This is it, Cynkz thought. *There is but one way to guarantee Eshra'Tel's attention and to keep them in place. I just hope this works…*

Cynkz reached into a leathery pocket in his coat and pinched the thread between his fingers. He couldn't help but pause a moment, fearing the worst. Still, something about the light compelled him to keep going. It was as if the thread were demanding to be revealed.

In a quick motion, Cynkz pulled the sliver out and blinded the world with its all-consuming radiance. The light was so bright Cynkz worried he would be blinding himself by merely holding it out in front of him, and it only seemed to grow brighter against the backdrop of shade that covered Potarium.

He couldn't see much due to the intense light, but he could hear just fine. The screeching winds, the shattering of glass in the sky, the rumbling of the ground below, even the screams of po and imps in the distance, all of it was muted.

It took a moment, but his eyes began to adjust to the light, only to be met with the fierce gaze of the woman melding with the dark sphere. A quick glance below Yla revealed a bright frayed split in the orb forming beneath him. The fierce eye of Eshra'Tel was now on Cynkz. A tense moment of silence weighed heavily between the two.

Cynkz expected a voice or some kind of sound to call out to him, maybe Eshra'Tel demanding the thread as he always did. Instead, the frayed edges of the eye grew, then burst out!

Rows of po souls, now forced together to form tight, spiraling limbs, shot out and came directly for Cynkz! The sight of countless eyes and hands barreling toward him instilled a fright he had hoped to never experience again.

The thread still exposed and in his grip, Cynkz twisted himself around and dashed forward. Cynkz could feel himself moving faster than he ever had before, and yet it was not enough. The wailing cries and breathy moans of the damned pierced the sky like an arrow and were upon him in seconds. He could feel countless cold hands gripping his legs, then his waist, then his arms and shoulders. He struggled to break free, but something about the grip of the forlorn po drained him.

Just like before, Cynkz was dragged into the dark eye of Eshra'Tel. The thread went with him, and its gleaming light soon faded from the realm as it was brought inside.

CHAPTER 27

A S DARKNESS RETURNED TO POTARIUM, Fiddle couldn't help but look up and cry out. He stopped so abruptly that Kadd nearly ran into him.

"Cynkz! That light had to have been him! Something must have happened."

"We must hurry, Fiddle!" Kadd exclaimed. "We do not know how much more time Cynkz can garner for us, or if this plan will even work…"

"It has to work!" Fiddle cried. "It will!"

Kadd nodded. "Yes, I have faith that it will. But let's hurry, there is only one temple left."

The entrance of the final temple was in sight. Just like the others, the great flag was splintered, and its collapsed pole rested over the half-torn structure. The usual pillars that lined the edges of the temple's exterior, just like the others, were mostly crumbling stumps. Still, it was a surprisingly calm-looking area compared to the rest of the city.

Fiddle smiled, and was ready to speed ahead, when something caught his eye. Familiar cloaks worn by troublemakers hid inside the temple's main hall. Fiddle didn't know what to make of them, other than they were apparently working with Yla, and he had to burn a few of them to get them to leave.

Fiddle stopped, held up a tiny claw, signaling for Kadd, Viola, and a small horde of other imps to halt.

"Looks like we have more trouble," Fiddle remarked. "I'll have to sneak in and clear 'em, out."

"Seems like an easy enough job for you, Fiddle," Kadd responded.

"It'd be easier if the other imps could spit fire, maybe help me out a bit with this."

"Hey!" one imp cried out. "We're helping! We—"

"Yes, yes, I know Viola," Fiddle said. "I apologize."

"Oh, wow... An apology..." Viola seemed dumbstruck. As she was always ready for a confrontation, it was odd for her to see Fiddle so calm and assured.

"Why are you the only one who can spit flame, anyway?" Kadd asked.

"Pops says it's 'cause I'm the oldest! My fire glands are near fully grown, see?"

Fiddle hooked the edge of his mouth with a tiny finger and pulled. Kadd, unfortunately, had no idea what he was supposed to be looking at. He looked up and down the rows of sharp, jagged, yellow teeth, leaned back, and smiled.

"I see," Kadd said. "Very impressive."

"Hehe, exactly," Fiddle remarked, crossing his arms.

"Come on!" Viola yelled. "Hurry up and roast 'em so we can move."

"Yeah, yeah, I know Viola, I'm going." Fiddle turned and waved a dismissive claw at the group before drifting ahead.

A dull shadow crept up the ruined steps and disappeared into the temple. It wasn't long before it happened upon a small room holding a half dozen of Yla's cloaked henchmen, all speaking worriedly with one another.

"This is insane…" one said.

"I agree…" another muttered.

"W-what're we supposed to do now?" a third stuttered.

"We do what we always do," the first one said. "Await Lady Yla's orders."

"She disappeared as soon as that *thing* in the sky appeared!"

"That 'thing' is our Lord Eshra'Tel."

"Screw Eshra'Tel! We were lied to! Yla only brought ruin to us all!"

"Did she abandon us?"

"No, I don't believe that. She said we would be free, that we would all have a place in her future."

"Lies!" one shouted, his remark so loud it echoed harshly against the high walls of the temple's interior and could be heard rolling through the main hall outside.

The disgruntled po continued. "It was all lies! She merely used us. There's nothing more to it."

"What good are we, otherwise? Lady Yla gave us sanctuary. If Potarium has no place for us, and Lady Yla has abandoned us, then…"

"Then we are truly forsaken…"

"Even heaven couldn't save us, and it was all our own doing."

"Hey," a husky voice rang out from a shadowed corner. "At least you guys can admit you screwed up."

The hooded po immediately shot to attention, their eyes wide and heads swiveling every which way to try and find the source of the new voice.

"W-who was that?! Who's there?!" one po shouted.

"Hehehehe." Fiddle slowly emerged from the dark corner, his scruffy brown-red form settling as he attempted to elegantly make his entrance.

"What in munder are *you* supposed to be?!" a po cried out.

"What I am," Fiddle paused—dramatically, of course—and placed a firm fist on his hip, his other dark claw pointed at the group, "isn't important! What is important is that you heathens scram! Me and my friends need this place."

The po shared a confused look before tightening their expressions and their fists as they looked at the bumptious creature smirking at them.

"Oh yeah?" one asked. "Why don't you make us, you little hairball?"

Back outside, Kadd waited behind debris not too far away with the other imps. Things were surprisingly quiet without Fiddle around, though the silence was soon interrupted by great streams of burning orange fire shooting in all directions.

Cloaked figures could be seen scrambling for their lives, some of them leaving small trailers of tinged cloth as they scurried away. Kadd couldn't help but smile at the sound of imps cackling behind him like children at the sight of it all.

It seemed as if the last few cloaked po were finally making their way out. Kadd lifted himself up and began to move ahead, only for something odd to catch the corner of his eye. It was a shining, jagged black crystal hanging off of the belt of one of the po. A strange, gleaming strand of hair was woven into it.

"A medium!" Kadd exclaimed. "That po has it!"

Before the imps behind him could react, Kadd was after the cloaked po, darting into the windy maelstrom of nearby city streets.

Kadd, unfortunately, was not as young and athletic as he used to be, but he was no stranger to a good run. The loud clopping of his sandals made him regret his choice of footwear. Still, he pressed on, his billowing purple sleeves waving to and fro as he desperately tried to keep up with the man. It wasn't long before the imps caught up with him.

"Yay! A chase!" one imp shouted.

"G-get away from me!" the cloaked man cried out.

The man quickly pivoted into a nearby building and pulled over several wooden beams and an unhinged door as he ran by. He escaped through a jagged hole in the wall and emerged in another street. The cackling voices and the claps of heavy sandals continued behind him.

"Eeheeheehee! Come back! Come back!"

"We don't want much from you, just—"

"Just your soul!"

The man shrieked and nearly stumbled over himself, allowing Kadd and the imps to gain on him. Surprisingly, the man gathered his wits and immediately threw himself into a dark alley a dozen feet ahead.

The sound of fleeing footsteps ceased, and Kadd reached the corner, taking a moment to stop and catch his breath. All that he could see was an empty alleyway, though there were sizable stones and bits from the golden tower strewn about, as well as splintered wood from who knows where.

"Hey! Where did he go?!" one imp squealed out.

"Kadd, Kadd, what do we do now?" another asked.

Kadd didn't respond and walked slowly, keeping sight of the alley from the corner of his eye. The imps shrugged to one another and followed.

After a short silence, the shifting of rocks and stone could be heard not too far in the dark space. The cloaked man, his short curly hair whisking thick beads of sweat from his brow as he moved, emerged and sheepishly tiptoed ahead. He turned an ear to the wind and figured the coast was finally clear. With a heavy breath, he relaxed his posture and traipsed forward, only to be met by the robed pursuer tackling him from the side and to the ground!

A horde of fuzzy reddish-brown bodies descended on the two, cackling as they always did while taking swipes at the poor po.

The cloaked man whipped and flailed. He even managed to get free from the many hands and claws grasping at him. With a steep kick of his heel into the priest's chest, he twisted his body and scrambled to get up. Frenzied scratches against the cracked pavement immediately gave way to the meaty thud of a hefty round body falling on the man's head. The man let out a trailing gurgling hiss before falling to the ground unconscious.

"Hey, Coda," Viola said.

"Hi! I finally found someone I recognize," Coda said.

"Why are you so bad at flying, Coda?" Viola asked. "It's really not that hard!"

Coda raised a tiny claw to his chin, his beady eyes moving about as if searching for an answer, but shrugged a response.

Kadd let out a hearty laugh, catching the attention of every one of the imps, before he leaned over and grasped the hand-sized stone from beneath the man's cloak.

The jog back to the temple was much easier than the chase away from it.

A small reddish-brown body could finally be seen waltzing triumphantly toward the outer steps of the temple. He smiled and brushed his tiny hands together, as if cleaning himself after finishing a job well done. The sight of a shining purple robe approaching, escorted by a horde of other small reddish-brown bodies above him caught Fiddle's attention. He lifted himself off the ground and flew over to greet them.

"Hey! Where did you guys go?" Fiddle snapped. "Leavin' to go play and letting me to do all the work, huh?"

"Pfft, of course not, Fiddle," Kadd snapped back, revealing the dark stone in his hands. "One of those goons tried to run off with this stone. But we got it—"

"I helped!" Coda blurted out from the back of the group.

"Oh. Hey, Coda," Fiddle responded.

"Come on, let's hurry inside and get set up," Kadd said, stepping forward past Fiddle to lead them inside.

"I looked around a bit and didn't see any other mediums," Fiddle said.

"I suppose we will just have to make do with this one,' Kadd said.

"Since this is the last one, I'll lead the huumming."

"Any one of you could probably do it."

"I'd ask why you don't do it, but I feel like I already know the answer."

"I could *never* bring myself to potentially huum for a dark lord of all things."

"Eh, he's really not so bad. Just a grumpy old man."

"Well, I hope this 'grumpy old man' is capable of seeing this through."

"Same. But... I know my dad. The second he sees something—anything—beckoning him in the abyss, he'll want to reach through and get his little pet back."

Kadd stopped in front of the fallen flag post. "Right here should do well enough."

It was like a stage of frayed wooden ends and cracked oak, spikes jutting out every which way in a massive pile that blocked out the rest of flag yard and building behind it. The remains of the flag's ripped cloth flapping wildly in the wind drowned out much of the screeching winds.

Kadd's eyes met dozens of beady shining eyes as they looked at him expectantly. Even Viola seemed compliant, the short, smooth waves of ruffled fur on her head leading down to eyes that almost seemed worried.

"This is it…" Kadd mumbled to himself. He revealed the weighty stone and knelt. Once he placed it in front of himself, Fiddle landed and waddled over, kneeling down and gripping the stone with both claws. The once self-assured imp paused long enough for Kadd to notice.

"What's wrong?" Kadd asked.

"Well, now it feels awkward," Fiddle replied. "Everyone's staring…"

"It's alright, Fiddle. Everyone struggles with it at first. You should have heard Cynkz the first time he tried to huum."

"Was he able to do it?"

"Erm, uh… Not really…"

"Hah!" Fiddle's glee seemed to catch everyone by surprise. "I guess we imps have a skill beyond our beloved lord of imps!"

A round of giggles followed, then settled. Fiddle relaxed.

"Just remember," Kadd continued, "focus on the stone, and imagine you are pushing warmth out of your body and into the medium as you huum."

"Like a burp?" one imp blurted out from the back.

"More like… trying to lull a baby to sleep with a song," Kadd said. "Relax, take a deep breath, focus, and huum as if you were trying to blow gentle air through a flute."

CHAPTER 27

Fiddle did exactly as he was told. He relaxed his tiny shoulders, drew in a deep breath past his thin lips, cleared his mind, and huummed. Something inside him, warm and resonant, began to seep from his chest and through his hands. It was like warm honey slowly dripping over him. The other imps giggled, then immediately hushed one another as they came in and huddled around Fiddle.

The collective warmth from their bodies pushed together was almost like a hot steam pressing into Kadd's eyes. He slowly and quietly stood and backed away. At first, their huums were out of sync, but only slightly. As they continued, their songs gradually harmonized, their eyes all closed and their arms reached toward Fiddle.

It would have been a heartwarming sight to Kadd, if not for the already dim light of the realm growing darker. The dark stone seemed to draw in whatever light was left around them, and it wasn't long before Kadd felt blinded by... something. A pitch black blanket of darkness seemed to crawl over everything. Kadd looked up and around, trying to keep vision of anything he could, but his sight was only met with darkness. Soon, the only thing that remained were the continuous huums of the imps, their song like an eerie chorus of children calling out from the abyss.

A haunting chill took the air, and soon the world was gone, claimed by the abyss.

CHAPTER 28

*I*T IS JUST LIKE THE DREAM, JUST LIKE *before…*

Once again, Cynkz found himself sinking into darkness. He could feel the cold grasp of countless hands digging into him from the depths. His mind was as blank as the abyss stretching infinitely before him, and he could do nothing except look into it.

A single light in the far-off abyss caught his attention. The frightening cadence of its crackling edges forced an uneasy feeling within his soul. With little else to reference—Cynkz couldn't detect his own body—the sight of the light growing larger made him think he was approaching it, or, more specifically, that he was being dragged into it. He yearned for the ignorance he held from the previous encounter, where he could focus on questioning the phenomena rather than fearing it.

The thread, still firm in his grasp, strangely did help him focus, and maintain some form of control over his body, though he could do little more than grip his hand tightly around it.

The sharp vertical slit burned its way toward him. The once flat plane of darkness was engulfed in the frayed, dancing edges of a menacing eye that peered directly into him and spoke in a voice that was felt, rather than heard:

Again, we meet…
Again and again we cross paths…
Why do you defy me?
What are you struggling for?
The universe is open to you, yet you choose to flail about,
trying and failing to protect these useless souls…

A sharp feminine voice echoed from above. "We don't need him, my love. His … unique attributes will be shared among our eventual children. He has nothing more to offer us."

It was Yla, reaching out from the darkness above. Cynkz tried to make sense of her new form, but it was difficult. She was half-submerged beneath a thick layer of darkness. Her body was exposed, yet covered in a thin dark film that hugged her form tightly. A piercing smile peered from the center of her sharp features. The worst part was her hair. It was completely undone, and the many long dreads waved behind her like sinister tendrils that poked harsh lines against the light emanating from the eye deep below.

The two stared at one another for what felt like a moment too long, before she finally gave in to a harsh cackle.

"In truth," Yla continued, "it would be much more productive if you did work with us. It is as my beloved says: the universe itself is open to you. All you have to do is willingly hand over the thread and serve us."

"Why would I *ever* do such a thing?!" Cynkz snapped back. "What do you mean by my unique attributes? And this talk of bearing dark children? You truly sound mad."

"Hah!"

It was her usual unrestrained outburst, but strangely, it didn't catch Cynkz off guard in the slightest. Despite the circumstances, he felt more resolute than ever, and tightened his grip on the thread in his hand.

Yla gathered herself. "Everything in this universe, every single minute detail, is confined to *His* plan and *His* will."

"You mean Paithos?" Cynkz replied.

"Yes. Paithos, The Creator, whatever you want to call him. He has his precious plan for all things and will go so far as to inhibit the natural inclinations of his 'children' to ensure things go as needed."

"The great huum…" Cynkz mumbled to himself.

"Yes, the supposed 'great huum,' the one thing protecting this realm from everything else is merely the result of His heavy hand pressing down on the very natures of every living thing here. But… there is a way around this, all of this…"

It was difficult to make out what precisely Yla was doing, but Cynkz could see the edges of her limbs shining against the light of Eshra'Tel's eye as she brought them close to her body. She appeared to be holding herself, and in a way, Eshra'Tel.

She continued. "Those born outside of His param-
eters are ultimately free and entirely unaffected by
His will. This is why I wish to bear many, many children for my beloved. Our family will be powerful. We
will ultimately be free to cultivate the universe to our
heart's desire! There will be nothing to hold me back
any longer!"

"What makes you think you could lead a universe
better than a god?" Cynkz could feel the many hands of
the damned reaching, pressing onto his chest. It took
great effort to draw in the breath necessary to speak.

"This 'god' allows so much suffering." Yla said.
"Munderworld is a good example of that. He went so
far as to destroy the world of his precious children—
Peara—when things didn't go exactly to his liking—"

"And yet here you are, ready to sacrifice heaven itself,
and the countless souls within, just to force things to
your own liking."

"This is why you are so weak! Like a pathetic lost
puppy! Even now, you hold the same docile, servile,
meek, compliant, and soft expression of an ignorant
child, just like how I found you back in that cell you
were rotting in! Like a naive child, you would *never*
understand the nuance of life's foundational truth:
every single damn thing requires sacrifice!"

"I suppose that is how you were able to so easily
throw poor Tuco into a hole once you found him useless."

"Think about what you are saying!" Yla's thin,
dark-embraced arms flailed out and toward Cynkz.
"You are defending an absolute louse who would sooner
run out on you at the first opportunity if it served him!"

"We all have faults, even you. *Especially* you. Yet, it is never right to throw away a life, a soul, on a whim."

Yla's expression flattened, now stern and hard as she rested her arms and stared at Cynkz.

"And what did Potarium do the moment they discovered one of *your* faults, Cynkz?"

He kept his eyes locked on Yla's, but he felt a heavy frown weighing down on his face. For a moment, he couldn't think of anything to say as he thought about Orilay, the duke, and her father, and the pain he had wrought upon them.

Yla crossed her arms and looked away. "My point exactly."

"My mistakes," Cynkz said, "are my own. I was content to pay for my sin, to try and make amends for it in some way. They only imprisoned me. They never tried to kill me!"

"Hmmm…"

Once again it was difficult to tell, but Cynkz swore he could see the woman rubbing a dainty finger along her chin.

"Perhaps," she continued, "you merely have the privilege of appearing redeemable, which means that you appeared potentially useful in the future."

"That right there is your problem, Yla. You only see po, actual living souls, as 'useful' or 'useless.' You judge life itself the way one does simple tools. You are careless and could never appreciate the role of a being who rules over the world. You have *nothing* worthwhile to give the universe."

"What would you do then? Would you cast me out for *my* sins?"

"I am in no position to pass judgment on anyone. What I can do is everything within my power to stop you!"

"How noble," Yla scoffed, "and how naive."

"What would your sisters think? I can only imagine how Foa would feel if she saw you in this state."

"Don't you dare bring them up again!" The anger in her voice carried deep into the abyss, its echo ricocheting against the non-existent walls of darkness. "They are just as useless as everyone else, like the lazy, worthless po in Potarium, and they too are content to merely sit back and accept things as they are. It is sickening."

Cynkz was beginning to notice her growing frustration. With emotions running high, his ability to stall her seemed to be waning.

"But they are your sisters, Yla," Cynkz continued. "Surely they deserve to—"

"Shut it!" Yla's shouting was finally achieving a frightening crescendo. She had remained relatively composed so far but now saw fit to put her body into her gestures.

Yla practically hissed her words at Cynkz. "You are as shortsighted as the rest of them. I am done trying to justify myself to an ignorant child! A blind lamb who refuses to see the larger picture! I gave you a chance, and it's gone. This is why mercy is wasted on the worthless. Eshra'Tel, you are free to do as you please with him. He is but a lost cause."

She closed her eyes and pulled herself back into the darkness. Once she was gone, the bright, sharp eye began to writhe and burn as it focused on Cynkz.

Countless streams of souls sprung out of the eye's edges and toward Cynkz. They descended upon him, each and every hand flailing and reaching out toward his own. Once several souls took hold of his body, he could feel himself being dragged further into the menacing, searing light below.

As he was being pulled, the many grips upon him quickly wormed their way toward his hand, scratching and pulling and prying at the thread. They managed to pull his arm forward, but his grip remained. The pain and struggle kicked his mind into focus, allowing Cynkz to exert himself, even if only in a small way. He gripped the thread so tightly that the marks his nails were digging into his palm hurt more than the clawing hands of the damned. His focus was weakened as he recognized the faces of the po being forced upon him.

They were the same po that aided him on the pier not long ago. Several pairs of desperate eyes lost in oblivion: the curly hair and soft eyes of Pairne, her once amber eyes now flushed and faded like the rest; the fierce grimace and gritting of teeth as King Burlowesque pushed and pulled alongside the other helpless souls; even Tall, his soul darker than the rest, and his form still mangled, seemed almost calm as he reached ahead. Whether he was aiming for the thread or his throat, Cynkz couldn't tell.

Having to look in the eyes of the very same po he let down, and having to struggle against his stubborn, unwanted rival, all while Yla surely watched with glee from the darkness… It was almost too much. Cynkz's body grew heavy, and he could feel warmth being drained from his hand as the weight of every soul grew more intense. His hand began to shake, and he could slowly feel his fingers, one by one, being pulled open.

Glimmers of the shining thread beamed defiantly from his hand.

I am sorry… Everyone…

Then—silence.

Everything stopped, and for a moment, it seemed that the world stood still. The many faces of damned po froze and looked ahead blankly. Cynkz couldn't help but squint and raise an eyebrow as he tried to deduce what was going on.

"What's wrong?" Yla cried out from the dark. "What is going on—"

An eerie, chilling huum slowly crept into the ear. It sounded like a quiet chorus of lost children weeping.

Below the great dark sphere, the city was completely covered in a blanket of abyssal film that had been stretched over it. It was pitch black and blended in with the shade Eshra'Tel's form cast over Potarium. Even the pillars of smoke billowing from the city turned into pure black columns dissipating into the air. The chilling huum quieted, as did the wind, the screams, the crumbling of rubble. Everything went silent.

And then…

Boom!

A thunderous snapping of the world burst forth from under the dark sphere. Two powerful forms stretched forth like limbs breaking through the surface of water. They were colossal wiry masses of impossibly dense muscle and burnt reddish skin whose color was surprisingly reminiscent of Fiddle's own coarse fur, and they shot out at otherworldly speed. Its hands, larger forms than anything the po could have made in Potarium, stretched out and clamped their black realm-piercing nails on the sphere.

They dug deep into the sphere, crushing and twisting the form. The sound of matter being collapsed drowned out the world. No matter where one may have been, they surely would have felt as if something heavy were squeezing their head at the temples.

The only thing that could be heard in the rising, intense shaking of the world were the final words of Eshra'Tel, his feeling somehow piercing through the violent trembling in the air:

No!

No!

You wouldn't dare!

It was perhaps the only time the dark entity's voice expressed fear.

Krull!

Krull!

You were too afraid to rebel against Him, yet you will risk His wrath by killing me?!

Why?!

The dark voice could be heard writhing and screaming as the twisting of the world outside began to mimic the sound of a fragile crystal breaking apart. Eshra'Tel let out a final, heart-curdling shriek. His cry immediately gave way to a world-shattering boom.

Finally, he was gone, burst into millions of tiny dissolved pieces of dark nothing that sat eerily still in the air. Hordes of glowing bodies filled the air between each dark piece, lost souls finally set free and able to breathe. They too sat suspended in the air, gravity be damned.

A sharp feminine voice cried loudly not too far above.

"No… No, no, no!" Yla shouted, her voice reducing to a trembling whimper.

The massive wiry limbs persisted, and as they slowly drug themselves down, the heft of their mass caused the air to rumble like a stone rolling down a mountainside. A heavy wind and dark shadow followed the limbs, slithering between the many bodies. Before they reached the abyss below, the dark claws of one of the hands could be seen reaching for the crying woman, casting a heavy shadow over everything below it.

"No! Damn you! What have you done?"

The great hand of The Munder King clamped down on the woman and only the woman. The sound of his grip tightening was deafening.

Cynkz watched as the frightening hand dragged its prey into the abyss, disappearing beneath the dark veil covering the city. It was faint, but Cynkz was certain he could hear a deep, distant chuckling emitting from below. As he looked around, still trying to get his bearings, he could see Tall's dark soul between the sea of floating bright bodies. Tall appeared to be just as lost as everyone else, and Cynkz saw an opportunity. He dove feet first and crashed into Tall's chest, sending the minstrel careening into the abyss before he had the opportunity to understand what was happening.

Cynkz watched Tall disappear into the veil, and with a brush of his cloak and a relieved breath, he gave a final word to his rival. "May the abyss judge you appropriately, this time."

A great rumbling followed the shrinking of the dark blanket covering the city. Hordes of imps could be seen flying into the contracting veil, each one laughing and cackling gleefully as they called out excitedly to their father.

A shrieking below caught Cynkz's ear. He turned to see what it was and saw a dozen tiny furred bodies giggling as they dragged a tall thin man with perfectly coiffed hair into the portal. It was Harquin, of course, and he struggled mightily as he tried to escape, but it was no use. Hardly a moment passed, and he was gone. As the darkness faded, the usual cream-coated buildings began to poke through, setting Cynkz's mind at ease.

The solace was soon replaced with curiosity, then dread as the hundreds of thousands of floating po bodies began to fall toward the ground. Realization kicked in. Without the flags, everyone was vulnerable!

Cynkz noticed the dark ocean just ahead of them, and a wild idea sprung into his head. With no time to think, or ponder if it would even work, the jester thrust himself toward the giant gashed marble that stood in the sky. He disappeared into a great burst of smoke and emerged in a new, unique form.

Many stories and legends have remained following Cynkz's action. Many speculate as to what precisely the jester turned himself into. Most po were lost in a daze as they fell toward the ground, their senses still twisted from their time trapped within the great eye of Eshra'Tel. Some say it was a massive bird, its wings long enough to cover the horizon itself. Others believe it was a projection of Hagharaia the Sky Flame, the old phoenix coming to save the po in their time of need. Others believed it was some form of dragon, with a few claiming they peered directly into a fierce, soul-piercing eye that seemed to be focusing all of its energy on its task.

A few, persistent tales have wormed their way into many po ears over the eons, however. Rumors of something entirely alien embracing heaven with its wings. Some say it had no real body and was practically a stem-like creature built specifically to flap its giant, kite-like wings. Some say it possessed a small, pointed, spear-like head and beak, mimicking the elegant forms of the hummingbirds that define the great city.

As the creature's body was pressed directly against the harsh light of Potarium's sky, it was near impossible to make out specific details. The shadow it cast upon the city was nearly blinding, and the warmth of the wind from its wings dulled the senses of all caught in its gale. All it took was a single, mighty twist of its wings to lift up every soul from their dangerous descent and send them far into the dark ocean.

By the time most po souls washed onto the shore, the creature was gone, and there was little more to see in the sky than the cold, pitch black scar left by the dark sphere.

After his task was done, Cynkz receded into a final burst of smoke that quickly dissipated, revealing a heavy-breathing jester watching over Potarium.

Watching the faint lights of glowing bodies falling into the dark water reminded him of falling stars in a dark night sky. For the first time, he didn't miss Dulrot, and found comfort in the new starscape of his own creation.

CHAPTER 29

THE ABYSS IS A STRANGE THING. IT consists of a type of darkness that consumes sights, sounds, even thoughts. To sleep in the abyss instills the soul with a feeling of nonexistence.

For her, in that moment, there was nothing but the void embracing her, almost like the arms of a beloved partner wrapped around her. The cold, yet familiar embrace of the abyss was the most comforted she had felt in eons.

That was until a sharp whimpering voice pierced the darkness and struck pain into her ear.

"Yla? Yla!" the man cried. "Lady Yla! Wake up! Please…"

When she finally opened her eyes, the first thing that came into focus was the familiar stubborn strand of hair. The only thing she could use to orient herself was the blurred visage of the man desperately trying to swim through empty space toward her. His long, thin limbs, poofy black hair and mangled singed hand came into view. Harquin was a sight for sore eyes, though not a particularly wanted one.

As she reached up to hold and comfort her still ringing head, she noticed the soft brush of odd cloth covering her body. She had been reduced to wearing little more than the iconic cloth the po of Munderworld were forced to wear.

Harquin flailed and soon was close enough to speak with Yla normally.

"Yla! What happened to Eshra'Tel? What took you so long to come retrieve me? P-please tell me you have a plan for this? There must be… a way out of…"

Yla stayed silent, her sharp features piercing the man's soul through the dark. Harquin struggled to maintain eye contact and resorted to looking around, fidgeting with his hands, or what remained of them.

Another voice, much huskier and rattling against the invisible dark walls rang out.

"It's about time you woke up, you madwoman."

"W-who are you?" Harquin asked, relishing the chance to get Yla's attention off of him.

"What's it to you, you sniveling wreck?" Tall snapped back.

"You have no room to talk, Tall," Yla said. "Both of you failed spectacularly."

A thundering cackle shook the abyss. Something, or someone, was laughing from the distant dark. It was a heavy voice, one that sounded long-lived, and it wormed its way slowly into the ear and continued to the gut.

The rumbling of something massive and dense shook the abyss as it crept into view. Great black wings with bony tips reached from each end of the void. Huge wiry limbs rested to each side of the three. The dark being's face was finally revealed.

A wry smile framed the bottom of a pair of large, half-closed eyes weighed down by some inconceivable sadness. It was almost as if his features were fighting one another, each trying to represent opposite emotions. Ultimately, the entity seemed to be taking glee in the show unfurling before him.

Before the three could stare at the massive entity for too long, rows of cackling giggles crept along, eventually surrounding them. Countless furry bodies emerged from the dark. An audience of jagged smiles and beady, child-like eyes watched from the darkness.

Harquin immediately began to cry, wanting nothing more to do with the scruffy creatures. Tall braced himself, fruitlessly trying to take a defensive stance. Yla remained unphased and kept her eyes locked on the dark entity. Eventually, the imps settled down, as did Harquin's blithering. It was oddly quiet for too long to be considered comfortable.

"What happened?" The Munder King asked. "You three were so talkative before! Now you're being boring…"

"Just get on with it." Yla's interruption seemed to have little effect on The Munder King, though he did noticeably curl up the corner of his thin lips hard enough to dig a deep line into his cheek.

"Hmph, very well then."

POTARIUM

The dark lord raised a heavy hand, revealing one of his impossibly long, otherworldly nails of pure black that somehow shone in the dark. He brought a nail near the trio, its sharp end pointing downward. Harquin shuddered and cowered behind Yla. Tall kept his wide stance, making full use of his equally wide form, and Yla continued to watch coldly.

One by one, The Munder King tore small rifts in the darkness in front of the group. Frayed energies split up and down and spread, revealing the hunched bodies of four old po women who peered out at them. Upon getting a good look at one another, Yla looked surprised for the first time. Even in her current form, the Sisters of Elm recognized their lost sibling immediately.

"Say hello to your judges," The Munder King said.

Yla gathered herself and looked on with a self-assured resolution. The silence seemed to last for ages. No one knew how best to start the conversation, and everyone waited for the others to start things off.

"It's been a long time, Yla," Foa said. Her voice was soft, hesitant, and hardly able to work its way past the old woman's cracked lips. "I worried we would never get to see you again."

"I'd have been fine if I never spoke with any of you ever again," Yla responded.

"How can you be so heartless?! Are you not a part of our family?!" Lea shouted loud enough to catch some of the imps by surprise.

"Tch… Your little hole in the ground is hardly what I would call a familial place," Yla said.

"What... What do you mean?" Una whimpered. She clutched her staff tightly, as if using it for emotional support.

"I grew to despise all of you," Yla continued. "You all are so content to waste away for an eternity as a group of half-assed 'rescuers' in Munderworld."

"We knew what we were signing up for when we made our pact, Yla," Foa responded.

"Who cares about some wretched pact?" Yla snapped back. "Unlike you worthless lot, I was given the opportunity for something greater, the opportunity to help create an actual future. And... And..." Yla looked down at her feet dangling above the abyss and brought her arms in close to hold herself. "And it was all taken away in an instant..."

"How did you become so selfish, Yla?" Foa said, her voice heavier than before. "How could you even *think* of doing something so heinous? You were willing to throw away innocent souls, Potarium, and even your own sisters for your selfish gains?"

"You hags would never understand! Content and thoughtless, as you always were. You are little more than complacent children! You could never understand what it means to have something truly precious taken from you!"

"Yla... We know all too well what that means. How do you think we felt when we lost you? When we lost mother?"

"I don't want to hear about mother! I don't even want this stupid ring of yours on my finger any longer!"

Yla whipped her arms up and quickly pulled off the crude ring on her middle finger. She took hold of it and flung the item with all of her might directly toward Foa. The old po was unphased and didn't need to wave her crooked staff to catch the ring with her magic. A faint, shimmering blue energy wrapped around the ring and slowly settled it in the center of Foa's scratchy palm.

"These rings were some of the first things we made together," Foa said in a soft hushed voice. "Even after all of this, you decided to hold onto it. That must mean something."

Yla interrupted, "I only took it off of that misguided, childish jester to taunt him with it. It had nothing to do with you lot."

"I suppose the cute jester did his job, then," Una said. "Where is he now?"

"You always did have poor taste in men, Una," Yla scoffed, crossing her arms and refusing to look her sister in the eye. "He is but a lost child, perhaps crying up in the ruins of the supposed great city of Potarium."

"That 'child' has a remarkable talent for finding his way forward, regardless of the odds," Lea said.

"The boy's mind is weak and ill-defined," Yla said. "He hardly has a proper definition for basic things, such as what one should consider 'good' or 'bad.'"

"Such concepts are abstract, Yla," Tia said, finally speaking up. "Such ideals are ever-changing and constantly maturing. As long as one's heart is in the right place, they need not have a hard definition for the terms. They will find a way, just as the jester always seems to do."

Yla scoffed again, this time turning her eye toward the speaker. "Save the vague platitudes for someone who needs them, Tia."

"You know," Foa stepped forward, a sharp clack echoing from the bottom end of her stave hitting the dirt floor. "You were always so different from the rest of us, but it never truly concerned me. You were so ambitious and so concerned with being efficient. In truth, I thought it was the perfect counterbalance for the rest of us. But I see now what the problem was. This very mindset of yours has been taken to an unfortunate extreme. Everything to you is an obstacle to overcome, something to be stepped over as you move forward, whether it be po, or even us, your own sisters."

Yla couldn't look her sister in the eye. She hung her head low, the heavy shade of the abyss accentuating her pressed brow. The sisters seemed to have little else to say. It was clear that there was no convincing their long lost sister to a better perspective.

Harquin shifted his eyes about and saw an opportunity to interject, perhaps a way to ease something better out of the situation.

"I-If I may be so bold," Harquin said, hobbling forward ever so slightly through the air, "I can sense a lot of unresolved—"

"Shut it, you weasel!"

Yla's retort was quick, snapping her attention to Harquin so quickly it struck him like an invisible hammer to the face.

"L-lady Yla, please," Harquin continued, "we should just calm down and—"

"You were always weak. So subservient, whether to me, the Royal Court, or the cheering crowd. It is the only way you know how to make anything of yourself. You too are but a mere child, willing to cry and dance for whatever authority is willing to pat you on the head for acting in their favor."

"Yla, you don't—"

"You had *one* job, you imbecile! One job! And you failed! All that you needed to do was keep the runt in captivity long enough for Eshra'Tel to get what he needed and break through!"

"B-but Yla, it was the imps!"

"Shut up. Go back to cowering in a corner, like the craven louse that you are."

Harquin could feel his eyes watering. He looked down and anxiously rubbed the charred stump sitting in place of his hand.

Tall couldn't help but let out a hearty grunt as he scoffed at the two. He grumbled, "Well, if nothing else, I was able to get a few good hits in."

"You did nothing," Yla hissed. "You may as well consider yourself as useless as Harquin. Eshra'Tel saw strength in you, minstrel. He gave you much needed respite from your torture and gifted you a substantial amount of his dark power. He presented you the opportunity to get revenge. All of that power, and talk, and posturing for what?! Any damage you think you may have caused could easily be healed by a quick swim in the dark ocean. You accomplished nothing. Worthless."

"Pfft, you are nothing more than a madwoman," Tall said, crossing his arms. His voice nearly spit his words out, "It seems that you, Eshra'Tel, and the hags over there all share the same trait of having terrible taste in men and allies."

"Ha!" A great, world-shaking cackle shook the darkness around them. If The Munder King had a stomach, he would probably be holding it as he laughed heartily.

The Munder King said, "I must say, I have not been presented with such invigorating drama in quite some time! This is a most enjoyable show. However…"

The Munder King's smile began to soften, and he stared deeply into the three sitting before him.

"This has gone on long enough," he continued. "I still very much prefer the peace and quiet of the void and would like to finish this little trial soon."

"W-what will happen to us?" Harquin squeaked, still anxiously rubbing his stump.

"In truth, not even I truly know what happens to those I obliterate."

"Obliterate?!" Harquin finally released his stump as he recoiled back, his fear pitching his tone to an uncomfortable degree.

"Yes. I will erase your entire worthless existence from my precious reality, and there will be naught but a memory remaining of you."

"I refuse to go without a fight! I refuse!" Tall's outburst was quickly followed by him dashing forth through the darkness. Propelled by faint traces of Eshra'Tel's power, the burly figure could be seen cutting a straight line for the godlike entity smiling down at them.

The Munder King seemed quite amused and did little more than laugh as he raised a black nail to the minstrel. Immediately Tall's momentum halted, and he could do nothing more than keel back as his body disintegrated into nothing.

"Well, he had guts, at least. 'Tis a shame they are littering my beautiful pit…"

"No… No!" Harquin cried out and leapt for Yla, trying to hold onto her with his remaining hand. "Please! Yla! You must have a plan! Some idea of what to do! Something! Anything!"

Yla did nothing but glare fiercely beneath a stern brow. When the realization that his doom was imminent settled in, Harquin drifted back and retreated into himself, holding himself like a lost child. A handful of imps could be heard giggling in the distance, though they soon jabbed at one another to quiet themselves, for fear of interrupting their king.

"You should be grateful," The Munder King said. "I am showing you an awful lot of mercy, considering what you did to my boy."

"His boy?" Foa mumbled. Una, Tia, and Lea looked at one another, whispering quick gossips across their rifts.

"Who is he talking about?"

"Heck if I know."

"Does he mean Fiddle?"

"Ugh, the scruffy thing with dirty, loose skin?"

"Shush, all of you," Foa said, quieting the group.

The glint of faint abyssal light bouncing off of The Munder King's dark nail as it rose caught Harquin's eye. In that moment, his instincts kicked in, fiercer than ever, and he tried his best to flee. Most of the imps found his flailing and thrashing about quite amusing. They couldn't help but laugh heartily at the sight.

In an instant, the dark nail came crashing down, slicing through the thin man's form with such speed and precision that it threatened to cut the abyss itself. Harquin, much like Tall, reeled back and began to fizzle into nothing.

There was just enough time for him to whisper his final words: "So... so... cold..."

Then, he was gone, and not a trace of his existence was left.

A moment later, all eyes were on Yla. She appeared to be staring blankly into the distance. One could only guess what was going through her mind.

"I will give the floor to the Sisters of Elm," The Munder King proudly declared, his voice echoing throughout the realm like the pounding of a judge's gavel. "They may have a say in the final judgment."

The remaining sisters looked on, each bearing a slightly different expression. Una's bouncing bun flopped as she looked around worriedly. Tia's straight curtain of gray hair swiveled as she looked on, desperately trying to get a feel for what the others may be thinking. Lea's faded dreads bounced off one another as she looked to Foa, who remained still and stern as she tried to catch Yla's eyes.

"Is this truly how you feel? About us? About everything?" Foa muttered.

"Yes."

Yla's short, curt response cut deep and forced Foa's stern expression to loosen into one of grief.

Foa continued. "It is clear to me, then, that you forsook us long ago. And so ... we must return the sentiment."

"Splendid, then," the Munder King said. "Do you have any last words, my dear?"

Yla remained unresponsive for a moment, her arms still crossed and her eyes still vacantly peering into the abyss. She lifted her head to look at The Munder King, yet the sway of a shining gray strand of hair caught her attention. She tried to ignore it, but as it always did, it compelled her to focus. Finally, she chuckled, and loosened her grip on herself. She opened her arms and shrugged toward the dark king.

"At least this damned hair will bother me no longer."

The Munder King couldn't help but raise his own brow, its great dense mass heaving about sent soft ripples through the dark.

"Strange choice of words," he said. "Give Eshra'Tel my regards."

Once again, a harsh black spear of a claw was raised, and once again, a fierce glint of ethereal light bounced off its perfect edge. It swung, instantly slicing through its final victim. Strangely, Yla felt no fear in that moment, or any real pain. All that remained was an overwhelming chill that wormed its way through her body as quickly as fire. As she reeled back, she caught a final glimpse of Foa's large, sad gray eyes before closing her own, and giving herself fully to oblivion.

For a time, everything was silent. Even the imps could sense a deep sadness filling the otherwise dead air. The light sound of Foa's head resting in her soft palm caught everyone's attention. The other sisters could be seen walking over to her to give comfort, and a final trail of sobbing capped off the closing of the rifts acting as windows into the abyss.

One by one, the imps faded into the distance. It was not long before The Munder King was alone. He pulled his arms back to rest them and looked up to glance upon the faint visions of his kingdom, whose images were now dulled and vague without Eshra'Tel's form to magnify them. The Munder King could do little else but release a soft sigh before closing his eyes and returning to his rest.

CHAPTER 30

T HE EARLY MORNING LIGHT CREPT over the ruined city. It was so bright, and so perfectly spread, that the deepest and darkest corners and crevices of Potarium lit up like thin threads of light against a creamy canvas. Even the dark ocean itself revealed countless beads of shining lights dancing along its waves as they pushed and pulled against the city's wide shores. The beads of light bouncing off of every drop of holy water blended into the foamy perimeter of slow waves hitting the bleached sand and beamed brilliantly beneath the city. If one were looking from high in the sky, they very well may have noticed the faint auras of countless souls slowly drifting in and settling on the line of seashore.

With each row of new bodies sliding into view as they washed up on dry land, others could be seen helping them up and comforting them. Families and friends reunited with great hugs and loud happy cries.

Guards could be seen attempting to shake out water and sand from their armor. Both nobles and common folk alike were reaching out to one another to give and receive aid. A scattering of deep red furry creatures could be seen curiously floating about at enough distance to not appear threatening, but close enough that their curious, child-like expression caught the eye of many of the soberer po.

Others took it upon themselves to surround and contain the hooded po that had worked diligently to sabotage many of Potarium's citizens during the chaos. The hooded sneaks were so outnumbered that they did not dare try anything, and most merely huddled together and sat, as they too were exhausted from the aftermath of the calamity.

A clean-cut gentleman in comfortable, loose and shining violet robes stood out, as he seemed especially energized and ready to lend aid to any he could. This caught the attention of a number of imps, many of whom recognized the man. They came to him, friendly as ever. It seemed that the po and imps were capable of getting along well enough.

Fiddle found Kadd easily and pestered the man as he was kneeling down to help someone stand. A few laughs and giggles followed, but soon a row of gasps quieted the scene. Everyone looked up and began to point and whisper as they were approached by the sight of a strange man in a pointed hat and a dark red and purple outfit gently drifting down toward them. His near-black cloak billowed behind him like a great wing reaching out to embrace the world.

"Cynkz!" Fiddle cried out. He immediately dashed through the air and above many watching heads to greet his friend. Cynkz continued downward as they shared a quick hug.

Kadd lifted himself up, brushed off his silk robes, and walked over as quickly as he could manage.

Fiddle, of course, never let a silent moment pass, even after they finally landed, and all eyes were on them. "Well, that was easy!"

"Heh, I would have to disagree, friend," Cynkz replied.

"We saw the thread from your light disappear into the calamity," Kadd said, still catching his breath after stopping short a few feet from the two. "You should have heard Fiddle crying out for you!"

"I did not cry!" Fiddle snapped back. "It was more like, like a, uh—"

A smaller, sleeker imp came drifting by, and her lighter voice rang out. "It was almost like a weird mixture of burping and whimpering."

"Oh hey, Viola," Fiddle replied.

Many of the po watching looked at each other in confusion. One man was bold enough, or perhaps just curious enough, to step forward and speak. "Um, who exactly are you? What happened? Were you the ones who … dealt with that hellish sphere?"

"You bet!" Fiddle barked. "Though, it was Cynkz's idea. Me and Kadd just did the groundwork in summoning my dad!"

"Y-your … dad?"

"Yeah! The Munder King! You know, the lord of darkness? He who sits on the abyssal throne? The architect of Munderworld?"

Another po stepped forward, bringing her own questions. "Why would such a being help us?"

"Because he's my dad, duh. And Cynkz here is my best friend, and as grumpy as the old man is, he'd never leave us hanging if we called him for help."

Another plump fuzzy form fell from the sky. It was slightly larger and more rotund than many of the other imps. The fall seemed to not affect him, as he immediately picked himself up and looked to Fiddle and Cynkz with puppy-like eyes.

"Hey, Coda," Fiddle said.

"Hey, Fiddle," Coda replied. "Oh! Mister imp lord! I saw you dive right into Eshra'Tel! How are you alive? Also, who were you fighting?"

"Just a minstrel with a grudge," Cynkz replied.

"Tall?! He was here?!" Fiddle shrieked.

Several other imps came forward, all bearing jagged smiles of their own.

"Yes, yes! The lord of imps engaged with a dark minstrel in battle!"

"It was crazy! We got to see him turn into wolves and bears and snakes and even a sentinel! They broke a lot of stuff while they fought."

"What difference does that make? This place is a mess right now, anyway."

"Eh, we can clean it up," Viola interrupted. "I never thought we'd be able to come here without possessing something. It's so bright, but also pretty!"

"But we should only stay here if we have our lord's blessing," Coda muttered. He turned to Cynkz and gave his best puppy-dog impression, going so far as to clasp his tiny hands together. "Milord, may we be granted access here? We promise not to mess anything up."

Cynkz looked a bit surprised, then looked around to notice countless beady eyes both from above and below staring expectantly. He couldn't help but smirk at the sight and chuckled before responding.

"Well," Cynkz said, "if the good people of Potarium will have you, then I don't see why not."

"Hurrah!" Countless little voices cheered out in unison. "All hail the lord of imps! All hail the infinite benevolence of the Munder vassal!"

"Cynkz!" A sharp voice cried out from behind the crowd. A bushel of bouncing auburn hair came hurtling toward the jester and threw itself into him before he could tell who it was.

"Cynkz! It's so nice to see you're alright," Pairne said, trying and failing to keep her bright amber eyes from overflowing. Cynkz smiled and placed a soft hand on her back.

"It's great to see you too, Pairne," Cynkz responded.

Pairne wiped away faint traces of tears and looked up at him. "What happened? What's this talk of fighting? And animals?"

"He can shapeshift," another po voice from the crowd said. Several po stepped forward and stood before the group. Immediately, Cynkz recognized them as some of the same men and women he had helped on the pier.

"Yes, it was quite a show," one young woman said. "One minute he was a ferocious bull, swiping away at goons attacking us, and the next he was as he is now. Bloodied and beaten, he still found the strength to reach over and save me from being pulled up into the wind."

"You helped me just as much," Cynkz responded. "I was poisoned and severely injured. I may not have been able to drag myself into the healing water without your help."

A guard stepped forward, trying to appear decent but having to use a hand to hold up his torn armored greaves so they wouldn't fall. "I saw you fighting that madman in the sky. While I was cowering in a butcher's shop, you and the imps were throwing yourselves every which way into danger. I thank you for succeeding where we could not."

"Hey! If you guys need any pointers, just ask. I could get you battle ready in no time," Fiddle said.

A few rounds of light laughs and hearty chuckles echoed around them. Just as the merriment settled, yet another voice shot out from behind the crowd, this one much heavier than the others.

"Cynkz! Cynkz, is that... is that you?"

It was King Burlowesque! The po immediately stepped aside to let the noble come forward. He peered from beneath a head of messy curly black hair, and had a much softer expression than at their last meeting.

Cynkz didn't know what to think. All of the guilt and shame that he had successfully distracted himself from returned in an instant. He wasn't sure if any amount of groveling or tears could express how sorry he felt. Cynkz finally drew in a deep breath and approached the king, keeping his head lowered all the while, the sharp tip of his hat's brim saving him from having to bear the weight of the man's gaze.

"Sir Burlowesque, I…I am so sorry, for everything…" Cynkz muttered. "I had lost my memory upon waking up in Munderworld. If I had known I had caused you and your family such trouble, I would have been more careful. Even if I cannot remember exactly who I was back on Peara, I still acknowledge that I committed a great sin. Nothing could make up for the damage I have caused, for what happened to Orilay—"

The king immediately grabbed Cynkz's hand and held it tightly. At first, Cynkz thought he was going for a handshake, but Burlowesque held on with both hands, and looked down at the ground in shame.

"No, Cynkz, I must apologize," Burlowesque said. "I have let the past hurt me for far too long. I should have known that you were not the same person you were back on Peara. Kadd always spoke highly of you and told me wild tales of your ventures through the abyss. Even now you threw yourself into danger, not only digging up the truth of the rumors, but also putting yourself on the line to save a city that allowed you to be cast out at first convenience. Whatever happened in the past, it can be forgiven, and we can move ahead and grow. I am sorry, Cynkz."

The king finished his statement by kneeling down, keeping a firm grip of Cynkz's hand. Some nearby guards looked shocked, then looked to one another and decided to follow suit, not wanting to stand higher than their king. Rows of nearby po did the same and began to huum. The warm air of the collective huum reached up to the imps watching above. They didn't know what exactly was going on but were amused by the sight of it all and decided to join in. Even Pairne and Kadd followed suit. For a time, only Cynkz and Fiddle remained upright.

"I think we did a pretty good job, eh?" Fiddle blurted out, patting his friend on his sharp shoulder. Cynkz shared a warm smile with the imp, then turned his attention back to Burlowesque as he gathered himself.

"What will you do now?" Cynkz asked.

"We will figure something out," the king said. "But it will be fine. We have plenty of time to clean things up, and maybe we can make something new." Burlowesque looked over and glanced at the many imps hovering about. "The little imps seem willing to help. That's good."

Cynkz smiled and motioned toward his companion. "Fiddle here is a good leader and has good ties to powerful figures in Munderworld. Whatever you need, he is the one to talk to."

"Hah!" Fiddle cackled. "You're damn right!"

Crack!

A shattering, piercing sound echoed from the sky. All eyes shot up to witness the massive gash in the sky rippling at its edges as it slowly morphed and began to shrink. It was only then that Cynkz noticed that Pairne had taken hold of his hand. He turned to smile and nod at her, before softly releasing her hand and floating back up to the marbled, broken orb above. As he flew a distance away, Fiddle seemed to catch on to what was going on and immediately turned to Kadd.

"Hey, Kadd."

"Yes, Fiddle?"

"Wanna get in one last goodbye?"

"How do you know he's—"

"Eh, I have a good instinct for these things, ya know? I always get a particularly heavy feeling in my gut when Cynkz is about to run off somewhere."

"Of course, but how—"

Fiddle smiled, then quickly turned away and began to bark orders at a nearby group of imps.

"You twelve over there! Get over here and lift Kadd up and follow my lead." Just as Fiddle began to fly up and away, another thought kicked its way into his mind, prompting him to stop and look over his furry shoulder. "And make sure he's comfortable! Hurry up now."

Cynkz couldn't help but notice that, with all the rubble and destruction below, it was the first time the mountain city actually resembled a mountain. He also couldn't help but take note of how much different the mountain looked without the golden tower reaching out from its top. Finally, all thoughts were on the giant gnarled gash in the ethereal orb's surface. A strange, all-consuming chill unlike anything he had ever experienced prior to reaching Potarium filled the air. It instantly reminded him of his first night in the city, and he could recall the pain in his shoulder from the incident. It appeared as though the gash mended itself more quickly the closer he got to it. If he was to ever enter Omundisia, this may be his only chance.

A familiar cordial tone and husky voice rang out from the distance behind him. "Cynkz! Wait up!"

Cynkz turned to see Fiddle leading a small horde of imps, their little red bodies clumped together to form a floating base for Kadd who sat cross-legged upon their many hands and backs. The group drifted close enough to speak with the jester reasonably.

"So ... what's in there, really?" Fiddle asked.

"No one truly knows," Kadd said, "but we believe it leads to Omundisia."

"It's cold. Really cold," Fiddle responded. "It sort of reminds me of space."

"Space?" Kadd raised a curious brow to the imp.

"Yeah. In Dulrot, at the top of Munderworld, you could fly up to outer space if you wanted."

"That sounds extraordinary!"

"Eh, it's kinda boring. It looks pretty, but it's so big, it takes way too long to get anywhere just flying around."

"Perhaps Omundisia is more than just space."

"Perhaps. I guess you'll have to tell us all about it when you get back, huh, Cynkz?"

Cynkz smiled warmly and so greatly that he could feel his cheeks pressing up and into his eyes to the point where they nearly forced water out of them.

"Of course, Fiddle," Cynkz said. "Also, Fiddle, could you do me a favor while I'm gone?"

"Sure! Whatcha need?"

"Go back into the mines underground and see if you can find Tuco. Yla tossed the poor sod into a pit not too long ago."

"Ugh, but he smells! And he's a bum!"

"Fiddle..."

"And he's a jerk! He's probably just gonna steal something once he's back."

"Fiddle, please."

"Also, maybe if he falls far enough he'll just reach pops, and then he could just—"

"Fiddle!"

The imp recoiled into a hearty laugh. "I'm kidding! I'm kidding! We'll see what we can do. I'm sure we'll have him out and showered in no time. Hopefully."

"Thank you, Fiddle. And you too, Kadd. Thank you both, for all that you've done."

"Ah, quit with the mushy stuff! Just gimme another hug!"

Fiddle dove in and wrapped his tiny arms around the jester as best he could. After a deep breath, the imp looked up to meet eyes with the sharp jester. He finally released his grip and slowly drifted back.

"Make sure to bring me a cool souvenir! Maybe another thread from another apostle or something like that."

"But of course! Nothing but the best for my oldest friend." Cynkz threw out an arm and flared his cloak like the dark wing of a noble bird. He gave a fanciful bow, and when he looked back up, he could hardly refrain from laughing as he saw the biggest, goofiest smile he had ever seen on the imp's face.

After staring for what felt like a moment that was not long enough, Cynkz gathered himself and turned to face the ever-shrinking gash. The speed at which the orb was mending itself was alarming. As he looked at it, the gash couldn't have been more than a couple times larger than himself. Whatever doubts that came into his mind were silenced by a persistent curiosity. It was the exact same feeling that had been spurring him forward since the beginning and was too great to ignore.

The jester finally drew in a deep breath and flew directly into the dark opening. A final crash of otherworldly glass collapsing boomed forth, and the sky returned to its heavenly form.

The silence was soon interrupted by the sputtering of a round furred figure lilting to and fro through the air toward them. He was breathing heavily but seemed to be enjoying himself well enough.

"Hey, Coda," Fiddle muttered.

"Awww!" Coda whimpered. "Did I miss it? Did Cynkz leave?"

Fiddle looked up and kept his eyes on the great shining marble in the sky, then finally responded, "Yeah, but don't worry. You'll have plenty of time to catch up when he returns."

AUTHOR BIO

KYLE SORRELL, ALSO KNOWN AS 'Pendoodle,' is a fantasy author based out of northern Florida. Having grown up with countless fantasy and sci-fi influences, as well as a lifelong obsession with video games, he loves to stitch together stories of odd elements dipped in the weird and the wild. Having been born on a naval base in a watery town in Japan, as well as growing up a multiracial child and working many different jobs from assistant plumbing to theme park caricatures to truck driving, he has worn many hats. You can catch sneak peeks at his next crazy idea, or just the occasional illustration, at his personal website at pendoodlez.wordpress.com.

BOOK CLUB
QUESTIONS

1. Would you be willing to live in a place like Potarium?

2. What did you think of the twist after Cynkz met Burlowesque?

3. What did you think of Lord Harquin's circus performance?

4. Who was your favorite character?

5. Is Fiddle ready to lead and guide his brothers and sisters?

6. Did any scenes stick out to you in particular?

7. What was your favorite sentence or line of dialogue?

8. Did this book impact your mood? And if so, how?

9. What surprised you the most in this story?

10. Did this book remind you of any other books?

11. Are you interested in finding out where the story leads to next?

12. What lingering mystery do you find the most intriguing/has the most potential down the line?

13. Would you read another book by this author? Was his prose unique or were there any influences that came to mind as you read?

More books from 4 Horsemen Publications

Fantasy

D. Lambert
To Walk into the Sands
Rydan
Celebrant
Northlander
Esparan
King
Traitor
His Last Name

Danielle Orsino
Locked Out of Heaven
Thine Eyes of Mercy
From the Ashes
Kingdom Come
Fire, Ice, Acid, & Heart
A Fae is Done

J.M. Paquette
Klauden's Ring
Solyn's Body
The Inbetween
Hannah's Heart

Lou Kemp
The Violins Played
Before Junstan
Music Shall Untune the Sky

R.J. Young
Challenges of Tawa

Sydney Wilder
Daughter of Serpents

Valerie Willis
Cedric: The Demonic Knight
Romasanta: Father of
Werewolves
The Oracle: Keeper of the
Gaea's Gate
Artemis: Eye of Gaea
King Incubus: A New Reign

Kyle Sorrell
Munderworld

Discover more at
4HorsemenPublications.com